MURDER

ANCIENT
AND
MODERN

EDWARD MARSTON
(Courtesy of Simon Whitfield)

MURDER

ANCIENT

AND

MODERN

By Edward Marston

Crippen & Landru, Publishers | Norfolk, Virginia | 2005

Cover design by Gail Cross

Crippen & Landru logo by Eric D. Greene

ISBN: 1-932009-38-8 (limited clothbound edition)
ISBN: 1-932009-39-6 (trade softcover edition)

First Edition

10 9 8 7 6 5 4 3 2 1

Crippen & Landru Publishers
P. O. Box 9315
Norfolk, VA 23505
USA

Email: info@crippenlandru.com
Web: www.crippenlandru.com

CONTENTS

INTRODUCTION

The stories in this anthology were written over a period of almost thirty years, and cover the best part of two millennia. I've arranged them in chronological order of their settings, from Biblical times to modern day, rounding the anthology off where we started, in the Holy Land. When they were first conceived, I had no idea that any of these tales would end up in an anthology so it would be wrong to look for any kind of pattern. Certain themes do, however, emerge from the collection and deserve comment.

My obsession with history can be put down to the fact that the formative years of my childhood were spent largely in the company of old people. The majority of younger men, like my father, had been conscripted to fight in the war against Nazi Germany. My paternal grandfather, who lived with us, fired me with stories of the Great War, in which, as the son of a blacksmith, he had served in a cavalry regiment. In the same conflict, my maternal grandfather has been a dispatch rider and he ignited my imagination with his recollections of daring runs on a motorbike through enemy territory. From the start, I got used to looking back in time. Things always seemed more exciting then.

Not surprisingly, war is a dominant theme in my novels and it creeps into many of my stories as well. Religion, too, has a habit of working its way into several of my yarns. I grew up in a family that had a firm belief in regular attendance at the local Anglican church, and learned as much from the vicar and his various deacons, as from any of the teachers at my school. As choirboy, reader, altar boy and, later on, sidesman, I got an insight into the way that devout Christians lived their lives, a great asset when I came to write, in my Domesday Books, about an Age of Faith.

Even a casual reader of this anthology will note another distinct feature. Having been born and brought up in Wales, I do like to introduce the occasional Celt into my work. "The Shoulder Blade of a Ram" is actually narrated by the wonderful and idiosyncratic Giraldus Cambrensis, Gerald of Wales. "Black Death" features the Prince of Wales at the battle of Poitiers. "Squinting at Death" was inspired by my favorite offstage Shakespearean character, Davy Gam, killed at the battle of Agincourt. The crew of the *Golden Hind*, under the command of Francis Drake, also includes a Welshman in "Murder at Anchor"; and "Sea Voices" takes place at a Welsh holiday resort out of season.

History, war, religion, Wales. If you add politics, architecture, theater, sport, travel, crime, a fascination with loners, a fondness for lost causes and a love of the sea, you'll have some idea what to expect in the following stories. Pick and mix to suit your individual tastes. I hope that you find something to relish.

Edward Marston

MURDER AND MIRACLES

It's not often that I can recall the exact moment when a new character first took shape in my mind, but, in the case of Iddo the Samaritan, I can give you chapter and verse. In 1997, I was staying at a hotel in mid-town Manhattan and was due to have breakfast on the following day with my literary agent, Stuart Krichevsky. I always like to turn up with a fresh idea at such meetings and — lo and behold — this merchant from Samaria suddenly appeared before me to demand my attention. Quirky, devious, obstinate, lecherous and an outcast, he seemed such an unlikely protagonist that I found him irresistible. When I pitched the idea to my agent, Iddo made him laugh. That settled it. I felt that I had to put this man down on paper. Here he is.

Call me Iddo. I'm a bad example of a Good Samaritan. Indeed, there are those in Samaria who would be happy to disown me and dispatch me into permanent exile. The thorny problem for my detractors is that they need me. I'm a merchant, you see. A highly successful one. I bring goods into Samaria that nobody else could manage to buy and I sell those that my rivals fail to unload. They are insanely jealous of me. I enjoy exciting such jealousy. It adds spice.

I own a house in Sebaste, a beautiful city built by Herod the Great of not-so-beautiful memory. My house is large and well-furnished. Its garden is the envy of my neighbours. It has everything a home should have but it also contains one glaring defect. My mother. Zilla. For a small woman, she bulks exceedingly large. In fact, there are moments when I feel that I do not so much have a house with a mother in it as a mother around whom four cowering walls have obediently arranged themselves.

Here she comes. Be warned.

"Iddo!"

"Yes, Mother?"

"When are you going to get married?"

"You ask me that every day."

"Then give me a reason not to ask it."

"I'm not ready for marriage yet."

"You've been ready for the last ten years," she says with a roll of her eyes, "but you refuse to commit yourself. Why? Samaritan girls make excellent wives. Look at me."

I stifle a waspish comment. "Yes, Mother."

"Your father snapped me up when I was fourteen. He called me the pick of the bunch. Our families agreed to the match. Your father was twenty at the time. When you came along, I was barely sixteen. A young, proud, loving, caring, Samaritan mother. Marriage is a duty and we were both dutiful, your father and I. Why must you be so different?" She pauses long enough for me to get in an apologetic shrug. "You're thirty, Iddo. Thirty! That's a lifetime for most people. Thirty years without even a betrothal to raise my hopes. I sometimes think you are doing it deliberately to vex me. Are you?"

"No, Mother."

"Then where is my daughter-in-law?"

"She will arrive one day."

"When?"

"In the fullness of time."

"Thirty years is full enough," she argues. "At my age, a woman is entitled to be a grandmother. To pass on her love and wisdom to a new generation. But you have no wife in sight, let alone any children. It's unnatural, Iddo. Thirty years of sleeping alone. It's indecent!" Her voice darkens. "Unless, of course, you've been sharing a bed with another kind of female."

"Mother!" I protest. I'm good at injured innocence.

"I've heard the rumours."

"Cruel lies!"

"Are they? I saw the way that prostitute looked at you in the street yesterday."

"Prostitutes look at every man in that way."

"She wouldn't have done it to your father. Or to any other respectable married man. And how did she know your name?"

"Everybody knows my name."

"Iddo the Wifeless!"

"The merchant, Mother. Iddo the Merchant."

"What kind of trade did you have with that prostitute?"

"No kind!" I say with controlled outrage. "How can you even suggest such a thing? It's humiliating. I honour my father and my mother. And you should trust your son."

My righteous indignation silences her for almost thirty seconds and gives me the opportunity to escape. Amok is waiting for me outside. Mother comes after me.

"Where are you going?" she demands.

"Galilee."

"But you've only just come back from there."

"I'm returning a barrel of fish. It was unacceptable."

Amok, my assistant and bodyguard, big, brawny, taciturn Amok, is sitting astride his donkey. Two camels are loaded with goods and provisions. I mount my horse, Jubal. In a country where most people travel by donkey or camel, Jubal gets me noticed. He suggests wealth, distinction, individuality. I like that. More to the point, his gentle gait does not chafe my buttocks or make me queasy.

"Who sold you the fish?" asks Mother.

"Zebedee."

"Does he have any marriageable daughters?"

"What Jewish girl would look at a Samaritan?"

"She should be so lucky!" says Mother, defensively, then she taps the cargo on one of the camels. "This barrel of fish is unacceptable? Why?"

I give her a broad smile and a wave of farewell.

"It has a man's head in it!" I tell her.

The journey from Samaria to Galilee is as long and tedious as the one I have just made from Galilee to Samaria. In the interests of safety, Amok and I join a caravan as it wends its way along dusty roads in the blistering sun. Reflecting on my mother's exhortations to marry, I recall that Amok himself is recently betrothed. A phenomenal development. Not simply because he is so vast, hideous and unlovable but because such a close relationship as marriage presupposes speech.

Amok is frugal with words. I've known him go for a month without uttering one of them. Reserved with men, he is struck completely dumb by women. How, then, did this rock of silence induce an attractive young girl like Deborah to become his wife? What grotesque form did his wooing take? Did he expend a year's vocabulary on the enterprise?

As we bed down on the first night, I catch him unawares.

"When did you ask Deborah to marry you?" I probe.

The answer slips out before he can stop it.

"She asked me."

Three words from Amok are three thousand from anyone else. I will not get another syllable out of him now. She asked me. The first complete sentence I've heard from his lips in ages. The effort has exhausted him. He falls asleep.

We reach our destination by nightfall on the third day. Zebedee is still at the quayside, watching the last catch being unloaded by the light of torches. He never strays far from the Sea of Galilee. A misnomer, of course. It's not a sea at all but a deep lake with illusions of grandeur. Galilee itself is a densely-populated Jewish district, surrounded by Gentiles. Zebedee and his sons are encircled by enemies. Just like Amok and me. Two Samaritans among thousands of Jews. The Gentiles look down on the Jews and they on us. I choose to forget what Samaritans look down on.

While Amok unloads the barrel, I close in on Zebedee, a truculent old character with a white beard and a sparkling eye. A man of substance. With nine large townships around the lake itself and a further ten cities in the Decapolis, there is an immense demand for fresh fish. It's a thriving industry. Zebedee thrives as well as any. He knows how to charm the best fish out of the blue water and is proud of his skills.

"Iddo!" he says, identifying me in the gloom. "What are you doing back here so soon?"

"I have a complaint to make, Zebedee."

He bridles at once. "About my fish?"

"The fish were fine," I assure him.

"Then what is the problem?"

"He is," I say and point to the barrel.

Having prised open the lid, Amok extracts the object and holds it up by the hair. Zebedee recoils. It is a gruesome sight. When a man's head has been pickled and cured along with the fish, it loses all dignity and definition. Eyes, nose, ears, mouth and beard are all one, an amorphous mass of flesh and bone. The hair is glutinous seaweed. The stink, unimaginable.

Zebedee recovers quickly. Fishermen are men of the world.

"It must be Matthias!" he says.

I'm astonished. "You *recognise* him?"

"His own mother would not recognise him, Iddo, but there is something about the hang of his lip and the droop of his nostrils. Besides, Matthias has been missing for several days. Where's the rest of him?"

"He wouldn't tell me," I joke. "He's even less of a conversationalist than Amok. But I could hazard a guess."

"What is it?"

"You won't like what you're about to hear, Zebedee."

"I'll hear it just the same."

"Brace yourself, then. I've been brooding on this for days now and I'm sure that I'm right."

"Where is Matthias's body?" he presses.

"Distributed among other barrels of fish."

"Contaminating my livelihood!" he erupts. "I'll not endure it. Why is he doing this to me? Matthias was one of my best fishermen. I paid him well. He has no cause for complaint."

"I'd say he has every cause for complaint," I argue with a gesture towards the decapitated head. "Matthias did not do this of his own volition. When a man wants to sleep with the fishes, he usually drowns. He doesn't cut himself up into pieces before jumping into a series of barrels."

"We're not certain that that's where he is."

"True, Zebedee. But my guesses are rarely wrong."

"Let's find out."

Zebedee leads me across to the warehouse where his fish are stored in barrels awaiting dispatch. He barks orders to a couple of men and they react with amazement. Open the barrels? Pour out the fish? Has their master taken leave of his senses? Zebedee repeats his command and they set to work, lifting the lid of the first barrel and sending its contents slithering across the floor.

No sign of Matthias in this or in three subsequent barrels and Zebedee grows sceptical. I urge him to try one more and my theory is proved correct. As another consignment cascades onto the floor, a human hand appears like a phantom starfish. It is enough to convince Zebedee, who is so enraged that he joins his men in the task of opening up the rest of the barrels.

Matthias is ubiquitous. Parts of him are scattered in a dozen different barrels, an arm here, a leg there, a foot, a toe, a kneecap, elsewhere. The torso itself is never found but all but a few of the appendages are soon laid out on the warehouse floor. The men goggle in horror. I preen myself. Zebedee is close to hysteria.

"Who has done this to me?" he wails.

"Matthias is the one who suffered," I point out.

"Only in order to hurt me. This is a direct attack on my business. What will happen to me if customers find human remains among their fish? My reputation will be ruined." He becomes vengeful. "I'll kill the man who did this. I'll flay him alive!" Reason takes over. "An investigation must be set in motion. I'll report this to the authorities."

"No," I say, firmly. "I have a better idea."

"This villain must be caught, Iddo."

"He will be. Trust me."

Our whole commercial relationship is based on trust and Zebedee has not found me wanting in the past. He agrees to hear me out. Having sworn his men to secrecy, we send them away so that we can talk in privacy. Only poor Matthias — whose pendulous ears lie a yard apart at our feet — eavesdrops.

"Let me solve this crime," I ask. "Discreetly. Contact the authorities and the whole of Galilee will know that you sell contaminated fish. Do you want that to happen?"

"No!"

"Then leave this to me, Zebedee. One of your enemies is behind this outrage. How many of them are there?"

"Hundreds. They hate my success."

"I'll need a full list of those enemies," I tell him. "And I must speak with your sons, James and John."

"They've gone, Iddo. They left home to follow The Healer."

"The Healer?"

"A man from Nazareth who performs miracles."

"What sort of miracles?"

"He makes the dumb speak, he feeds five thousand with a few loaves and fishes, and he raises men from the dead."

"Could he do anything for Matthias?" I wonder.

"Forget the Healer," he says. "Think of my fish. Some of these barrels were due to be sent off to the High Priest's Palace in Jerusalem tomorrow. My produce is held in high regard there. How long would that regard last if someone was served Matthias's Adam's apple at the next banquet?" He embraced me warmly. "Thanks to you, that danger has been averted. You stopped that shipment in time. If you can solve this crime, Iddo, I'll not only replace the barrel you returned to me. I'll give you thirty others as well."

That kind of deal is music to a merchant's ears.

"Done!" I confirm.

Then I realise that *I* must now perform miracles.

Amok and I begin our investigations at first light. Boats are already out on the water. The best fishing-grounds are near the mouth of the River Jordan at the north-east end of the lake. Fed by the melting snows of Mount Hermon, the river comes hurtling down into the lake with a mass of silt in its wake. The silt contains rich food for fish and shoals converge on it. Fishermen converge on shoals. Zebedee and his sons are among them, often working in partnership with Andrew and Peter, the brothers from Bethsaida. A strange coincidence. Andrew and Peter have also gone off to follow The Healer. This man from Nazareth must be something of a fisherman himself to land such an impressive catch.

By hanging around the wharves in Capernaum, I pick up every scrap of information I can about Matthias and his dispersed remains slowly merge into a whole man. He was an unappealing fellow, grumpy, outspoken and disliked by all for his grinding pessimism, which is why his disappearance has been noted with relief rather than alarm. Yet he was an able and conscientious fisherman whose job was to catch and land fish then load the very barrels in which he himself took up residence.

Did a discontented colleague hear one complaint too many from Matthias's whinging lips? Or was his death the result of a violent argument? Neither possibility seems likely. When a man takes up simultaneous lodgings in a dozen barrels of fish, calculation is patently at work. His accommodation has been carefully planned in advance so that horror can be scattered far and wide.

Galilee is a meeting-place of nations with trade routes crossing in all directions, from the Levant to Damascus, from Jerusalem to Antioch, from the Nile to the Euphrates. Zebedee exports to all these regions. Matthias would have provoked chaos across the whole of the known world. As barrels were unpacked, unkind remarks would have been made about Jews.

Am I searching for an anti-Semite?

I start with the men who gut and pickle the fish before leaving them to cure. It is a smelly occupation and the sheds in which they work make my stomach heave. But hours of patient watching eventually pay off. His name is Alphaeus. Alone of the men in the sheds, he has a real zest for his work, using his knife with the practised ease of an assassin and grinning vacantly as he grabs each new victim from a wooden box. Slit, gouge, slice. He is an expert.

Alphaeus is tall, thin and sinewy. There is brute strength in those long arms. Instinct is a vital part of my trade and my instinct tells me that this man makes a hobby of bearing grudges. The face has a deathly whiteness but there is deep darkness in the soul of Alphaeus.

When I finally catch him alone, he is not welcoming.

"Piss off, you Samaritan turd!" he hisses.

"I want to talk to you," I say.

"Come near me and I'll cut your tongue out," he warns, brandishing his knife. "Go back to Samaria while you can!"

"Did you know a man called Matthias?"

"No!"

"Everybody else did."

"Then sod off and talk to them."

"We need your help, Alphaeus."

"I don't help Samaritans."

"That will disappoint him."

"Him?"

"Amok," I say. "He's standing behind you."

Alphaeus swings around with his weapon at the ready but he has met his match in Amok. My bodyguard comes into his own on occasions like this. He stuns Alphaeus with a blow between the eyes, seizes the knife from his grasp then lifts him a foot from the floor. Alphaeus squirms impotently like a giant eel.

"Now will you talk to me?" I invite.

"No!" splutters the eel.

A nod is all that Amok requires. He has ways of making even the most reticent men speak. Alphaeus is tough but his resolve soon weakens when he has been held headfirst in a barrel of fish for two minutes. When Amok hauls him out again, he is gasping for air and begging for mercy.

"Now you know how Matthias felt," I suggest. "Tell me about him. While you still can."

"I've no idea where he is," he lies.

"Then go and search for him."

Amok plunges him deeper into the fish this time and all resistance vanishes. When Alphaeus is finally released, he looks as if he has been to hell and back in a basket. Amok holds him while I begin my interrogation.

"Why did you kill Matthias?"

"I didn't kill him," protests Alphaeus.

"You were involved somehow."

"Only afterwards," he bleats. "My job was to cut him into portions and share them out among the barrels. I never liked Matthias. It was a pleasure to slice him up. And I needed the money. Zebedee doesn't pay me enough."

"Did you want to ruin his business?"

"Yes, I did."

"Why?"

"Zebedee always criticises me."

"He'll have good reason when he hears about this."

"I didn't murder Matthias," insists the prisoner. "I did what I was paid to do and nothing more."

"And who paid you?"

"I don't know."

"Forgotten his name already?" I ask, jocularly. "Put him back in the barrel, Amok. It will jog his memory."

"No, no!" he implores. "Anything but that!"

"Who paid you?"

"I really don't know," he repeats in desperation. "We met in an inn and he was in disguise. A big man, that is all I can tell you. And rich. He paid me extremely well."

"Did he bring the body himself?"

"Yes. One night. Matthias had been strangled to death. The man was so pleased with himself. He was giggling. Giggling with excitement at the way he'd killed his victim. He couldn't stop telling me how easy it'd been. Matthias was strapped to the back of a donkey."

"One donkey brought him to another," I muse.

"Eh?"

"Samaritan wit. Too subtle for you."

"Spare me!" he begs. "Spare me and I'll give you all the money I have." He grins hopefully. "What do you say?"

Amok answers for both of us. A mighty punch fells the wretch. Taking a leg apiece, we drag him off to Zebedee and hand him over. I have to move on to the next stage of the investigation on my own. Amok would never approve. Beneath that bear-like exterior, he has too many moral imperatives floating around.

They'd be a severe handicap in the house I'm visiting.

Naomi is unique. Tall, slim and sensuous, she moves with the grace of a dancer and the dignity of a queen. Naomi has fathomless beauty but she also has a dimension beyond the merely physical and emotional. Locked in her wondrous embrace, I attain true ecstasy. I actually forget my mother.

"It is wonderful to see you again so soon," she purrs.

"Have you missed me?"

"Painfully."

"That is what I like to hear."

"Are you happy in my arms, Iddo?"

"Blissfully."

"Do you like this?"

I moan in sheer delight.

Her fingers are magical. A saint would capitulate under her delicate touch. Except that a saint could not afford to call on Naomi. She is highly selective. Her clients are few in number and chosen for their wealth or their personality. I prefer to believe that it is the latter criterion which was applied to me. My personality blossoms in Naomi's mansion.

I force myself to concentrate on the murderer.

"I need your help, Naomi."

"That's what I'm giving you."

"Information," I explain, trying to ignore the thrills of delight shooting up through me from her tantalising digits. "You consort with the great and the good in this city. You know what goes on in Capernaum."

"Stop flattering me."

"I want the name of a murderer from you."

"No murderer is allowed in here," she protests, angrily. "Is this some silly game of yours, Iddo? I thought you came to me for pleasure."

"I did, my dove. And I received it."

"No more talk of murderers, then."

"But this is important," I say, softly.

And I slip some more coins into her hand. It buys me five minutes to tell my tale. Naomi is inscrutable. A body which can speak fluently in a hundred different languages now lies stiff and unresponsive in my arms. She is deeply upset. I suspect that I know why.

"Did he come to you that night, Naomi?"

"I never discuss one client with another."

"Then he was here?"

"I am saying nothing."

"He was a big man," I remind her. "Rich enough to afford you and excited enough to need you. What better way to celebrate his villainy than with the pride of Capernaum? He could not stop boasting about it, Alphaeus said. I warrant that you heard the whole story from him. You know him, don't you?"

"Close the door behind you, Iddo."

"You remember him. From that giggle of his."

"We will not be doing business again."

"Would you turn me away and harbour a killer?"

"I harbour nobody."

"Then give me his name."

"I have no notion what you are talking about."

"How much money would it take to give you a notion?"

"Far more than you have at your disposal."

"Do not underestimate my wealth."

"Do not overestimate my affection for you."

"How much?"

"I know nothing, I tell you."

"How much, Naomi?"

"Goodbye."

"I'll pay *any* price," I affirm.

Naomi gives me a curious look. Her body relaxes and she fondles me absentmindedly. Her expression is inscrutable but her mind is racing. She heaves a deep sigh.

"This is no life for me," she confesses. "Waiting on the whims of men. Pampering their passions. I deserve better. I was born for a life of leisured respectability."

"I could not agree more."

"You will pay *any* price, Iddo?"

"I give you my word."

"Then this is what it will cost."

She whispers in my ear and I give a slight shudder. Naomi drives a hard bargain. As merchants, we are well-matched.

When I collect Amok and go back to the wharf, chance contrives better than I could myself. The very man I am seeking is talking with Zebedee. I recognise him at once from Naomi's description. Big, dark, handsome and vain, with a beard that curls at the edges. He strokes his beard as I approach. A telltale giggle escapes him. I plunge straight in.

"Caleb the Fisherman?" I say, accosting him.

He frowns. "Who are you?" he snarls.

"My name is Iddo. I'm a friend of Zebedee."

"And a Samaritan!" The familiar note of contempt.

"That is immaterial. We must talk."

"I have nothing to say to you."

"Then say it to Zebedee instead," I encourage. "Tell him why you killed one of his men and had him carved up by that ghoul, Alphaeus. Why did you do it, Caleb?"

"Do what?" His coolness is breathtaking. "I have never heard of this – what did you call him – Alphaeus?"

"You paid him to do your grisly work for you."

"Is that what the fellow says?"

"Not exactly."

"Does he identify me by name?"

"No," I admit.

"Has he pointed the finger of blame at me?"

"Only indirectly."

"Then you are very bold," he says, black eyes ablaze. "Very bold and very stupid. I am wrongfully accused here and will call Zebedee as my witness. This is the grossest slander. You will answer for this, Iddo the Samaritan. I'm a keen rival of Zebedee, it's true, but that rivalry has always been friendly. Why on earth should I wish to kill one of his men?"

"To strike at the very heart of his reputation."

Zebedee intervenes. "But Caleb and I have known each other for years," he argues. "He would never do such a thing."

"Wouldn't he?" I challenge.

"No!" attests Caleb, stroking his beard.

"Not in a hundred years," adds Zebedee.

"So where is your proof, Iddo?"

Thinking he's safe, Caleb giggles with excitement.

"The lady took confession from you," I remind him and his giggle becomes a spluttering rage. "Murder aroused you, Caleb. You went to her in the exhilaration of your villainy and you could not resist bragging about your triumph. Naomi is my proof. I call upon her to unmask you."

"Who will listen to the word of a slut?" he sneers.

"Naomi is no slut," I retort with composure. "You speak of the lady who is about to become my wife."

Caleb is cornered. Even Zebedee is coming to see him in his true light now. Stout denial is no longer enough for the killer. We have him over a barrel of fish.

He is a powerful man. His fist catches me a glancing blow on the jaw and sends me reeling. It has the most remarkable effect on Amok. Springing into life, he not only pounds Caleb unmercifully until the fisherman crumples to the ground, he actually accompanies the beating with a stream of coherent, not to say, impassioned words.

"You attacked my master," he says with a reverence for me that I never expected to hear. "You hurt him. You'll have to account to me for that. If you murdered Matthias, you will pay at a latter date but I'll exact full payment right now for what you did to my master. Nobody touches him with impunity. You'll apologise to him, do you hear? On your knees, you'll grovel and apologise to Iddo the Merchant."

And Caleb does. Without even a trace of a giggle.

Three dusty days in the saddle take us home to Sebaste. A long train of camels is towed in our wake. Mother comes out of the house to welcome us. We dismount with relief.

"Where have you been?" she asks.

"In Capernaum, Mother."

"What were you doing there?"

"Competing with The Healer."

"Who?"

"The Healer," I explain. "Some clever Nazarene who does conjuring tricks to amuse the crowd."

"Conjuring tricks?"

"Yes, Mother. He makes the dumb speak. He feeds five thousand with a few loaves and fishes, and he raises men from the dead."

"These are not tricks, Iddo. They are miracles."

"I matched each one of them."

"How?"

"I, too, made the dumb speak," I announce, proudly. "At my prompting, Amok turned into a monster of garrulity. As for feeding the five thousand, look at these barrels of fish." I indicate the cargo on the camels. "I took one to Galilee and turned it into thirty at no extra cost. Nor was I defeated by the task of raising a man from the dead. I brought Matthias back to life again so that he could accuse his killer. Your son is a miracle-worker, Mother. Are you not impressed?"

She grimaced and gave her famous dismissive shrug.

"I'd be more impressed if you'd found yourself a wife."

"Ah, yes," I add, triumphantly, "I'd forgotten her. I'm betrothed at last, Mother. A delightful creature called Naomi. A lady in every sense of the word. I have the feeling that Naomi will be the ideal partner for me in life."

My mother fell silent for a whole day.

It was the biggest miracle of them all.

THE HUNCHBACK AND
THE STAMMERER

Charlemagne has always fascinated me, not least because of his foundation of the celebrated Palace School at Aachen. Here was a military hero, who was somehow unable to conquer the arts of reading and writing, yet who created an institution that was the engine room of the Carolingian Renaissance. His relationship with his sons, legitimate and illegitimate, lies at the heart of this story. There are two standard lives of the Emperor. The one by Einhart the Frank is far more reliable because he was a trusted friend of Charlemagne and worked at the Palace School. But the anecdotal version by Notker the Stammerer, written much later, is more entertaining and, in its own way, more insightful at times. Notker's book was written for the Emperor Charles the Fat, the epileptic grandson of Charlemagne. Its story of how a stammering monk overcame his disability would have appealed to a man with a disability of his own.

The monastery of Saint Gall, 883.

My name is Notker, the St-St-St-St-ammerer.

Have no fear, my friends. I jest with you. Though my tongue betrays me whenever I open my mouth, my pen is as fluent as the stream that flows beside our monastery. Here I sit, old, weary and toothless, shivering in this inhospitable place where I have lived out my days. The Benedictine house of Saint Gall is in the upland valley of the Steinach, in the German Swiss canton of Saint Gallen. It is bleak and remote. We suffer all the privations enjoined by the founder of the Order and I, of course, your humble narrator, suffer the additional burden imposed upon me at birth. A stammer can cause endless amusement among those who can speak without impediment but it is a heavy cross to bear for the stammerer himself.

Monks are capable of great cruelty. They tease me incessantly. My nickname is N-N-N-Notker even though that particular consonant is one over which I never stumble. Labials are my real enemies. My lips tremble at the very thought of them.

But nothing terrorizes me more than the letter "S". Ask me to tell you about saints such as Simeon Stylites or Simplicius or the Seven Sleepers of Ephesus and I will hiss embarrassingly at you for hours on end. Like others who were born to stammer, I have learned to choose my words with care or, on occasion, to express myself in ways that require no speech at all. That is why I am drawn to tell this hitherto unpublished story about *Carolus Magnus*, the Emperor Charlemagne. It features a man, not unlike myself in younger days, naïve, devout and deeply loyal to his ordained ruler. An unlikely hero, perhaps, but one who deserves praise. How many of you realize that Charlemagne's life was once saved by a monk with a pronounced stammer?

We also serve who only stand and bite our tongue.

Charlemagne is remembered primarily as a military leader, as a supreme general who fought over fifty campaigns in the course of his long life. Danes, Slavs, Saxons, Avars, Dalmatians, Lombards and Spaniards alike found it impossible to resist the inexorable extension of his empire. Yet he was impelled by no mere lust for glory. Behind the recurring wars was a holy purpose. He strove to defend the Christianity of the West against the enemies who threatened it on all sides and, in the wake of his victories, he was able to promote the most wondrous renaissance of learning.

Charlemagne's renowned Palace School in Aachen was a haven for the finest scribes, teachers, scholars and illuminators of manuscripts. No *scriptorium* before or since has ever rivaled the quality and quantity of the work that was published and disseminated from the Carolingian capital. Only one achievement was greater than the establishment of the Palace School and that was Charlemagne's choice of the man who was its head.

His name was Alcuin but his master called him by an affectionate nickname.

"Greetings, Albinus."

"Welcome to the School, mighty King."

"It seems busier than ever," said Charlemagne, looking around the *scriptorium* with satisfaction. "Or are your scholars merely trying to impress me?"

"What you see now is what you would see on any day that you cared to visit us," said Alcuin proudly, indicating the rows of monks bent diligently over their work. "I impose stern discipline. It is the only way to ensure that our high standards are maintained. Lazy scholars have no place here."

"How does it compare with York?"

"Very favorably."

"In what way?"

"The most obvious," replied Alcuin. "When I began copying and editing texts in York Cathedral all those years ago, we never had more than three or four scribes at work. Here, as you see," he went on, waving a skeletal arm, "we have almost four dozen. This year we expect to produce over two hundred and fifty books."

"Excellent!"

"Much of the credit must go to you."

"Me?" said Charlemagne with a chuckle. "A man who cannot even write?"

"You appreciate the importance of books."

"What I appreciate is the genius of a certain Albinus."

Alcuin gave a weary smile. "My remaining hair is silver rather than white."

"You will always be Albinus to me."

"And you, my Imperial Highness, will always be King David to me."

Charlemagne gave another chuckle. His own nickname delighted him. It was an honor to be compared to such a commanding figure from the Old Testament. King David was a courageous soldier, a shrewd politician, a fond husband and father, a lover of beauty, poetry and music. Believing himself to be in the same mould, Charlemagne was not blind to the fact that he, like David before him, also had an impressive retinue of concubines. It was something about which Alcuin ventured to tease him.

The contrast between the two men could not have been sharper. Charlemagne was tall, well-built and powerful. He had a natural authority and a dignified bearing. His eyes were unusually large and set either side of a prominent nose. There was a worldliness about him that made others feel desperately provincial. Alcuin, on the other hand, was an ascetic, a native of Northumbria who had dedicated himself to learning at an early age and who had grown up within the hallowed walls of York Cathedral. The fair skin and white hair of a typical Anglo-Saxon had earned him the nickname of Albinus. Slight of build, he was a quiet, resolute, conscientious man who had distinguished himself as a scholar, teacher and poet. Whatever reservations he might have about the darker sides of Charlemagne's private life were kept to himself. At the Palace School, he had been given an opportunity that every scholar in Christendom would envy.

"Are you happy here, Albinus?" asked Charlemagne.

"Sublimely so, David."

"Then why do I sense a note of wistfulness?"

"Wistfulness?" repeated Alcuin.

"Yes," said Charlemagne, studying him carefully, "I noticed it as soon as I came in. It is as if your body is here in Aachen but your mind is somewhere else."

"I am sorry if I give that impression."

"Do you still pine for York?"

"No, David."

"Are you sure? I would not blame you, if you did."

"I still *think* of York," admitted Alcuin. "It holds many dear memories for me. When you were gracious enough to let me return there, I was filled with contentment but I do not yearn to spend the last of my days in York. That chapter in my life is ended."

"Will you remain here in Aachen?"

"That is for my lord and master to decide."

"I would not hold you here against your will."

"My heart and mind belong to the Palace School for the moment," said Alcuin, not yet ready to confess that his real ambition was to become abbot of Tours. "But, if we are looking to the future," he continued, deftly turning attention away from himself, "we ought also to consider your own."

"Soldiers have no future, Albinus. The next battle could be my last."

"Then it behooves you to think about a successor."

"My eldest son, Charles."

"Not necessarily."

Charlemagne tensed. "You doubt his qualities?"

"Not at all, great King. All your sons are worthy of their illustrious father. What I beg leave to doubt is whether or not Charles will outlive you."

"Yes," sighed the other, "he is prone to recklessness on the battlefield. But he has fought bravely and deserves to take my throne in the fullness of time." He saw the glint in Alcuin's eye. "You *know* something, Albinus."

"Do I?"

"You can see into the future."

"Hardly."

"Your predictions are invariably correct."

"They are simply wild guesses."

"Wild but accurate."

Alcuin shrugged his shoulders. "Place no reliance on me, David."

"I place every reliance on you," said Charlemagne. "Look what you have achieved here. Your learning is beyond compare, your counsel always sage. So tell me, Albinus," he pressed, taking a step closer, "who will succeed me?"

"Do you really wish to know?"

"I insist."

"Then I will give you my prediction," said Alciun. "It is Lewis."

Charlemagne gaped at him. "Lewis?"

"The youngest of your sons."

"Not Charles or even Pepin?"

"No," said Alcuin.

"But Lewis is so *pious.*"

"Piety is not out of place on an imperial throne."

"Only soldiers can build and hold together an empire."

"Nevertheless," said Alcuin with quiet conviction, "Lewis will be your successor."

The prophecy troubled Charlemagne. Though he was soon preoccupied with affairs of state, he never forgot the gentle confidence with which Alcuin had spoken. Could his friend be mistaken for once or did Charlemagne have to accept that two of his beloved sons would die before he did? It was unsettling. Charlemagne was no ordinary father. Determined to give his children a proper training in the liberal arts, he insisted that his daughters should be educated alongside his three sons. While their brothers were taught to ride in the Frankish fashion, to bear arms and to hunt, the girls learned to spin, weave and acquire every womanly accomplishment so that they would not fritter away their time in idleness.

Though his sons were encouraged to marry, Charlemagne kept his daughters within his own household, arguing that he could not live without them. For such beautiful and spirited girls, this was bound to lead to extreme frustration and they relieved it by clandestine romances within the Court. Unlike his youngest son, none of his daughters could be accused of excessive piety.

The prediction about his successor haunted the family man. It was in Ratisbon that it took on a frightening immediacy. Charlemagne was returning from his war against the Slavs. Situated on the River Danube, Ratisbon was a pleasant town near the eastern rim of his empire. Its palace was a secure fortress where Charlemagne could refresh and restore himself in the wake of another triumph. But he was not allowed to relax for long. When he had been there only a few days, he had an unexpected visitor.

"I must speak with you, Father."

"My ears are always open to you, my son."

"That is why I came."

"You have a request to make?"

"No, Father."

"Then how may I help you, Pepin?"

"By heeding my warning."

"Warning?" echoed Charlemagne.

"They mean to kill you."

Pepin the Hunchback was one of Charlemagne's many illegitimate children. His mother was called Himiltrude and she was a favored occupant of the royal bed. Whether it was out of love or pity, I do not know, but when Himiltrude brought the misshapen child of his lust into the world, Charlemagne felt constrained to bless it with the name of his own celebrated father, Pepin the Short, the first Carolingian King of the Franks.

Pepin the Hunchback was also short, twisted by Nature into complicated knot that no midwife could even begin to untie. Despite his physical defects, however, the boy grew up to be able, intelligent and proud of his birthright. During his childhood, he enjoyed the routine mockery of his playmates with surprising equanimity. Hunchbacks are stammerers made manifest. It is as if their bodies are permanently locked in hesitation between the womb and the world, not knowing whether to remain curled up in perpetuity or to straighten their backs into manhood.

Charlemagne had a sneaking fondness for Pepin the Hunchback. His handsome face resembled that of his mother so closely that it took Charlemagne's breath away. Was that cruel hump a judgement on the two lovers? The notion always caused a pang. If his bastard brought a warning, Charlemagne was ready to listen to it but it was important to display no fear.

"So they mean to kill me, do they?" he said with a grin. "This is old news, Pepin. They have been trying to murder me from the day I came to the throne."

"I am talking of a new plot, Father," said the hunchback.

"Who is it this time – Saxons or Danes?"

"Neither."

"Slavs, then?"

"No, Father"

"Then who?"

"Frankish conspirators."

"Never!" exclaimed Charlemagne.

"I would not speak out without evidence."

"My own people would not betray me."

"They have tried to do so in the past," said Pepin.

It was a painful reminder. Charlemagne bit back a reply. Plots had been hatched against him throughout his reign but they were usually inspired by agents of foreign powers. Intrigue at Court had brought treachery nearer home and it had been a sobering experience for Charlemagne. When the conspirators were exposed, he had ordered their execution but he could never feel entirely safe again in Aachen.

Doubling his bodyguard, he took even more precautions than ever. As he considered the last plot against him, he recalled that Pepin the Hunchback had been instrumental in revealing that as well. His bastard was perhaps the best bodyguard of them all.

"Who are these men?" demanded Charlemagne.

"One moment, Father," said the hunchback solemnly. "Before I speak, I must exact a promise from you. What I am about to say may cause you distress. It will certainly be met with disbelief. Promise me that you will hear me out."

"Of course."

"No matter how angry you may feel?"

"Why should I be angry?"

"Any father would be in your position."

Charlemagne bridled. "What do you mean?"

"You see?" asked Pepin ruefully. "Your eye is aflame. You are roused already. How can I tell my tale when I know that you will rage and interrupt? Father," he said, kneeling down in front of him, "I am an unwilling messenger. I hate the tidings that I bring. Only concern for your safety makes me pass them on."

"Well?"

Pepin glanced over his shoulder. They were alone in a private room at the palace but he feared that someone might be listening outside the door. He lowered his voice to a whisper. Charlemagne did his best to rein in his temper.

"There was a man called Werinbert," began Pepin, hand on his father's arm. "He was a creature of mine, an unlovely fellow but a cunning intelligencer. It was he who first caught wind of the plot but he was discovered by the conspirators when he eavesdropped on them. They attacked him without mercy. Werinbert was left for dead. Fortunately, I got to him while there was still a spectre of life in him."

"What did he tell you?"

"Everything that he had overheard."

"Go on."

"You are to be killed here in Ratisbon."

"By whom?"

"A group of Frankish nobles."

"Give me names, Pepin," ordered Charlemagne. "Unmask the villains."

"I wish that I could but Werinbert, alas, was not able to identify any of those he overheard. He had no time," explained Pepin. "What he did do, however, was to get a clear idea who is behind the conspiracy."

"Speak his name. He will be arrested at once."

The hunchback sighed. "It is not as simple as that, Father."

"Why not?"

"This is where you must hold back your anger. When you learn what Werinbert told me, you will be furious. You will refuse to believe that it is even possible and I will be tainted for having brought you such disturbing news. Believe me," said Pepin with tears in his eyes, "the revelation hurt me deeply as well. It hurt me and disgusted me. After all, I, too, have blood ties with him."

"With whom?" said Charlemagne, lifting him to his feet. "With whom?"

"Calm down, Father."

"How can I remain calm in the face of such an allegation?"

"It is more than an allegation," urged Pepin. "It cost Werinbert his life."

"And what did the wretch hear?"

"Something that I could not even imagine to be true at first."

"Tell me."

"The leader of the conspiracy is one of your own sons."

Charlemagne was torn between shock and incredulity, stunned by the revelation yet unable to accept it. His sons were his closest friends, trusted allies of his heart from whom nothing was hidden. It was impossible that one of them should turn against him.

"Werinbert did not secure a name," Pepin went on. "But he was left in no doubt that it was from your own flesh and blood that danger would come. The men were boasting about it. 'Poor blind Charlemagne!' one of them said. 'He does not realise that he is nurturing a viper in his bosom. Force is power. Like father, like son.' Those are the very words that were spoken."

"Werinbert was lying to you," asserted Charlemagne.

"He was telling the truth, Father. Dying men have no cause to lie."

"My sons revere me."

"I know that *I* do," said Pepin firmly. "And so should they."

"Yet one of them is preparing to lift his hand against me? No, it is inconceivable."

"Therein lies its chance of success. Because you do not fear attack from that quarter, you have no defense against it. Your sons have ready access to you. They know your movements. Who better to direct assassins against you?"

"Stop!" yelled Charlemagne. "I'll hear no more."

"Let me and my men protect you, Father."

"There is no need."

"We will shield you against the Devil himself."

"None of my children would *dare* to strike at me, Pepin."

"I hope and pray that that is true," said the hunchback with burning sincerity.

"But I felt that I had to tell you what Werinbert overheard. His information has always been reliable in the past and I see no reason to distrust it now. Your life is in danger, Father. I offer you a secret bodyguard that will ward off any assault. Accept that offer," he argued. "One of your sons means to kill you."

Worried by Alcuin's prediction, Charlemagne was alarmed by the warning from Pepin the Hunchback. When he was left alone to reflect on what he had heard, he wondered if the words of the two men might not be in some way linked. Was the master of the Palace School telling him the same thing as his bastard? The distraught father agonized for hours on end. Of his three sons, Charles had least cause to enter a conspiracy. He was the acknowledged heir and would succeed in due course. Why kill his way to a throne that was his by right? It was perverse.

Pepin, the second son, whose legitimacy was attested by a powerful physique that set him apart from his namesake, the hunchback, was another unlikely assassin. He had led Frankish armies against the Huns and the Avars. His father had made him King of Italy and Pepin was thrilled with his beautiful kingdom. Charles, too, of course was a dashing warrior who commanded armies in Bohemia and Lunenberg. If it was Pepin who conspired to kill his own father, he would have to remove Charles as well because his elder brother stood between him and the throne.

Charlemagne's mind was tormented by Alcuin's prophecy. According to the saintly old scholar, Lewis would succeed his father. Yet he was the most peace loving of all three sons. As the appointed King of Aquitaine, he was more concerned with ruling by Christian example than with anything else. For him to succeed to the throne, a father and two elder brothers had first to be removed. Was it possible that Lewis could contemplate the assassination of the three people he loved most in the world? His conscience would never permit such hideous thoughts.

And yet he, in Alcuin's opinion, was the designated heir. How could that be? Charlemagne wrestled with the question. Was there some bizarre agreement between all three brothers to kill their father in order to place Lewis on the throne? His piety would make the youngest son the most acceptable to the Pope. Charlemagne liked to portray himself as the defender of Christianity but there were many, even in the Vatican, who considered him to be no more than a holy barbarian

"Dear God!" he said to himself. "Pope Leo!"

It was a timely reminder that piety was no guarantee of civilized behavior. Pope Leo III had been attacked by the citizens of Rome, true Catholics to a man, who tried to blind their pontiff and cut out his tongue. Fleeing to Charlemagne's camp at Paderborn, he had sought solace and help. The following year, Charlemagne entered Rome and set the Pope back in power. Almost exactly a month later, on Christmas Day, 800, Leo III crowned him Emperor and Augustus in St Peter's Cathedral. Behind the pomp and magnificence of the occasion lay the ugly fact that the Pope had once been expelled by the very people who were, in effect, his own children.

If rough hands could be laid upon a Pope, why should an emperor be spared? If the spiritual leader of Christendom could be arraigned, among other things, for keeping mistresses, then Charlemagne himself was bound to be condemned for the same reason. Alcuin might tease him about his many concubines but he still disapproved of them. Lewis had never been able to accept his father's random promiscuity. Was he intent on replacing a sinful emperor with a devout Christian? How and when would he strike?

Charlemagne swung between disbelief and apprehension. His heart told him that none of his three sons would plot against him but his mind was less certain. The son who demanded the closest scrutiny was Pepin the Hunchback. Why had he brought the grim tidings and how seriously should they be taken? Charlemagne was bound to wonder if his bastard was activated by envy of his half-brothers, legitimate offspring who had no physical defects and who enjoyed great power in their own right. At the same time, he had been moved by the patent reluctance with which the hunchback had imparted the news. Pepin did not want to accuse any of them of plotting against their father. And what did he stand to gain by making a false allegation?

It was time to act. Charlemagne dispatched spies of his own to make discreet inquiries. Reports seemed to justify the hunchback's warning. Werinbert, a man in his service, had indeed died that very day of terrible injuries. Charles, the eldest son, had mysteriously disappeared from Ratisbon. His brother, Pepin, King of Italy, had also quit the town without warning, his excuse being that he was travelling to Rome for an audience with the Pope. Most disturbing of all was the fact that Lewis, the pious King of Aquitaine, had sent word that he was on his way to Ratisbon. Why? Fear took a stronger grip on Charlemagne. As he weighed all three sons in the balance, he found each one of them wanting and asked himself if Pepin the Hunchback might yet turn out to be the most upright of his progeny.

As night began to fall, his fears were intensified. Charlemagne needed help from the one person in whom he had total faith but Alcuin was far away in Aachen.

"Albinus!" cried the emperor. "What am I to *do*?"

The five conspirators met in St Peter's Church at the heart of Ratisbon. Most of them were Frankish nobles, men of high position who each nursed a grievance against their emperor. In the flickering candlelight, their faces were hard and determined. Their plans were discussed in the shadow of the huge golden crucifix.

"When will we strike?" asked one.

"Tomorrow," decided their leader.

"Where?"

"Here in the church."

A third man had scruples. "On hallowed ground?" he said with alarm.

"Yes," replied the leader. "It is the one place where he will be at our mercy."

"That may be," agreed the other, "but it will hardly gain us God's blessing."

"Where better to kill a Devil than in the Lord's own house? What kind of prayers can this monster offer up when he kneels before the altar? Does he ask forgiveness for the hanging of four and a half thousand Saxons in one day at Verden? Does he seek divine approval for the way he betrays his marriage vows? Does he apologize for the wickedness with which he has treated us? No, my friends," said their leader. "It is not humility that puts him on his knees but exultation. I am closer to him than any of you and I have seen the true Charlemagne. My father, our Christian emperor, our so-called defender of the faith, is no more than a gloating tyrant. He must die."

There was general agreement. Objections to the venue for the assassination were soon dropped. It only remained to work out the final details. Each man was anxious to wield the fateful dagger. When everything was finally settled, the conspirators were about to depart. Their leader, however, was circumspect.

"First, let us search the church," he ordered.

"But there is nobody here," said one of his companions. "The place is empty."

"That is how it appears but we must make certain. Dangerous words have been spoken in here tonight. If nobody has overheard us, then my father's life is forfeit. If, however, somebody *is* lurking in here," warned the leader, wagging a finger, "then our own lives are at risk. Search thoroughly, my friends."

They did as he told them and conducted a careful search of the entire church. Candles were used to illumine the darkest corners. The leader's caution was wise. From beneath an altar in the Lady Chapel, they plucked the shivering figure of a young cleric. His name was Stracholf the Stammerer and he had never stammered so violently in his entire life. Though they beat him soundly, they could get no comprehensible words out of him. One of the men held a dagger to the young man's throat.

"Stop!" said the leader. "Do not kill him."

"It is the only way to ensure his silence," insisted the other.

"We do not want more blood on our hands than is necessary. To slay a tyrant is one thing: to murder a holy man is quite another. I will not condone it. Besides," said the leader, "there is a much simpler way to keep that mouth of his shut."

Stracholf was dragged across to the Bible that lay open on the lectern. The cleric was ordered to place his hand on Holy Writ while an oath was dictated to him. He was ordered to swear that he would reveal nothing of what he had heard. Terrified to resist them, Stracholf could not get out the two words that would appease them.

"I s-s-s-s-s-s-s-s. ..."

"Swear, man!" yelled the leader.

"I s-s-s-s-s-s-s-s. ..."

"Swear!"

The dagger was held once more against his throat to cut through his stammer.

"I s-s-s-s-s-s-swear!" gasped Stracholf.

Then he collapsed in a dead faint.

Charlemagne had no sleep that night. Spurning the comfort of a woman, he retired to his bedchamber alone. Seven doors stood between him and the outside world but that thought did not console him. A hundred doors would not keep out a son bent on killing him. If there really was a plot, he decided, then it had to be the work of his youngest son, Lewis. The King of Aquitaine was, in the considered opinion of Alcuin, the one who would succeed to his father's throne. Piety was a capacious cloak for ambition. Lewis would certainly envisage himself as a far worthier defender of the faith. He would not be the only ruler to seize power by assassinating a wicked father. Complete exoneration would surely follow. Charlemagne was shocked to realize that he had broken the bond so completely between father and son. Lewis might be guilty but he himself was not free from blame.

He was still writhing on his bed with remorse when he heard the laughter from the adjoining room. The womenfolk sounded as if they were playing some kind of game. Shrieks of mirth and uncontrollable giggling found their way through Charlemagne's door. He went to investigate. The Queen and his daughters occupied the neighboring room, attended by their maids. All of them seemed to be involved in the commotion. When he flung open the door, Charlemagne was confronted by the strangest of sights. Laughing and giggling, the womenfolk were flitting about the room, pulling up their garments to cover their faces, pretending to hide in corners or behind curtains.

The object of their amusement was a pale, thin, frightened young cleric, wearing no more than a linen surplice. He was hardly a threat to the virtue of the ladies present yet they were behaving as if he had come to take his pleasure at will. Puce with embarrassment, the newcomer stood in the middle of the room and quaked visibly.

"Be quiet!" roared Charlemagne. "Who is this man?"

"He is unable to tell us," said one of the women, setting off the cachinnation once more. "The poor fellow can not even s-s-s-s-say his own n-n-n-n-n-n-name."

Stracholf flung himself at the emperor's feet and looked up at him. Words might befuddle Charlemagne, but he could read despair in a man's eyes. Only something of great importance could have brought the cleric to him. Rebuking his womenfolk with a stare, he took the hapless visitor into his own chamber and shut the door behind them. Stracholf got to his feet and stammered incoherently.

"Slowly, my friend," said Charlemagne, holding up a palm. "Let your tongue catch up with the words before you try to utter them."

It was sound advice but Stracholf was in no state to accept it. The emperor's life was in danger and that fact robbed him of articulate speech. His oath had been discarded. Imposed by force, it had no real power to bind him and he had made his way to the palace to raise the alarm. Unfortunately, he got no further than the adjoining room where the women had ridiculed the matching defects of his virginity and his stammer. Stracholf had at last been admitted to Charlemagne's presence. Tears of gratitude coursed down his cheeks. The emperor wanted an explanation.

"Why have you come?" he asked.

With his tongue in open revolt, Stracholf made a series of vivid gestures.

"You bring a warning?" said Charlemagne.

The cleric nodded. Robbed of speech and seeing the futility of writing down words that could not be read, he went into an elaborate mime. He crossed to the table on which a small crucifix stood and knelt before it in prayer. Then he lay beneath the table as if about to go to sleep. A hand to his ear, he sat up to listen.

Charlemagne was quick to understand. "You were sleeping in church when you heard something?" he said. Stracholf nodded. "Was it to do with me?"

Nodding once more, the cleric got to his feet and pretended to draw a dagger from its sheath. When Charlemagne was threatened with the invisible weapon, he stumbled back a few paces. This mute individual was repeating the warning he had already received from someone else. Conspirators had been plotting inside the church. Tensing himself, Charlemagne asked the question that had dogged him all evening.

"Which of my sons was involved?" he demanded.

Stracholf picked up one of the pillows from the bed and stuffed it up the back of his surplice, bending over until his body threw a grotesque shadow upon the wall. The emperor put a hand to his mouth in horror.

"Pepin the Hunchback!"

Stracholf nodded and tossed the pillow back on to the bed.

"Who else conspired with him?" Stracholf held up four fingers. "Four of them? Could you pick them out for me?" An affirmative nod was given. "Thank you," said Charlemagne with a mixture of gratitude and sadness. "You have saved your emperor but deprived him of a son whom he once loved and trusted. My womenfolk will be justly chastened when they hear what you have done." He put a hand on the other's shoulder. "What is your name, my friend? Can you tell me?"

"Yes, your Imperial Highness," said the cleric boldly. "It is Stracholf."

And for the first time in his life, he spoke without a stammer.

Justice was swift and brutal. Pepin the Hunchback was arrested. Identified by Stracholf, the other conspirators were quickly rounded up. Summary execution ensued for them but Pepin's life was spared. In warning his father that his life was threatened by one of his sons, he had, in a sense, been telling the truth but only in order to win Charlemagne's confidence. Instead of coming from his legitimate offspring, the threat arose from a bastard with the ill-omened name of Pepin. To establish credence, he had even hacked his own man, the innocent Werinbert, to death. The hunchback was exiled to the poorest and most austere place in the entire Empire, in short, to this very Monastery of Saint Gall where I have penned this history.

There is an ironic footnote. Because it is so cold in this God-forsaken place, Pepin the Hunchback, bitten hard by the fangs of winter, spoke through chattering teeth and ended up as a fully-fledged stammerer. Whereas I, Notker the Stammerer, spent so much time bent over my table as I wrote his story down that I acquired a hunchback of my own.

Don't you think that is s-s-s-s-s-s-ignificant?

Notker was writing seventy years after the death of Pepin the Hunchback but much of his account has some truth in it. Charlemagne was betrayed by his illegitimate son and the plot was unmasked by a stammering cleric, though not perhaps in the way envisaged here. Alcuin's prediction was accurate. The two eldest sons predeceased Charlemagne. Pepin, King of Italy, died in 810. Charles died the following year. Charlemagne himself died in 814 and was succeeded by Lewis the Pious who ruled until his death in 840. Alcuin of York had already ended his days in the way that he hoped – as abbot of Tours.

WAR HATH MADE ALL FRIENDS

This story came into being when I was invited to write the introduction to an anthology called More Shakespearean Whodunnits. *In a preceding volume,* Shakespearean Whodunnits, *most of the Bard's plays had already been used to spark off mystery tales. That set me looking at the Apocrypha, the group of plays that may, at least partly, have been written by Shakespeare. The anonymous play,* Edmund Ironside *was only a marginal contender but its subject and language interested me. An English hero with a name that still resonated in Elizabethan times, Edmund would have been an attractive character for the young Shakespeare. In its portrayal of national strife, the play, probably never performed, anticipates the three parts of Shakespeare's* Henry VI; *and the character of Eadricus, the deceitful Earl, has a clear resemblance to Warwick the Kingmaker, changing sides when it was expedient to do so. As an unrepentant villain, Eadricus cried out to be the narrator so I'll let him tell his own story.*

The end justifies the means. That is my firm belief. Peace justifies war. Friendship justifies hostility. Survival justifies treachery. The pleasures of love justify the vilest act of seduction. And power – sheer, naked brutal, beautiful power – justifies any villainy which is used to attain it.

And I should know.

My name is Eadric and I am Ealdorman of Mercia, a title which I have held for almost a decade. I am one of the most powerful men in the kingdom, entrusted with the governance of all the lands between the Thames and the Humber. Everyone who dares to lay claim to the throne seeks my support. They call me Eadric Streona, curling their lip as they do so, but I bear that "Streona" with a certain pride. It means that I am acquisitive, a quality sneered at by most people, yet one which they all share to a greater or lesser degree. What red-blooded man is not stirred by ambition? Who but a fool has no wish to acquire wealth and influence? Is not growth the most basic law of nature?

Because I am more ambitious than anyone else I have been more acquisitive, and that kind of success always breeds envy. Let them mock. Let them set me down as The Grabber. While they strike at me with a feeble taunt, Eadric Streona will go quietly on acquiring more property, more money, more friends, more status and much more power.

I will revel in my nickname and treat it as my prime acquisition.

Canute appreciates my worth. That is why he courted me above all other. With a man like me in his camp, his position was strengthened beyond measure. And so was mine for a time. Our armies were in Wessex when the first crisis arrived. Canute swept into the room, pulsing with fury and spitting his words out.

"Eadric!" he yelled.

"Yes, my Lord?"

"We have been betrayed!"

"By whom?"

"Leofric and Turkullus."

"Ah!"

"The two earls have run back to Edmund to bleat their apologies like a pair of sheep. I trusted them, Eadric! I relied on their support."

"That, perhaps, was a mistake."

"A serious one."

"Serious," I agreed calmly, "but by no means fatal. And better that they should defect now than on the battlefield where their treachery could inflict more harm. These are bleak tidings, my lord, but you have the means to punish their betrayal."

"The hostages!"

"Yes, dread sovereign. It is always wise to extract pledges of loyalty in human form. Leofric and Turkullus each leave a favoured son in your keeping. The flight of the fathers means instant death for their progeny."

"No," said Canute, eyes blazing with revenge. "Not death, Eadric. That would be too swift a release for them. I have other designs." He clapped his hands and a guard came running. "Take three men and fetch the sons of Leofric and Turkullus. Away!" The guard hurried off and Canute turned back to me. "When those foul traitors left, they willingly sacrificed their sons to the sword. But I will betray their expectations as they betrayed me. The pretty boys will live as testaments of my anger."

"Let them rather die," I urged.

"Never!"

"But their fathers' villainy demands it. Anything less than summary execution would seem too light a sentence, my lord. They will say that Canute is weak and soft-hearted."

"Not when they look at those two sons."

"Dispatch them straight," I argued with a persuasive hand on his shoulder.

"Send word to their fathers of the terrible consequences of their flight. It will shake their hearts. Kill them, my lord. Or let *me* send them to their graves. The situation demands it."

Canute bristled. "I make the decisions here!"

"Of course. But you did seek my counsel."

"And you have given it, Eadric."

"Then let me give it once more."

"No!" he snarled with a peremptory wave of his hand.

There was nothing more than I could do. I was not really pleading for execution because it was a more serious punishment. I wanted to spare two fine and handsome young men from the agonies which they would surely face. Long years of fighting against Danish warriors have made me well acquainted with their savagery. In the circumstances a quick death would be a form of blessing.

The prisoners were dragged in by the four guards. One look at Canute's expression told them what had happened, but they did not flinch. In times of war, even the most loved of sons is expendable. They understood that. They were prepared to meet their fate with a mixture of courage and resignation.

"Leofric and Turkullus are traitors!" roared Canute, drawing his sword. "They have fled and left you behind to face my wrath. What kind of fathers would treat their sons with such contempt?"

"They made an honourable decision," said one of the prisoners.

"We are ready to pay the price for it," added his companion. "Kill me first, my lord. I am not afraid to die."

"You will be afraid to live when I have finished with you," said Canute, seizing him by the arm. "*This* is the price a king exacts."

His sword flashed and cut clean through the prisoner's wrist. A second vicious stroke claimed the other hand, but Canute's rage was still not appeased. Only when he had sliced off the captive's nose was he satisfied, leaving him drenched in blood as he turned to mutilate the other hostage with equal severity. I looked away from the punishment. Two young warriors would never bear arms again. Two handsome faces would be spurned by every woman for their grotesque ugliness. It would be a species of Hell for them.

"Take them away!" ordered Canute. "Bind their wounds and turn them out. Let the world know what happens to those who desert me."

Hiding their pain with great fortitude, the two hostages were hauled out by the guards. Canute wiped his blood-sheathed sword then gave me a grin of triumph.

"Was not that a more fitting penalty, Eadric?" he said.

"Yes, my lord," I lied.

"Nobody will say that I am soft-hearted now."

"Nobody."

And I wondered how soon it would be before *I* betrayed him.

Edmund was not idle. Having secured the support of London, he moved into Wessex to try to restore its allegiance to the old dynasty. We met him first at Penselwood, then at Sherston, in indecisive skirmishes with losses on both sides. Edmund was a doughty soldier and more men flocked to his banner each day, inspired by his valour to attest their abiding hatred of the Danes. It was when he lifted the siege of London then parried our thrust into Mercia that I came to view his leadership with more than admiration. If any man could rout the Danes it was Edmund. So he proved. Canute launched another attack but our army was soundly beaten and forced to retreat to the Isle of Sheppey.

It was time for me to leave.

The name of Eadric still commanded enough respect for my messenger to be admitted to the royal presence. He handed over the letter which I had carefully composed and awaited a reply. Edmund read it slowly through. My words beguiled him. After reminding him that it was I who had helped to keep his father, King Ethelred, in power for so many years, I congratulated him on his feats on the battlefield and wished him success in driving the Danish menace forever from our shores. Imploring his forgiveness, I promised to pledge myself to his cause and renew my loyal service to his family.

Edmund Ironside, as he was now called, was visibly moved by the letter. Though his counsellors warned him that I could not be trusted, he knew the value of my support and overruled them. My unkempt and shabbily-dressed messenger cringed before him.

"Take this reply to your master," said Edmund firmly. "We do not wholly pardon his treachery but we will give him welcome if he cares to join our army. His life is safe."

"Does he have your word on that, my lord?" asked the messenger.

"He does. Eadric will be treated with respect."

"Then tell him so to his own face," I said.

Pulling myself up to my full height and casting off the mean apparel of a messenger, I revealed myself as the author of the letter which he held in his hand. Edmund was both astonished and pleased, amazed at my cunning in gaining access to him and delighted that my betrayal of Canute was no ruse to lure him into ambush.

"Noble Eadric!" he said, spreading his arms wide. "The King of England welcomes you back."

"Thank you," I replied, enjoying his embrace and the discomfort it caused his watching counsellors. "But first attain your kingdom before you try to rule it. Canute still lives and danger is ever-present."

"That danger has shrunk since Eadric came back into the fold."

"I hoped that you would see it that way, my lord."

"I do, my friend, I do." He nodded eagerly then his face suddenly darkened. "Why did you betray me?"

"I did not, Edmund."

"You joined forces with the Danish army."

"Only in order to learn their strength so that I could report it back to you. They had an English spy in their ranks and not a faithful ally."

"Yet you fought against us."

"With reluctance. And only to convince Canute."

"You killed some of my men."

"And lost an equal number of my own," I reasoned. "Few enough on both sides. War is bound to claim some victims. But I never led an attack, Edmund. I always held back in battle, waiting for the moment when I could follow my heart and ride with an English king once more."

"So you shall, Eadric."

"When?"

"When you have told me all you know about Canute's forces."

"That can be done here and now, my lord."

"Good," he said with a smile. "How large an army can he muster and how does he mean to deploy them? What are his weaknesses and how can we best exploit them? Turn messenger again, Eadric. Tell us the news. Help us to defeat our Danish foe."

"Nothing would please me more."

When I gave him the details he sought, the last traces of suspicion fled from his mind. I was accepted. Eadric Streona had lived up to his name once again. In a short space of time I had acquired a new king, a new command, a new security, a new set of hopes and instant repute as the man whose defection would bring about the ruin of the Danish army. I was, of course, too sage a politician to be lulled into complacency.

That night, I wrote to Canute to assure him of my loyalty. These are troubled times. A sensible man always keeps his options open.

The final battle came sooner than I expected and sooner than Canute would have desired. Sailing from Sheppey, his fleet anchored in the River Crouch and he led a raiding party ashore. Intelligencers reported his movements to Edmund who moved swiftly to cut him off. Loaded down with booty, Canute found himself hemmed in near Ashingdon. The only way for him to avoid battle and escape by land was to discard his spoils and abandon his fleet. He had little choice but to fight.

Edmund Ironside had mustered a large army with contingents from Wessex and East Anglia swelled by my own forces from Mercia, but his poorly trained levies would have been no match for seasoned Danish warriors in an equal contest. What gave him the slight advantage was superiority of numbers. Whom should I support? Edmund or Canute? An English king or a Danish usurper? The trick was to appear to favour both sides so that each would be grateful in the event of victory. As I lay in my tent on the eve of battle, I worked out how to pull the trick off.

Our army was camped on Ashingdon Hill, no more than a mile and half away from the enemy. They were in full view. When dawn came on that October morning in the year of Our Lord, a thousand and sixteen, we saw that Canute was assembling his forces on the hill at Canewdon. Edmund Ironside deployed our own army in three divisions with the Wessex contingents under his own command in the vanguard. On the left flank, Ulfcetel had charge of the East Angles while I led the Mercians on the right flank. Sheer weight of numbers told in our favour but I was not convinced that it would be decisive.

Edmund commenced battle by charging down the hill. We obeyed his signal to follow but geography was to have a critical influence. The gradient was much sharper on the left flank and Ulfcetel's men surged down it at a speed which we could not match on the right. I made virtue of a necessity, slowing our descent even more so that we could see how the battle fared before we engaged in it. Edmund and the men of Wessex clashed with the enemy first, then the East Anglian contingents flung themselves upon the Danes. They fought with spirit but they lacked the ferocity of the marauders. Instinct had warned me to hold back and my decision was proved wise.

Seeing the gap on their left flank, the Danes immediately poured men into it so that they could attack the English from behind. Edmund and his army were suddenly engulfed. Both sides fought fiercely but the clear advantage now lay with the Danes. Since I have never believed in the needless waste of lives, I deemed it a prudent moment to depart from the field with my men. When the battle began, I was in the ranks of Edmund Ironside but I withdrew my support in order to yield the day to Canute. In effect, I fought on both sides and on neither. Whatever the outcome, I stood a chance of currying favour with the victor.

As I quit the field, however, I knew that the result was not in doubt. Canute would be triumphant and that would make him grateful to me. Outflanked and outnumbered, the English fought manfully until late in the afternoon but their cause was hopeless. Ulfcetel perished along with a large proportion of the English nobility, while the majority of Edmund's men were killed. It was a massacre. Edmund Ironside himself escaped with his life and his reputation for steadfastness, but he now had to negotiate from a position of weakness.

Shortly after the battle, he and his foe met at Deerhurst to agree to the partition of the realm. While Edmund was allowed to rule in Wessex, the north came under the direct control of King Canute. Since he now held sway over Mercia, it was to the latter that I naturally turned.

Canute received me with a mixture of suspicion and curiosity. We met on the bank of the Humber, an undisputed part of his kingdom now. I lapsed easily into the Danish tongue. It is always politic to learn the language of an invader. Honeyed words can often achieve more than armed conflict.

"I wondered when we would see you again," began Canute warily. "Where did you hide when you fled from the battlefield?"

"That was no flight," I corrected with a smile. "It was a carefully planned retreat to hand the advantage to you."

"What I saw was a frightened man, scurrying for cover."

"Then your eyes were blurred by the heat of battle, my lord."

"You betrayed me, Eadric."

"Only in order to serve you the better."

"You joined Edmund's camp."

"And sent immediate word that I was still your agent. I could help you best by knowing your enemy's inner counsels. To do that, I had to deceive you into believing that I was playing the traitor. It was only when Edmund heard of your rage at my supposed treachery that he took me fully to his bosom."

"Whose side do you *really* favour?" he demanded.

"Yours, my lord. I always prefer to sup with a victor."

"But my victory was not assured at Ashingdon."

"It was when I held back," I argued forcefully. "Until then the issue was in doubt. You were heavily outnumbered. Had I fought for Edmund, he might now be wearing the English crown and you might have been driven out of the realm in disgrace. Think on that, my lord."

He pondered. "You were my spy?" he said at length. "My loyal intelligencer? Is that what you are claiming?"

"The evidence was there on the battlefield."

"But that battle need never have taken place if you had forewarned me of

Edmund's movements. He took us unawares. Why did you not send word to me that he was pursuing us so closely?"

"There was no time, my lord."

"No time or no inclination?"

"Report reached us that you were anchored in the River Crouch. That is all we knew. Edmund whipped us into action at once. How could I get a message to you when I was not sure of your exact position? I had to ride with the hounds before I could find their quarry."

"Then you joined the attack on that quarry."

"Seemingly."

"You rode at the head of the Mercian army."

"But kept them out of the battle."

"Was that by design or cowardice?" he taunted.

"Design!" I retorted vehemently. "A coward would not have fought alongside you as I have done with distinction. A coward would not have risked discovery by Edmund Ironside and certain death at his hands. A coward would not come to you now to pledge his loyalty when he could save his skin by going into exile. No!" I insisted, shaking with righteous indignation. "Call me devious. Call me cunning. Call me anything that you choose. But do not name me as a coward, my lord. Only a brave man could survive the dangers that I have courted."

"Treachery involves a certain bravery," he conceded.

"First and last, I was your man!"

"Prove it."

"I have done so many times."

"Then do so once more, Eadric."

"If you wish, my lord."

"Give me certain proof of your loyalty."

"How?"

He bared his teeth in a wicked grin and I had my answer.

The surest way to learn the truth about a man is either to seduce his wife or bribe his doctor. I have used both methods with equal success in the past, and while I prefer the excitement of the former, it is the latter which often brings the greater reward. So it was with Edmund Ironside. Since his wife was beyond my reach, I had perforce to work through his doctor, and my money purchased far more than I could have hoped. A small, fussy man with an irritating habit of scratching his beard, the doctor was nevertheless an experienced physician who had nursed his wounded patient back to health after many battles.

He was privy to secrets denied even to a wife or a confessor.

"Edmund Ironside lies grievous sick," he confided.

"From injuries sustained at Ashingdon?"

"No, my lord," he said with a sigh. "Though they have also taken their toll. He is in the grip of a strange malady and weakens by the hour."

"Can you not recover him?"

"He may be beyond my skill."

"Do I hear you aright?" I pressed, conscious of the significance of what he told me. "Edmund Ironside is on his deathbed?"

"No, my lord," he said quickly. "I would never put it like that, and he has a will to live which is the best medicine of all. But he is patently unwell. His limbs ache, his throat is swollen and he has a fever that draws a river of sweat out of his body. And yet, when I least expect it, the fever gives way to a fit of shivering that is woeful to behold. You see my dilemma," he added, scratching at his beard. "As soon as I treat one set of symptoms, they are replaced by another. I am not sure if my remedies are curing the disease or feeding it."

"Is he in pain, doctor?"

"Great pain."

"It must weaken him."

"So much so that I have to conceal the truth from his followers. Only his wife and his priest know the worst. Sickness is a cruel leveller, my lord. It has robbed Edmund of his Ironside."

I was quick to see the personal advantages in the situation.

"Take me to him," I ordered.

"I dare not, my lord!"

"Why?"

"It is more than my life is worth," he protested. "Your name is spoken with anger in the camp. You are reviled as an enemy. If I were to conduct Eadric Streona to the sick bed, I would be accused of treachery. I will not do it, my lord."

"You will not have to, doctor."

"I am relieved to hear you say that."

"Yet I must see him."

"It is impossible."

"Only if I appear as Eadric Streona," I reminded him. "Were I to visit him in the guise of a fellow doctor, a learned physician whom you have consulted, then nobody would question my presence for a moment."

"*I* would, my lord."

"Your silence has already been bought."

"No!" he exclaimed. "You ask too much of me."

"I ask nothing, my friend. What you hear is a demand."

The doctor argued long and hard, scratching his beard with such vigour that I was surprised it remained attached to his chin. In the end, he capitulated. Having accepted my bribe, he was at my mercy. I merely had to proclaim him as my creature and Edmund's counsellors would have dismissed him at once and sought a fit punishment.

A gown and a hat turned me into a physician and I whitened my beard with chalk to add age and distinction. When the doctor was next sent for, he took me along as his assistant. We were admitted to the room where Edmund Ironside lay. Stretched out on his bed, he was streaming with perspiration and moaning quietly to himself as he constantly shifted his position. The doctor knelt beside him and conducted a thorough examination before bathing his face and neck with a wet cloth. Edmund consented to drink a cup of water but it took the two of us to hold him upright while he did so. Not for the first time, I was propping up a feeble King of England. It was almost as if his father Ethelred were still alive.

"Edmund," I whispered. "Can you hear me?"

"Do not bother him, my lord," pleaded the doctor.

"Can he say nothing?"

"Not without effort. Make him speak and you torment him."

"Let me ask but one question."

"No, my lord."

"Just one," I said, leaning in close to the patient. "You know my voice, Edmund, and you know my mind. Tell me this. Will you live?"

Defiance flickered briefly in his eyes before being washed away by a surge of pain. His whole body twitched in agony and the doctor took a long time to soothe him, throwing a glare of resentment over his shoulder at me as he did so. I ignored him. As I watched Edmund Ironside in agony on his bed, I was seeing history change before my eyes.

The patient eventually drifted off into a fitful slumber.

"He is in such discomfort," sighed the doctor.

"Is there no way to ease his suffering?"

"None that I have not tried."

"Do you have no kind remedy in your satchel?" I asked gently. "Something that might put an end to his misery and allow him to quit this world with a degree of dignity?"

The doctor was shocked. "My lord!" he spluttered.

"It is no more than I would ask for myself in a like predicament."

"I have sworn to save lives, not to take them."

"This life is already lost."

"That is not true."

"Look at him. Listen to that breathing. Smell that stink."

"The fever may yet break."

"And he will shiver to death instead. Show sympathy, man. Help him on his way to Heaven and you will be rewarded for your deed."

"By execution!"

"Not if his death appears to be natural."

"I will not do it, my lord," he said querulously. "I will not administer a draught to snuff out the flame of Edmund Ironside's life."

"You do not have to do it," I assured him.

"Then why do you badger me so?"

"Because I wish to help a dying man."

"You help him best by leaving him in peace."

"No," I said, reaching for his satchel. "I help him best by sending him to eternal peace. Find me the remedy in your satchel, doctor. You will not have to soil your conscience by administering it. As you see, I too, am a physician. Let me do the office."

"That is tantamount to murder!"

"Is it?"

"I would sooner die myself than be party to this act."

A doctor with scruples was the last thing I needed at such a crucial moment. When it came to murder, the fellow was obviously beyond bribery. Opening his satchel, I thrust it roughly at him.

"Will you take it upon yourself to deny Edmund Ironside an escape from his ordeal?"

Canute was in a joyful mood when we next met. Less than a month after the battle of Ashingdon, he was the unchallenged King of England. What his father, Sweyn Forkbeard, had only half-achieved, the son had now made secure. A Danish warrior sat firmly on the throne and a new form of Danegeld would be exacted from the whole country. It made Canute extremely grateful. He held a banquet in my honour.

"Eat your fill, Eadric," he encouraged. "You deserve it."

"Thank you, my lord king."

"The finest dishes have been prepared for you, my friend. You will eat nothing that will disagree with your stomach."

He went off into a peal of laughter and I smiled tolerantly. An hour later, when he had feasted royally, he slipped a drunken arm around my shoulder and spoke in a hoarse whisper.

"How did you do it, Eadric?"

"Do what?" I asked, feigning ignorance.

"Prove your loyalty to me."

"I have done that a hundred times."

"This was proof positive, man. Two kings cannot rule one realm. It is a perverse situation. You took steps to remedy it."

"I took steps," I admitted, "but the remedy lay elsewhere."

"Come, Eadric," he coaxed. "We are friends for life now. I will garland you with honours. For this duty to his sovereign, Eadric Streona will acquire more than ever before. Exult in your triumph."

"I do, my lord."

"And tell me how you did it."

"With prayer."

He blinked in disbelief. "You *prayed* him to death?"

"I asked God to gather a suffering soul unto Him."

"There was more to it than that, Eadric."

"Possibly," I said.

"Divulge. Share the secret with me."

"There is no secret. Edmund Ironside died of natural causes."

"With unnatural assistance from you."

"What makes you think that?" I said artlessly.

"I *know* you, Eadric."

"That is certainly true."

"And you confessed that you bribed his doctor."

"How else was I to get into Edmund's presence?"

"What physic did you administer?"

"None. I am no doctor."

"But you found the medicine that cured his ills. What was it?"

"I told you. Prayer. Compounded with luck, hope and opportunity."

"Opportunity to kill?"

"That did exist."

"And you seized it with both hands."

"They were closed in prayer."

"Around the neck of Edmund Ironside."

He went off into another peal of laughter, shaking with mirth and pounding me on the back with robust affection. Then he sat back and drained his cup before licking his lips with his tongue. King Canute regarded me shrewdly.

"Keep your secret," he decided with chuckle. "Only you and the doctor know the full truth."

"Me, the doctor and God."

"You rendered me great service, Eadric."

"That is my sole aim in life."

"On my behalf, you committed a murder."

"But I did not."

"I am no fool," he said. "When you went to his bedside, Edmund Ironside was still alive. By the time you left, he was dead."

"A happy coincidence!"

"Why are you being so modest, Eadric?"

"It becomes me."

Yet another burst of laughter rang through the hall. King Canute had settled on a version of events which suited him and nothing would alter his opinion. I was the killer, Edmund Ironside was the victim and this boisterous Dane was the beneficiary. I went along with the myth. It served my purpose and won back his indulgence. I could look forward to a long and comfortable life on my estates in Mercia. Had poor Edmund survived, it would not have been so. Bickering with Canute would inevitably have led to blows and more civil strife would have followed. I would have been forced once again to play one side off against the other. Myth was far more accommodating.

I would soon come to accept it myself.

Canute rose to his feet and dragged me upright beside him. He bellowed above the tumult then banged the table until the pandemonium subsided. Drunken warriors turned to listen to their king.

"We must drink a toast, my friends!" he announced. "To the man in whose honour this banquet is held. The loyal servant who killed one king to make another secure. Raise your cups – to Eadric Streona!"

They drank, laughed, shouted, cheered and pounded their tables in wild approbation. There was no point whatsoever in telling them that I had no part in the death of Edmund Ironside. My notoriety went before me and it had now acquired an even darker hue. It was ironic. After a lifetime of lies and deception, I actually wanted to tell the truth for once.

But nobody would believe me.

Edmund Ironside died with mysterious swiftness in November, 1016. There were no suggestions of foul play at the time. Eadric Streona was welcomed into Canute's court once more, but the Danish king kept a close eye on him. Late in 1017, Canute had him murdered. One of the great villains of Saxon England met an appropriately treacherous end.

DOMESDAY DEFERRED

This story was written at the invitation of Miriam Grace Monfredo and Sharon Newman, joint editors of Crime Through Time II. *It gave me an opportunity to feature a character, who only appears in one of eleven novels in my* Domesday Book *series even though he casts a long shadow over all of them. William the Conqueror was a man who understood the disadvantages – as well as the advantages – of conquest. As both Duke of Normandy and, later, King of England, he had enormous responsibilities, all of which had to be backed up by a credible show of force. His life was always under threat and there was no time when he could allow himself top be off guard. This story, set in his capital city of Winchester, features Ralph Delchard and Gervase Bret, the Domesday commissioners who are the protagonists in the mystery series. Fortunately, they are on hand to defer William the Conqueror's own domesday.*

"W inchester is a city of eunuchs!" complained Ralph Delchard.

"You are being unjust to it."

"Look around you, Gervase."

"I do so. I live here."

"Churches down every street. Three monasteries – Old Minster, New Minster and Nunnaminster. The Bishop's Palace Wolvesey. It is such an eerie place for a virile man to be that I feel threatened. Religion has castrated the whole city."

Gervase Bret laughed tolerantly. His companion was a soldier, a restless man of action who was never happy in the presence of so much ecclesiastical power, attested to, as it was, by the massive towers which loomed above them and by the Benedictine monks who were hurrying past on their way back to the cathedral. Gervase and Ralph nudged their horses along the crowded High Street. When the bells for tierce rang out with deafening authority, Ralph had to shout above them to make himself heard.

"Why on earth did you do it, Gervase?"

"Do what?"

"Take the cowl."

"I did not," reminded the other. "I left the Order at the end of my novitiate."

"Yes," said Ralph, "but you were actually on the point of joining those tonsured virgins. How could you even consider it? Trading your manhood for a life of pointless meditation? It's unnatural!"

"Celibacy is a virtue!"

"Then I willingly embrace vice!"

Gervase laughed again. His youthful flirtation with the monastic life was something on which he looked back with a mixture of affection and relief, nursing fond memories of his time within the enclave, yet grateful that he had renounced it. Life as a Chancery clerk was much more to his taste, and his betrothal to the lovely Alys had banished any wistfulness about his departure from the Benedictine Order. His rejection of the cowl had another important benefit. It enabled him to meet and to work alongside Ralph Delchard.

"Why have we been summoned?" yelled Ralph.

"The King must have more work for us."

"We have done our share, Gervase. I am tired of riding around the shires of England to decide who owns which land and how much they should be taxed. I want to stay at home. I want to rest. Is that unreasonable?"

"No, Ralph."

"Is it too much to ask?"

"I think not."

"Then I will demand that the King release me!"

Gervase raised a mocking eyebrow. Ralph chuckled.

"Well," he said on reflection, "I will *mention* it to him in passing. Only a fool would try to demand anything of William. He has Norman blood in his veins. Hot, red, surging, angry blood. Defy him and you may suddenly lose all interest in life."

"It is rumoured that he is unwell."

"Even more reason to obey him, Gervase. When a bear is sick or wounded, it is the worst time to upset him." The bells chimed relentlessly on. "Dear God!" howled Ralph. "Why must Christianity be so earsplitting?"

As soon as they entered the royal palace, they sensed that something was amiss. The guards had been doubled, gates and doors habitually kept open were now locked, and the newcomers, though familiar visitors, were challenged at each stage of the way to identify themselves and to declare what business had brought them there. After leaving their horses at the stables, it took them several minutes to reach the antechamber next to the hall. Armed guards in helm and hauberk once again blocked their way and asked who they were. Gervase carried no weapon but they eyed Ralph's dagger with cold suspicion. The visitors were ordered to wait. Their brusque manner did not endear the guards to Ralph.

"What is going on here?" he challenged.

"You will be told in good time," said one of them.

"I wish to be told *now*."

"Be patient, my lord."

"How can I be patient when some numbskull like you is asking me who I am every time I come to a door?" He drew himself up to his full height. "My name is Ralph Delchard and I have done the King good service. So has Gervase Bret here. We are royal commissioners, engaged in the great survey which the King has initiated, come to answer his summons. Tell him that we are here."

"He knows, my lord."

"How?"

"Your approach was noted and reported."

"Note and report it again, you idiot!"

"I do not answer to you, my lord."

"His summons was urgent."

"We have our orders."

Hands on the hilts of their swords, the guards stood shoulder to shoulder in front of the door. There was no way past them. Ralph was smouldering. Gervase took him by the elbow and led him to the other side of the room.

"All we can do is to wait," he advised quietly.

"I've a mind to bang their stupid heads together!"

"Where will that get us?"

"It will relieve my irritation," said Ralph, throwing a resentful glance at the two men. "I'll not be treated like this. We are wont to be shown directly into the King's presence. Why do these oafs bar our way? And why is the whole palace crawling with armed guards?"

"They are protecting the King."

"From *us*? We are his loyal subjects, Gervase."

"Everything will be explained in due course."

Ralph was only partially mollified. He retreated into a sullen silence. Gervase, by contrast, remained alert and inquisitive. He crossed to the window to look out into the courtyard, studying the disposition of the guards and trying to draw some conclusions from the impressive show of security outside. When more visitors arrived at the palace, they were closely questioned before they were even allowed to dismount.

Drifting across to his friend, Ralph peered over his shoulder to take a desultory interest in the activity outside. He was in time to see two ladies riding into the courtyard with their train. Even they were subjected to a ritual interrogation.

Ralph suffered a rare lapse into a biblical mood.

"It is easier for a camel to go through the eye of a needle than for innocent visitors to enter the royal palace in Winchester."

Gervase grinned. "I did not know that you were so well-versed in the Gospel According to Matthew," he said, turning to his friend. "We will convert you to the Faith yet."

"I put my faith in my sword arm."

"That, I suspect, is why you were sent for, Ralph."

"What do you mean?"

"You will see."

Raised voices came from the hall. The two men caught only a few of the words before the door burst open and a short, slim, nervous figure in episcopal garb stormed out with a monk at his heels. The two of them went off down the corridor with more speed than dignity. Gervase recognized the bishop at once.

"Maurice of London," he observed.

"Our late chancellor."

"What brings him to Winchester?"

"I do not know," said Ralph. "Nor why he has been sent home again in such haste. But I like this stern treatment of the Church. It augurs well."

"The Church would disagree."

"It always does."

"I meant that it would disagree most strongly with your choice of Bishop Maurice to represent it." Gervase smiled discreetly. "He is hardly a typical prelate."

Ralph went off into an irreverent peal of laughter.

A third guard appeared in the open doorway and beckoned the visitors over. Gervase and Ralph composed themselves before going into the hall.

William the Conqueror, King of England and Duke of Normandy, was huddled in a high-backed chair at the far end of the room. There was no air of conquest about him now. He seemed more like a victim than a victor. Wrapped in a fur-trimmed cloak, he looked old, tired and pale. Long and unrelenting years of soldiering had taken their toll. A big man, with unusually long arms and legs, he had somehow shrunk in size and power. The face retained its character but the glint of invincibility had faded from the eyes. Nothing could actually frighten him, but he appeared at last to have discovered a need for caution.

He was not alone. Standing behind him was a tall, thin, angular monk in his late twenties, massaging the royal temples with supple fingers and whispering words of comfort to the King. As the pain was slowly coaxed out from his pounding head, William began to sigh with gratitude, almost like a lover yielding to the amorous caresses of his mistress.

Ralph and Gervase bowed and stood before their King. He studied each of them in turn for a moment before lowering his lids to surrender to the seductive touch of the healing hands. With a benign smile, the monk worked gently on, probing the forehead and scalp with his fingertips. Ralph, who had ridden in battle many times behind the military genius known as the Conqueror, was astonished to see his revered general in such a depleted condition. He shot Gervase a look of disbelief.

In an instant, the picture before them changed.

"Enough, Brother Godfrey!" said the patient, sitting up and waving a dismissive hand. "Away!"

Brother Godfrey took a step back, bowed to the King, gave a nod of acknowledgment to the visitors, then shuffled out of the hall. The guard followed him and closed the door after them. Ralph and Gervase were alone with their King.

William appraised them again and shrugged an apology.

"I am not at my best," he said wearily. "My head aches and my body is fatigued. No remedy has been found for my ailments. That monk is the only physician who can bring relief. His hands have almost as much magic as Brother Osmund's."

"Brother Osmund?" said Ralph.

"From New Minster," explained Gervase. "I have met him. A clever doctor. A skillful man in the fight against pain."

"Quite so," added William. "But, alas, Brother Osmund is himself unwell and was unable to attend to me. He sent this pupil in his stead. Brother Godfrey has stilled my demons."

"We are pleased to hear it, my liege," said Ralph.

"Maurice was to blame."

"We saw the bishop leave."

"He would insist on arguing with me," said William testily. "The moment he did that, warfare broke out inside my head once again. I need peace and quiet. I crave isolation."

There was a long pause. The King gathered his strength.

"You are wondering why I sent for you," he said.

Gervase was deferential. "We are at your command."

"Yes," said Ralph, with gruff politeness. "Dispatch us where you will, my liege, and we are on our way. Which part of the kingdom must we visit this time?"

"Winchester," said William.

"But we are already here."

"This is where I wish you to stay."

"To look into the returns for Hampshire?"

"No, Ralph," said the other. "This is nothing to do with the great survey – the Domesday Book, as it has come to be called. The Final Judgement. The task I have for you concerns my own Domesday." He gave a defiant smile. "I am not yet ready to be called to account."

Ralph was puzzled, but Gervase understood very clearly.

"There is no question of that," he reassured. "Your reign will continue for many years yet. The health and strength for which you are rightly famed will soon return."

"Not if the assassin has his way, Gervase."

Ralph tensed. "Assassin?"

"Did you not see all the guards?"

"Saw them and suffered them, my liege."

"I am a prisoner in my own palace," complained the King. "That was what Maurice and I were arguing about. He wanted me to move to the castle and cower behind its fortifications. I'll not be driven out of here by anyone. Least of all by the bishop of London." A harsh laugh. "Maurice only wants me to vacate the palace so that he will have free rein among the ladies here. There is a rampant stallion under that mitre of his. The man burns with holy lust. When Archbishop Lanfranc reproved him for his lechery, do you know what Maurice told him?"

"What, my liege?"

"That his exploits in the bedchamber were essential to his health. Lechery was his medicine. When he heard that wondrous excuse, Lanfranc blushed for a week."

"You talked of an assassin," said Ralph anxiously. "Has any attempt been made upon your life?"

"Several, over the years. Kings are never popular."

"No monarch in Europe is more secure upon his throne."

"That only makes me an irresistible target."

"To whom?" asked Gervase.

"To anyone and everyone," said William with an expansive gesture of his arm. "Conquest produces enemies. Some have waited many years for the chance to kill me. Saxons, Danes, Welsh, Scots, and the King of France would happily dance on my grave. And I do not need to look as far afield as that."

"In what sense, my liege?" said Ralph.

"I have a mutinous family," sighed the King. "Odo, my half-brother, bishop of Bayeux and earl of Kent, a man I have loved and garlanded with honours, now languishes in a dungeon in Normandy. Hand him the dagger and he would cheerfully plunge it into my heart. Then there is my eldest son, Robert." A shudder went through the King. "He has betrayed me and turned my old age into an ordeal. And there are others besides those two. Many others. Too many."

"You have lived with such threats for years." noted Ralph. "What makes you think that one of your enemies will strike now?"

"There have been signs."

"Of what nature?"

"The kind I cannot ignore," said the King. "I have been spied on at prayer in the cathedral. Someone tried to force his way into my bedchamber at night. At a banquet earlier this week, my wine was poisoned and the man who tasted it for me lies grievous sick. How many more signs do I need?"

"None," agreed Ralph. "Let me be your bodyguard."

"I have enough of those."

"Then how may we help?" said Gervase.

"By looking where others are unable to look. By staying here at the palace as my guests. This mouse is guileful. It will take a cunning pair of cats to catch him." The King hauled himself upright. "I know your merit. You have a nose for crime and corruption. I can fill the palace with guards but they would never find an assassin. He would see them coming. Only you can pick up his scent and move with the requisite stealth."

Ralph pondered. "I hate to agree with a bishop," he said at length, "but Maurice of London is right. You would be far safer in the castle. Move there at once, my liege."

"I do not run from danger, Ralph!"

"This is a strategic withdrawal."

"I will never be safe while this man still lives," said the King with bitterness. "Hide away and I simply prolong my existence a little. Stay here and I tempt him out into the open. It is the only way."

"But it involves such a risk," said Gervase.

"That is why I sent for you. Find him."

"Where?" asked Ralph.

"Wherever he is."

The rest of the day was spent in familiarizing themselves with the geography of the palace and with its daily round of activities. Assigned an apartment, the two friends were also given an immunity from the prying attentions of the guards. Ralph and

Gervase could move at will around the building. To attract less attention and to cover more ground, they separated and pursued individual lines of inquiry.

Ralph Delchard began with the captain of the guard.

"How long have you been at the palace?" he asked.

"Five years, my lord."

"Then you should know your duties by now."

"Has there been some complaint?"

"None that I have heard."

The captain relaxed. He was a big, broad-shouldered man with a white tunic over his hauberk. Dark blue eyes glistened either side of the iron nasal of his helm. They were standing in the courtyard. Ralph noticed that guards were stopping the latest arrivals to question them.

"How many men have you lost?" he asked.

"Lost, my lord?"

"In the time you have been here. How many have been dismissed from royal service?"

The captain shrugged. "Two or three."

"What was their offence?"

"Laziness and insubordination," said the other.

"Would they harbour grudges?"

"Probably."

"When were they dismissed?"

"A long time ago, my lord."

"Do they still reside in the city?"

"No," said the captain. "They left Winchester as fast as they could. I gave them the sharp edge of my tongue. They did not linger for a second dose." A thought struck him. "Except for Huegon, that is."

"Huegon?"

"He has been seen here recently. That surprised me."

"Why?"

"Huegon was thrown out of the palace in disgrace and warned never to come near it again. He was caught taking bribes to allow certain women into the palace at night."

"Prostitutes?"

"Yes, my lord," said the captain with a grim chuckle. "Most paid him in coin but some rewarded him with favours. Huegon was found bare-arsed in the straw with one of the women, rutting like a stag."

"What was his punishment?"

"He was left to rot in a dungeon and repent of his wrongdoing. Then he was upbraided in front of his fellows. When he was dismissed, Huegon was very bitter."

"What did you say to him?"

"Nothing. He was ejected by the King himself."

"Indeed?"

"Huegon has good reason to feel vengeful towards him."

"Why?"

"The King hates corruption among his knights," said the captain with an approving smirk. "He made an example of him in a way that Huegon will never forget."

"An example?"

"His ears were cut off."

Gervase Bret moved among the other denizens of the palace. He spoke with servants, cooks, ostlers, a chaplain, two minstrels, and anyone else in the royal service who could provide a morsel of information. By the time he had finished, he knew everything of consequence about the daily routine of King William. His footsteps then took him on impulse in the direction of New Minster, the monastery which stood at the heart of the city, adjacent to the palace itself.

He found Brother Osmund in the infirmary.

"You will not remember me," he said.

"I remember you well, Gervase Bret," returned the old monk. "You once discussed the virtues of Augustine of Hippo with me. You had actually studied *De Civitate Dei*."

"Not as closely as you, Brother Osmund. You exposed my ignorance but did so with such gentleness that I did not feel in any way humiliated. I thank you for that."

"And I thank you for coming here, Gervase."

"I heard that you were ailing."

"Yes," said the other, grimacing as a sudden pain hit him. "I have been here in the infirmary for days. It is a poor doctor who himself is in need of doctoring. Illness will damage my reputation as a physician."

"Nothing could do that, Brother Osmund."

The old man was plainly in great discomfort. He lay hunched up on his mattress under a rough woollen blanket. All the colour had been chased out of his wrinkled face and there was a quiet panic in his eyes. It seemed cruel to engage him in conversation, but Brother Osmund knew things about the King which could be of help to Gervase.

"The King misses you sorely," said Gervase.

"I despise myself for letting him down."

"Is he often indisposed?"

"Headaches descend on him from time to time. They match his black moods. I thank God that my fingers have been able to relieve his pain. The King has come to rely on me."

"When did you last visit him?"

Brother Osmund went off into a fit of coughing and it was minutes before he was able to answer the question. Gervase knelt beside him and listened with care to the frail voice. Brother Osmund was fiercely loyal to the King, divulging nothing of a confidential nature, yet giving Gervase enough insights into the royal malady to make his journey to New Minster worthwhile. When another spasm of pain shot through the patient, Gervase put out a consoling hand.

"Say no more, Brother Osmund. I have troubled you enough."

"It was kind of you to come."

"I wanted to pay my respects."

"You have medicined my mind."

"Good," said Gervase. "When you have recovered, we will talk again about Augustine of Hippo."

"Perhaps."

Osmund smiled sadly. He brightened when he saw someone coming towards them. Brother Godfrey was carrying a wooden bowl in his hands. He gave a nod of greeting to Gervase before turning to the patient with concern.

"How do you feel now, Brother Osmund?" he asked.

"The pain still torments me."

"Here is something to banish it," said Godfrey, holding up the bowl. "I have mixed the potion in accordance with your instructions. Drink it down."

The newcomer lifted the old man's head up with one hand so that Osmund could more easily sip from the bowl. Gervase was struck by Brother Godfrey's tenderness and affection. It was almost like watching a devoted son attending to his father.

"Godfrey is my salvation," said Osmund. "Without him to look after me, I believe that I should have perished already."

"The Lord still has work for you at New Minster."

"I may survive to do it. Your skill has given me hope."

"You taught me all I know," said Godfrey with pride.

"Use that knowledge to heal me."

"I will, Brother Osmund. I will."

The potion seemed to have a calming effect. Pain ebbed away and the old monk lay back with a look of contentment. His eyes glazed over. Brother Godfrey whispered to Gervase.

"Let him sleep, I beseech you. He needs rest."

"Of course."

They stole quietly out of the infirmary. Gervase threw a glance over his shoulder.

"What ails him?"

"A disease is eating at his entrails," sighed Godfrey. "It is hideous to watch him suffer so. I can arrest the pain but a cure still eludes me."

"He fears the worst," said Gervase.

"I know."

"Is he like to die?"

Brother Godfrey's face puckered with alarm.

"Osmund must not die," he said. "I love him."

Ralph managed a brief exchange with Maurice of London. Still exasperated, the bishop was mounting his horse for departure. A dozen knights were in the saddle to escort their master out of Winchester. Maurice was flanked by two monks. Ralph bore down on him with a purposeful stride.

"I crave a word, Your Grace!" he called.

"Do not delay me," said Maurice. "I am eager to quit the palace and return to a city where my advice is respected."

"You argued with the King, I believe?"

"That is no concern of yours."

"I was outside the hall when you swept out."

"I do not like eavesdroppers."

The bishop tried to ride off, but Ralph took the reins of his horse to detain him. Maurice's ire swelled. Veins stood out on his forehead and words hissed out of him like steam.

"Stand aside!"

"I wish to speak with you, Your Grace."

"How dare you obstruct my path. Who are you, sir?"

He glared down at Ralph, but the latter held his ground. Maurice peered at him more closely, then nodded resignedly.

"Ralph Delchard!"

"I wondered when you would recognize me."

"This is not the first time you have got in my way," said the bishop. "I seem to recall tripping over you when I was chancellor here. You have a talent for obstruction."

Ralph beamed. "It has often been admired."

"Not by me."

Ralph looked up into the pinched face of the bishop. It was difficult to believe that such an unprepossessing man was such a successful libertine. His consecration had not been allowed to interfere with his pleasures. Maurice had found a way to reconcile his episcopal duties with his lecherous promptings.

"I am trying to serve my King," continued Ralph, "and I can best do that if I know the substance of your quarrel with him." He led the horse away a short distance so that their conversation had a token privacy. "We both know that he is in danger, Your Grace. What is its source?"

"His own folly."

"I have never heard King William called a fool before."

"He is too stubborn for his own good," snapped Maurice. "Why ask for my counsel if he discards it? I would have put a ring of steel around him that only an army could pierce."

"And where would that army hail from?"

"Come, my lord. I am sure that you have heard the reports from our intelligencers. The Vikings have been making preparations for several months."

"They would never reach Winchester."

"Not in numbers, perhaps. But they do not need to."

"What do you mean?"

"One would be enough to kill a king."

Gervase spent an improving hour with the steward, an arrogant man with a crushing self-importance but one whose knowledge of the household was invaluable. Gervase gleaned an immense amount of information about every aspect of the royal palace. To achieve that, it was well worth enduring the steward's supercilious manner.

When Ralph went back to the apartment, he found Gervase poring over a sheet of parchment with a stylus in his hand.

"Writing a letter to Alys?" he teased.

"No," said Gervase. "I have turned artist."

"Let me see."

Ralph studied the diagram that his friend had drawn. It was a plan of the royal palace, crude but identifiable, replete with a series of tiny crosses.

"What do these represent?" asked Ralph, pointing.

"Guards."

"Are there really as many as that?"

"I counted them."

"What else did you do?"

Gervase gave his friend a concise account of his movements since they parted and Ralph was fascinated. He responded with the details of his own investigations, and it was Gervase's turn to have his curiosity aroused to the point where the questions bubbled out of him. Pooling their evidence, they began to sift it with care. Ralph was the first to reach a verdict.

"Huegon may be our man," he decided.

"He has a motive certainly," agreed Gervase, "but hardly the means. Look at my drawing. Guards everywhere. How would this Huegon slip past them?"

"In the most obvious way. By looking like one of them. Only another soldier could deceive all those soldiers. He knows every room and corridor in the palace, Gervase. Huegon knows where to hide."

"The King has a guard beside him at all times."

"One man can murder two if he takes them unawares," said Ralph, thinking it through. "Besides, the bodyguard is not always in attendance. The King dismissed him when he spoke to us."

"That is true."

"Huegon is the villain here. I feel it in my bones."

"Acting on his own behalf?"

"Or in the pay of foreigners. A man who can be led astray by prostitutes would be easy prey for the bribes of enemy spies. Bitterness breeds traitors."

"Huegon has enough bitterness. That is clear. But I am still not convinced that he is our man, Ralph." Gervase indicated the parchment. "Study the drawing."

"Why?"

"It holds the answer we are seeking."

"One of those crosses is Huegon."

Gervase grew pensive. "Perhaps we should be looking at a cross of another kind," he said. "Bishop Maurice."

"He is no assassin. For all his bluster, Maurice is as loyal as anyone in the kingdom. He was a shrewd chancellor until his consecration. No, Gervase," Ralph said firmly, "the bishop is too busy fornicating to have time for betrayal. Why do you even mention Maurice?"

"I remembered what the King said about him."

Huddled under his cloak, William the Conqueror sat in the pool of light from the flickering candles. Food and wine lay untouched on the table before him. When the door opened at the far end of the hall, he did not even look up. Two figures were conjured out of the gloom. Brother Godfrey and the guard waited until the King became aware of their presence. A nod dismissed the guard and the man vanished into the darkness. They heard the door close behind him.

"I am sorry to call you so late," said William with evident strain, "but my head is bursting apart. Work your magic, Brother Godfrey. Bring me some rest."

"I will," promised the other.

The monk stepped behind the chair and began to massage the patient's temples, gently at first, then with more pressure. After a few minutes, a sigh of relief escaped the King. His eyes closed, his tension seemed to ease. The fingers worked tirelessly on, exploring the whole scalp for pain, and drawing it slowly out. William began to doze.

"Sleep," whispered Brother Godfrey. "That is what you need. Sleep, sleep. Surrender yourself to sleep and you will soon be restored. Your mind and body want rest. Sleep, sleep."

The massage continued until the head eventually lolled to one side. Hands which had eased the King into his slumber now took on a different role. Brother Godfrey untied the rope at his waist to slip around the neck of the sleeping man. It was as far as he got. Ralph Delchard leapt out of the shadows to fell the monk with one blow of his forearm, and the King was suddenly awake, standing over his would-be assassin with a sword held at the monk's throat. Gervase Bret emerged from a dark corner to look down at the villain.

"*Why?*" demanded the King. "Who paid you to kill me?"

"A voice from Heaven bid me do it," said Godfrey.

"Did it also bid you to poison Brother Osmund so that you could take his place as my physician?"

The monk's eyes moistened with regret. "It was the only way to reach you," he explained. "I had to inflict pain on someone I love in order to kill someone I hate. You have done too much damage to the Church," he accused, pointing a finger at William. "You have killed and looted your way through England like a barbarous heathen. You betrayed your God. He instructed me to call you to account."

The King bawled a command and a dozen armed men burst into the hall. Ralph hauled the monk up from the floor. Brother Godfrey was dragged unceremoniously out by the guards.

William sheathed his sword and gave a broad grin.

"It seems as if my Domesday has been deferred."

"We have Gervase to thank for that, my liege," said Ralph.

"It was that remark about Maurice of London, my liege," recalled Gervase.

"You said that lechery was his medicine. The bishop's health depended on it. Yours depended on the skills of Brother Osmund. Yet he was indisposed when you needed him most. I visited him in New Minster. I wondered why such a noted physician could not heal himself. My suspicion fell on Brother Godfrey. He was biding his time to strike. All we had to do was to contrive the opportunity for him."

"Yes," said Ralph ruefully. "I was searching for an assassin among the soldiers when, all the time, he was lurking inside the cowl of a Benedictine monk."

"I am deeply grateful to you both," said the King.

After he had showered them with praise, the friends left the hall together. Gervase could not resist a teasing nudge.

"Do you still call Winchester a city of eunuchs?"

"No," conceded Ralph. "Not while it has men like Brother Godfrey in its midst. I loathe what he tried to do, but I admire the wild courage which drove him on to do it. Who would have thought the Church had so much pulsing manhood in it?" He gave a ripe chuckle. "No wonder they elevated Maurice to a bishopric!"

THE SHOULDER-BLADE OF A RAM

Gerald of Wales remains one of the most colorful and dynamic characters in the history of his beloved country. Learned, opinionated, tenacious and fearless, he was inspired by an ambition to become Bishop of St David's, to be consecrated without having to accept the supremacy of Canterbury, and to persuade the Pope to appoint him as Archbishop of Wales. Failing in this grand design, he stayed as Archdeacon of Brecon to the end of his long and controversial life. In 1188, he toured Wales with Baldwin, Archbishop of Canterbury, trying to recruit support for a Third Crusade. The book that resulted from this tour is also about Gerald's own crusade. His mention of the beliefs attached to a shoulder-blade of a ram caught my attention. Though this story is my own invention, Gerald insists on telling it himself.

Wales, 1188

Until I witnessed the phenomenon with my own eyes, I would never have believed that a murder could be solved by means of the shoulder-blade of a ram. The right shoulder-blade, to be exact. It happened when we reached Haverfordwest.

Baldwin, Archbishop of Canterbury, a man respected for his learning and piety, was travelling around Wales in the service of the Cross, endeavouring to recruit soldiers for a Crusade. I, Gerald de Barri, more usually known as Giraldus Cambrensis, was privileged to be his companion on this holy journey. In Haverfordwest, the Archbishop first gave a sermon, then the word of God was preached with some eloquence by the Archdeacon of St David's, whose name adorns this story, in short, by me. A great crowd of people assembled, soldiers and civilians. Many found it little short of miraculous that when I preached first in Latin then in French, those who could not understand a word of either language were just as moved to tears as others. I was duly touched.

That evening, over an excellent meal, we heard more about the Flemings.

"They're dreadful people," complained our host, the ancient but waspish Owain ap Madog. "Wild, arrogant and hostile."

65

"Yet several of them pledged themselves to join the Crusade," I noted. "That must surely be evidence of Christian impulse."

"Evidence of their warlike spirits, that is all."

"I thought that they were affected by my preaching."

"Flemings kill for the sake of killing, Archdeacon."

"The same has been said of the Welsh," suggested Baldwin.

Even archbishops make foolish comments at times. Owain and I ignored him.

Having been born and brought up in Pembrokeshire, I was aware of the enmity between the indigenous Welsh inhabitants and the Flemish colonists who had been thrust upon the area by the edicts of Henry I, King of the English. The two races remained in a state of perpetual conflict, each inflicting outrages upon the other with deplorable regularity. Honesty compels me to admit that Flemings are not wholly reprehensible. Highly skilled in the wool trade, they are ready to work hard and to face danger by land or sea in pursuit of their commercial ends. Though they have turned their hand to the ploughshare, however, it still reaches too easily for the sword.

"Then there is this nonsense about the shoulder-bone of a ram," said Owain, plucking at the food lodged in his silver beard. "They claim to have powers of divination. Flemings boil the right shoulder-blades of rams. Instead of roasting them, they strip off all the meat and, by examining the little indents and protuberances, they can foretell the future or reveal the secrets of events long past." He gave a cynical snort. "Or so they say. I think it's just one more idle boast."

"Why the right shoulder-blade?" asked Baldwin, sipping his wine as if receiving Communion. "Would not the left serve just as well?"

"Yes," said Owain sourly. "And so would the head and the horns, Archbishop. They could use any part of the beast to justify their monstrous claim. Nobody can foretell the future or conjure up the past." He turned to me. "Can they, Archdeacon?"

I was too intrigued by the notion to dismiss it out of hand. Long experience had taught me that anything is possible on Welsh soil. Even when it is settled by foreigners. Owain wanted me to agree with him. Baldwin awaited my answer. I was circumspect.

"I would like to put this claim to the test," I said, nodding sagely.

The murder gave me the opportunity to do just that.

The crime occurred that same night. While her husband was away on business, a woman called Margaret was strangled to death in her own bed. When the body was discovered by a maidservant, the whole town was thrown into a tumult of fear and indignation. Baldwin wanted to ride on to Pembroke to continue our work but I persuaded him to linger until the full facts of the murder were known. In the event, the personal interest that I took in the affair turned out to be crucial and I am not being immodest when I claim some of the credit for unmasking the killer and bringing him to justice.

Margaret was a popular member of the community. The wife of a successful merchant, she was a kind, friendly woman who gathered good opinions from all who met her. It was difficult to see what possible motive lay behind her foul murder. She was a handsome lady, by all accounts, and generous to a fault. Nobody was more devout or more loving towards her husband. I spoke to several people who knew her and they all agreed on one thing. Only a madman would slaughter such a domestic saint.

The victim's husband, Richard, returned to find his household in disarray. He was horrified to learn that his wife had been strangled and was at first inconsolable with grief. When he finally mastered his anguish, he was overcome by feelings of revenge. He drew his dagger and swore a terrible oath. Fortunately, I was on hand to calm him down and to offer practical guidance.

"I can understand this surging anger," I said, gently.

"Can you?" he growled.

"Yes, my friend. But you will need more than blind fury to catch the vile rogue responsible for this heinous crime. You will need a cool head. I share your sorrow and long for retribution."

"It is no business of yours, Archdeacon Gerald."

"It is the business of every man to hunt down a ruthless killer."

"Leave him to me!" warned Richard. "This quarry is all mine."

"Let me direct your steps, good sir."

"How can you so that?"

It took me a long time but I eventually convinced him that the very fact that I was a stranger told in my favour. I viewed everything from the outside. I could be objective and dispassionate. Lacking any acquaintance with the dead woman, I was not caught up in a welter of emotions. Richard looked at me with a mixture of respect and caution.

"What do you advise?" he asked.

"First," I said, "I would like to question everyone in the household."

"Why?"

"All the doors were locked last night yet the killer somehow entered and left the building without being seen or heard. If," I added, reasonably, "that is what happened."

"What other explanation is there?"

"That the killer is a member of your own household."

"Never!" he exclaimed. "My servants loved their mistress. None of them would dare to lift a finger against her. I can vouch for them. We keep three men and four women beneath our roof. The women would not have the strength to commit such a crime and one of the men is so old that he could be discounted as well. Of the other two, I have the highest opinion. Tried and trusted fellows with every cause to worship my wife."

"I would still like to speak to them all," I persisted.

"A waste of time, Archdeacon!"

"I might garner vital information."

"Far too slowly. I want that villain run to ground now."

"Then there may be a quicker way to identify him, my friend. I hear that your people have gifts of divination. Seek out the best of them. Kill a ram from your own flock and present the right shoulder-blade for examination. Will that content you?"

A strange look came into his eye as he listened to my counsel. He was patently surprised that a man of the Church should offer such advice, wondering if I really believed in the stories about divination or if I was subtly mocking the Flemings' habit of resorting to the shoulder-blade of an animal for critical information.

"It shall be done," he said at length. "Thank you, Archdeacon."

"I would still like to talk to your servants."

"It may not be necessary."

Richard moved swiftly into action. One of the rams was selected from his flock and he insisted on slaughtering the creature himself, standing over the cook while the man cut out the right shoulder-blade before boiling it in a pot of hot water. I was not allowed to be present in the kitchen but I did accompany Richard when he hastened across to a house on the edge of the town. It was there that we found the person most accomplished in the arts of divination by means of animal bone. Her name was Adela.

I was astonished to see how relatively young she was, barely thirty years old in my estimation, a soulful widow whose beauty was marked by clear indications of suffering yet who had an air of distant wisdom about her. Could this pale woman really have magical powers? I doubted it. Adela was highly sympathetic towards Richard and offered her condolences time and again. Anxious to help him, however, she was very reluctant to become involved in the case, fearing that any mistake on her part might lead to the arrest and execution of an innocent man. Richard pleaded with her until she finally consented to use her skills on his behalf.

"Do not expect too much," she said, diffidently.

"Everyone knows your reputation," argued Richard.

"I have never been asked to solve such a hideous crime before."

"Then this is a unique moment," I observed, always delighted to see an important precedent established. "Find the killer and you will do the whole community a service."

"I will try, Archdeacon Gerald."

"It will be some murderous Welshman!" asserted Richard. "I know it."

"Let us see," she murmured.

Taking the shoulder-blade from him, she held it in the palm of one hand so that she could use the fingertips of the other to explore every inch of it. I was fascinated. All that I could see was a shoulder-blade picked clean of meat and gristle yet it obviously had a series of invisible markings that could be read and interpreted by someone with the gifts of a seer. Adela clearly had such gifts. I watched her face closely. Eyes shut to aid her concentration, she worked her way deftly over the shoulder-blade until her fingers came into contact with something that caused her to stiffen. She sat up with a start.

"What is wrong?" I wondered.

"Nothing," she said, opening her eyes.

"You've found him, haven't you?" pressed Richard. "What's his name?"

"Truly, I don't know."

"Tell me," he demanded. "I must avenge my wife."

Adela was torn between willingness to help and a lack of faith in her own abilities. She licked her lips and took a deep breath before reporting her findings.

"The killer was a strong young man who hated the Flemings," she said.

"A Welshman!" shouted Richard.

"He cannot speak his name nor hear your denunciation of him."

Richard's jaw tightened and his eyes blazed. Before I could stop him, he charged out of the room as fast as he could go. I turned to Adela for elucidation.

"He has recognised the man," she explained.

"One of the servants?"

"Not exactly, Archdeacon."

"Then who is the fellow."

"A poor, wretched deaf and dumb creature with no more sense than the ram whose shoulder-blade helped to identify him." Her voice hardened. "Yet he is capable of a bloody crime and must pay for it."

"You saw all that with your fingers?" I said.

"Everything but his name."

"An extraordinary gift!"

"I'm pleased to put it to such a valuable use," she said with a wan smile. "Most of the people who come to me simply want to know the sex of an unborn child or to hear a comforting prophecy about their futures. I have now helped to catch a murderer."

"You and the shoulder-blade of a ram."

"Yes, Archdeacon."

"If you've finished with it, I'd like to inspect it myself." She was hesitant. I smiled quietly and held out my hand. "May I?"

The villain's name was Hywel and he was lucky that the sheriff arrived in time to save his life or, at least, to postpone his death until legal process had been observed. Hywel was a thickset man in his twenties whose disabilities made him a figure of fun in the locality. He earned his keep by doing mundane chores on a farm a few miles away from the town. When Richard caught up with him, Hywel was working in a field, sublimely unaware of the presence of an enraged man who was brandishing a sword. It is probable that the incensed husband would have slain him on the spot had not the sheriff and his men turned up providentially, having been told of the crime and having trailed Richard. Less inclined to accept the judgement of a ram's shoulder-blade, the sheriff nevertheless arrested Hywel and placed him under lock and key while an investigation was conducted.

It soon yielded results. Hywel, it transpired, was a kinsman of the old servant in Richard's household and – without the permission of the master – was sometimes admitted to the house in the dead of night to sleep in comfort for a change. Under questioning, the old man confessed that he had let Hywel into the building the previous night to escape the storm that was brewing. Customarily, the deaf and dumb Welshman slept in the stables with the other animals on the farm. The old man, Iestyn by name, took pity on him. Richard, by contrast, was quite pitiless in his questioning.

"So you are an accomplice in this murder!" he roared.

"No, sir," pleaded Iestyn. "I'm no killer. Nor is Hywel."

"You sneaked him into the house."

"But that is all I did."

"Is it?" said Richard. "Are you sure you didn't help him to strangle my wife?"

The old man wept bitterly. "I'd never do that, sir. I adored and respected my mistress. You know that. You trusted me. Have I ever given you cause to doubt that trust, sir? Tell me. Have I?"

"Not until now."

"Hywel slept beside me all night. I swear it."

"Planning the murder."

"No!"

"Yes, you Welsh cur!"

"How could I plan anything with someone who can neither speak nor hear?"

"You acted on instinct. Two evil men, consumed by hate."

"But I loved your wife, sir!"

Richard's blow caught him across the face and sent him reeling. The sheriff had heard enough. The old man was dragged off to join Hywel in a dungeon. When he had calmed down, Richard was able to suggest another motive for the crime. Soft-hearted as she was by nature, his wife had accepted that Iestyn was too frail to be kept much longer in their service. She had told him that he must leave within the month. The old man must have used Hywel to get his revenge on her, confident that, if caught, his kinsman would have no voice to incriminate him.

Impressed by the speed and the manner in which the murder was solved, I was troubled by lingering doubts. When I was allowed to examine the two hapless Welshman, I found no malice or violence in them. The one was far too dim-witted to know what he was doing and the other too loyal to harbour any feelings of revenge. Instead of confiding my worries to the sheriff, I repaired to the home of Owain ap Madog, where Baldwin awaited me with growing impatience. I related the events of the day without embellishment. To his credit, the Archbishop sat enthralled but Owain was sceptical. Not only was he furious that the murder was laid so hastily at the feet of two of his compatriots, he had grave misgivings about the part that Adela had played in the whole affair.

"It was a wild guess," he contended. "She plucked Hywel's name out of the air."

"But she didn't give him a name," I reminded him. "She merely said that the killer had been deaf and dumb. That led Richard to the malefactor. The shoulder-blade somehow yielded up the information required."

"Remarkable!" said Baldwin.

"Trickery!" countered Owain.

"But I was there," I said, producing the shoulder-blade from my satchel. "I saw the lady tease out the secrets locked away in this bone. Do not ask me how part of a dead ram can be used to divulge the identity of a killer but it did. I witnessed it."

"God must have been acting through the lady," decided Baldwin, never one to acknowledge powers from a source other than heaven. "This Adela was inspired by the wonder of the Almighty."

Owain took the shoulder-blade from my grasp and scrutinized it carefully.

"Inspired or misled?" he asked.

"What do you mean?" I said.

"Where did this shoulder-blade come from, Archdeacon?"

"A ram in the flock owned by Richard himself."

"Who killed the beast?"

"He did. Then he stood over the cook while the shoulder-blade was boiled and cleaned." Owain held the object up to the light and stroked it. "What is wrong?"

"I smell a rat."

"But you're holding part of a ram," said Baldwin.

"No, I'm not, Archbishop. And neither was the lady."

"What are you telling us?" I said, suspecting what his answer might be.

Owain savoured his moment. "If this came from a ram," he announced, waving the shoulder-blade before us, "then it was a most peculiar beast. It might deceive most people because the two are so alike but it would never deceive me. I'm a true Welshman, remember, brought up among goats. As a boy, I tended, killed and ate them on occasion. I also carved the bones of sheep and goats. That teaches you a lot about both animals. I'd stake my life on the fact that this is the shoulder-blade of a goat and not of a ram."

Baldwin was mystified. "Then why did this Richard slaughter a beast from his flock? A wool merchant can surely tell the difference between a ram and a goat?"

My mind was racing. A ram had indeed been killed and the cook had extracted and prepared the shoulder-blade but there was no proof that it was then presented to Adela for inspection. Could a clever switch have occurred? The lurking doubts that had assailed me now began to take on a more definite shape. Perhaps I had not witnessed an act of divination, after all. I rose to my feet and headed for the door.

"Where are you going?" bleated Baldwin.

"To solve a crime."

"But the villains have already been arrested."

"On false evidence, Archbishop."

I have never liked the practice of eavesdropping because it smacks of nosiness but there are times when it is unavoidable. Sensing that the true facts of the case had yet to come to light, I made my way discreetly back to Adela's house and approached by means of the garden at the rear. I concealed myself in the bushes and kept the lady herself under surveillance through the open shutters. Adela was tripping happily around her parlour, singing to herself and glowing with anticipatory pleasure. The rather sombre young woman who had been so reluctant to examine the shoulder-blade at first was now a spirited creature who was almost luxuriating in her sins. I did not have long to wait. A horse approached at a steady canter and the rider brought it to a halt outside the stable. I caught only a glimpse of him as he rushed into the house but I recognised him instantly.

Richard had also undergone a transformation. The demented husband was now an urgent lover, racing to claim his prize, so supremely confident of the success of his plan that he did not pause to think that he might be giving himself away. When they came face to face, he and Adela embraced like the conspirators they were. I had seen enough. As I scurried off to summon the sheriff, I worked out why and how the crime must have been committed. Richard was a strong, virile man who needed more sensual excitement than a God-fearing wife like Margaret could provide. Evidently, the widowed Adela supplied that excitement and relished it in turn. The only way that they could be together was to rid themselves of the obstruction posed by Margaret and arrange for someone else to bear the blame for her death.

My guess was that Richard knew only too well that his aged servant took pity on his deaf and dumb kinsman and that the time when Iestyn would most probably let Hywel into the house was during his master's absence. It was a cunning gamble. Pretending to be away on business, Richard instead let himself into the house with his key, strangled a wife who would have made no protest when she saw her husband unexpectedly entering the bedchamber, then fled into the night. The rage that he kindled on the following day was an effective cloak for his own wickedness. Other details that I had gleaned now fell neatly into place. With a skill born of years of practice and with an insight into human depravity culled from a life of random ubiquity, I solved a cruel murder without resort to the shoulder-blade of any animal.

The sheriff took a long time to accept the inexorable logic of my theory.

"Richard?" he said, shaking his head. "A murderer? What does he stand to gain?"

"Adela," I replied.

"She is a rich widow, it is true, and very beautiful. But so was Margaret. Indeed, she had even more private wealth than Adela." He paused as a secondary motive came into view. "Lust and gain? They are strong enough temptations for any man. Richard would be set for life if he were to inherit his wife's wealth and merge it with the money left to Adela by her late husband." He was persuaded. "And you say that you saw the pair of them together, Archdeacon?"

"Meeting up to celebrate their triumph."

"Hardly the action of a grieving man."

"Approach the house with stealth, my lord sheriff. I fancy that you may even take them *in flagrante*. Would that be proof enough for you?"

"It most certainly would."

We stayed in Haverfordwest long enough to see the arrest of the two accomplices and the release of Iestyn and his kinsman. Richard tried to bluff his way out of the situation but Adela broke down under interrogation and confessed all. I allowed myself the rare pleasure of receiving unstinting congratulations from all sides. It is not often given to me to be in a position to wield the sword of justice to such effect. As we took our leave of our host, I was gracious enough to acknowledge his crucial contribution.

"Your help was quite invaluable, Owain."

"I'm always happy to imprison a couple of lying Flemings," he said with a chuckle. "Especially when two innocent Welshman are set free into the bargain."

"You were magnificent," complimented Baldwin. "Who else could tell the shoulder-blade of a ram and that of a goat apart? I praise God that such rare knowledge could be put to such a critical use."

"It serves as symbol of the whole sorry business," I opined.

"What does?"

"The difference between sheep and goats, Archbishop."

"I do not follow you, Gerald."

"Nor more do I," added Owain.

"It is simple," I explained. "Richard was a wool merchant who was married to a submissive lamb of a woman. But he could never be entirely happy among the sheep of this world. He was a man of goatish inclination and sought out a woman as red-blooded and rampant as himself. According to the sheriff," I confided, enjoying the opportunity to scandalise Baldwin, "that libidinous pair were caught in the very act of adultery, their naked bodies so entwined that they had to be prised forcibly apart."

"Saints preserve us!" gasped Baldwin.

"Flemings are born lechers!" commented Owain.

"The lady brought about her own downfall," I concluded. "The sheriff tells me that, when they burst into the bedchamber, Adela had both hands on her lover's shoulders. Deception came full circle. For the second time in one day, a scheming woman had her hands on the shoulder-blade of a goat that was pretending to be a ram. No wonder she could not foretell the future from that bogus shoulder-blade or she would have known that the sheriff was coming."

I swear that Archbishop Baldwin came perilously close to laughter.

PERFECT SHADOWS

The title for this story comes from the play, Edward II, *by Christopher Marlowe.*

But what are kings, when regiment is gone,
But perfect shadows in a sunshine day?

It deals with the possibility that Edward II did not, in fact, suffer a horrible death at the hands of assassins in Berkeley Castle. The tale was suggested by the contents of an undated letter that was sent to Edward III by Manuel Fieschi, a Genoese priest who held an English benefice. Fieschi recounted facts that he claimed to have heard from the lips of the deposed Edward II in the confessional box. The details of events leading up to the arrest and imprisonment of the former king are remarkably accurate, and it is difficult to see how else the priest could have learned them. England, however, accepted that Edward II was dead and mourned him with unexpected fervor. "Perfect Shadows," then, is about a perfect mystery. Readers will have to make up their own minds about the fate of its unfairly maligned protagonist.

Y ou are to be moved to Berkeley Castle," said Henry of Lancaster gently.
"Why?" asked Edward with alarm.
"Orders have been given to that effect."
"By whom?"
"The king."
"My son would not be so unkind to his father. This is the work of that she-wolf, Isabella, my hateful wife. She and evil Mortimer conspire against me here. I do not like it, Henry."
"No more do I, my lord. But I must comply."
"What lies behind this change of prison?"
"You have been no prisoner here," Henry reminded him.
"I know, my friend, and I am deeply grateful."
Edward the Second had suffered indignities enough by the time he was consigned

to Kenilworth Castle and his custodian, Henry of Leicester, who had newly assumed his dead brother's title of Earl of Lancaster, saw no reason to add pain to ignominy. Courteous and considerate, Henry treated the deposed king more like a guest than a prisoner. Edward was allowed the freedom of the castle and lived, if not in state, then at least in relative comfort. He was about to exchange his kindly host for a much more heartless gaoler. It put a note of anguish into his voice.

"Mortimer has stolen my wife, my son and my kingdom. Now he robs me of my peace of mind. There is only one thing left to take!"

"Do not even entertain such a thought."

"I must, Henry. My life is at risk."

"Thomas de Berkeley is an honourable man."

"He *does* know what honour means," said Edward bitterly. "And he has cause for revenge. After my victory at Boroughbridge, I kept both Thomas and his father, Maurice, languishing in a dungeon. The old man died in captivity but his son was liberated by my erstwhile queen, who restored his estates to Thomas de Berkeley. Now that I am his prisoner, Thomas will not forget that he was once mine."

"I, too, suffered at Boroughbridge," sighed Henry. "You defeated us in battle and condemned my brother, Thomas of Lancaster, to a traitor's death. In your mercy, you commuted the sentence to one of beheading. I am eternally grateful for that act of kindness. Though I have grievances of my own to nurse, I have endeavoured to treat you with the respect due to your position."

"Is any respect due to a king who was forced to abdicate?"

"I believe so, my lord."

"My time has come and gone."

"You may still live out your life in dignity."

"Here in Kenilworth, perhaps," said Edward, reaching out to squeeze his companion's arm. "Thanks to you, my misery has been greatly eased. Warwickshire is a beautiful county even though it holds cruel memories of the death of my beloved Gaveston. I have enjoyed gazing out across its green fields as I walk around your battlements." His face darkened. "Will I be given the same licence at Berkeley Castle?"

The question was answered by the arrival of his new custodian. With an eagerness bordering on glee, Thomas de Berkeley came striding into the Great Hall where the two men had been conversing. One look at the newcomer's face was enough to confirm Edward's worst fears. There was a ruthless glint in Berkeley's eye. No compassion could be expected from him nor from the man who accompanied him. Sir John Maltravers, his brother-in-law, was a fugitive from the army which Edward had so soundly beaten at Boroughbridge some five years earlier.

Maltravers had joined Isabella's party in France and was one more beneficiary of her husband's fall from power. He and Thomas de Berkeley had a score to settle with the deposed king.

After an exchange of greetings, Berkeley's disapproval was curt.

"Why is the prisoner not chained?" he snapped.

"He presents no danger," explained Henry.

"What is he doing out of his cell? Does he have a degree of liberty here in Kenilworth?"

"At my discretion."

"He will not enjoy such favours in my custody."

"Nor will I expect any," said Edward defiantly.

Berkeley ignored him and gave a peremptory command.

"Have the prisoner taken back to the dungeons!"

Henry of Lancaster bristled. "Only I give orders in this castle," he said with vehemence. "Bear that in mind. While he is in my keeping, I will treat Edward as I think fit. Tomorrow, I hand him over to you, Thomas. Until then, I warn you not to interfere."

Edward was grateful for his host's intercession but he knew that it would gain him only a temporary relief. Thomas de Berkeley was clearly smarting at the rebuff. When the prisoner came into his charge, he would make Edward pay for the stern words of the Earl of Lancaster.

They left Kenilworth at the crack of dawn on Palm Sunday. Manacled on the orders of his new master and surrounded by four burly men-at-arms, Edward rode in discomfort and saw little of the county whose beauties he had savoured from the vantage point of the castle. Out in the fresh air, he yet felt more confined than he had done when in the care of Henry of Lancaster. There were no solicitous inquiries about his health and preferences at table. Berkeley and Maltravers had none of the gracious behaviour which had lessened the ordeal of imprisonment at Kenilworth. When they were not mocking or sneering at Edward, his captors fell into a grim silence.

At the end of a long day, they reached Monmouthshire and spent the night at Llanthony Priory. The monks showed a dutiful kindness towards Edward but he was allowed no privileges. On the following day, they completed their journey. The prisoner's first glimpse of his new abode struck quiet terror in his heart. Berkeley Castle was smaller, neater and more compact than Kenilworth and had none of the latter's craggy magnificence. Set in a wooded plain which swept on to Severn Estuary, the castle was an imposing fortress which somehow combined elegance with solidity. Edward saw none of its handsome features. What filled his mind was the fear that he was riding towards his tomb.

When they entered the courtyard, Thomas de Berkeley was crisp.

"Lock the prisoner up!" he ordered.

"Am I to be allowed books to study?" asked Edward.

"No!"

"Not even the Bible?"

"You will inhabit a dungeon and not a monastery."

"Have care for my soul," pleaded the other.

"We will remember you in our prayers."

Berkeley gave a derisive laugh and gestured to his men. Edward was lifted bodily from the saddle and hustled off to his quarters. The cell was small, fetid and without natural light. A single candle illumined the bleak scene. Dank straw partially covered the floor. A crude mattress stood against one wall. The only other furniture was a rough-hewn stool and a rickety table. A rat scuttled out through a drain-hole. Before Edward could complain, he was thrust unceremoniously into the dungeon and the heavy door clanged shut behind him. When he tried to shout, the stench hit his nostrils so hard that he started to retch.

The comforts of Kenilworth seemed a thousand miles away.

Weeks stretched into months and the privations began to tell on his health and appearance. He was permitted some brief daily exercise in the courtyard but the shuffling figure was unrecognizable as the proud warrior who had put his foes to flight at Boroughbridge. Edward suffered a dramatic loss of weight. His hair was unkempt, his overgrown beard salted with grey. His shoulders sagged and his head was bowed. Sharing most of his time with the flickering flame of a candle, he squinted badly in the daylight. It was a life of sustained humiliation.

Some time in July, he was allowed a visitor. When the Dominican friar was admitted to his cell, Edward was at first disturbed, fearful that the man had come to administer last rites before summary execution. Seeing his distress, the newcomer was quick to offer reassurance.

"Have no fear, my lord," he said. "I come to bring succour."

"I am sorely in need of it. What is your name?"

"Brother Thomas."

"I am much abused here, Thomas."

"So I see," said the other sadly, "and it does not become your rank. They do you wrong to treat you so. Is this some whim of your custodian or does he act under orders from above?"

"Both," explained Edward. "He inclines towards cruelty and is ratified in that inclination by the commands of his father-in-law, Roger Mortimer. The same villain who sleeps in my bed with my wife and rules the kingdom through the person of my young son."

"England has learned to rue the name of Mortimer."

"So have I, Brother Thomas."

"He is a harsh ruler."

"Matched with a harsh woman."

"Both have made the kingdom bleed. God will punish them for it." He glanced around to make sure that the guard was not listening outside the door. "I come as a friend, my lord."

"I hear it in your voice, Thomas."

"A *special* friend. I have done you service in the past."

"Have you?" Edward peered at the gnarled face in the gloom. "At Oxford, perhaps? Were you one of the kind Dominicans who took in the headless body of my dear Gaveston and embalmed it because sentence of excommunication still attached to it and it had to lay unburied?"

"No, my lord. I was not at Oxford."

"Where, then, did you show this special friendship?"

"In Avignon."

"Ah!"

"I was sent hither at the express command of Sir Hugh Despenser to negotiate with the Pope the annulment of your marriage."

"Would that I had never wed Isabella in the first place!"

"I acted as your emissary, my lord."

"Then you are doubly welcome, Brother Thomas. Yours are the first soft words I have heard since I came into Gloucestershire. I am in a dire condition yet you still reverence me like a king."

"I am not the only one, my lord."

"Your meaning?"

"England is in turmoil," said the friar. "Those who supported the alliance between the Queen Isabella and Mortimer are having second thoughts. Our new rulers take arrogance to the point of tyranny. Instead of rewarding their followers, they bully and tax them. Rebellion is in the air. People are starting to remember how well you treated them, my lord. They are angered by reports that you are kept here under restraint."

"Those reports are not false, as you can see."

"I see much more than that."

"In what way?"

"That will soon become clear. Tell me about the castle."

"The castle?"

"Its design, its defences, its garrison, its routines. You have been here long enough to see how Berkeley Castle is run. Tell me all, my lord. The intelligence will be put to good use."

"By whom?"

"Myself and my brother."

"Another friar of the Order?"

"Hardly!" said the other with a chuckle. "My brother, Stephen, is too wild and wilful a man to submit to the Rule of St Dominic. You may understand why when I tell you his full name. It is Stephen Dunheved."

Edward's eyes widened. "Lord of the manor of Dunchurch."

"Banished lord. His estates were seized."

"Does he live abroad in exile?"

"So it is believed."

"And what is the truth of the matter?"

"You will see."

The talked earnestly together for a long time in lowered voices. Thomas Dunheved was a resourceful man who provided much more than spiritual sustenance. By the time that his visitor was about to leave, he had revived a long-dead hope in Edward.

"Will you do me one more service, Brother Thomas?" he asked.

"Do but name it, my lord."

Edward thrust his hand under his tattered tunic to bring out a roll of parchment. He gave it to the friar with a conspiratorial whisper.

"See this delivered to Henry of Lancaster."

"A letter?"

"A poem," said Edward. "I wrote it during my stay at Kenilworth. It is not safe to hold on to it any longer. I am denied writing materials here and they would take this from me if they knew I had it. Have it put into the hands of Henry of Lancaster. He deserves this record of my time with him at Kenilworth Castle. Can I trust you to see this done?"

The friar nodded then slipped the parchment into the sleeve of his cowl when he heard the door being unlocked. Edward was sorry to see Brother Thomas go but he was heartened by what he heard. It would give him food for thought during the lonely hours of the night. He still had friends. There were those to whom he remained Edward the Second.

Escorted to the main gate, Thomas Dunheved left the castle and picked his way across the meadow and through the trees. Only when he was out of sight of the sentries did he stop to take out the parchment from his sleeve. Unrolling it with care, he read the first verse of the poem.

> In winter woe befell me
> By cruel Fortune thwarted,
> My life now lies a ruin
> Full oft have I experienced,
> There's none so fair, so wise,
> So courteous nor so highly famed,
> But, if Fortune cease to favour,
> Will be a fool proclaimed.

The friar was moved. Edward's plight was far worse than he had imagined. He had now seen with his own eyes the way that the deposed king was treated, kept like a wild animal in a dungeon below ground. Slipping the poem back into his sleeve, he turned northward and moved off through the undergrowth with long and purposeful strides.

The attack was cleverly-timed and well-executed. Primed by his brother, Stephen Dunheved knew exactly when and where to strike. Under the dark blanket of night and taking advantage of a depleted garrison, the banished lord and his men stormed over the walls and dealt viciously with any resistance. Dunheved was a big, brawny man with a love of valiant action and an edge of desperation about him. Having killed, robbed and cheated in order to survive as an outlaw, he now felt that he had a worthy cause and committed himself wholeheartedly to it. Once inside Berkeley Castle, he opened the main gate to admit his brother, Thomas, with the rest of the armed band.

When the guards were overpowered, Stephen Dunheved battered his way into the keep then raced down to the dungeons. Roused from his sleep, Edward was confused by the yells and the sound of fighting. A blood-covered Dunheved soon unlocked the door and beckoned the prisoner out. Thomas arrived with a cloak, hat and sword for him.

"What is happening, Thomas?" said the bemused Edward.

"We have come to rescue you, my lord."

"Where are you taking me?"

"Away from here."

"I am truly free?"

"Only if you move your royal arse away from this cesspit," said Stephen

Dunheved, averting his nose from the stink of the cell. "Come, my lord. We have a long ride ahead of us this night."

But the leader of the attackers had other business to discharge first. While Thomas ushered the prisoner into the courtyard where horses awaited them, his brother gave the order for his men to loot and destroy indiscriminately. Only when they had filled their satchels with spoils and set fire to parts of the castle were they ready to retreat. Thomas Dunheved had planned the assault but it was his brother who provided the efficient brutality needed for its success.

Edward was thrilled to have a horse beneath him again. A brilliant horseman, he sorely missed the opportunity to ride. Now he was free once more, galloping through the night on a black stallion, putting distance between himself and the castle which had entombed him. At the first gesture of daylight, they reined in their mounts and waited for the others to catch them up. Stephen Dunheved and his men were a clamorous assembly. Drunk on stolen wine and inebriated with their success, they came hurtling along with loud whoops. They behaved less like loyal subjects than wild marauders but Edward did not mind. These men had risked their lives to rescue their king. It was exhilarating. Edward laughed as loud as any of them as they continued on their way.

Pursuit was swift and decisive. The reckless flight of the attackers was their own undoing. A large posse was formed and it had no difficulty following the vivid trail south to Dorset. Before they could embark and sail to the safety of the French coast, Edward and his supporters were caught and outnumbered at Corfe Castle. Many of the band died in the skirmish or fled ignominiously. Stephen Dunheved was among them. It was ironic. The man who wreaked most havoc at Berkeley Castle escaped but his hapless brother, Thomas, the Dominican friar, who had organized the violence in which he did not participate, was dragged savagely back to Gloucestershire to face the full wrath of Berkeley himself.

A monastic cowl was no protection. Stripped naked and flung headlong into a dungeon, Thomas Dunheved was cruelly tortured until his body could take no more. Locked in another cell, Edward could do nothing but lie there and listen to the agonised cries of his erstwhile saviour as he went to his Maker by the most excruciating route. The friar had served his king well but paid a frightful penalty for his loyalty.

Having vented their fury on the man who planned the escape, Berkeley and Maltravers took steps to ensure that such a bold rescue could not happen again. Edward was moved to another cell, even darker and more malodorous than the first, serving the castle as a sewer and leaving its occupant ankle-deep in accumulated filth and excrement. Even the robust constitution of the deposed king began to suffer. Sir Thomas Gurney now shared responsibility for the safety of the prisoner and he was as merciless as his colleagues. Gurney was as Berkeley Castle in September when the fateful message came from Mortimer.

It was delivered by William Ogle, who arrived in haste from Wales. They received him in the Great Hall and read the letter with interest. It was written by William of Shalford, one of Mortimer's lieutenants and it disclosed details of a second plot to rescue Edward which was being hatched by Sir Rhys ap Grufydd. The intelligence had first been sent to Mortimer himself who was Justice of Wales and in Abergavenny at the time. Mortimer moved swiftly to crush the threatened rebellion, after first dispatching Ogle to Berkeley Castle. The message was clear. As long as Edward lived, he was a source of potential danger. A letter in Mortimer's own hand gave the point more emphasis.

Thomas de Berkeley read out the crucial sentence.

"*Edwardum occidere nolite timere bonum est.*"

"Fear not to kill the king," said Maltravers. " 'Tis good he die."

"There is another translation," noted Gurney, poring over the words. "*Edwardum occidere nolite timere bonum est.* Put a comma in the right place and it becomes the opposite. Kill not the king, 'tis good to fear the worst."

"There is no punctuation here," observed Berkeley. "We must provide our own by which I mean a full stop at the end of life. Our orders are plain. Fear not to kill the king, 'tis good he die."

"The sooner, the better," agreed Maltravers.

"Edward is a Latin scholar," said Berkeley with a smirk. "Should we show this message to him and ask him to oblige us by translating his own death sentence?"

"He must himself be translated," said Maltravers, stroking his beard. "From earth to heaven. Or to hell, rather. For the angels will not allow that unholy stink in heaven."

Berkeley nodded. "We know what we must do. All that remains is to decide exactly how we do it."

"Drown him in that sea of ordure down there," suggested Maltravers with a hollow laugh. "Or cut his throat. Or toss him from the battlements and say that he fell while attempting to escape. Any of these ways or all three together will be enough to snuff out a royal life."

"Yes," said Gurney, succumbing to a rare moment of guilt. "A *royal* life. That is what concerns me. Have we really been given licence to kill a king? This is no ordinary crime, sirs. It is regicide."

"A year ago, it may have been," argued Berkeley. "But not any more. What was regicide then is now a service to the nation.*Edwardum occidere nolite timere bonum est.* Let us be more precise translators. Fear not to kill Edward, 'tis good he die.''

"Edward is not a king," added Maltravers. "He is merely the father of the king. His son has now been crowned."

"And will that son condone this murder?" asked Gurney, still troubled by scruples. "How will he view us if we are seen to be his father's assassins?"

"That is not how we will be seen," said Maltravers airily. "By those who rule the kingdom – Mortimer and Isabella – we will be hailed as heroes because they will know the truth of the matter. Everyone else will be led to believe that Edward died of natural causes."

"But he is as strong as an ox," said Gurney.

"Even an ox must die at the end of its useful life," asserted Berkeley with a dismissive wave of his hand. "Enough of this hesitation. Our instructions are clear and the manner of their delivery reinforces their urgency. This good fellow here has ridden hell-for-leather to deliver the message. While Edward is alive, his name will continue to act as a rallying-point of rebellion. It has fallen to us to rid England of that threat. And to earn the undying gratitude of Mortimer."

"You are right," said Gurney, sweeping aside his reservations. "Let us about it this very night. Whom should we employ to do the deed?"

"There are enough of us here to do it ourselves," said Berkeley, looking around their faces in turn. "Four strong men against one weak prisoner. Whatever method we choose, he will be unable to resist us."

"Beat his brains out," urged Maltravers. "A quick and violent death."

"With the marks of violence left upon him for all to see. No," said Berkeley, pursing his lips reflectively, "we must devise a means to take his life while leaving no trace of how it was done. And let us remember that Edward was once king over us and made us all suffer under his yoke. He deserves a special kind of death. An appropriate end."

Maltravers gave a sudden laugh and slapped his thigh.

"I have it, friends!" he boasted. "I know the perfect way."

The atmosphere of Berkeley Castle underwent a subtle change. There was a sense of imminent violence in the air. Everyone was aware of it except the man at whom it would be directed. Small and unexpected acts of kindness lightened the burden of Edward's last day. He was given a candle and a Bible. One of the gaolers brought him extra food and drink. One of the porters gave him a small crucifix and talked kindly to him. Two of the men-at-arms who had recaptured him at Corfe Castle came to take their leave of him. They found him hunched in a corner, reading the Bible with intense satisfaction.

When night fell, mercy was replaced by vindictiveness. The four assassins had everything in readiness. Down in the dungeons, a poker was laid in the roaring fire. A stout wooden table was placed beside the forge. Ropes were procured. When the poker was white hot, it was time to act. They grinned in the half-dark with anticipatory pleasure.

The prisoner was fast asleep when they struck. Berkeley led the way with Maltravers, Gurney and William Ogle as his confederates. When the door of the cell was unlocked, Berkeley rushed in to rouse his guest and to slip a black bag over his head. Resistance was useless. The prisoner was dragged from his cell by determined hands and carried across to the table. They held him face down on the timber and used the ropes to tie his flailing arms and twitching body. His rags were torn away to expose his bare buttocks. Maltravers and Gurney held down a leg apiece while Ogle pressed down hard on the prisoner's shoulders.

It was Thomas de Berkeley who wound thick leather around his hand before picking up the poker. It glowed murderously in the gloom.

"You have a visitor, my lord," he taunted. "Your dear Gaveston has returned to pleasure you once more. Bid your lover welcome."

And he thrust the poker deep into the prisoner's anus.

They drank in celebration until dawn and congratulated each other on their night's work, convinced that it would bring them rich rewards. Maltravers took the credit for devising a means of death which had a certain poetic justice about it. He had no regrets.

"Those that live by the arse, die by it!" he said with a guffaw. "We gave him a new delight. Even Gaveston's beloved prick was never as hot as that poker. Mortimer will appreciate this jest, I think."

"Yes," said Berkeley, sipping another cup of wine. "And the beauty of it is that it will not show. When the body has been bathed and the wound tended, we may lay Edward on his back and display him to the witnesses we must call. There will be no visible marks of violence upon him. To the naked eye, it will seem that he died a natural death."

"While savouring an unnatural vice."

They shared a crude laugh then decided to gloat over their handiwork. When they got down to the dungeons, however, a surprise awaited them. The prisoner had been untied and the bag had been removed from his head. Bathed and bandaged, he was turned over on his back. Berkeley held a flaming torch beside the face of the corpse and bent over to whisper another taunt into Edward's ear.

But Edward was not there. The sightless eyes which stared up at him belonged to an older and somewhat shorter man. His beard and colouring resembled that of the prisoner and there was the same fine nose but the likeness ended there. The four assassins gaped in horror. They had killed the wrong victim. The vile death had left the man's face contorted with pain but Berkeley was still able to recognize him.

"It is Dickon!" he said in astonishment.

"Dickon the Porter?" asked Maltravers.

"The same. He sought my permission to visit the prisoner so that he could give him a crucifix. I saw no harm in the request and granted his wish." Berkeley looked around in dismay. "But he tricked us all. Dickon must have taken the prisoner's place so that Edward could escape. This is a calamity!"

"Only if it is known," said Maltravers firmly.

"Yes," said Gurney, searching for a means of redemption for them. "Our orders were to kill Edward and we duly dispatched the prisoner. Let it be thought that we murdered the right man. Cut out his heart and send it to Mortimer, encased in a silver casket." He shrugged his shoulders. "Who will know the difference?"

"We will," said Ogle nervously.

"And so will others when the body is displayed," said Berkeley.

"Not if we prepare it properly," argued Gurney. "Faces change during long captivity. Nobody but we have seen Edward for several months. We can swear that this is he. Let us have the body embalmed and dressed in raiment which conceals it. Close this porter's eyes and he may yet have the faint appearance of a king about him."

"It will be done!" affirmed Maltravers.

"It must be done!" insisted Berkeley. "Or we stand accused of folly. Nobody must ever know the truth of this. It is a secret which we four must take to our graves. The body will be shown to witnesses and we will give out that Edward died of a fever contracted in the dungeon. Are we all agreed on that?"

"We are," said Gurney. "And there is nobody to gainsay us."

"Yes, there is," remarked Ogle.

"Who?" said Gurney.

William Ogle ran his tongue over his dry lips before speaking.

"Edward himself."

Edward rode hard and thanked God repeatedly for what he believed was divine intercession. Dickon the Porter had been sent from above to save him from the hideous fate which beckoned. The man had not only taken his place in the cell and slipped him a dagger, he had saddled a horse and left it hidden among the trees nearby. Having sneaked out of the castle under the cover of darkness, Edward followed the directions and soon found the animal. His flight was swift but more considered this time. Instead of leaving an easy trail to follow, Edward altered his course time and again, zigzagging his way south.

When dawn came, he felt safe enough to rest the horse, cleanse himself in a stream, change into the apparel which the considerate porter had put in the saddle-bags and shave off his beard. Staring at himself in the rippling water, he saw a very different face smiling up at him. He was free once more and he would not surrender that freedom again. Before he set off, he got down on his knees to offer up a heartfelt prayer of thanks. Then he rode on at a steady canter.

Pope John XXII, ruling the Catholic Church from Avignon, was both surprised and curious when he was told who came in search of him. He granted the visitor an audience at once and heard the strange story with rapt attention. Edward the Second was evidently still alive.

"Word reached us that you had died of a fever," said John.

Edward gave a wry smile. "It seems that I did, your Holiness. My body was seen by several eminent witnesses who vouched for the fact that it was me. But nobody wished to claim my body, fearful that they would incur the disfavour of Mortimer if they did so. Malmesbury and Bristol both refused to accept the corpse of a deposed king."

"Or a deposed porter."

"I was in Ireland when I heard the news," continued Edward. "The goodly abbot of St Peter's at Gloucester took pity on me, I learned. He defied the threats from Mortimer and gave me the most honourable burial. I am almost sorry that I was not there to enjoy it."

The Pope did not share his amusement. "This is a wondrous tale, Edward," he said seriously, "and proof positive of God's benevolence. But while you escaped, another died in your place. I will name him in my prayers. What was he called?"

"Dickon, your Holiness. Dickon the Porter."

"A brave and noble man. Buried in Gloucester, you say?"

"At the abbey church of St Peter."

"Then he will find true fellowship in Heaven," said John soulfully. "St Peter is the porter at the gates and he will have a special welcome for this blessed porter. Your rescue is a small miracle, Edward. Few men are capable of such an act of self-sacrifice. Dickon was your salvation."

"Yes," said Edward sadly. "The perfect shadow of a king."

This story was suggested by the contents of an undated letter which was sent to Edward III by Manuel Fieschi, a Genoese priest who held an English benefice. Fieschi recounted the facts which he claimed to have heard from Edward II himself in the confessional box. The details of the events leading up to his imprisonment at Berkeley are remarkably accurate and it is difficult to see how else the priest could have learned them. England, however, was firmly convinced that their former king had died and he was mourned with unexpected fervour.

Edward III soon tired of being manipulated by Mortimer and his mother. He overthrew Mortimer in a coup and had him executed in 1330. His father's assassins – if that is what they really were – never paid the price for their crime. Thomas de Berkeley was prosecuted but his plea of ignorance was accepted and he was acquitted. William Ogle was arrested but escaped to die a free man. Sir John Maltravers found it safer to live abroad but rendered good service to Edward III in Flanders and secured a full pardon before his death in 1364. Sir Thomas Gurney was arrested twice. The first time he escaped but the second time he died in the hands of his captors.

A BLACK DEATH

Thwarted ambition drives this particular story. It takes place on the eve of the battle of Poitiers in September, 1356, when two Welsh archers decide to avenge their nation by assassinating the Black Prince. Meurig, one of the archers, has royal blood in his own veins, being descended from the princes of Gwynedd. Unfortunately, he was brought up in England, a country that he despises. Born on the wrong side of the blanket and raised on the wrong side of the Welsh border, Meurig yearns for true recognition and that can only be achieved by the removal of a quintessential English hero. First, however, he has to confront the famous suit of black armor.

O nly one arrow was needed. Plucked from its sheaf, it was fitted to the bow-string with deft fingers, then drawn steadily backward with its head pointing up at a slight angle. When the longbow was bent to its full extent, its target was measured in an instant and its tilt adjusted accordingly. The arrow was released with a fierce surge of power, and it explored the air in a rising trajectory until it located its victim. Descent was swift, silent, and deadly. Heavy armor was no protection. After a flight of over two hundred yards, the arrow came hurtling out of the sun like a white-hot brand and pierced the camail with contemptuous ease. It cut into the throat of the rider with such force that it knocked him backward from his horse and stilled forever the proud war cry on his lips. The assassin was pleased with his work.

He had killed the Prince of Wales yet again.

Meurig was born with murder in his heart. His earliest memories were of death and deprivation. His first instinct was to seek revenge. Meurig had been dispossessed. He was cheated out of his birthright by an accident of nature and robbed of his eminence by a cruel twist of fate. He was the grandson of Rhodri, brother of Llywelyn ap Grufydd, and so his lineage should have been impeccable. But his mother lacked the wedding ring that would have gained him an honorable place among the descendants of the princes of Gwynedd. Royal blood pulsed through his veins, yet he was not recognized as a rightful claimant to his father's rank and estate.

More humiliation followed. He was raised in England, in the very country which had ground his own beneath its iron heel. He was forced to live among the enemy. Born on the wrong side of the blanket and brought up on the wrong side of the border, Meurig was tormented by a sense of loss. He was estranged from his own land and cut off from his own language. His crown had been snatched away from him. Hatred and rebellion mingled in his breast. He needed someone to blame and someone to kill.

His chosen victim was Edward.

Wales had good cause to rue that name. It was Edward I who had conquered the land with such vicious finality and who built a series of huge castles to keep it in subjection. It was his son, Edward II, born in one of those same castles at Caernarvon, who became the first Prince of Wales and who thus symbolized the fate of the defeated nation. And when Edward II was murdered by foul conspiracy, it was *his* son, Edward III, who seized the throne and continued the oppression of the Principality. Meurig loathed them all, but there was one Edward for whom he reserved real animosity.

Edward, Prince of Wales.

The eldest son of Edward III had other honors bestowed upon him. At the age of three, he became Earl of Chester; at the age of seven, he became Duke of Cornwall. But these were irrelevant titles in the fevered mind of Meurig. What rankled with him was that Edward of Woodstock became Prince of Wales at the age of thirteen. He supplanted Meurig himself. He was guilty of a royal crime – the theft of a crown.

For Edward was the anointed prince of a land that he had never visited. He held sway over a people whose customs he did not respect and whose language he did not understand. His title gave him added status and a greater income, but Wales gained nothing in return. Through his envious eyes, Meurig saw it all very clearly. Edward did not just commit a royal crime. He epitomized it.

Destiny linked the two of them from the start. Meurig and Edward were the same age, the same build, and the same coloring. Both were skilled in arms, and both had a noble bearing. Each was a natural leader of men. The resemblance ended there. While Edward, Prince of Wales, had a glittering future before him, Meurig had only a lifetime in the shadows ahead. The young Welshman wanted to burst into the light and free his nation from the yoke of the tyrant. There was only one way that he could achieve his ambition. Meurig, the true heir of Gwynedd, had to vanquish the usurper. One Prince of Wales had to be destroyed by another.

An accomplice was needed. Meurig soon found him.

"How will you kill him, Meurig?"

"In single combat."

"With sword, with dagger, with lance?"

"With my bare hands, if need be."

"Why not put an arrow between his eyes?"

"We must fight on equal terms."

"He gives Wales no equal terms."

"Edward will be slain by me," said Meurig grimly. "But I will be a just executioner."

"Stab him in the back!"

"I have to think of my honor."

"Poison the English *mochyn*!"

Idwal was a short, stocky young man with a mop of dark hair falling down to a matted beard. He was a distant cousin of Meurig's on the maternal side and gave the latter total respect and obedience. Royalty had brushed Meurig and left its mark indelibly upon him. Idwal was glad to serve the next Prince of Wales. He never tired of discussing methods of disposing of the incumbent holder of the title.

"Beat his brains out with a boulder."

"Leave it with me, Idwal."

"Ride him down with your horse."

"I will decide."

"Remember how they killed his grandfather," said Idwal with a wicked grin. "Use a burning poker!"

They were only sixteen when they first began to plan the assassination. Eager to quit England and to perfect his military skills, Meurig had come to France to join a band of roving mercenaries. He was part of a small force of Welsh expatriates – Idwal among them – who were willing to fight for money until the time came when they could fight to liberate their country. Meurig provided a focus for their patriotic impulses, and he quickly rose to a position of command. It was a prince-dom of sorts.

He served in Spain, Alsace, and the Swiss cantons. He cut down the enemies of a Breton paymaster before selling his allegiance to the Duke of Anjou. Battle only served to sharpen the edge of his ambition. Every blow he struck was for the honor of his country. Every man he killed was Edward, Prince of Wales. Every time he fought, he avenged a royal crime.

"We must raise an army, Idwal."

"How?"

"We must hire a fleet."

"When?"

"We must invade Wales and drive out the English."

"Where is the money for all this?"

"It will come," said Meurig. "It will come."

And Idwal, like all the others who sat around the camp fire, believed him. Their captain inspired confidence. He gave them a vision and purpose to carry them through their grisly existence. They were hired murderers, but they had hope in their hearts. Nothing could stop them now. They came to believe that they were invincible.

Then the final enemy struck. It came from the east, and it brought devastation in its wake. The disease was so savage in its effect and so widespread in its attack that it seemed as if the Day of Judgment had arrived. Whole towns were brought to their knees and whole villages emptied of their inhabitants. Nothing could escape the Black Death. It killed evenly among high and low, it snuffed out the lives of holy men just as easily as those of heretics.

Meurig led his company north at full gallop, but they could not outrun the disease. By the time the Welshmen reached the coast, a third of their number had died in hideous ways. By the time their ship sailed, another ten had fallen to the invisible foe. Others expired at sea, others again survived the voyage to find the plague waiting to welcome them ashore. Meurig's dreams were shattered. He and Idwal were left with a mere handful of soldiers.

It was time to fight with different weapons.

"Kill for the English!" Idwal was disgusted.

"We have no choice," argued Meurig. "We will not get close to the Prince of Wales unless we join his army."

"It is a betrayal."

"Edward is the one who will be betrayed."

"We swore an oath to fight *against* him."

"He will not expect an attack from within his ranks."

"Let us burn him alive in his tent!"

"Mine is the surer way, Idwal."

"Drive a stake through his black heart."

"It may be slow," said Meurig, "but it will be sure."

And Idwal eventually came to accept the wisdom of the advice. There was a long wait. The war with France was languishing and the Prince of Wales – now hailed as a hero after the battle of Crécy – busied himself with visiting his estates and distinguishing himself in knightly pursuits at a series of tournaments. Meurig was not idle. He and Idwal kept their skills in an excellent state of repair. While Edward was jousting for applause, the two Welshmen were practicing at the butts with their longbows or exercising their sword-arms. Peace wearied them, but their common purpose still smoldered.

"How will you kill him, Meurig?"

"Like a prince."

The chance finally came. War with France was resumed. The Duke of Lancaster led an army that landed at Cherbourg and struck out toward Brittany. Edward, Prince of Wales, went deep into Aquitaine to attack from the south. An important part of his army was a troop of mounted archers. Meurig and Idwal rode behind the man they despised.

Edward cut a striking figure. His black armor was beautifully made to fit the contours of his body, and it covered every inch of him. His helm was surmounted by a royal lion. His jupon, sleeveless and tight-fitting, displayed the quartered arms of England and France. A straight-bladed sword with a large hilt hung from his left hip. Seated astride his horse, he looked the very flower of chivalry.

Even Meurig and Idwal were impressed at first. What sustained their rancor throughout the years was the idea of a Prince of Wales. Now they were confronted by the reality, a courageous knight who was loved and trusted by his men. But the assassins soon saw another side to the flamboyant young hero in the black armor, for he did not mount a direct attack on the French army at all. His policy was to destroy and to terrorize. Edward led a series of *chevauchées*, daring raids on towns and villages, looting and burning with indiscriminate brutality before riding on to his next prey. The chivalric commander was fighting like the most depraved mercenary. Meurig and Idwal hated him even more.

They watched and waited, but their opportunity did not come. Their leader was too alert and too well-guarded. It was the intercession of the French that helped them. King Jean assembled a huge army and rode south to do battle. Edward could not avoid the encounter and quickly sought a good defensive position. He chose a wooded slope some two miles south of Poitiers. Meurig could at last move in for the kill.

"They say there are thirty thousand Frenchmen!"

"Those are but rumors, Idwal."

"Their army will massacre us."

"Think on our sworn duty."

"I am not ready to die yet, Meurig."

"The Prince of Wales is."

"We have to fight a battle tomorrow."

"Kill Edward and there may *be* no battle."

Idwal listened intently, and the persuasive tongue of his master soothed him once more. The plan was bold enough to try and cunning enough to succeed. A royal crime would at last be avenged on behalf of their nation. On the eve of a battle between England and France, it was Wales that would strike the decisive blow. Idwal scorned danger. He was not prepared to die in the service of a foreign power, but he would willingly lay down his life for his country.

"Wait for my signal," ordered Meurig.

"I've waited these ten years."

"Take up your station with great care."

"I'll merge with night itself."

"Have your bow ready."

"It is cut from the finest yew."

"Choose your sharpest arrows."

"They will fly straight and true."

"Pray that they may not be needed," said the other. "If it please God, I will dispatch him myself."

Meurig had no doubts on that score, but he still believed in having a second line of attack. If his dagger should miss its mark, then Idwal's arrows might yet succeed. One way or another, a great ugly stain on their national pride would be removed.

The eager Idwal pressed for important details.

"How will you kill him, Meurig?"

"With cold steel."

"Cut his foul throat."

"I'll strike at his heart."

"Feel no pity."

"I do not, Idwal."

"Show no mercy."

"There is none to show."

"Butcher his body," urged the other with sadistic glee. "Hack it to pieces and drench the ground with his blood."

Meurig shook his head solemnly. "I will accord a royal corpse all due respect. We are not barbarians, Idwal."

"Edward has fought like one in these wars."

"He will die as a true soldier."

"He will die. Let us agree on that."

Meurig nodded. "He will die."

The two men embraced, then parted to rejoin the others. They were soon hammering stakes into the earth so that their sharp points stuck up at an angle to give a hostile greeting to any attackers. The English army would fight on foot. The mounted archers had tethered their horses in the safety of the trees. Crouched behind their barricade, they would discharge their arrows at an enemy whose size was swelled by each new report. Fear spread through the ranks, but Meurig and Idwal worked calmly on. They stalked a different foe.

It was the Sabbath, but this was no day of rest. While soldiers of both parties went about their business, the Church bestirred itself and made a vain attempt to avert bloodshed. Cardinal Talleyrand de Perigord shuttled to and fro between the armies with his robes flapping in the wind as he tried to maneuver the two sides toward a peaceful settlement. Edward did not seek battle with the French host. Hopelessly out-numbered and completely surrounded, he was in such a desperate situation that he offered huge concessions to King Jean – even the return of Calais and Guines – but nothing short of abject surrender would content the French.

The cardinal warned, argued, cajoled, and pleaded, but it was all to no avail. He resorted to the power of prayer, but it could not alter the course of history. Two armies were preparing to fight the Battle of Poitiers to a bitter conclusion. Nothing could stop them now.

Edward strengthened his defenses still further, then toured his camp to put heart into his men. There was no hint of dread in his manner, no touch of weakness in his voice. He had never lost a battle and did not intend to lose one now. Even Meurig was forced to admire his brave defiance. Edward turned a frightened army into a confident force. Soldiers who were resigned to defeat now dared to believe in victory. The charisma of their leader had worked its magic.

There were tactics to be discussed and battle plans to be finalized. Edward consulted with his commanders long into the night, then he withdrew to his pavilion to snatch a few precious hours of sleep before the conflict. Meurig bided his time, then moved swiftly into action. The royal chaplain was about to put on his vestments when the Welshman slipped soundlessly into his tent. One thrust of the dagger sent the chaplain to his Maker. His body was summarily stripped.

Dressed as a priest and walking with the measured tread of the sacred, Meurig went off to his unholy task. As he picked his way through the camp, he gave a signal to the watching Idwal. Guards were on duty outside the royal pavilion, but they did not obstruct the prince's chaplain. Nor did they observe the shadowy figure who crept up in the undergrowth and lurked behind some bushes only thirty yards away. Sentinels were posted all round the camp, but they were on the lookout for French soldiers and not for Welsh assassins. The plan was working.

As Meurig came into the pavilion, however, he saw something that rocked him back and made him reach for the dagger that was concealed in his sleeve. The Prince of Wales was standing before him, armed and ready for battle. They faced each other at last. The encounter for which he had yearned was finally taking place. But as Meurig took a threatening step forward, there was no response from Edward. And the latter did not even flinch when his chaplain jabbed at him with a dagger. Then Meurig realized that he was confronting an empty suit of armor.

It stood tall, dark, and proud in the flickering light of the torches. Meurig was moved. So this is what it meant to be Prince of Wales – to reside in a sumptuous pavilion and to lead an army into battle in a magnificent suit of armor. With a covetous hand, he stroked the helm and the camail that was laced to it to protect the chin, cheeks, and neck of royalty. His fingers rippled over the chainmail, then met the sculptured smoothness of the breastplate.

The craftsmanship was quite breathtaking. Meurig was only a mounted archer who fought in a nailed jerkin of filled leather above a mailed shirt. He wore a plain bascinet on his head, not a work of art like the helm before him. There were no superb iron gauntlets for his hands. All that he had was a bracer to guard his left arm and catch the string when an arrow was released. Jealousy stirred within him. Here was his true inheritance.

A cough from the adjoining chamber alerted him to his purpose, and he resumed his role as the royal chaplain. Parting the rich hangings, he stepped through into the inner part of the pavilion. Edward, Prince of Wales, lay sleeping on his couch with only his page in attendance. The latter saw no more than he expected – a visit from the chaplain at the approach of dawn to pray for God's help in the mighty struggle ahead Meurig exploited the element of surprise. Whipping his dagger from his sleeve, he raised it up and brought the hilt smashing down on the page's skull to knock him senseless. The page fell to the ground in a heap.

Meurig smiled. The Prince of Wales was at his mercy. All he had to do was to push a blade between some ribs, and a lifelong promise would be fulfilled. Destiny beckoned. The ghosts of his princely ancestors urged him on. He lifted the knife, but it froze in his hand. Meurig could not move.

Doubts assailed him. Should he not wake his enemy so that he could kill him in a fair fight? Should he not make Edward understand that a royal crime demanded royal recompense? After ten years of planning, the assassination should surely have more to it than a momentary plunge of steel. What honor was there in a squalid murder? Meurig wrestled with the irony of the situation. He had killed an imaginary Prince of Wales a hundred times, but he could not now dispose of the real one.

Screwing up his courage, he raised the dagger high in the name of Wales, but something stayed his hand yet again. Edward opened his eyes. He came out of his dream to gaze up at his executioner for a fleeting second before lapsing back into a drowsy slumber. Meurig was chastened. That brief glance between them contained a whole world of recognition. In the eyes of his victim, he saw valor and integrity and pride. He saw the one man alive who could lead his army to victory on the morrow against impossible odds. He saw the cold arrogance of power and the unmistakable glint of royalty.

He saw kinship.

Idwal watched anxiously from his hiding place with a nervous hand clutching at his beard. What had happened inside the pavilion, and why was it taking Meurig so long? They had rehearsed the murder endlessly in a thousand discussions. Had the plan gone awry? Was Meurig standing in triumph over the corpse of his victim? Or had he made his escape through the rear of the pavilion? What if his disguise had been detected? Had he been slain by guards, or was he being held to face trial and execution? Why did he not step out of the pavilion?

The answer eventually came. Meurig had faltered. On the last few, vital steps of a ten-year journey, he had tripped and fallen. For it was not a royal assassin who strutted out into the night air. It was the Prince of Wales in full armor. There was no moon to shed its light on the scene and no fire to cast its glow, but Idwal knew what he saw — Edward of Woodstock, the scourge of his nation.

A Black Prince who deserved a black death.

Only one arrow was needed. Plucked from its sheaf, it was fitted to the bowstring with deft fingers then drawn steadily back. With a hiss of derision, Idwal sent it off on its fatal errand. The most famous suit of armor in Christendom was no match for the skill of a Welsh archer. Whistling its way into legend, the arrow shot out of the darkness with the future of a nation riding on its flight. It pierced the camail with vengeful force and sliced out the throat of its victim. Idwal barely had time to watch his quarry fall to oblivion before he himself was hacked to death by a dozen English swords. His life was forfeit, but a sense of deep satisfaction went with him to his grave.

He was not the only man to die happily in the darkness. When they lifted the visor of his helm, they found that Meurig was still smiling with regal joy. He had regained his rightful crown after all. He had risen to power among the lords of the house of Gwynedd. He had vindicated family honor. One royal crime answered another. By stealing a suit of armor, he won back the country of his heart. Edward might still awake to glory. He might still lead his army to heroic deeds in the forthcoming Battle of Poitiers and plant the English flag more firmly on French soil.

But Meurig ended his life as the Prince of Wales.

A GIFT FROM GOD

This story has a tenuous link with "A Black Death" in that one of its characters, Walter Huckvale, fought and lost an arm at the battle of Poitiers. "A Gift from God," however, is very different in tone to its predecessor. It's the most unashamedly romantic tale in the whole anthology. Catherine Teale, a beautiful young wife, has a strange ability to cure the sick and dying. When she falls out with the brutal Hugh Costaine, he accuses her of witchcraft and she is duly arrested. The murder of Walter Huckvale is also laid at her door. Her vintner husband, Adam, vows to save her but it is Catherine herself who finally engineers her vindication from the unjust charges. In doing so, she realises that she has, after all, a gift from God.

England, 1371.

Nobody had told him how beautiful she was. When he heard about her reputation as a weaver of spells, he imagined that she would be an ugly old crone who lived in some hovel with only a mangy cat or a flea-bitten dog for company. Instead, much to his astonishment and pleasure, Catherine Teale was a handsome woman in her late twenties, alert, bright-eyed and glowing with health. Her attire was serviceable rather than costly but it enhanced her shapely figure. Hugh Costaine was duly impressed. As he reined in his horse, he gave her smirk of admiration.

"*You* are the sorceress?" he said in surprise.

"No, sir," she replied with a polite shake of her head. "There is no sorcery involved in what I do. I have a gift, that is all."

"You have many gifts, as I can see."

Costaine leered at her. He was a tall, sharp-featured man, little above her own age but coarsened by debauchery that added a greyness to his beard and a decade to his appearance. As befitted the eldest son of Sir Richard Costaine, lord of the manor of Headcorn, he was wearing the finest array and riding a spirited black stallion. Catherine was about to go into the house when he accosted her. She had just returned from a walk across the fields to gather herbs. Costaine feasted his eyes on her.

"I need your help," he said at length.

"It is yours to command, sir."

"Prepare me a flask of poison. Something swift and venomous. Our stables are overrun with rats and I would be rid of them."

"Then you must look elsewhere," suggested Catherine. "I do not make potions to end life, only to preserve it. I medicine the sick. That is my calling."

"If you can cure, you can also kill," he insisted. "I'll not be baulked. Now, get into the house and mix what I require."

"I do not know how to, sir."

"Hurry, woman!"

"There is no point."

Costaine angered. "You deny my request?"

"It has been brought to the wrong person."

"But I heard many tales about you. They say that you practice sorcery. That you conjure spirits out of the air to help you."

"Idle gossip. Do not believe it."

"Too many mouths praise your skills."

"Skills of healing. Nothing more."

"Unnatural skills. Deeds of wonder. Magic. No more of this evasion," he ordered, dismounting to confront her. "I have ridden five miles on this errand. I need that poison forthwith. Fetch it at once."

He was close enough to appreciate her charms even more now. Her face was gorgeous, her skin luminous. Catherine exuded a scent that was almost intoxicating. Costaine inhaled deeply. Lust stirring, he gave her an oily grin and took a step nearer.

"You will be well-paid," he promised her. "Give me what I seek and I will reward you with a kiss. A hundred of them." He reached out but she eluded his grasp. He chuckled. "Do you find me so repellent?"

"No, sir."

"Then why keep me at bay? Is it to whet my appetite?"

"I would never do that."

"Not even to please me?"

"Not even then, sir."

"Do you know who I am?" he boasted. "And what I am?"

"Yes, sir."

"Well?"

"You are the son of Sir Richard Costaine, an honest gentleman and a courteous knight who would never show such a lack of gallantry."

"To hell with gallantry!" he retorted, snatching her by the arm. "You dare to refuse me? I'll have more than a kiss from you for that. When you have made my flask of poison, I'll have a sweeter potion from you in a bedchamber."

"But I am married, sir," she protested.

"What does that matter? So am I."

"You would take me against my will?"

"Of course not, lady," he said with a snigger. "I will woo you like any lovesick swain. Now, do as I tell you and be swift about it."

As Costaine released her arm, a figure emerged from the house. Adam Teale was a big, broad-shouldered man in his thirties. He ambled across to them with an easy smile but his eyes were watchful.

"What is the trouble, sir?" he asked. "I heard raised voices. Has my dear wife upset you in any way?"

"Yes," snarled the other. "She is trying to thwart me."

"Catherine would not do that without cause, sir. I am Adam Teale, the vintner, and I can vouch for my wife's good temper. There never was a gentler or kinder woman." He loomed over Costaine. "What is it that you want, sir? Perhaps, I can help you."

"It's not wine that I'm after, vintner. It's poison."

"Then you've wasted your journey, sir. Only wholesome liquid is on sale here. Your father has been pleased to buy it from me on occasion."

"Enough of my father!"

"Does he know why you have come?"

"That is nothing to do with you," said the visitor, dismissively. He turned back to Catherine. "Will you obey me or will you not?"

She gave a shrug. "I have told you, sir. I do not concoct poison."

"It is true," added her husband. "Such gifts as my wife possesses are put to the relief of pain and sickness. You must search elsewhere."

Hand on the hilt of his sword, Costaine squared up to him but Adam Teale met his gaze without flinching. He was not afraid of his belligerent visitor. Costaine was livid. Not only was he being turned away without the potion he sought, he was being deprived of the joys of ravishing the comely wife. They were two good reasons for his hatred to smoulder. He vowed to exact revenge.

"A vintner, are you, Master Teale?" he sneered.

"And proud of my trade," said Adam.

"Take care your wine is not tainted by this sorceress you married."

"Catherine is a devout Christian."

Hugh Costaine let out a sudden laugh and mounted his horse.

"We shall see about that!" he cried.

As the visitor rode away, Adam put a protective arm around Catherine's shoulders. She planted a grateful kiss on his cheek.

"Did I arrive at the right moment?" he said.

"Oh, yes," she answered, fondly. "You always do."

Agnes Huckvale sat dutifully beside her husband throughout the meal. He was in an expansive mood, loud, laughing, boastful, generous with his hospitality and flushed with wine to the point where he kept shooting sly and meaningful glances at his wife. Agnes could no longer remember if she had ever loved Walter Huckvale. She had been struck by his wealth and impressed by his military feats but she could not recall if her heart had really opened to him. It seemed so long ago. Agnes had been barely sixteen when she married a man who was well over twice her age. The gap between them had steadily widened and it was not only measured in years. Walter Huckvale pounded the table with his one remaining hand.

"More wine!" he called.

"You have already drunk more than your fill," warned his wife.

"I could never do that, Agnes." He looked around the empty tables through bleary eyes. "Where are our guests?"

"They retired to bed."

"So soon? Why did they not bid their host adieu?"

Agnes sighed. "They did, Walter, but you were too caught up in your memories to listen to them. When our guests took their leave, you were still fighting the Battle of Poitiers."

"And Crecy," he reminded her. "I won true renown at Crecy. It was at Poitiers that I lost my arm."

"You told us the story. Several times."

"It bears repetition."

The grizzled old warrior jutted out his chin with pride. A servant arrived with a jug of wine and poured some into his goblet. He did not offer any to Agnes. The servant bowed and left the room. Husband and wife sat amid the remains of the banquet, their faces lit by the flames of a hundred candles. Walter Huckvale sipped his wine and became playful.

"Let them go," he said. "I would be alone with my wife."

"I am tired."

"Then let me rouse you from your tiredness."

"It is too late an hour."

"Nonsense!" he announced, taking a long swig from his goblet. "I'll soon rekindle your spirits. Have you ever known me to fail, Agnes?"

He thrust his face close to her and she caught the stink of his breath. There was no point in trying to contradict him. She had pledged obedience at the altar and there was only one escape from that dread commitment. Agnes was doomed to suffer his bad breath, his coarse manners, his drunkenness, his bursts of rage and his interminable reminiscences of military campaigns. Worst of all, she had to enjoy the random brutality of his love-making. It was an ordeal.

Huckvale remembered something and an accusatory stare came into his eyes. Putting down his goblet, he reached out for her wrist.

"Where have you been all day?" he asked, sternly.

"Here."

"That's not true. I wanted you this afternoon and you could not be found. You sneaked off somewhere, didn't you?"

"No, Walter."

"Yes, you did. Where was it?"

"You're hurting my wrist," she complained.

He tightened his grip. "Tell me, Agnes."

"I was in the garden, that is all."

"Where *were* you?" he roared.

But the question went unanswered. As the words left his tongue, they were followed by a gasp of sheer agony. Releasing her wrist, he went into a series of convulsions, his eyes bulging, his face purple, his whole body racked with pain. Walter Huckvale put a hand to his stomach and looked appealingly at his wife. Then he pitched forward on to the bare wooden table, knocking his goblet to the floor with a clatter. Agnes drew back in horror. It was minutes before she was able to cry for help.

The Sheriff came to arrest her with four armed men at his back, a show of strength that was quite unnecessary but which deterred her husband from any intervention. Catherine Teale was bewildered.

"What is my crime?" she wondered.

"Witchcraft," said the Sheriff.

"I am no witch, my lord."

"That remains to be proved, Mistress Teale."

"Who laid the charges against me?"

"Hugh Costaine. He traces the murder to you door."

"Murder?" echoed Catherine in alarm.

"Walter Huckvale was poisoned to death last night. It is alleged that you slew him by means of a venomous brew in his wine."

"How can that be, my lord sheriff?" asked Adam Teale. "I do not provide the wine for Walter Huckvale's table."

The Sheriff was sarcastic. "And why might that be?"

"He and I fell out over an unpaid bill."

"Yes, Master Teale. Harsh words were exchanged between you and Walter Huckvale. There were many witnesses. I can understand why you wanted to get back at him but you lacked the means to do so." He turned to Catherine. "Your wife, however, did not. Because he refused to buy from you, she cast a spell on the wine he got elsewhere. She made him pay in the most dreadful way. He suffered the torments of Hell."

"That is a monstrous allegation!" exclaimed Adam.

"It is one that Mistress Teale must face. Be grateful that I do not arrest you on a charge of complicity. If I did not know you to be so upright and decent a man, I would suspect you had some part in this."

"No!" said Catherine, firmly. "Take me alone, my lord. My husband is not implicated in any way."

"You confess your guilt, then?" demanded the Sheriff.

"I protest my innocence!"

"You will be examined by Bishop Nigel."

"So be it."

Catherine silenced her husband's protests with a patient smile. There was no point in incurring the Sheriff's anger. Adam was as baffled by the charge as she was but it was important that one of them remained at liberty. Catherine submitted to the indignity of having her hands tied then she was lifted on to the spare horse which had been brought for her. As the little cavalcade pulled away from him, Adam Teale bit his lip in exasperation. He remembered the parting words of Hugh Costaine. Evidently, their unwelcome visitor had spread his own brand of poison.

Bishop Nigel was a wiry little man in his sixties with a bald head that was covered with a network of blue veins, and a pair of watery eyes. His voice was quiet but tinged with irritation. Several hours of interrogation had produced nothing but calm answers from the prisoner. Nigel was annoyed that he had not yet broken her spirit. They were alone together in a fetid cell but it was the manacled Catherine Teale who bore herself with equanimity in the foul conditions. Perspiration glistened on the prelate's brow. He resumed his examination.

"Are you in league with the Devil?" he hissed.

"No, my lord bishop. I am married to the best man alive."

"Then your husband is part of this conspiracy."

"There *is* no conspiracy," she assured him.

"Adam Teale had a disagreement with Walter Huckvale."

"My husband has a disagreement with anyone who does not pay his bill. That is only right and proper. I seem to remember that he once had a mild altercation with your own steward when an account was left unsettled but he did not wish to poison you, my lord bishop."

"Heaven forbid!"

"Adam had no *reason* to strike at Walter Huckvale."

"That is why you took retribution upon yourself. Do not deny it, Mistress Teale. Worrying reports about you have been coming in to me for several months now. I can no longer ignore them. You have been covertly engaged in sorcery." Bishop Nigel consulted the document in his hand, angling it to catch the light from the candle. "I have a full record of your nefarious activities here."

"Has anyone laid a complaint against me?"

"I lay a complaint," he snapped. "On behalf of the Church. I am enjoined by God to drive out the Devil."

"A worthy purpose but hardly relevant here."

"Is it not true that you cured an old woman from Pluckley of an ague that threatened to kill her? Is it not true that you brought a stillborn baby back to life in Marden by laying-on of hands? And is it not true that you helped to trace a man who had been missing from his home in Staplehurst for over a week?"

"I willingly admit all these things."

"Then your witchcraft is established!" he said, triumphantly.

"How?" she challenged. "A herbal compound cured the old woman in Pluckley. Such a mixture as any physician would prescribe. As for the stillborn child, it had never really been dead. It needed only some love and prayer to bring it fully to life. Most midwives would have done exactly as I did."

"And the man from Staplehurst?"

"He was a woodcutter, dazed when the bough of a tree chanced to fall on him. He wandered off, lost his bearings and could not find his way back. I sensed that he had found his way to Maidstone."

"*Sensed?*"

"Yes, my lord bishop."

"What evil powers enabled you to do that?"

"They are not evil or the result would not have been so good."

"Do not bandy words with me!"

"When people come to me for help, I give it to them."

"By means of sorcery."

"By means of my gift."

"And from whom does that come?"

"From the same source as your own – from God Almighty."

Her voice was so earnest and her manner so sincere that he was checked for an instant. Bishop Nigel had to remind himself that he was in the presence of a witch, clever enough to dissemble, cunning enough to assume whatever shape she wished. He was engaged in a tussle with the Devil and must not relax his hold.

"Hugh Costaine alleges that you know how to mix poison."

"My whole life is dedicated to healing."

"Unless you wish to strike at your husband's enemies."

"Adam has no enemies. Just one or two awkward customers. As it happens, your own steward was far more of a nuisance than Walter Huckvale. He claimed that the bill had been paid. And much more wine was sent to your palace than to –"

"Forget my steward!" barked the other. "He is immaterial."

"The point still holds."

"The only thing which holds in my view is the allegation from Hugh Costaine that you boasted about your skill in concocting vile poisons. You claimed that you could turn fine wine to foul simply by casting a spell. Why gainsay it? Hugh Costaine has sworn as much on the Bible."

"Bring that same Bible here and I will swear on Holy Scripture that I am innocent of this charge. I have nothing to do with this murder."

"But you do admit that you saw Hugh Costaine recently?"

"Yes, my lord bishop. He called at the house."

"And you discussed poison?"

"I made it clear to him that I had no means of making it."

"That is not what he says."

"Then it is a question of my word against his."

"His allegation is buttressed by this list of your crimes," said the Bishop, waving the document at her. "I have mentioned only three cases of your witchcraft so far. Over two dozen are recorded here."

"Have any of the people I helped spoken against me?"

"They dare not."

"Because they have no cause."

"Because you put the fear of death into them."

Bishop Nigel took a deep breath. He was about to launch into a recital of her alleged misdeeds when a key grated in the lock and the oak door swung back heavily on its hinges. A tall, stately figured entered. Sir Richard Costaine was an older version of his son but he had none of the latter's arrogance or marks of dissipation. Instead, he was a symbol of nobility, a distinguished soldier who had fought beside the Black Prince and a man who was renowned for his fair-mindedness. He glanced at Catherine with a mixture of apology and apprehension, not knowing whether to release her or accuse her of further villainy.

"Has your examination been completed?" he asked.

"Not yet, Sir Richard," said Bishop Nigel, airily. "The creature was on the point of capitulation when you interrupted us. Why have you come? Is something amiss?"

"I'm afraid that it is, Bishop Nigel. My son has disappeared."

"Disappeared?"

"He has not been seen all day. Nobody has any idea where he can be. A search has been organised but there is no sign of Hugh." His eye travelled to Catherine. "I hope that this is not your doing, Mistress."

She was adamant. "I give you my word that it is not, Sir Richard."

"Do not be misled," warned the prelate, wagging a finger. "If she is capable of casting a spell on Walter Huckvale's wine, she has the power to work her evil on your son."

"When my hands are manacled?" she said, reasonably. "What sorcery can I practice when I am locked up here? You have been with me since this morning, my lord bishop. Your holiness would quell any evil spirits. Though, in truth, there are none here to quell."

Bishop Nigel snorted. "I beg leave to doubt that."

"How did Hugh mysteriously vanish?" asked Sir Richard.

"Not by any sorcery," returned Catherine.

"He should have been here hours ago. It is my wife's birthday. Nothing would keep him away from the celebrations. Hugh has his faults but he loves his mother dearly. I suspect foul play."

"So do I," decided the bishop. "Hatched in this very cell."

Catherine Teale shook her head and gave a gentle smile.

"No evil has befallen your son, Sir Richard," she announced. "That I can tell you. Hugh Costaine is alive and well."

"Then where is he?" said the anxious father.

"I do not know. But I could help you to find him."

"How?"

"By using my gift."

"Do not trust her, Sir Richard!" warned the bishop. "The only gifts she possesses are for witchcraft and dissimulation."

"I find it difficult to accept that, Bishop Nigel."

"Look at the facts. Her husband argues with a customer and the man's wine is poisoned. Your son accuses her and she casts a spell on him. There are clear connections here. We are dealing with cause and effect."

"Are we?" said Sir Richard, doubtfully. "I am not so sure. Could we not simply be looking at two coincidences?" He regarded Catherine with a mixture of curiosity and embarrassment. "I am sorry that you have been treated so harshly, Mistress Teale. When a serious charge is laid against you, it must be answered but I would have thought this interrogation could have been conducted in better surroundings than these." He wrinkled his nose in disgust. "You say that you can find my son."

"I can try, Sir Richard."

"By what means?"

"By sensing where he might be."

"*Sensing?*"

"That word again!" exclaimed the bishop.

"Let me touch something belonging to your son," she said. "A garment, a weapon, a personal item of some kind. It will help me in my search. Could you bring such a thing to me, Sir Richard?"

"I will do more than that, Mistress Teale. I will take you to my house and let you examine all of Hugh's wardrobe."

"But she is being held as a prisoner," complained Bishop Nigel.

"The Sheriff will release her into my care when he understands the situation. We are in extremity here, Bishop Nigel. My wife is beside herself with fear. So is Hugh's own wife. They are both certain that he has met a dreadful fate. We want him back to celebrate what should be a happy occasion for the whole family. Hugh is missing. If Mistress Teale can find him for us," he added, soulfully, "we will believe that she really does have a gift from God."

Glad to be rescued from her imprisonment, Catherine rode the short distance to Headcorn with Sir Richard Costaine at her side. The house was in a state of mild uproar when they arrived. Everyone was firmly convinced that Hugh was the victim of some attack. It was felt that he was such a strong and capable man that only violence could prevent his return. It was the hapless wife for whom Catherine felt most sympathy. The tearful Isabella Costaine still loved her husband enough to be blinded to his blatant shortcomings. When she heard that the visitor was there to aid the search, she begged Catherine to find her missing spouse soon.

Sir Richard calmed the household then led his companion off to the private apartments used by his son and his wife. Catherine was given ready access to Hugh Costaine's wardrobe. When she saw the apparel he was wearing at the time of his confrontation with her, she gave a mild shudder. Then she reached out to take the rich material in her hands. Closing her eyes, she let her fingers play with the mantle until she felt a distinctive tingle. She raised her lids once more.

"We must ride towards Sutton Valence," she said.

"But what would Hugh be doing there?" wondered Sir Richard.

"I do not know but that I where I am being guided."

"By what? A voice? A sign?"

"By instinct."

Within a few minutes, their horses were cantering out of the courtyard. Four men-at-arms acted as an escort. Catherine was a good horsewoman and they covered the ground at a steady pace. It was only when they reached the woods that she raised a hand to bring them to a halt. After looking all around, she elected to strike off to the right, nudging her mount forward so that it could pick its way through the trees. Sir Richard was directly behind her, trying to control a growing scepticism. Could a vintner's wife really have divine gifts? Or was he being led on a wild goose chase?

When they came to a clearing, Sir Richard's doubts fled at once. Tethered to a bush was a black stallion, cropping the grass contentedly.

"It is my son's horse!" he said, dismounting.

Catherine nodded. "I expected to find a clue of some sort here."

"But what about Hugh himself?"

"We still have some way to go before we reach him," she said. "This is only the start. The first signpost, so to speak. But it shows that we are on the right track."

"Where do we go next, Mistress Teale?"

Catherine closed her eyes and was lost in meditation for a few minutes. When she came out of her trance, she spoke with certainty.

"We must continue of the road to Sutton Valence."

"How far?"

"I will know when we reach the spot, Sir Richard."

"And will Hugh be there?"

"Not this time."

Sir Richard Costaine mounted his horse then went back to rejoin his men, towing his son's stallion behind him by its rein. Catherine paused in the clearing long enough to notice the little wine flagon that was all but concealed behind a bush. It was the sign she wanted.

The six of them rode on until they came to a fork in the road. Without hesitation, Catherine struck off to the left and followed a twisting track down a steep hill and on through a stand of elms. When they emerged from the trees, the track petered out beside a stream. Catherine indicated a tall pile of brushwood, a short distance away on the opposite bank.

"The trail leads to that dwelling," she explained.

"What dwelling? I see nothing but a heap of old wood."

"That is where he lives, Sir Richard."

"Who?"

"Thomas Legge."

"What manner of man would live in such a place?"

"A strange one."

"You know the fellow?"

"Only by repute."

The crossed the stream and headed along the opposite bank. As they got closer, they could see a thin wisp of smoke emerging from the top of the brushwood. A small dog suddenly leaped out and yapped at them. The noise brought Thomas Legge out of his lair. The entrance to his little home was so low that he had to crawl out on his hands and knees. The newcomers looked down at the bedraggled old man who peered up at them with suspicion. Thomas Legge seemed to be more animal than human, a misshapen creature with white beard and hair that were grimed with filth. He scrambled to his feet and kicked his dog into silence. His speech was slurred, his tone unwelcome.

"What do you want?" he growled.

"We need your help," explained Catherine. "This is Sir Richard Costaine and we have come in search of his son."

"He's not here," said Legge. "Nobody's here but me."

"But I believe he came here." She pointed to the black stallion. "On that horse. Do you recognise the animal?" Legge gave a reluctant nod. "I thought so. He came in search of something, didn't he?"

"That's private," grunted the old man.

"Not if it concerns my son," said Sir Richard, sharply. "Keep a civil tongue in your head or you'll feel the flat of my sword. We want answers."

"I think I can give you one of them," ventured Catherine. "Your son came here to buy some rat poison. True or false, Thomas Legge?"

"True," mumbled Legge.

"He told you that his stables were overrun with rats, didn't he?"

"But they're not," said Sir Richard. "We keep too many dogs to have any trouble with vermin. Hugh knows that." He glared at the old man. "Is that what my son told you? We were plagued by rats?"

"Yes," agreed Legge.

"Did you give him the poison there and then?" asked Catherine.

"No. It took a long time to mix."

"So what happened?"

"He told me a man would come to fetch the poison that same afternoon. I had it ready. The man paid me."

"Who was the man?" said Sir Richard.

Legge gave a shrug. "No idea."

"Which direction did he come from?"

"I can tell you that, Sir Richard," said Catherine. "We have learned all that we can here. Follow me."

She swung her horse around and led the party away. Thomas Legge scratched his head in surprise. Why was he so popular all of a sudden? He could go for weeks without seeing anyone yet he had had two visits already that day. He did not much care for the lady with her armed escort. His first visitor was much more preferable. Climbing back into his lair, he reached for the flagon of wine which the man had left him by way of reward. He took a long, satisfying swig.

It took them only a short time to identify the man they sought. When they arrived at the house, they found it deep in mourning. The body of Walter Huckvale still lay in the mortuary at the family chapel. His wife, the lovely Agnes, was bearing up well under her grief and was able to give her unexpected visitors a welcome. She was puzzled by their request.

"You wish to talk to my servants, Sir Richard?" she said.

"That is so," he replied, softly. "We have reason to believe that one of them may be able to help us. I was shocked to learn of your husband's untimely death. He and I fought together at Crecy and at Poitiers. Walter Huckvale deserved a hero's end."

Agnes nodded, showing a loyalty she did not really feel. She was clearly discomfited by Sir Richard's presence. Catherine believed that she could guess why.

"Let us get on with it," suggested Sir Richard, briskly. "Perhaps you could have the servants sent into us one by one so that we can question them. We hope to throw new light on your husband's murder."

But the examination proved unnecessary. When the word spread among the servants, one of them took fright and bolted. Sir Richard's men had to ride for a mile before they ran him to ground. The man was dragged unceremoniously back to the house. He was squirming with guilt. Sir Richard was merciless.

"You helped to poison your master," he accused.

"No, Sir Richard!" bleated the other.

"Do not lie to me!" A blow to the face knocked the man to the ground. "You served him that fatal draught of wine, didn't you?" The man shook his head. A kick made him groan. "Didn't you, you rogue?"

"Yes," confessed the servant.

"On whose orders?"

"I cannot tell you, Sir Richard."

"Do I have to beat the truth out of you, man?"

The servant looked up with a mixture of pleading and defiance.

"I wouldn't do that, if I were you," he said with a hollow laugh. "You might hear something that you wish you hadn't."

It was Catherine who once again led them with unerring accuracy to the right place. The cottage was on the edge of the Huckvale estate, small, comfortable, isolated and well-hidden by woodland. The found Hugh Costaine in the bed-chamber, securely bound, gagged and blindfolded. When he heard them enter the house, he kicked violently on the floor to attract their attention. Sir Richard was the first person to see him. He gazed down at his son with contempt before removing the blindfold and the gag. Hugh Costaine squinted in the light. He recognised the figure who towered over him.

"Father!" he exclaimed. "Thank heaven you came!"

"I can find no reason for thanks," said the other, grimly.

"Untie me so that I may pursue the rogue who attacked me."

"The only rogue I see is the one who lies at my feet. Whoever delivered you to me like this deserves a rich reward for he has solved the murder of Walter Huckvale."

"I did that!" ranted his son, nodding at Catherine. "There's the villain, standing beside you. That black-hearted witch put a spell on Walter Huckvale and struck him down with poison."

"Be quiet!" ordered his father. "We have caught the wretch who bought and administered the poison at your behest. He is under arrest and will hang for his crime. It shames me that my own son will hang beside him. What kind of birthday present is this for your mother? What kind of reward is it for your dear wife? You disgust me, Hugh. You and that heartless woman, Agnes Huckvale. She may have had no part in the murder but she was ready to share a bed with you before her husband had even been consigned to his grave." He turned away. "Take him out. He offends my sight!"

Two men-at-arms hauled Hugh Costaine to his feet and hustled him out. Catherine ignored the vile taunts that were hurled at her by the departing prisoner.

When Sir Richard looked at her, his face was ashen with despair. He tried to master his feelings.

"We owe you a huge apology, Mistress Teale," he said. "You were wrongly accused in order to throw suspicion away from the true villain. My son is the real sorcerer here. He knew that the only way to possess Agnes Huckvale was to remove her husband. You were unwittingly caught up in his evil design. There will be restitution for the way in which you have been cruelly abused."

"My liberty is restitution enough, Sir Richard."

"You have my heart-felt thanks and I will make sure that Bishop Nigel offers his words of regret as well. I will also insist on making some financial reparation. After all," he added with a sad smile, "you did find a missing son for me. I had no idea that you would solve a heinous crime in the process. It is a sorry day for my family."

Catherine put a consoling hand on his arm. She had no quarrel with Sir Richard Costaine. He had behaved honourably towards her and had made no attempt to shift the blame away from his son when the latter's villainy was exposed. The experience had aged him visibly.

"One of my men will take you back home," he offered.

"Thank you, Sir Richard."

"You were right, Mistress Teale. You do have a gift."

Adam was waiting for her in the house. After a warm embrace, he conducted her to the wooden bench and sat beside her with his arm around her shoulders. Catherine gave him a detailed account of all that had happened since her arrest. He listened patiently.

"It was that lie about the rats which betrayed him," he noted. "When you told me that Hugh Costaine came in search of rat poison, I knew that it was a ruse. A man like that would never run his own errands. He wanted that poison for a darker purpose."

"I counted on you working that out, Adam."

"I worked out much more than that, my love. Costaine would only stoop to murder for one reason. Lust. It seeps out of the man. Well, look at the way he tried to molest you. No," reflected Adam, "there had to be a woman involved and Walter Huckvale's wife was the obvious person. Then there was the poison, of course. If you would not provide it, there was only one person who would."

"Thomas Legge."

"I loosened his tongue with a flagon of wine and he told me all I wanted to know. His testimony pointed me in the direction of the Huckvale estate. Hugh Costaine was not a person to bide his time. He wanted his reward immediately.

When I saw his horse outside that cottage, I guessed that he was inside with his prize. Agnes Huckvale. I waited until the young widow slipped out then crept in to overpower Costaine and tie him up. That was how you found him."

"Delivered up to justice," she said. "Bishop Nigel would not believe me when I told him that I could sense things. For that is what I did. I sensed exactly what you would do to prove my innocence. You would go first to Thomas Legge to establish if and when he sold some poison. I knew that you would leave a sign for me and guessed where it would be."

"In a place very dear to both of us, my love."

"That clearing in the woods where you once asked for my hand." She gave a smile. "I did not expect to find a black stallion there, I can tell you. But it satisfied Sir Richard that we were on the right trail."

"Did you see the flagon?"

"Of course. It was certain proof of your success."

"My real success was getting wed to you, Catherine."

"I have been thinking the same about you," she admitted. "It has been a marriage of true minds. When I am being accosted by a foul-mouthed man like Hugh Costaine, you come to my aid at just the right time. When I am falsely accused, you spring to my defence. I love you so much," she said, kissing him on the lips. "You always know when I need you and how best to help me. That is my real gift."

"What is?"

"A husband called Adam Teale."

"Me?" he said with a grin. "Am I really a gift?"

"Oh, yes. A gift from God."

SQUINTING AT DEATH

When invited to write about a minor character in Shakespeare, my immediate choice was Davy Gam, who gets no more than an honorable mention in Henry V. *Since he was a real person, one of many Welshmen who fought at Agincourt in October, 1415, I wondered how his fictional compatriot, Fluellen, would react to the news of his death. Pistol, too, is heavily involved in the story and I have borrowed some of Shakespeare's own dialogue to establish him. Using Davy's squint as my starting point, I was able to look at the battle from an unusual angle, mixing fact and fiction in differing proportions.*

Where is the number of our English dead?
                    (Herald shows him another paper)
Edward the Duke of York, the Earl of Suffolk,
Sir Richard Ketly, Davy Gam esquire:
None else of name; and of all other men
But five and twenty.

Henry the Fifth.

The battle was mercifully short but its actual progress was mercilessly brutal. Arrows, swords, daggers, lances, stakes and clubs killed or maimed indiscriminately. Dead and dying men littered the muddy field of Agincourt, their blood intermingling with that of the countless horses that had been wounded or slaughtered. It was a scene of utter carnage and it was difficult to see how such an accurate list of the deceased could be made so soon after the conflict. One thing was certain. It was a signal victory for King Henry and his army. France had suffered a defeat even more crushing than those of Crecy and Poitiers.

Fluellen listened to the record of enemy casualties with pride and exultation. The Welsh captain had been at the heart of the fighting, wielding his sword in the service of an English king and sending several Frenchmen to their Maker before their time. Fluellen was astonished at what he heard. Could they really have accounted

115

for ten thousand of the enemy? That was the number announced by King Henry and it was buttressed by the news that the fifteen hundred prisoners included Charles, Duke of Orleans, nephew to the French King, Jean, Duke of Bourbon and the redoubtable Jean Boucicaut, Marshall of France. Hopelessly outnumbered, the English army had somehow achieved a miracle. Like everyone else who had fought with King Henry, the Welsh captain was entitled to feel elated. The day was theirs.

But Fluellen's joy was tempered with concern. A Welsh name had jumped out at him from the abbreviated list of English dead. Davy Gam. Davy the Squint. Or, to give him his full name, Dafydd ap Llywelyn ap Hywel from Breconshire, a veteran soldier and a close friend to Fluellen. The two men had grown up together. Other friends had fallen in the heat of battle but it was the death of Davy Gam that really saddened him. War was cruel. It gave him no time to bid farewell to a loved companion. When occasion served, Fluellen seized the opportunity to take King Henry aside.

"I crave a word with your majesty."

"As many as you wish, Captain Fluellen," said the King. "Your deeds at Agincourt have earned my deepest thanks and admiration."

Fluellen gave a shrug. "God chose to spare me. Others were not so fortunate."

"I grieve for all our casualties."

"So do I, your majesty, but I mourn for one man in particular."

"I think I can guess his name – Davy Gam."

"Is he really dead?"

"I fear so," confirmed the King, "but he died with honor. He was struck down near to the place where I was striving with the enemy myself. As he lay bleeding, I was able to reward him for his valor by touching him on both shoulders with my sword and creating him a knight. He may have followed me as Davy Gam Esquire but he quit this world as Sir Dafydd ap Llywelyn ap Hywel."

"His family will be consoled by that news."

"Bear it to them, Captain Fluellen."

"I will, your majesty," said the other. "But you say that you were nearby when he was mortally wounded. Did you see whose weapon inflicted death on him?"

The King shook his head. "I was too busy trying to protect my brother and myself. Thus it stood. The Duke of Alencon led a charge with fresh men against a part of the field where my brother, Humphrey, Duke of Gloucester, was embroiled with the men of Marle and Fauquemberghes. A knife thrust pierced Humphrey's belly beneath his cuirass and he fell to the ground. As soon as report of this was brought to me, I hastened to my brother's side with a bodyguard of archers and yeoman, men like Davy Gam and his son-in-law, Richard Vaughan of Bredwardine. Nobody fights as fiercely as the Welsh when they are in a tight situation."

"I can bear witness to that."

"My bodyguard shot and clubbed a pathway for me until I reached my brother. The fighting continued unabated all around me. It was only when we had subdued the French that I was able to take stock of our losses." The King heaved a sigh. "That was when I saw the gallant Davy Gam, lying in the arms of his page."

It was all the detail that Fluellen got. King Henry went off with his escort to walk the rain-soaked battlefield and see for himself the true extent of God's benevolence towards his army. His men did not rest. They spent the remainder of the day, stripping clothes and armor from the corpses, searching for articles of value and confiscating discarded weaponry. Rings, brooches, coins, gold ornaments and jeweled daggers were snatched uncaringly from the dead by looters. Any Frenchmen found alive in ditches or other hiding places were summarily killed and robbed. Loose horses were rounded up. Plunder was rampant.

Fluellen took no part in it. While most soldiers grabbed all that they could carry, he searched among the piles of bodies for a friend. Davy Gam was not easy to find. At the point where he fell, fighting had been particularly fierce and dozens of corpses lay haphazardly on the ground. All had met violent ends. Many were hideously mutilated, some had lost limbs in combat. When he eventually picked out his friend, Fluellen breathed a sigh of relief. Not only had Davy Gam been spared the butchery handed out to others, his body had not yet been reached by looters. He lay on his back with a serene expression on his face. The familiar black patch covered one eye. He no longer squinted at the world through the other. Fluellen knelt respectfully beside him and offered up a silent prayer for the salvation of his soul.

He examined the body more carefully, noting the wounds in the neck and the legs. They had bled profusely but had hardly been enough in themselves to kill so powerful a warrior as Davy Gam. There had to be a more serious injury somewhere. Fluellen was gentle but firm, putting hands under his friend so that he could roll him slowly over. Davy Gam was not heavily armored. His torso was protected by a nailed jerkin of filled leather over a mailed shirt and a bascinet warded off any glancing blows to the head. Sword and dagger were his preferred form of defense. He had none of the expensive plate armor worn by the king, lords and knights. While they had been encased in heavy, cumbersome metal suits, he valued freedom of movement. It had been his undoing.

Fluellen was shocked by what he saw. Davy Gam had been stabbed in the back. A dagger had been worked in under his jerkin and sunk to the hilt with vicious force. It took an effort on Fluellen's part to extract the weapon. An even greater shock awaited him. It was no French dagger, thrust hard into the Welsh-man's back while he grappled with an enemy. The weapon was of English design. Davy Gam had not, it seemed, been killed in combat with a Frenchman.

He had been murdered by one of his fellows.

While plunder and celebration continued throughout that October evening, Fluellen was engaged in a hunt for the man who killed his friend. The dagger was a vital clue. It was a long-bladed weapon with an elaborate handle into which the letter "P" had been carved. Since the hapless Davy Gam had died in the arms of his page, Fluellen first sought out Madog, the loyal young man who had fought beside his master. When he found the page shivering beside a camp fire, he did not at first recognize him. Madog had been bruised and bloodied, the once-handsome face now scarred for life. One arm was in a sling. A wound in the thigh was heavily strapped. He looked close to exhaustion.

Fluellen bent over to peer more closely at him. He spoke in Welsh.

"Is that you, Madog?" he asked.

"What's left of me," replied the page. "I'll have painful souvenirs of Agincourt."

"None more painful than the memory of Davy Gam's death, look you."

"No, Captain Fluellen. That was a tragedy. To fight so bravely and then to be denied the privilege of sharing in the victory. It was heart-breaking."

Fluellen sat beside him. "Who actually killed Davy?"

"Some nameless Frenchman."

"Did you *see* the fatal blow delivered?"

Madog shook his head. "I was too busy fighting for my own life, Captain Fluellen. Then I heard this terrible cry from my master. By the time I struggled across to him, he had collapsed to his knees in a pool of blood. King Henry was close by."

"So I hear. He knighted Dafydd on the spot."

"Yes," said Madog, sadly. "No sooner had he done that than my master died. I had no chance to carry him from the field. I had to defend myself and, as you see, I came off worst. When I'm recovered, I'll go in search of the body."

"There's no need," said Fluellen, "I've already found it." He produced the dag-ger for inspection. "Have you ever seen this before?"

"No, I haven't. Where did you get it?"

"I pulled it out of Davy Gam's back."

Madog shuddered. "Is this what killed him? No wonder he cried out."

"It was a cry of horror, not of pain. He was betrayed, Madog. Look at the dagger. No Frenchman would carry an English weapon like that. Davy Gam was murdered by someone in our army."

"Never!"

"It's not only a dreadful crime," said Fluellen, puce with anger, " 'tis expressly against the disciplines of war."

"Who could have done such a thing?" wondered Madog, dazed by the news.

"That's what you must tell me."

"How, Fluellen?"

"You may not have seen the murder but you were not far away when it happened. Who else was nearby? What other members of the King's bodyguard were close to Dafydd when you went across to him?"

"I didn't take much notice."

"You must have seen *someone*, Madog."

"Well, yes, I suppose I did. Let me think," said the page, face puckered with concentration as he teased out the names. "Iestyn Morgan must have been there. And I think I caught sight of Rhys Pugh. The only other person I can think of is Owain ap Meredyth ap Tydier."

"Nobody else?"

"I'm afraid not, Fluellen."

"But this is an *English* dagger," emphasized Fluellen, holding up the weapon. "That means an English hand was, in all probability, holding it. A Welsh hero was felled by English treachery. Was there no English soldier next to Dafydd?"

"Only one that I recall."

"Who was he?"

"That bragging knave who struts like a turkey-cock."

"Pistol?"

"That's the man, Captain Fluellen."

"Indeed, it is," said the other, vengefully. "I know the rogue well. Look at this letter carved in the dagger's handle. "P" is for Pistol just as clearly as "M" is for murderer. I'll match these initials to that scurvy, lousy, beggarly heap of ordure and call him to account. Davy Gam's death must be paid for in full."

Pistol was in his element. Having survived the battle, he had been among the first to search for plunder and was weighed down with booty stolen from French corpses. Pistol had hidden his cowardice behind a loud voice and a threatening manner. Reasoning that the largest bodyguard would belong to the King, he had stayed, for the sake of safety, close to Henry in the field and traded only a few blows with the enemy. Laden down with money, weapons, and assorted pieces of armor, he walked along with a jaunty stride and sang aloud. When he was suddenly confronted by a Welsh captain, he showed no fear.

"Out of my way, base Trojan!" he demanded.

"God pless you, Ancient Pistol," said Fluellen with mock deference.

"Ha! Art thou bedlam?"

"I desire a word with you, sir."

"Not for Cadwallader and all his goats."

"Do you remember my kinsman, Davy Gam?"

"What?" said Pistol, contemptuously. "That one-eyed madman who spoke with a squint? Yes, I recall the knave. I'd know that ugly Welsh face of his anywhere."

"Then why did you stab him in the back?" yelled Fluellen, grabbing him by the throat and holding up the dagger. "If you meant to kill him, why not have the courage to look him in his one remaining eye while you were doing it?"

"Kill him?" gasped Pistol. "I killed nobody, you leek-eating loon!"

"This dagger has your initial on it."

Pistol could hardly breathe. "That doesn't mean that it's mine," he croaked. "I've never possessed a dagger as fine as that. I swear it!"

"No," said Fluellen, pushing him to the ground and forcing him to drop his stolen weapons. "What are these, you lying knave? There are three French daggers here worth twice as much as the one I hold."

"Presents for some friends."

"Whose backs are you going to sink these into?"

"Nobody's," said Pistol, covering before him. "Spare me, Captain Fluellen. I'm no wild Frenchman. I fought on your side in the battle."

"Close to Davy Gam."

"He sought protection alongside a veteran soldier like me."

"A veteran liar, you mean!" exploded Fluellen, kicking him hard. "A veteran cheat, coward, braggart, traitor and murderer. You stabbed Davy Gam in the back."

"As God's my witness, I didn't."

"Tell the truth for once in your life."

"That's what I am doing."

"Is it?" said Fluellen, drawing his sword to hold the point at Pistol's throat. "Confess, you railing villain, or I'll slice you up and feed your entrails to the birds."

"No, no!" begged Pistol, squirming on the ground. "Take my money, good Captain Fluellen. Take my loot. Take my clothes. Take my hair, if you wish, but leave me my entrails. We've been close friends these many years and, truly, sir, I'd not be parted from them."

"Speak honestly or prepare to die!"

"All hell will stir for this."

"I'll send you off to Satan with your tongue cut out."

"Take pity on me!" implored Pistol as the sword pricked his throat. "I've lost every friend I have and would not lose the one I love most, namely, my poor innocent, self. Jack Falstaff died before we left England. Bardolph was hanged for some trifling offence and our boy was killed when the French attacked our baggage train."

"Kill the poys and the luggage!" yelled Fluellen. "That was shameful. It was directly against the laws of arms."

"That was why I fought so hard against the villains. Why should I murder a fellow-soldier when there were so many French vipers to excommunicate from the battlefield? Spare me, good sir," he pleaded. "I may have mocked Davy Gam for his squint but I praise him for his bravery. When last I saw him, he was cutting a path through the enemy like a mower with a scythe."

Fluellen drew back his sword. "That sounds like Dafydd."

"I never got within five yards of him. Truly, I didn't. And even if I had," said Pistol, sitting up and spreading his arms, "I could not have stabbed him with that dagger. My only weapon was a bent sword I found at Harfleur."

"Then why does the dagger have your initial on it?"

"Ask Peter. Ask Paul. Ask Philip. Ask every Percy in our army how his initial came to be inscribed on the weapon. You'll have hundreds to choose from. Why pick on me when there are so many others whose name begins with the fateful letter?"

"Because you're a cowardly, counterfeit cutpurse who hates the Welsh."

"Why, no, Captain Fluellen," said Pistol, beaming. "I revel in your company."

"You do nothing but pour scorn on us," retorted the other, angrily. "Only yesterday, you sneered at our leeks and called me a mountain-squire to my face."

" 'Twas all done in good humor."

"Is that how you killed Davy Gam? In good humor?"

"No, no!" bleated Pistol as the sword jabbed at him again. "I never touched him. It's you who have the squint now, my friend. You're looking at the wrong man."

"Am I?"

"On my word of honor."

"That's worthless."

"I swear that I did not murder your valiant countryman. And what is more, I'll prove it in the best way possible."

"How's that?"

Still sitting on the ground, Pistol did his best to strike a pose.

"By helping you to find the *real* killer," he declared.

Madog had mentioned three other people he had seen in the vicinity of Davy Gam during the battle. Fluellen decided to speak to each one of them. Having hidden his stolen armor in some bushes, Pistol trailed in his wake. Of the three men named by Davy Gam's page, one ruled himself out immediately. Iestyn Morgan had perished from wounds received in the first French charge. That left Rhys Pugh and Owain ap Meredyth ap Tydir. When he tracked down the first of them, he spoke to him in Welsh.

"A word in your ear, Rhys," he said.

"Where else are you going to speak it, Fluellen?" replied the other with a chuckle. "In my mouth? Up my arse?"

"This is no time for vulgarity. I want to talk to you about Davy Gam."

Pugh's face darkened. "Aye, poor man. Death finally closed his other eye."

"This is the weapon that killed him."

Fluellen handed him the dagger and watched him carefully as he examined it. Rhys Pugh was a big, powerful man with a black beard that was spattered with blood.

"An English dagger," he observed, gruffly.

"Does it belong to you?"

"No, Fluellen. This "P" on the handle doesn't stand for Pugh, I can assure you of that. Besides, why would I want to stab Davy Gam? We were fellows."

"That wasn't always the case."

Pugh nodded soulfully. "I confess it freely. We fought against each other in the past but we were indentured to fight beside each other this time. I was proud to call Davy Gam my fellow. He was a true soldier."

"You were close to him when he fell."

"That may be, Fluellen, but I was even closer to the two Frenchmen who were trying to kill me. I heard Davy cry out and wish I could have gone to his aid. Those two Frenchmen had other ideas. It took me an age to beat them off."

Fluellen could see that he was telling the truth. Rhys Pugh was not the assassin. He would be more likely to hack a man to death than to dispatch him with a sly dagger. Taking the weapon from him, Fluellen slipped it into his belt.

"Did you see anyone close to Davy?" he asked.

"Dozens of people, pressed all around him."

"Can you give me some names?"

"No," said Pugh, rubbing his beard. "In the middle of a battle, you don't stop to take a roll-call of everyone nearby. I caught sight of Madog, his page, that I do remember. And I think that Iestyn Morgan was there somewhere. The only other person I remember was that other page."

"Who was he?"

"Owain ap Meredyth ap Tydir."

When his companion strode quickly away, Pistol had a job to keep up with him.

"What did he say, Captain Fluellen?" he asked.

"It wasn't him."

"I didn't understand a word of your heathen language."

"Welsh is an older and finer tongue than the one you speak."

"I could smell the leeks on his breath."

"Don't ridicule my nation," warned Fluellen, turning to him, "or I'll send you off to have a private conversation with Davy Gam."

Pistol quivered. "I'd prefer to stay alive, if it's all the same to you."

"Then hold your peace, you whoreson rogue!"

"I'll be as silent as the grave."

Owain ap Meredyth ap Tydir was a page in the King's household. Having acquitted himself well on the battlefield, he was resting with some friends in the shadow of a tree. Fluellen detached him so that he could speak to him in private. Pistol stayed within earshot but was bewildered when they lapsed into their native language. Owain was a personable young man, dark, well built and well featured. He was momentarily saddened by the mention of Davy Gam's death but expressed no personal grief.

Fluellen was roused. "Aren't you sorry that he was killed?"

"I'm sorry that anyone from our army fell in battle," said Owain, easily.

"But Davy Gam was your countryman!"

"Others who died also came from Wales."

"I expected more anguish from you."

"That will come at a later date, Captain Fluellen. I am still exulting in our victory now, as you should be. I have a personal triumph to celebrate as well," he boasted. "In recognition of my deeds at Agincourt, I've been promoted to the ranks of the Squires of the Body to the King. What do you think of that?"

"Don't look to me for congratulation," said Fluellen with vehemence. "While you glory in your own achievement, Davy Gam lies on the battlefield, squinting up to heaven. And it was no enemy weapon that killed him," he added, brandishing the dagger. "It was this, Owain. Someone thrust it into Davy's back. Was it you?"

"No!" denied the other.

"Are you sure?"

"Absolutely sure. I was on the same side as Davy Gam."

"So was his killer. This dagger was the work of an English craftsman."

"Then look for an English assassin," said Owain with indignation. "I'd not use a dagger like that. All my weaponry was made in my native Anglesey. Don't accuse me of this murder, if that's what it was."

"What else could it be?"

"Who knows? It's not my concern."

"Don't you *care* about Davy Gam?"

"Of course. But he was only one of thousands who fell today."

Fluellen was so enraged by his indifference that he wanted to strike the man. Owain turned away from him to walk back to his friends. He then paused and swung round again, fingers stroking his chin in meditation.

"I was not the only person close to Davy Gam," he said.

"I know. I've spoken to the others."

"To his page, Madog?"

"Yes."

"What about Iestyn Morgan?"

"He's dead," said Fluellen, tartly. "Not that you'd be upset to hear that."

"That leaves Rhys Pugh."

"I've just questioned him."

"Only one more remains, then."

Fluellen's ears pricked up. "One more?"

"Yes," said Owain, thoughtfully. "I only had the merest glimpse of him, mark you, so I can't be certain of what I saw. But I had the impression that the person who got near enough to Davy Gam to see his squint was Rhodri ap Iorwerth."

Pistol had seen enough. When the bustling Fluellen tried to set off again, Pistol blocked his path and held up an appeasing hand.

"One moment, Captain Fluellen."

"Stand aside, you cur!"

"But I'm here to help you," said Pistol, "and I can't do that if you insist on talking in that foul language of yours. I take it that this young friend of yours was not the killer."

"He was not."

"But he gave you the name of another suspect."

"I'm on my way to question him right now."

"Let me hold the interrogation for you," volunteered Pistol.

"You?"

"Yes, Captain Fluellen. You are too direct in your examination. When you show them the dagger that killed Davy Gam, you give them time to invent their excuses. Where Welsh bluntness fails, English cunning may succeed."

Fluellen inflated his chest. "Nobody is more guileful than a Celt."

"We'll see about that."

"Begone, you pedlar's excrement!"

"Step on me and I'll stick to your shoe forever."

"I need to speak to Rhodri ap Iorwerth."

"Is that his name?" said Pistol. "Then hear my device. Give me the dagger and let me try my wiles on him. Stand off and watch us in secret. If he be innocent, you'll know it soon enough. If he be guilty, good captain, I'll wager every penny I'll tease out the proof of his guilt. Will this content you?"

"No, you dolt."

"Even a dolt can do a good deed sometimes."

Fluellen pondered. His own investigation had so far borne little fruit. The longer it was taking, the more frustrated he became. Pistol had a point. He had been too hasty to confront the others with the evidence of the dagger. Whoever killed Davy Gam would have an alibi and it would be readily produced when he saw the Welsh captain bearing down on him. If a different method of questioning could be employed, the only thing that could be lost was a little time.

"Very well," he said at length.

"First, we must trade."

"Find me the killer and I'll spare your stinking hide."

"I want more than that, Captain Fluellen," said Pistol. "Give me your word that you'll not beat me about my pate with a leek on Saint Davy's day."

"I'm more likely to stuff it down your lying throat."

"I need your promise."

"Then you have it," said Fluellen, testily. "Saint Davy's day lies a long way off. The only Davy I'm interested in now is Davy Gam. The patron saint of revenge."

Rhodri ap Iorwerth was a short, stocky, vigorous man in his thirties with bow legs. He was sitting on a tree stump and chatting happily with two friends about their respective deeds in the battle. Glad to be alive, they were still surprised at their victory against such overwhelming odds. Fluellen approached furtively with Pistol until they reached the cover of some bushes.

"Which one is Rhodri?" whispered Pistol.

"The one in the middle."

"A wild-eyed rogue, if ever I saw one."

"With a hot temper," cautioned Fluellen. "Take care what you say."

"Watch and listen, good captain."

"What will you do?"

"Teach you how to catch a Welsh fish with the right bait."

Leaving him concealed in the bushes, Pistol sauntered across to the three men. Tucked in his belt with the English dagger were the three French ones he had stolen from their dead owners. Pistol gave an elaborate bow.

"Good even, good sirs," he said. "Is there anyone here who speaks English? From the sound of your crucified consonants, you must be talking in Welsh."

"Mind your manners, you English pig," sneered Rhodri, "or we'll crucify your own consonants and disembowel your vowels."

"But I come as a friend."

"Then depart just as swiftly."

"Are you not interested in what I have to sell?" asked Pistol, plucking one of the French daggers from his belt. "Look here. This once belonged to a man of high degree, as you may see from the jeweled handle and fine workmanship. It's too precious an object for me but veterans like yourselves might prize such an object."

"What are you asking for it?" said of one the men.

"Make me an offer."

"Let me inspect it more closely first."

"Here," said Pistol, handing it over and taking a second weapon from his belt. "And here's its brother, made by the same craftsman, I daresay. Put them side by side and you can hardly tell them apart."

The man took the second dagger as well. "Where did you get them?"

"He filched them from corpses," said Rhodri.

"I found them lying on the ground, sir, and that's not theft. Its good fortune." He bared his teeth in a lop-sided grin. "I've always been lucky."

"What's your name?"

"Pistol."

Rhodri laughed. "Do you hear that? This long streak of English piss is called Pistol. I doubt if he can fire a good fart, let alone a lead ball." The others joined in the mockery. "Pistol, is it? Beware his cock, boyos!"

Wanting to answer the taunts, Pistol schooled himself to be patient. He bestowed an understanding smile on Rhodri then whisked a third French dagger from his belt.

"This is the best of them all," he explained. "It came from the hand of a Duke."

"He gave it to you as a present, did he?" said Rhodri.

"No, my friend. He tried to stab me with it but I twisted it from his grasp. We are fellow-soldiers, you and I. Laugh at my name, if you wish, but recognize me as your comrade in arms."

"All I recognize is a scavenger. One that hides behind others when there's fighting to be done then sneaks across the field when the battle is over to plunder the dead and dying. Comrade in arms? You're nothing but a vulture."

Pistol smirked. "What will you give a vulture for this dagger?"

"A kick up the arse."

"Then I'll not trade with you," said Pistol, turning to the others. "Your friends know how to barter properly. They like what they see. Here, sir," he added, passing the third dagger to one of the men. "Feast your eyes on perfection."

"What's that last dagger in your belt?" asked one of the men.

"It's not for sale."

"Why not?"

"It belonged to a man who once did my a good turn. A Welshman, as it happens. And though he looked askance at me, I want his dagger as a keepsake. It will help me to remember the name of Davy Gam."

"Davy Gam?" said the man. "That was *his* dagger?"

"I found it lying beside his dead body."

"Give it here!" demanded Rhodri, coming forward.

"I'd not part with it for a King's ransom."

The Welshman raised a first. "Hand it over while you still have strength to do so or I'll beat you all the way from here to London."

Pistol tried to back away but Rhodri reached out to grab him by the arm. With a swift movement of his hand, he snatched the English dagger from Pistol's belt. He held the weapon covetously.

"I'll keep this," he announced.

"But it's mine," argued Pistol.

"Not any more."

"Davy Gam would've wanted me to have it."

"You will have it, if you're not careful – straight through the heart."

"Why are you so keen to have it, Rhodri?" asked one of his friends, going over to him. "These French daggers are far more costly. What's so special about that one?" His eye saw the letter carved into the handle. "It's your dagger," he said, pointing at it. "I swear it is, Rhodri. 'P' stands for Pomeroy. Isn't that the selfsame dagger you took from Sir Richard Pomeroy when you cut his throat at that skirmish in Harlech?"

"It is," admitted Rhodri.

"How did it come to be in Davy Gam's possession?"

"I'll tell you that!" roared Fluellen, bursting out of his hiding place to threaten Rhodri with a sword. "I pulled that dagger out of Davy's back and now I know who put it there. Rhodri ap Iorwerth," he said, "I arrest you on a charge of willful murder."

Pistol chuckled. "I told you I'd expose his villainy."

Rhodri blustered but there was no escape. His guilt was plain for them to see. Unable to lie his way out of the situation, he fell back on frantic self-justification.

"I did it for us, Fluellen," he gabbled. "I struck in the name of Wales."

"Welshmen don't stab their fellows in the back," retorted Fluellen.

"That's what Davy Gam did to us. Is your memory so short, mun? Owain Glyndwr may be hiding in a cave now but he was once a Prince of Wales that we were proud to follow. From Caerleon to Caernavon, we fought at his heels But did Davy Gam join us in that war of liberation? No!" he said, scornfully. "He stayed loyal to the King. He was ever a great stickler for the Duke of Lancaster. He betrayed us."

"That was one war," decided Fluellen. "This is another. A general amnesty was declared for all Welsh rebels who pledged themselves to fight for King Henry. You gave that pledge, Rhodri, and you broke it."

"Only in order to punish a traitor."

"Davy Gam fought honestly against the French."

"And dishonestly against the Welsh. Come, Fluellen," said Rhodri with an ingratiating smile. "What's one more death among so many? Davy Gam had too strong a squint to be allowed to live. Instead of looking to his own country, his eye fell instead of England. I did our nation a service by killing him."

"That's enough' " yelled Fluellen, using his sword to slash at his wrist so that the dagger was knocked to the ground. "Murder has no excuse to hide behind. Davy Gam, like his father before him, may have stayed loyal to the English but he paid a heavy price in loss of land and ransoms. He surrendered that eye of his in battle, remember, and it was a mere three years ago that he was kidnapped. A fearsome ransom had to be found."

"We should have killed him while we held him prisoner."

"That defies every article of war, Rhodri."

"Who cares about that?"

"Captain Fluellen does," said Pistol, cheerily before turning to the other men. "Now, my friends, what are you going to offer me for those daggers?"

Fluellen took hold of his prisoner and marched him away. The sound of Pistol, haggling merrily, began to fade away in the background. Fluellen was content. He had no respect for Pistol but he had to admit one thing. A petty criminal had been responsible for solving a far more serious crime.

King Henry believed in summary justice. When the evidence was presented to him by Fluellen, he did not hesitate. Rhodri ap Iorwerth was convicted of murder and hanged on the spot. Distressed that a fellow-Welshman had been the killer, Fluellen nevertheless took comfort from the fact that he had been brought to justice. He was ready to admit that Pistol's help had been of crucial importance.

"I might never have caught him without you, Pistol," he confessed.

"It takes an English hero to outwit a Welsh villain."

"Don't lay claim to heroism. That's too big a lie, even for you. You tricked the truth out of him I'm grateful to you for that. Davy Gam can lie easy in his grave."

"Nobody can tease him about his squint now."

"He was loyal to his commander. That's vital in a soldier. Rhodri ap Iorwerth was treacherous. He fought under the King's banner but held firm to old loyalties. When he saw the chance to kill Davy Gam, he took it. Thanks to you, Pistol, disgusting maltworm, that you are, Rhodri is now dancing on air."

"Yes," said Pistol. "I'm glad of that. Like most of his nation, he was an ugly brute. Why does Wales breed such hideous ghouls? The only pretty Welshman I've ever seen was that one you talked to earlier."

"Who was that?"

"Owain something."

"Owain ap Meredyth ap Tydir."

"That's him. Except in a mirror, I've never seen such a handsome man."

"His handsome face will be his downfall," predicted Fluellen.

"Why?"

"Because it comes with a wandering hand and a seductive tongue. Brave soldier he may be but his finest conquests are in the bedchamber. The goatish instinct of Owain ap Meredyth ap Tydir will be the death of him in the end."

"Can you give his name a more English sound?"

"Owen Tudor," said Fluellen, waving a dismissive hand, "but it's not a name you need to remember. I don't think you'll ever hear of the Tudors again."

A certain amount of fact underlies this fictional tale. Fluellen and Pistol were, of course, created by Shakespeare but Davy Gam was a real person. He was a member of the premier family in Breconshire. His father, Llywelyn ap Hywel, stood firm in his support of the English crown. Davy Gam was equally loyal and was rewarded by Henry IV with the gift of confiscated lands. Until the revolt led by Owain Glyndwr finally petered out, Davy Gam was involved in regular skirmishes with his kinsman.

He died at Agincourt in the way described by King Henry in this story and was knighted before he passed away. He was killed by the enemy and not by an assassin.

Owain ap Meredyth ap Tydir is best known as Owen Tudor, grandfather of Henry VII. At the death of Henry V, he stayed on at Court and was appointed by the young Queen-Dowager, Catherine de Valois, to a prestigious position as Clerk of her Wardrobe. Their love affair led to a secret marriage and the birth of five children. Owen was eventually beheaded after the battle of Mortimer's Cross in 1461 on the orders of Edward IV. His son, Edmund Tudor, had already been created Earl of Richmond. Edmund's only son, Henry, was the victor at Bosworth in 1485 and set the Tudor dynasty in motion.

MURDER AT ANCHOR

Written for the first Crime Through Time *anthology, this story gave me the opportunity to explore the earlier life of Nicholas Bracewell, stage manager, who is the protagonist in my series about an Elizabethan theater company. Since the novels contain many references to his circumnavigation of the globe with Francis Drake, I decided to show Nicholas as a sailor and highlight one incident during that epic voyage. The capture of the Spanish treasure ship, Nuestra Señora de la Concepcion, was a remarkable feat for all sorts of reasons. Nicholas and his friends play a full part in it but murder aboard the Golden Hind takes the edge off their triumph. Someone wants more than his fair share of the booty. It falls to the resourceful Nicholas to solve the crime and to earn, from Drake, an accurate prediction about his future employment.*

S tanding on the quarter-deck, Drake addressed the whole crew.

"The *Cacafuego* is our destined prize!" he announced. "Whosoever first descries her shall have a chain of gold for his good news. About it, lads. Be vigilant."

Nicholas Bracewell had never seen such a sudden change come over his shipmates. Promise of rich reward turned them all into eager lookouts. Men who had been sapped by hunger, assaulted by disease, battered by tempests, nibbled by disillusion, and subjected to all the other privations of an interminable voyage now revived miraculously. They became wondrously alert and committed, forgetting past torments as their eyes scanned the horizon with greedy hope. The hot blood of avarice was coursing through their veins.

The *Cacafuego* was much more than just another Spanish vessel on which they could prey with impunity. It was a treasure ship, a floating horde of gold, silver, and precious stones. Her proper name was *Nuestra Señora de la Concepcion* but Spanish seamen were far too irreverent to call her Our Lady of the Conception. *Cacafuego* – or Shitfire – was the title which filled their uncouth mouths with more satisfaction.

The chase was on. With greater speed and sense of purpose, the *Golden Hind* surged through the waves in the dying sunlight. Francis Drake knew the value of maintaining his vessel in good order. Thanks to his seamanship, it had come through the cumulative horrors of the Straits of Magellan to find calmer water. Choosing a safe anchorage, he had the *Golden Hind* careened, recaulked, and tarred against attacks of marine worm. Bowsprit and masts were repaired, yards were sent down, running-rigging was overhauled, and standard-rigging was set up taut and hard.

She was ready for action.

"Will we ever catch her, Nick?" asked John Strood.

"No question but that we will," said Nicholas.

"The *Cacafuego* sailed well ahead of us."

"Yes, John. But she will have put into port from time to time to pick up flour and fresh water. Each delay allowed us to get that much closer. We will soon catch sight of her."

"Tomorrow," boomed the deep Welsh voice of Merfyn Pugh. "I'll wager every last coin I have on it. Tomorrow."

"How can you be so sure, Merfyn?" said John.

"Because of the date, mun. Tomorrow – if I am right, and my heart tells me I am – will be the first of March."

The boy was none the wiser. "So?"

"St. David's Day," explained Nicholas.

"Yes!" confirmed Merfyn, giving John a reproving slap on the arm. "Patron saint of Wales. *Diu*! I never thought I'd be spending a St. David's Day this close to the equator." He chuckled happily. "But it will bring me luck. The *Cacafuego* will be sighted tomorrow and Merfyn Pugh, the only true and decent Welshman aboard, will be the man to descry her. I can feel that gold chain around my neck already."

"Nobody will see it beneath that black beard," said Nicholas with a grin. "You'll have to shave, Merfyn."

"Never, Nick! This beard is my blanket. It kept me alive in those damnable straits while others were freezing to death. I hope we never have to go through an ordeal like that again. My pizzle was like a giant icicle."

Nicholas gave a nod of assent. He was a powerful young man with fair hair and beard, and a face that had weathered the most terrifying extremes of climate. Like the rest of the crew, he had set sail from Plymouth in the firm belief that they were headed for the Mediterranean. It never occurred to Nicholas that they had embarked on the longest voyage ever made. When that fact was borne in upon him with cruel force, it was far too late to change his mind. He had joined the expedition on impulse in order to escape a troubled domestic life. What lay ahead now frightened him far more than anything he had left behind.

They had already been at sea for the best part of fifteen months now. Of the five vessels which had left Devon under the command of their captain-general, Francis Drake, only one remained. Almost a quarter of its crew had been lost along the way. There were those who blamed Drake for bringing them to the South Seas and who held him personally responsible for the deaths of their shipmates, but Nicholas was not among them. He knew that their captain had saved far more lives than he had sacrificed.

With a combination of ruthlessness and religion, Drake enforced stern discipline aboard the *Golden Hind*. He was at once aloof and familiar, dining off gold plate while musicians played yet digging for water beside his men when they went foraging ashore, conducting the daily services with a priestlike solemnity yet lending a hand to pull on the ropes in a storm. Nicholas was astonished at the way Drake could come down among his crew without losing one jot of authority or respect.

"When will we sail for home?" bleated John Strood.

"Soon," promised Nicholas.

"When the hold is full of treasure," added Merfyn Pugh. "That's what we came for and that's what we will get. It's the only thing that will make up for the miseries we've been through on this voyage."

"Will we be rich?" asked the boy, wistfully.

"As rich as emperors!" said the Welshman.

The three men were on deck, cleaning the muskets and checking that they were in working order. All weaponry was kept in good condition and Drake drilled his men regularly in its use. When Nicholas had joined the expedition on that fateful day in November 1577, he was sturdy but untrained in the arts of war. The voyage had transformed him into a soldier. He was now adept with sword, dagger, crossbow, and musket. Few men aboard could handle a pike as skillfully as this son of a Barnstaple merchant. His prowess won the admiration of John Strood.

"If we board her," said the boy excitedly, "Nick will lead the way. He will mow down the Spaniards like grass."

"I do not look to kill anyone," corrected Nicholas.

"I do," asserted Merfyn, thumping the stock of a musket against the bulwark for effect. "If anyone gets between me and that gold, I'll send him straight up to Heaven with a prayer to help him on his way. Forgive, O Lord, the imperfections of my worship – but here's a Spanish corpse as recompense. Amen."

Nicholas smiled indulgently. The Welshman was a huge, brawny man with features of almost exotic ugliness. Older than most of the crew, Merfyn was mocked for his nationality and teased for his religious streak, but Nicholas saw the finer qualities behind the surface bluster. He would never forget the way that Merfyn had confounded the chaplain, Francis Fletcher, by quoting scripture at him for an hour without pausing for breath. The chaplain had never dared to lock horns with Merfyn over the Bible again.

A voyage deepened friendships and intensified hatreds. John Strood soon discovered that. Only fourteen when they set sail, the boy was alternately coveted or reviled, sought after by those who wanted to bestow more than a caress upon his slim, lithe body and bullied by those who saw his innocence as an excuse to snarl and strike at him. It was only when Nicholas came to his rescue that the lad began to understand how indiscriminately he had been abused by friend and foe alike. With Merfyn as an additional guardian, John Strood was completely safe.

"There!" shouted the boy, pointing. "There, there!"

"Where?" demanded Merfyn.

"There! Can you not see it?" John was almost climbing over the bulwark. "The gold chain is mine. It's mine!" His whole frame sagged with despair. "Oh! ... I was wrong."

What he took to be the sails of the *Cacafuego* were no more than the distant breakers of the Pacific Ocean. In the fading light, the white foam had deceived his tired eyes. The boy was completely abashed and Nicholas had to console him. Merfyn Pugh clipped the lad's ear playfully, then repeated his prophecy with even more assurance.

"Tomorrow!" he predicted. "On St. David's Day. And a Welshman will carry off the prize. Mark my words!"

Only part of the boast was fulfilled. Merfyn Pugh had picked the right day but nominated the wrong lookout. At noon on March 1, they were standing off Cape Francisco when John Drake, the captain's young nephew, standing at the masthead in a fever of anticipation, discerned a sail four leagues to seaward. His yell of triumph brought the whole crew up on deck. Drake surmised that it was the treasure ship and gave his orders accordingly. His men rushed to obey.

Nicholas, Merfyn, and John Strood were given the task of filling wine casks and pots with water before roping them together and tossing them over the stern.

"Why are we doing this, Nick?" wondered the boy.

"To slow us down."

"But we want to overtake the *Cacafuego*."

"If she sees us bearing down on her, she will clap on full sail and make a run for it. We must move by stealth."

"Then why not shorten our own sail?"

"That, too, would give the game away, lad." Nicholas indicated the mattresses which were also being flung over the stern with ropes attached to them. "You see? These will act as a drag as well. They will make the *Golden Hind* seem far more sluggish than she is. We will creep upon our prey like a cat."

Merfyn was impatient. "We should pounce like a lion!" he said. "There's a fortune floating on the waves ahead of us. Why delay? We should seize her!"

"All in good time," soothed Nicholas. "My guess is that the captain does not mean to get within hail before dusk."

"I cannot wait till *then*!"

"You will have to, Merfyn."

"Yes," said John with a flash of mischief. "Unless you dive over the side and swim to the *Cacafuego* to board her on your own. Call on St. David to help you."

The Welshman's anger abated and he laughed into his beard. Francis Drake would not let a prize such as this slip through his fingers. Their captain had to be trusted.

The strategy worked perfectly. It was nine hours before the *Golden Hind* came within reach of its target. Throughout the leisurely pursuit Drake had manouevred his vessel in such a way as to conceal the English pinnace being towed behind it. He now sent the pinnace to pull up on the port side of the treasure ship while he crossed her stern to engage her other flank.

The *Cacafuego* was taken unawares. Lulled into complacence by the friendly approach of the other ship, it realised too late it was being attacked by an English privateer. Captain San Juan de Anton's plight was hopeless. His ship had no artillery and few firearms abroad. When the Spaniard showed a token defiance by refusing to haul down his flag, Drake gave the signal. A whistle sounded, a trumpet blew, and a volley of artillery brought down the treasure ship's mizzenmast. A simultaneous shower of arquebus balls and arrows wounded one of the crew and sent the rest scuttling below deck in a panic. Only the brave captain dared to remain in view.

Nicholas Bracewell was in the pinnace when it grappled alongside. He and Merfyn Pugh were among the first to scramble over the enemy bulwark. They seized the Spanish captain, deprived him of his weapons, and then escorted him back to the *Golden Hind*. Drake was removing his helmet and coat of mail. He embraced his captive in the most courteous manner.

"Have patience," he said. "Such is the custom of war."

It was over as quickly as that. The *Cacafuego* was taken and its dazzling cargo was gloated over by the corsairs. In the holds of the treasure ship they found 14 chests of silver reals, 80 pounds of gold, and 26 tons of silver bars. The registered cargo alone amounted to 360,000 pesos, half the annual revenue of the English crown.

To this could be added a large amount of unregistered bullion. No privateer had ever taken a prize of such magnitude. In a single brief engagement Drake had made himself one of the richest men in England and taken his crew into the realm of legend.

"How much will we get?" asked John Strood.

"Enough, lad," said Nicholas.

"Yes," added Merfyn, rubbing his great hands together. "From now on, every day will be St. David's Day for me! I thought we were mad to try to sail around the world. Not now! This contents me more than I can say. Now I can retire to grow leeks!"

The three of them were helping to unload the booty from the *Cacafuego*. After being checked and listed, it was carefully boxed and rowed from one ship to the other. Though the whole process was closely supervised, odd items did somehow go astray as greed got the better of duty. Nicholas was fairly certain that Thomas Relph was the thief but he had no means of proving it. Relph was a tall, rangy man in his thirties with a pock-marked face half-hidden by a straggly beard. More than once on the voyage, Nicholas had warned him to stop pestering John Strood.

Relph was now emboldened to try his luck once more with the boy. It was night. Stars dotted the heavens. The ship lay at anchor, its timbers creaking noisily as it rocked on the water. A stiff breeze plucked at the rigging.

"What will you take, John?" whispered Relph.

"Nothing," said the boy, blushing in the half-dark.

"I only wish to buy a little of your time."

"It is not for sale."

"But you would *enjoy* it," urged Relph, leaning in close to him. "I'll make sure of that. Come, Sir. We are shipmates. Let us be true friends as well."

"True friends do not threaten."

"Have I threatened you, lad? Far from it. I am offering you money. A reward for your kindness. If that will not suffice, I will trade something that even you could not refuse." He opened the palm of his hand to reveal a small pearl. "This, John. Take it. All yours."

The pearl glittered as he held it up to the lantern.

"Where did you get it?" asked the boy, hypnotised by its severe beauty. "What is it worth?"

"An hour with you."

Relph slipped an arm around him but withdrew it at once as a figure bore down on them. Nicholas had come up on deed to search for his young charge and the wooing was at an end. Cursing under his breath, Relph closed his hand around the pearl and scurried off into the darkness. Nicholas recognised his distinctive gait.

"Has Tom Relph been bothering you again?" he said.

"Yes, Nick. He offered me a pearl."

"A pearl!"

"I have never seen such a thing before."

"Where did a man like that come by it?"

Nicholas answered his own question and set off in pursuit of Relph. The pearl was the proof he needed. It was patently stolen from the *Cacafuego* and would establish the guilt of Thomas Relph. Nicholas suspected that many other incriminating items would be found on the thief. He would overpower the man and drag him off to the captain. John Strood would never be harassed by Thomas Relph again.

His search was thorough but fruitless. Nicholas looked from stem to stern but there was no sign of Relph. He had vanished into the night air. Nicholas had to wait until first light before the mystery was solved. The dead body of Thomas Relph lay spread-eagled in the pinnace that was moored alongside the vessel. His throat had been cut. When Nicholas searched him, he discovered that the pearl had disappeared along with any other valuables Relph may have concealed about his person. Full punishment had been exacted for his crimes by an anonymous executioner.

"Who could have killed him, Nick?" said John, nervously.

"Almost anyone. Tom Relph had many enemies."

"Merfyn thinks it might have been his brother."

"We must not rush to judgment," said Nicholas. "It is true that there was no love lost between Tom and his brother but that does not mean Amos Relph is a murderer. I am not sure that he would have the stomach for such a vile act."

"What happened to that pearl?"

"The killer has it now."

Francis Drake was horrified by news of the murder and launched an immediate inquiry. His crew was depleted enough as it was. He could not afford to lose an able-bodied man. Their captain felt sure that the killing was linked in some way to the capture of the *Cacafuego*. He knew only too well the dangers of taking rich prizes along the way and he tried to offset them by maintaining strict discipline and by paying wages on a regular basis. Men with money in their pouches were less inclined to be crazed by the sight of so much gold and silver. Evidently Drake's precautions had not worked this time. Tom Relph and his killer had wanted substantially more than their due.

"I am glad that I gave my wages to you," said John.

"There will be much more to come when we get back to England," reminded Nicholas. "Every member of the crew is entitled to a share of our good fortune."

"That is under lock and key in the hold and my wages are just as secure in your keeping. Thank you, Nick."

John Strood was not the only person to entrust his money to Nicholas Bracewell. Two or three others had seen his broad shoulders and his unswerving honesty as ideal safeguards for their meagre wealth. Apart from anything else, they could not be tempted to throw their wages away at a game of dice if the money was looked after by Nicholas. Several pouches were concealed about his person. Nobody would dare try to take them from him.

There was an immense amount of work to do on the ship. Now that the *Cacafuego* had been sent on its way, the *Golden Hind* needed to be cleaned, repaired, and victualled for the long voyage home. Spain would most certainly launch a counterattack to avenge the indignities which Drake had inflicted on her vessels. It was time to run.

Nicholas was pleased. The further he got away from England, the more appealing it became to him and he was as anxious as the rest of the crew to return home. He was ready to do all he could to speed up the process. Nicholas and Merfyn were assigned to mend one of the leaks in the hull. There was a problem. When they got down there with their tools, they learned that their assistant was Amos Relph.

"There's a foul stink down here," grumbled Merfyn.

"Rotting timber," said Nicholas.

"It smells more like betrayal. The stench of a man who would kill his own brother. Can anything reek as much as that?"

Relph tensed but said nothing. Younger and smaller than his brother, he was cunning but weak-willed. He would stand no chance in a fight against the muscular Welshman, especially when the latter was armed with a mallet. When Merfyn continued to bait him, Amos Relph did his best to ignore the provocation. Nicholas eventually decided that it was best to separate the two men and sent Merfyn away on an errand. The taciturn Relph was grateful.

"Thank you," he grunted. "Though I wished him dead, I did not kill Tom. More's the pity!"

That was all he was prepared to say on the subject. Nicholas was inclined to believe him. The two men worked on quietly side by side and patched up the hole in the hull, which was just above the water line. In heavy seas, waves lashed it and water poured through. Hot pitch was used to seal the repair. They were interrupted by the breathless arrival of the chaplain. Francis Fletcher was relieved to see Nicholas.

"At last!" he exclaimed. "Merfyn told me I would find you down here. I have sad tidings, Nicholas."

"What is the problem?"

"Gabriel Usher. He's very near his hour."

Nicholas was distressed to hear it. Gabriel Usher had been a good friend to him. A veteran sailmaker, he had taught Nicholas the rudiments of his craft and bewitched him with countless sea stories while he was doing it. Usher had now succumbed to the disease that afflicted all voyagers: scurvy was about to claim yet another member of the crew.

"I'll come as soon as I may," promised Nicholas.

"Do not tarry," said the chaplain. "He cannot wait."

"Tell him I am on my way."

Nicholas hurried to complete the repair, then checked that it was sound. Merfyn returned to find that his help was no longer needed. Nicholas was loath to leave him alone with Amos Relph but there was no remedy. The dying man took precedence over all else. As he moved away Nicholas could hear the firstlings of a row in his wake. Merfyn was in accusatory mood.

Gabriel Usher was lying below deck in a corner reserved for the sick and injured. The odour of decay hung over the whole area and clutched at Nicholas's throat. As soon as he knelt beside his friend, he saw that he was too late. Usher's mouth was swollen. His face and body were covered with large, ugly blotches. Old sores on his hands and arms had reopened. The telltale marks of scurvy were everywhere.

Nicholas sent up a silent prayer for his soul then bent forward to feel inside the man's shirt. Gabriel Usher had asked an important favour of his friend. Nicholas had agreed to take charge of his money in order to hand it over to Usher's widow when he reached England. It was a solemn pledge that had to be honoured. The leather pouch was held by cord around the dead man's neck. Nicholas lifted it gently off him but the feel of the pouch alarmed him. It was empty. The body had been robbed.

The funeral at sea was short but moving. Mariners who had already consigned dozens of their shipmates to earth or to water now watched as another slid out of their world under a foreign sky. Gabriel Usher would not be able to share in the spoils of the *Cacafuego*. John Strood shivered throughout the service and the emotional Merfyn Pugh all but wept. As Nicholas let his gaze drift across the assembled crew, he paused to take a closer look at Amos Relph. One eye was blackened and a gash had appeared on the man's temple. He was still clearly suspected of the murder of his elder brother.

The boy was baffled by the sheer malignity of fate.

"Why did he have to die, Nick?" he puzzled.

"Scurvy picks its victims at random."

"But why Gabriel? He was one of the kindest men aboard. For all his strength, Gabriel would not harm a fly. He was so gentle. Why was he picked out from the rest of us?"

"It was God's will," sighed Merfyn.

"There is no sense to it," persisted the boy.

"Do not question the ways of the Lord," scolded the Welshman, lapsing into a Biblical vein. "He made us and He can call us back to his side whenever He chooses. Gabriel was summoned. That is all you need to know. He will not be the last."

"Alas, no," agreed Nicholas. "We shall soon be mourning another shipmate. Henry Lye is set to follow Gabriel."

Merfyn was shocked. "Henry Lye?"

"Within the next twenty-four hours."

"Never! He's too good a man to die."

"So was Gabriel Usher," argued Nicholas.

"But Henry ...?" He scratched at the black beard. "No. It must not be. I could not bear the loss. He and I have sailed together ten times or more. He is not just a friend. Henry Lye is part of my life."

"The chaplain will confirm what I say."

Francis Fletcher came up to speak to Nicholas.

"Gabriel's effects are in my cabin," he said. "The poor wretch left precious little but his widow will want what there is, some kind of keepsake."

Nicholas nodded. "I'll seek her out back in England."

"Gabriel went to his grave, trusting that you would."

"And is this true about Henry Lye?" said Merfyn, still shaken by the news. "He, too, is failing fast?"

"Very fast," signed the chaplain. "He sent for me in the night to take his confession. Scurvy is draining every last ounce of his strength and his will to live. I do not expect Henry to see another dawn in the Mare Pacifico."

John Strood began to shudder violently until Nicholas put a comforting arm around him. Even a seasoned mariner like Merfyn Pugh was stunned. Nicholas saw the tears welling up in the Welshmen's eyes. Mastering his emotions, Merfyn went off to talk to his stricken friend for the last time.

When night wrapped its blanket around the ship, the *Golden Hind* did not sleep. Watch was maintained around the clock and the bell rung precisely on the hour. Drake even posted a man at the masthead lest the twinkle of a distant lantern be missed. The groan of the timbers was punctuated by the clack of heels on the deck and the muttered conversations of the sentries. With a veritable fortune as its ballast, the ship was taking no chances. It was built for attack but it was also schooled in the rules of defence. Nothing would catch it off guard.

Slumber was fitful below deck. In their cramped and fetid quarters, the crew snatched what little sleep they could before beginning another long and arduous day. Only the sick and the doomed slept with any conviction.

Henry Lye was curled up on the bare boards in a corner. He was quite motionless. His head was all but invisible and his body was twisted into an unnatural position. In the gloom it was difficult to see if he was still alive. No sound of breathing seemed to come from the solid frame and the grinding snores of his companions did not trouble his ears.

A figure crept silently through the darkness, stepping over prone bodies and halting in his tracks if any of them so much as stirred or twitched. When he finally located the person he wanted, he knelt solicitously beside him.

"Henry!" he hissed. "Can you hear me, Henry?"

There was no response. Even a shake of his shoulder did not rouse him. Henry Lye was either dead or so near death that it would be simple to ease him into its welcoming arms. Scurvy was a thief. It robbed a man of his health, his strength, his appearance, and his willpower. When it had filched everything he had to give, it left its victim in such a debilitated state that any sudden movement could kill him.

One thief conspired with another. A sharp bang of his head would put Henry Lye out of his lingering misery. It had worked for Gabriel Usher. It would be equally effective here. A sinewy hand hovered over the prostrate figure, intending to grab his hair in order to dash his skull down on to the hard timber. A mumbled prayer came first; then the hand descended with a vengeance.

It was met by another, which gripped it by the wrist and twisted it sharply away. Henry Lye came vigorously back to life in the shape of Nicholas Bracewell and grappled with his attacker. The element of surprise was decisive. In a matter of seconds the visitor was pinned to the floor with a knife at his throat. Awakened by the commotion, others called out in fear and anger. Lanterns were quickly brought to illumine the scene.

Nicholas Bracewell sat astride the heaving body of Merfyn Pugh. The Welshman shook with righteous indignation.

"But why you, Nick?" he protested. "We are *friends!*"

"Henry Lye was your friend," said Nicholas. "But you were ready to steal his money when you thought him about to die. Gabriel Usher was a friend as well but you were happy to deprive him of the weight of his savings."

"I would have shared everything with you."

"Including your haul from Tom Relph? No wonder you were in such a hurry to accuse his brother of the murder. While we were all looking at Amos, attention was taken away from the real villain – Merfyn Pugh."

"Tom Relph *deserved* to die."

"You will follow him to the grave."

"Nothing can be proved," said Merfyn truculently.

"Your action tonight is proof enough and we have witnesses aplenty to that. Then there are all the items you stole, including that pearl from the *Cacafuego*. You are too greedy a man to part with it for a second. I'll swear that it is hidden about you somewhere with the rest of your booty."

The Welshman was caught. With a howl of rage he tried to throw his assailant off but Nicholas was far too strong and alert. Other hands came swiftly to his assistance and the prisoner was securely bound. Merfyn flung a last exasperated question at his erstwhile friend.

"Where is the real Henry Lye?" he demanded. "When I saw him earlier, he was at death's door. Where is he now?"

"Alive and well," said a voice in the darkness. "I will be there to enjoy your execution, Merfyn. I'm only sorry that we can't arrange it for St. David's Day."

Francis Drake summoned Nicholas to his cabin to congratulate him. At one stroke two murders had been solved and a third one had been prevented. The captain beamed with delight. He felt that his vessel had been properly cleansed at last. A devout man, he believed that the *Golden Hind* had been exorcised.

"You have done me great service this night," he said. "I am deeply grateful to you, Nicholas."

"Henry Lye played his part," said Nicholas. "When Merfyn called on him earlier, Henry feigned illness with the skill of an true actor."

"But he was prompted by you."

"I needed him to bait the trap."

"Why did you suspect Merfyn Pugh?"

"When I remembered that he had directed the chaplain to me. Merfyn heard the grim tidings about Gabriel Usher before I did. He had time to go below, dispatch Gabriel, and steal his money. That is how I imagined it but I had no evidence."

"So you forced his hand," observed Drake.

"Henry helped me to do that. Because he was an old friend of his, Merfyn's ears pricked up at the very mention of Henry Lye. I knew that Merfyn would go to him at once and I rehearsed Henry in his role." Nicholas heaved a sigh. "Both of us were deeply saddened by the thought that Merfyn Pugh could sink to such villainy. We liked him. But he had to be exposed."

"The chaplain was pressed into service as well," said Drake with a smile. "I own it freely, I never thought to see the day when Francis Fletcher would turn into a strolling player."

"I employed him to lend credence to my tale."

"The blessing of the Church is always useful." Drake became serious. "The prisoner will be tried and sentenced without delay. I will not have a thief and a murderer contaminating the *Golden Hind*. This will serve as a lesson to the rest of the men. When they see Merfyn Pugh dangling at the end of a rope, they will be truly chastened." He regarded his visitor with admiration. "It is good to have you aboard, Nicholas. You are a fine seaman and a loyal member of my crew. I would like to feel that I could call upon that loyalty for my next voyage but I fear that I have lost you, my friend. Your future is clearly elsewhere."

"Elsewhere?" said Nicholas.

"Yes," explained Drake. "You did not simply contrive the capture of a villain with your performance. You *revelled* in it. You set everything up to perfection. The sea will not hold you. I fancy that Nicholas Bracewell will sail in a different vessel from now on – the playhouse."

THE COMICAL REVENGE

Many writers create a character in a short story then go on to develop them in a full-length novel. I tend to work in the opposite direction, blooding new characters in book form before confining them to a smaller canvas. "Domesday Deferred" and "Murder at Anchor" both featured protagonists already well established in a novel series, and "The Comical Revenge" is in the same vein. Written for this anthology, it's the first outing in a short story of Christopher Redmayne, an aspiring young architect in Restoration London, and Jonathan Bale, a Puritan constable, who teams up with him to solve various crimes. Like the novels, the story is set during the aftermath of the Great Fire of 1666 when the capital city had to be completely rebuilt, and when there were great opportunities for a talented architect like Christopher Redmayne. At a time when he least needs interruption, he is called away from work on his latest house by a family crisis. His dissolute elder brother, Henry, is once again in trouble.

W here on earth have you *been*?" asked Henry Redmayne, petulantly. "You must have received my letter hours ago."

"I came as soon as I could," said Christopher.

"Well, it was not soon enough. Heavens, I'm your *brother*!"

"I was busy, Henry. My client wanted to be shown over the house."

"And does the demand of a client take precedence over a heartfelt plea from your only sibling? I declare, Christopher, that your memory is wondrous short. But for me," said Henry, striking a pose, "you would *have* no clients."

"You did help me to launch my career, it's true, and I'm eternally grateful."

"Then why not show your gratitude by responding to my summons?"

"I've done so."

"Hours too late."

Arms folded, Henry turned his back to show his displeasure. Christopher was far too accustomed to his brother's irritable behavior to let it upset him. Over the years, he had endured Henry's bad temper, his capriciousness and his blatant selfishness,

144

with a weary affection. They were in the drawing room of Henry's house in Bedford Street and Christopher was waiting patiently for his brother's ire to cool. A gifted young man, he was one of the many architects helping to rebuild London after the ravages of the Great Fire, and he had achieved marked success in his short career. He never forgot that it was Henry who, by introducing him to a friend, provided him with his first client.

Christopher always dressed smartly but his brother wore nothing that was not flamboyant. As he swung round to confront his visitor, Henry was wearing a pair of red velvet petticoat breeches, edged with ribbon and hanging from his hips, a blue and gold doublet over a billowing linen shirt and a pair of shoes whose silver buckles positively gleamed. To hide his thinning hair, he had on a full periwig but it did not disguise the clear signs of dissipation in his face. With his handsome features, his healthy complexion and his long hair with its reddish tinge, Christopher looked as if twenty long years separated them and not merely a short few.

Henry put a hand to his chest. "I face a terrible dilemma," he announced.

"There is no novelty in that," said Christopher with a tolerant smile.

"Do not mock me. I speak in earnest."

"What is it this time – gambling debts?"

"No."

"A stern warning from Father?"

"The old gentleman has not written for a month, thank God."

"Then there must be some vexing problem at your place of work."

"The Navy Office is an agreeable sinecure."

"That leaves one possibility," decided Christopher. "There's a woman in the case. You've put yourself in a compromising position yet again." He heaved a sigh. "Will you never learn, Henry?"

"Stop sounding like Father," retorted the other. "It's bad enough to have one clergyman in the family. Read me no sermons, Christopher. Every supposition you make is entirely wrong. Do me the courtesy of listening to me and you'll hear why I'm in such a dire predicament."

"Very well," said Christopher, sitting down. "I am all ears."

"Last night, I went to the theater with a friend to watch the Duke's Company. The play was called *The Comical Revenge*."

"I remember it well. I saw it some years ago when it was first performed. George Etherege has a wicked eye and sparkling wit. *The Comical Revenge* is almost as good as his new play, *She Would If She Could*."

Henry stamped a food. "Damnation! Who is telling this story – you or me?"

"I'll say no more."

"Thank you. Now, where was I?"

"Going to the theater with a friend."

"Will you please be *quiet*, Christopher!" His younger brother put a hand to his lips to signal that he would remain silent. "Let me try again," said Henry, measuring his words before he spoke them. "What I tell you is in the strictest confidence and must be divulged to nobody. Do you understand?" Christopher nodded obediently. "The friend whom I accompanied last night was Sir Beresford Tyte, an odd fellow in some ways but generous to a fault. He has saved me time and again with a providential loan. Now, however," he went on, grimacing, "Sir Beresford wants repayment."

"I knew that it was a gambling debt!"

"But it's not – at least, not entirely. Sir Beresford had an unfortunate encounter at the playhouse. We chanced to meet the egregious Lord Plumer there. Sir Beresford – and here I must remind you how crucial discretion is – has become closely acquainted with that divine creature, Ariana, my Lady Plumer. It seems that her husband finally learned of the attachment," said Henry, rolling his eyes. "There was a frightful scene. My friend denied ever having seen the wife, as any decent man would have done, but my Lord Plumer insisted on revenge. He challenged Sir Beresford to a duel."

"That was very rash," observed Christopher. "Sir Beresford must be thirty years younger than him. He's bound to triumph."

"Sadly, he is not."

"Why?"

"Because he will not be crossing swords with that old cuckold, that's why. He has a substitute," said Henry, ruefully. "I've been engaged to fight in his stead."

Christopher was astonished. "*You?*"

"Yes," confessed the other, taking a seat opposite him. "My friend and I are of the same height and build. If I wear that black periwig of his and don his apparel – years out of fashion, though it be – I can pass for Sir Beresford Tyte easily enough."

"But why should you have to?"

"To settle my debt to him."

"On such demanding terms."

"I owe the fellow hundreds of pounds."

"Let me help you to pay it off."

"If only it were that easy, Christopher," said his brother, woefully, "but it is not, I fear. After the play, we adjourned to a certain house to take our pleasure with the ladies of the establishment. A modicum of drink was consumed."

"In short, you became hopelessly drunk and gave him your word."

"As a matter of honor, I have to keep it. Yes," he added, seeing his brother's look of disapproval, "honor is at stake here. When the idea was first put to me, I found it rather appealing. Just think of it, Christopher. Five minutes of swordplay and I wipe out debts that took me years to build up. I'd be free of obligation."

"Sir Beresford is the man with the obligation. It is he who was challenged last night. If honor has any meaning," insisted Christopher, "he should face his mistress's husband with a sword in his hand. Is he too cowardly to do so?"

"No, he's too fearful of losing Ariana's love. It's one thing to put horns on the head of my Lord Plumer. To thrust a rapier through his heart is a different matter."

"So he expects *you* to kill the old man in his place?"

"He'd prefer me to wound and disable him."

"That's a monstrous imposition to place upon a friend."

"It did not seem so at the time," said Henry. "I am no mean swordsman and have no fear that the old goat will get the better of me. If I drew blood from him, I foolishly assumed, he'd turn tail and quit the field. Duty done, debt discharged." He ran a worried hand across his chin. "Then I learned a little more about my Lord Plumer."

"I think I can guess what you are going to tell me," said Christopher. "If this lady is the young and beautiful wife of a much older man, she will have more than one suitor after her. Sir Beresford Tyte may just be the latest."

"You've hit the mark, brother."

"My lord Plumer will have challenged others to a duel before now. Why does he do so when he has little chance of prevailing with a sword in his hand?"

"Because his bullies have cudgels in theirs, Christopher."

"Ah, I see. He is determined to win at all costs."

"The last man whom he accused of a liaison with his wife was found battered almost to death. The one before that had his nose slit." Henry shivered. "I prefer my nose as it is, thank you. It's one of my best features. And I've no wish to be cudgeled until every bone in my body is broken." He spread his arms in despair. "What am I to do?"

"Let your friend suffer the consequences of his dalliance," said Christopher. "Sir Beresford must have known the risk that he was running. Husbands do not like it when their wives are led astray. This is a mess of his own making."

"But I'm the one who has to get out of it somehow. Whatever I do, I'll not go back to Sir Beresford. He's *counting* on me."

"To take punishment on his behalf. That's an unjust contract to enforce."

"Teach me a way to escape from it, Christopher. I need your counsel."

"Why? You always ignore it. I've been telling you for years to shed the company of rakes like Sir Beresford Tyte, but you'll not hear of it. You see the result of it now."

Henry put up his hands defensively. "Not another homily – *please*."

Christopher bit back what he was going to say. His brother was in great distress but censure would not help him. Only positive action could rescue Henry Redmayne. The difficulty lay in extracting him from a desperate situation while keeping his honor intact. Christopher pondered. Henry reached out to touch him.

"Will you protect me, Christopher?" he asked. "Will you act as my second?"

"That will not suffice."

"Do not betray me in my hour of need."

"I'd never do that," said Christopher, smiling as an idea suddenly popped into his head. "Where is this duel to take place?"

"At a time and spot of our own choosing."

"Then the problem is solved."

"How?"

"All will become clear in time, Henry. Talk to Sir Beresford." He instructed. "Let him send word that the duel will take place at seven o'clock on Sunday morning."

"*Sunday?*" Henry was surprised. "A sword fight on the Lord's Day?"

"There's a reason behind it."

"And where will Sir Beresford – or his deputy – meet his challenger?"

"At the new house that I've designed in," said Christopher. "It's only half-built but the garden has been walled. It's very private. Sunday is the one time when the none of the builders or gardeners will be there."

"But I hoped you'd find a way to get me *out* of this duel."

"Trust me, Henry. I'm doing just that."

The house was in Baynard's Castle ward, a district that had suffered badly during the Great Fire and lost its parish churches as well as a large number of other properties. Christopher Redmayne had designed one of the many new houses to fill the vacant gaps. Tall, stately and with an impressive façade, the building had a garden that ran down to the river where, in due course, it would have its own landing stage. Trees, bushes and flowers had already been planted but most of the garden was given over to a series of rectangular lawns. It was on the biggest of these swards that the duel was to take place.

Christopher did not recognize his brother when they met. Henry had not only put on apparel belonging to Sir Beresford Tyte, he was wearing the man's periwig and had adopted his friend's posture and gait. It was a convincing disguise. Christopher used a key to let them into the house. They went through it into the garden. Henry was tense and uncharacteristically reticent. His brother led him into the shadow of some bushes. They did not have long to wait. Within minutes, the garden gate opened and Roger, Lord Plumer, entered with two brawny companions.

"I thought you said I would not have to fight," complained Henry.

"Tale up your position," said Christopher. "That is all."

"And then?"

Henry's question went unanswered because his adversary was bearing down on them. Lord Plumer was a short, fat, waddling man in his late fifties with a neat gray beard. Identifying Henry as his opponent, he got close enough to sneer at him.

"So you had the courage to turn up, did you?" he said with disdain. "I'll make you rue that decision, Sir Beresford. You tried to steal my wife's affections away from me, you libertine. By the time I've finished with you, my friend, you'll not be able to consort with any lady. Make yourself ready, sir!"

"Not so fast, my lord," said Christopher, stepping forward. "If a duel is to take place, it must abide strictly by the rules."

"A plague on any rules!" snorted the other, drawing his sword. "Defend yourself, Sir Beresford. I'm coming to relieve you of your manhood."

And without further warning, he charged forward, brandishing his rapier. Henry barely had time to unsheathe his weapon in order to defend himself. Parrying the first thrust, he backed away. Christopher kept one eye on the two seconds as they tried to move in behind his brother to distract him. It was clear that, if their master faltered, they were to rescue him and overpower Henry. As a precaution, Christopher kept a hand on the hilt of his own sword but he did not have to draw it. Salvation appeared in exactly the way that he had planned.

"Hold, sirs!" yelled Bale. "You are breaking the law!"

Two constables had just burst in through the gate. Jonathan Bale, the first of them, was a big, powerful man with an authoritative voice. There was disgust in his face as he strode across the lawn.

"Shame on you both!" he cried. "Is this how you celebrate the Day of Rest? Would you defy God by fighting on the Sabbath?"

Relieved by the interruption, and recognizing Bale as his brother's close friend, Henry backed away. He had been rescued. In turning up in place of another man, he felt that honor has been satisfied. Tossing a smile of thanks to Christopher, he sheathed his sword. But his opponent was not so ready to abandon the duel. One of his seconds pulled a pistol from his belt and handed it to his master. Lord Plumer took aim. Before Henry realized what was happening, there was a loud report and something stung him on the temple. With blood streaming down his face, he collapsed to the ground.

Shocked by what he had witnessed, Bale ran towards the injured man. The other constable, meanwhile, tried to arrest Roger, Lord Plumer, but he was brushed aside by the two seconds. They ran to the gate with their master and got away in their carriage.

Christopher paid no attention to their escape. His only concern was the fate of his brother. Bending solicitously beside him, he eased the wig off so that he could examine the wound properly. Bale looked anxiously over his friend's shoulder at the fallen man.

"You did not tell me that it was your *brother*, Mr Redmayne," he said.

Christopher did not mince his words. As he stood outside his brother's bedchamber, he let Sir Beresford Tyte know exactly what he thought of the man's behavior.

"What you did was unforgivable," he said with controlled passion. "It was cruel, ungentlemanly and tinged with cowardice. Thanks to you, my brother might easily have been killed."

"I did not mean this to happen," said the other.

"Then you should have met your own obligations, and not shuffled them off on to Henry. You exposed him to unnecessary danger."

"I thought he would simply wound my lord Plumer and put him to flight."

"While you were hiding at home. Really, Sir Beresford, I thought better of you."

Sir Beresford Tyte had the grace to look shamefaced. He was a tall, thin man in his late twenties with an air of prosperity about him. Unlike Henry, his life of debauchery had left no visible signs on him. He was undeniably handsome and Christopher could see why the lady in question had been attracted to him.

"How is Henry?" asked Tyte with obvious concern.

"We shall know when the doctor has finished examining him."

"I was horrified when I heard the news."

"Had you fought the duel yourself, my brother would not have been shot."

"No," rejoined Tyte, "but *I* might have been. How was I to know that that old fool would have a pistol at hand?" He tried to mollify Christopher with a smile. "Do not be too harsh on me, Christopher. Your brother has profited from this venture. All his debts have been paid off in this action."

"That is no consolation to him – or to me."

"I'll be revenged on my lord Plumer for this!"

"And who will you get to do *that* on your behalf?" asked Christopher, sharply.

Tyte looked embarrassed. The next moment, the door opened and the doctor, an elderly man with a pronounced stoop, came out of the bedchamber. They turned to him.

"Well?" asked Tyte.

"He's a fortunate man," said the doctor. "The bullet only grazed his temple. It drew blood and will leave a scar, but there's no lasting damage. The patient, however, is still badly shocked by the experience. I've given him a sleeping draught."

"May I not speak to him?"

"You may try, Sir Beresford, but do not expect a conversation with him."

Tyte nodded and went quickly into the bedchamber to apologize to his friend. Reassured by the diagnosis, Christopher led the doctor downstairs and showed him out of the house. He then went across to Jonathan Bale who had been waiting in the hall. The constable was trying not to look at a painting on the wall of naked women in a Roman orgy. Christopher repeated what the doctor had told them.

"I'm relieved to hear it," said Bale, seriously. "I could never bring myself to approve of your brother's way of life," he added, glancing at the painting that troubled him so much, "but I do not wish him any ill. He was the victim of attempted murder and the culprit must answer for it."

"He will do, Jonathan," promised Christopher.

"Tell me his name and I'll obtain a warrant for his arrest."

"That would not achieve anything, alas. The gentleman is far too well connected to fear the process of law. His brother is a judge and he has a dozen politicians in his pocket. Besides," he went on, "Henry would not want this matter to go to court or he will be charged with taking part in a duel."

"Why did he do so in disguise, Mr Redmayne?"

"I will tell you when this whole business has blown over."

Christopher was very fond of the constable but he knew that his friend's Puritan conscience would be aroused if he heard the full facts of the case. Infidelity and large gambling debts lay behind the affair. Both were anathema to Jonathan Bale. At a later date, Christopher resolved, he would give his friend an edited account of events.

"I'll not let this crime go unpunished," warned Bale.

"Nor will it be, Jonathan. I am already devising a reprisal."

"I hope that you do not intend to change the fellow to a duel."

Christopher grinned. "I'd never do that," he said. "Dueling is illegal. You'd have to arrest me and I'd hate to put you in a position to do that."

"Thank you," said Bale with a rare smile. "My wife would never forgive me, if

I arrested you. Sarah would not let me hear the end of it." He became solemn. "As long as an attempt to kill your brother does not go unanswered."

"It will have the most appropriate answer of all, Jonathan."

"And what is that?"

"A comical revenge."

Convinced that he had killed his wife's lover, Roger, Lord Plumer, returned to his house in high spirits. He found his wife, Ariana, alone in the drawing room. She looked up with disappointment when he entered.

"Yes," he said, knowingly. "You may well be surprised to see your husband when you were hoping that Sir Beresford Tyte would call on you."

"I awaited only your return," she said, retaining her composure.

"That is how it will be from now on, Ariana. Whether we are in London or on our estate in the country, you'll keep to the house and await my return."

"Would you make a prisoner of me, sir?"

"I thought I'd done that when I married you. But I see that I'll need to put more formal constraints upon you. Do not stir abroad without my permission."

"This is intolerable!" she complained.

"It is what befits a Lady Plumer."

"I'll not be kept behind bars like that."

"You were allowed far too much license, Ariana. Those days are gone."

His wife rose from her chair and crossed to the window. Still in her twenties, she was a shapely woman of medium height with a quiet loveliness that was now vitiated by a deep frown. Having married her husband for his title and his wealth, she had soon regretted her decision. It was not long before she was seeking interest and affection from outside the bonds of matrimony. Without such diversions, her life would be unbearable. The future suddenly looked bleak.

"Forget him, Ariana," said her husband, moving to stand behind her. "You'll never see Sir Beresford again – unless you attend his funeral, that is."

She spun round in alarm. "His funeral?" she gasped.

"Yes, my wayward darling. I killed him in a duel this very morning."

The sleeping draught administered by the doctor was quick to take effect. No sooner had Sir Beresford Tyte told his friend how deeply he regretted what had happened than Henry Redmayne drifted off. When he woke up again a few hours later, he found Tyte still at his bedside. Christopher was also there.

"How do you feel now?" asked his brother, softly.

"In agony," replied Henry, determined to get maximum sympathy from the situation even though he was in no pain. "My stomach churns, my heart is about to burst and my head stings as though someone inserted a dagger in my ear. The wonder is that I'm still alive after that ordeal."

"I blame myself for that," admitted Tyte.

"So you should," said Christopher.

"Tell me how I can make amends and I'll do it."

"A loan of fifty pounds would be an admirable gesture," suggested Henry.

"Take it as a gift," insisted Tyte. "You've earned it, my friend."

"I've an idea how it might usefully be spent," said Christopher. "An attempt was made on your life this morning, Henry. A sly and cowardly attempt. The culprit must pay for that. Jonathan Bale wanted to arrest him but the deception would then be exposed in open court."

"We must not have that, Christopher!"

"Dear Lord, no!" agreed Tyte. "If it were known that I let Henry deputize for me, my reputation would be ruined."

"It's already been seriously compromised, Sir Beresford," said Christopher, "but enough of that. Let us turn to my Lord Plumer. Though he is swift to denounce anyone who dallies with his wife, I hear that he is not above straying away from the marital couch."

"Indeed not!" declared Henry, sitting up in bed. "For all his wrinkles, he's a rampant satyr at times. His mistress is one Betty Malahide, a comely creature and worthy of far better than him."

"The lady is aware of that," said Tyte. "From what I hear, Betty Malahide tired of him and brought an end to the liaison. That made him choleric. It also forced him to spend more time at home where he found evidence that Ariana and I were more than passing acquaintances. Had he still been involved with his mistress," he went on with rancor, "then I would still be enjoying favors from his wife."

"And I would not have had to face a madman with a pistol," said Henry.

Christopher was curious. "Do either of you know this Betty Malahide?"

"We both do, Christopher, and I would sue to know her better."

"If she discarded my lord Plumer, she will have only bitter memories of him. Do you think she would help us to wreak our revenge on him?"

"At a price," said Tyte. "Betty will do anything for a price."

"Then the fifty pounds you offered Henry will be a sound investment."

"But I *need* the money," wailed his brother.

"You need satisfaction," said Christopher, "and the only way you can get that is by humiliating my Lord Plumer to the point where he has to quit London."

"Yes," said Tyte. "I'll subscribe to any plan that does that. I want him well and truly out of the way. While he's in the city, he remains a danger to me."

"Return home, Sir Beresford. Give out that you've been injured and are lying at death's door. That will content my Lord Plumer and put him off guard."

"What of Betty Malahide?" wondered Henry.

"You must introduce me to her," said Christopher. "I have a proposition that might appeal to the lady."

Lord Plumer was at his favorite coffee house when the letter was delivered to him. It was a request from his erstwhile mistress and he responded with alacrity. Excusing himself from his friends, he went out to his carriage and told his coachman where to take him. He was certain that Betty Malahide had repented of her decision to end her relationship with him, and was going to beg him to return to her bed. That put him in a position to exact conditions from her. He whiled away the journey by musing on what those conditions might be.

Admitted to her house, he was immediately conducted upstairs and that confirmed his belief that she wished to be reconciled with him. As he tapped on the door of her bedchamber, he expected a welcoming call to enter the room where he had enjoyed so much pleasure in the past. All that he heard, however, was a frightened voice.

"Is that you, my lord?" asked Betty Malahide. "Do please come in."

As he opened the door, a second surprise awaited him. Hoping to find her contrite and anxious to atone for the unkind way she had spurned him, he instead discovered that his mistress was not even alone. Betty Malahide, a buxom woman with a swarthy hue that he found irresistible, was perched on the edge of the bed. A plump man in black attire seemed to be examining her. Pulling her gown around her with embarrassment, she shot the newcomer a glance of apprehension.

"Thank you for coming so promptly, my lord," she said. "This is Doctor Cooper and he has grim news for both of us." She flitted towards her dressing room. "I'll leave you alone so that he can divulge what he has found."

"What ails you, Betty?" asked Lord Plumer but she had already vanished into the adjacent chamber. He turned to Doctor Cooper. "Well?"

"The lady requires treatment, my lord," explained the doctor. "Not to put too fine a point on it, she has the French disease."

"Well, she caught it not from me!" exclaimed the other.

"Perhaps not, my lord, but she would certainly have *given* it to you."

"How do you know, man?"

"Because it's a virulent strain that I recognize," said Doctor Cooper, "and it is highly infectious. If there have been intimate relations between the two of you in recent weeks, there is no way that you could escape contracting the disease."

"The devil take her!"

"Mistress Malahide deserves compassion rather than reproach."

"The wanton will get no compassion from me," snarled the other, pacing the room in agitation. "If she did not catch the disease from me, then she caught it from another man. Betty has both infected and cuckolded me!"

"That's a private matter between the two of you, my lord. Fortunately, we have caught it early and I have a cure that will restore the both of you to perfect health."

"What sort of cure?"

When the doctor explained in detail, Lord Plumer was so shocked that he had to sit in a chair to recover. He agreed to present himself later that day so that the first stage of the treatment could begin. The doctor left him to reflect on the consequences of his doomed romance with Betty Malahide. He was still basking in remorse when she came back into the room. Her manner had changed completely. Hands on hips, she was now angry and vindictive.

"I curse the day I ever met you, my lord!" she yelled.

"I am the victim here, you harlot!"

"I offered you my love and you infected me in return. The French disease is a poor reward for all the efforts I made in this very room to pleasure you."

"What are you saying, woman?" he demanded. "You are the villain here. While swearing that you were true to me, you grant favors to another and let him pass on his hideous infection. I caught it from you in turn."

"How can that be when no other man has touched me?"

"Do not lie to me, Betty."

"You are the liar, my lord," she accused. "This condition from which we both suffer was picked up by you between the thighs of some common whore. Admit it."

"I'll admit nothing of the sort," he said with righteous indignation. "Unlike you, I kept my vow of fidelity. In all the time that we were together, I never looked at another woman. I swear it, Betty! I'd take my Bible oath."

Betty Malahide could see that he was telling the truth. It put a malicious glint into her eye as she came forward to confront him. She produced a cold smile.

"What about your dear wife, my lord? Did you not sleep with her?"

He flicked a dismissive hand. "Ariana does not count."

"Oh, but she does. In view of what Doctor Cooper told us, I think that she counts for a great deal. *There* is the root of our trouble," she urged. "It's my Lady Plumer who is to blame for all this. Your wife infected you and you passed on the disease to me."

"Dear God!" he said, clutching at his throat. "Can this be so?"

"It is so, my lord. And that raises another question. Who gave it to her?"

Lord Plumer gulped. A day that had begun so well had ended in disaster.

Christopher Redmayne had never thought of his brother as a tactful man but he was proved wrong. When the two of them called on Lady Plumer, Henry was both suave and politic, passing on the information with a degree of charm and wording it in a way to upset her the least. Henry had recovered from his brush with her husband. Wearing his new suit, he looked as resplendent as ever but his serious manner counteracted the impression that he usually gave of being a decadent fop. Christopher also admired Lady Plumer's poise. She did not falter for a second.

"I am vaguely acquainted with Sir Beresford," she said, "and I'm sorry to hear that he was injured in a duel with my husband." Her voice hardened. "I'm even more sorry to learn that Roger disgraced himself by shooting a pistol in that way. Yet you tell me that Sir Beresford will recover?"

"Yes," said Henry. "My brother has just been to see him."

Christopher took over. "Sir Beresford was badly wounded but the surgeon managed to save him. What he needs now," he said, "is a period of rest. His wife has been a tower of strength to him. When he feared that he was about to die, he confessed his sins to her but she was a true Christian and forgave him, provided," he added, "that her husband did not go astray again."

It was a polite hint to Lady Plumer that the affair was over. In view of the trouble that it had caused, Sir Beresford Tyte was eager to abandon his relationship with her and, while he had not, in fact, confessed all to his wife, he had resolved to commit himself to a period of fidelity. Though she gave no hint of understanding what Christopher meant, Lady Plumer was, for her part, quite content. Since her husband had learned of her clandestine romance, it could not, in any case, continue.

She was grateful to the brothers for confiding in her. What they told her gave her a lever to use against her husband. Even someone as ruthless as Lord Plumer would not wish his friends to know that he had broken the unwritten laws of dueling so brazenly. Knowing the truth about what he did would purchase her freedom once more. Of the two brothers, she thought Christopher by far the more handsome and appealing but she sensed that he was too responsible to become involved with a married woman. She dismissed Henry as a possible lover because of his resemblance to Sir Beresford Tyte. In time, she would have to look elsewhere.

"I thank you both for this intelligence," she said, smiling at Christopher.

"We felt that you had a right to know," he replied, "even though Sir Beresford was only a distant acquaintance. But your husband must be warned, my lady. The duel was interrupted by two constables. Had they managed to apprehend my Lord Plumer, he would have been arraigned on a charge of attempted murder."

"Goodness!" she cried, secretly wishing that he had been.

"It might be better if he were to quit London for a while."

"I'll insist upon it, Mr Redmayne," she said. "When he returns home, I will have a great deal to say to Roger. The time has come for stern words."

"Do not be too harsh on him, my lady," said Henry, suppressing a grin.

"No," said Christopher. "You may find him in a weakened state."

Lord Plumer could not believe the severity of the cure. Stripped naked in the doctor's private chamber, he was forced to sit in a hot tub from which mercury vapor rose to invade his eyes and ears. It was agony but it was also the only known way to deal with venereal disease. If this first ordeal did not work, Doctor Cooper had warned him that he would have to endure isolation, semi-starvation, enemas, ointments and pills, each involving the hateful mercury. Lord Plumer felt as if he were being boiled alive. The worst of it was that he did not know whether to blame his wife, his mistress or himself. His dilemma was an impossible one. He could not challenge his wife without revealing that he had caught the disease, yet he could not sleep with her for fear of contracting the infection again. All that he could do was to grit his teeth and suffer.

"No!" he howled as the doctor added more mercury. "I am burning in Hell!"

Jonathan Bale had been so helpful that Christopher felt he deserved an explanation. They met at the architect's house in Fetter Lane, one of the few buildings that had escaped destruction from the fire. It was so much larger and more comfortable than his own house that it always made Bale slightly uneasy. Christopher told him about his brother's folly in agreeing to represent another man in a duel though he did not disclose Tyte's name or that of Lord Plumer. Bale's sense of duty pricked him.

"I should, by rights, arrest your brother and this false friend of his," he said.

"Leave them be, Jonathan. Thanks to your prompt arrival, the duel did not, in fact, take place. You prevented the crime. But you inadvertently set off another. Henry's opponent did not behave like a gentleman."

"Neither will I when I call him to account. Who is the rogue, Mr Redmayne?"

"A man who has been truly chastened."

"He deserves to be locked up in Newgate."

"Have no fear," said Christopher with a chuckle, "he has suffered worse than mere imprisonment. He has been deprived of his peace of mind."

Christopher did not dare to tell him how they had employed an actor to play the part of Doctor Cooper or paid Betty Malahide to collude with them. Lord Plumer had been given a fright and that was the object of the exercise.

"You talked about a comical revenge," recalled Bale.

"Yes, Jonathan. It's the title of a play by George Etherege."

"You know my opinion of playhouses. They are dens of sin and iniquity."

"They are also places of entertainment," said Christopher. "And they excite the mind as well. It was only because I once saw Mr Etherege's play that I was able to arrange this comical revenge. I look upon it as a fine piece of architecture."

Bale was mystified. "How is this play linked to the punishment that has been inflicted?" he asked, scratching his head.

"*The Comical Revenge* has a significant sub-title."

"Oh? And what might that be, Mr Redmayne?"

Christopher smiled to himself. "*The Tale of a Tub*," he said.

THE RADICAL DANDY

Although this is another new story, it can lay claim to being the oldest in the book. It was conceived in 1974 but, instead of writing it as a story, I turned it into a radio play that was broadcast by the BBC. Set in the 1820's, its protagonist is Ben Spiggott, a Bow Street Runner, whose slow, methodical approach to detective work always pays dividends. Over a ten-year period, Spiggott and his assistant, Joe Glindon, had many adventures in radio drama but this is their first appearance in short story form.

L ondon, 1824.

Ben Spiggott was surprised to see how many people had turned up to hear Sir Timothy Hatton speak. Though he arrived in Hyde Park early, Spiggott found himself standing several rows back from the platform. He was part of an exclusively male audience, made up of grateful workmen who had come to acknowledge their champion's role in securing the repeal of the iniquitous Combination Laws. Thanks to Sir Timothy Hatton, Member of Parliament, and to those politicians he persuaded to support him, working men were no longer shackled by legal restraint. They were now able to form unions and associations to protect themselves.

Spiggott was not a beneficiary of the new legislation. As a Bow Street Runner, he belonged to a small team of law enforcement officers who were united by their desire to fight crime, rather than by membership of a particular trade. For two quite different reasons; however, Spiggott had come to the meeting. Before he became a detective, he had worked in the printing trade and knew what it was like to be at the mercy of a tyrannical employer. His former colleagues would now have a means of fighting back against such exploitation. Spiggott still felt a kinship with the London compositors and wanted to enjoy their moment of celebration.

But what really took him to Hyde Park on that beautiful afternoon was simple curiosity. He wanted to see Sir Timothy Hatton, the radical dandy, a person who had all the advantages of high birth yet who dedicated himself to improving the lot

159

of the ordinary working man. Spiggott admired him for that. None of the people gathered there even had the right to vote in parliamentary elections, so Hatton was clearly not trying to increase his majority in the House of Commons by helping them. His satisfaction came from the removal of what he – and Ben Spiggott – saw as a rank injustice.

"That's him," said the man standing beside the Runner.

"Where?" asked Spiggott.

"Just about to step up onto the platform."

Spiggott had to stand on his toes to get his first glimpse of the hero of the hour. A solid man of medium height, Spiggott merged easily with the people around him. Until his change of career, he had been one of them and, when Sir Timothy Hatton appeared on the platform, he clapped as loudly as anyone. The speaker was one of a group of people but the others were invisible beside him. Hatton's nickname was an accurate one. The radical dandy was a reforming politician who dressed in the very best taste. Tall, slim, fair and strikingly handsome, he was a portrait of sheer elegance. Spiggott was especially taken with the way that he wore his top hat at a rakish angle.

The bearded man who came forward to introduce the speaker looked positively dowdy by comparison. He raised both hands to quell the ovation then waited as it slowly died away. A huge smile came through the black beard.

"Friends," he declared, "this is a great day for the working man. He has been set free from his chains. And who has been responsible for our liberation?" he went on, turning to their savior. "No one more so than Sir Timothy Hatton."

The cheers resounded again and partially muffled the sound of a pistol shot that suddenly rang out. Spiggott was close enough to hear it. He saw the man with the black beard emit a cry of pain, clutch his chest and fall to the floor. Spiggott craned his neck to pick out the person who had fired the shot but there was so much commotion around the platform that it was impossible to see what was going on. One thing was certain. Not everyone in the crowd approved of what the radical dandy had achieved.

Though he was almost half his age, Joe Glindon had difficulty in keeping up with his friend's brisk walk. As they made their way along Oxford Street, Spiggott gave his young colleague the salient details.

"His name was Aaron Peak," he said.

"Who was he?"

"The chairman of the committee that arranged the meeting. He stood up to introduce Sir Timothy Hatton, then someone shot him dead."

"Why?" asked Glindon. "What did the assassin have against this Aaron Peak?"

"Nothing, Joe."

"*Nothing?* You don't shoot someone for nothing, Ben."

"I don't believe that Mr Peak was the target," explained Spiggott. "He happened to get in the way. The assassin was really trying to kill Sir Timothy."

"How do you know?"

"I have this feeling."

Spiggott gave him an abbreviated account of what took place in Hyde Park and Glindon listened attentively. The young Runner was disappointed to hear that the assassin had got away in the confusion.

"Did nobody recognize the man?" he asked.

"No, Joe. One minute, he was there; the next, he'd disappeared into the crowd. I wish I'd been as tall as you. I might have spotted him then."

Glindon chuckled. "I may be taller and have longer legs, but you can still walk twice as fast as me. We ought to call you the Bow Street Racer."

"There's only one nickname that interests me," said Spiggott.

"What's that?"

"The radical dandy. Sir Timothy is a remarkable fellow. What he did will help thousands of working men up and down the country. He deserves to be kept alive."

"Are you sure that he's in danger?"

"Quite sure."

"How?"

"Because his wife has reached the same conclusion," said Spiggott. "That's why we're calling on Sir Timothy this morning. Lady Hatton wrote to ask for some protection for her husband. We may end up as his bodyguards."

"What sort of man is he, Ben?"

"A very brave one. The stand he took on this issue made him lots of enemies."

"And is he a real dandy?"

"He'd have put Beau Brummell to shame." Spiggott wagged a finger. "Be warned, Joe. When you stand beside Sir Timothy Hatton, you'll feel decidedly shabby."

"I always feel shabby," grumbled Glindon. "How can I afford to dress in style on the kind of money we earn? I'm no swell with private wealth."

"Nor is Sir Timothy."

"Then how does he pay his tailor's bills?"

"I suspect that he does what most men like him do. He runs up debts. He may be courageous politician but he's no saint. Sir Timothy inherited a lot of money then gambled most of it away. Then there are his election expenses," said Spiggott.

"The last time he went to the hustings, it cost him all of ten thousand pounds to win the seat."

"You seem to know a lot about him, Ben."

"I read the newspapers. He's often mentioned in them."

"So, he's brave, well-dressed and a gambler, is he?"

"Sir Timothy was also a ladies" man in his day."

"What else can you tell me about him?"

"He's lucky, Joe."

"Lucky?"

"Extremely lucky."

"Ah," said Glindon. "Because someone else was shot instead of him, you mean?"

"That was only one aspect of his good fortune," said Spiggott, quickening his pace. "Wait until you meet his wife. Lady Hatton is not only immensely rich. She has a reputation of being one of the most beautiful women in London."

Lucy Hatton's beautiful face was puckered with anxiety. During the few short months when she and her husband had been married, they had never had a mild disagreement, let alone a quarrel. He had been unfailingly kind, gentle and indulgent towards her. Being the wife of Sir Timothy Hatton had, until that moment, been an extended honeymoon. When she inadvertently provoked his anger, therefore, she was horrified.

"I had your best interests at heart, Timothy," she argued.

He was almost curt. "Why did you not tell me about this in advance?"

"Because I knew that you would have stopped me."

"Indeed, I would have," he said, sternly. "Can you not see how humiliating this is for me? You write a letter, behind my back, soliciting the protection of the Bow Street Runners. Am I some kind of weakling who cannot look after himself?"

"Someone tried to kill you at that meeting."

"And they may do so again, Lucy, but that will not deter me from my mission."

"I care only for saving my husband's life."

"Think more about his self-respect," he said, "for that's been badly damaged by this intemperate action of yours." Seeing the distress in her eyes, he softened. "I know that you *meant* well, my darling, but I cannot be seen in society with a body-guard trailing behind me. It would be demeaning."

"I worry about you, Timothy," she said. "You take such risks."

He smiled. "You were the one who took the greatest risk, Lucy," he pointed out. "You married me." Enfolding her in his arms, he gave her a conciliatory kiss. "Do you regret your folly now?"

"No! It was the most sensible thing I ever did in my life."

They were in the library of their town house in Grosvenor Square. Knowing that someone from Bow Street would be calling very soon, she had been forced to confess that she had made contact with the Runners on his behalf. Lady Hatton was relieved that his fury seemed to have spent itself. Locked in his embrace, she listened to his apology and to his protestation of love. Neither of them heard the ringing of the doorbell.

It was the butler who interrupted them. After tapping on the door of the library, he entered to tell them that two visitors had called. When he was told who they were, Hatton wanted to send them on their way but his wife persuaded him at least to see them. The Bow Street Runners were shown into the room and introductions were made. Spiggott was honored to meet the radical dandy face to face, but Glindon did not even spare him a glance. He was completely dazzled by Lucy Hatton.

"I fear that you have made a wasted journey," said Hatton, brusquely. "I do not require your protection or that of anyone else."

"I must beg to differ, Sir Timothy," said Spiggott, politely. "At the meeting in Hyde Park, you could easily have been shot dead."

"Why do you say that?"

"Because I was there."

Hatton was surprised. "For what purpose?"

"To acknowledge what you did, Sir Timothy. I had a trade once and I yearned to belong to an association that could advance our interests. Yet it was forbidden by law."

"But for my husband," said Lady Hatton, proudly, "it still would be."

"I appreciate that," said Spiggott. "It's the reason I'm so eager to offer assistance. Sir Timothy has provided some much-needed protection for the common man. Surely, he ought to be defended himself."

"Against what, Mr Spiggott?" demanded Hatton.

"Another attempt on your life."

"God forbid!" cried Lady Hatton.

"We'll look after him," said Glindon, finding his voice at last.

"You'll do nothing of the kind, Mr Glindon," said Hatton, sharply. "Nobody in the House of Commons is so well able to look after himself as I am. It's an insult to suggest that I must have two Bow Street Runners to act as my nursemaids. I'll none of your protection, gentlemen." He turned his back. "Good day to you, sirs!"

"At least, take a few simple precautions," advised Spiggott. "Never go out alone. Cut down on your appearances in public. Make sure that you are always among friends."

"Friends!" said Hatton, swinging round to face him again. "I can see that you are no politician, Mr Spiggott. Enter the House and you *have* no friends. Only political allies and sworn enemies. I long ago learned how to tell one from the other. As for the incident in Hyde Park," he continued, "it was very regrettable. Aaron Peak was a good man but he, too, aroused dislike. That is why he was shot."

"No," said his wife. "I'm sure that the bullet was meant for you."

"So am I, Lady Hatton," agreed Spiggott. "Mr Peak spends most of his time speaking on public platforms. An assassin would already have had endless opportunities to kill him. Why wait for that particular meeting? The answer is that Sir Timothy Hatton was the main speaker. He *had* to be the target."

"Then why did the bullet miss me?" asked Hatton.

"Because the man was a poor shot. That suggests he was unused to firing a pistol and would probably have bought it recently. When we leave here, Joe will visit all the gunsmiths in central London to see if any have sold a weapon in the past week or so."

"That will take me ages," complained Glindon.

"We must exhaust every possibility, Joe," said Spiggott. "The assassin was standing close to the platform. Several witnesses confirm that. From that distance, he should have been able to hit the right man."

"I believe that he did," asserted Hatton.

"And supposing that he did not, Sir Timothy?"

"I'll take my chances."

"Listen to what Mr Spiggott is saying," urged Lady Hatton. "Do not venture abroad so much. Stay here with me and you are perfectly safe."

He smiled at his wife. "Perfectly safe and sublimely happy, my darling."

"Who would not be?" thought Glindon, still goggling at her.

"Come, Joe," decided Spiggott. "We are trespassing on Sir Timothy's privacy. Since we cannot force him to engage us as bodyguards, we'll try to solve the murder of Aaron Peak and capture the assassin that way." He looked at Lady Hatton. "Please excuse us. We came with the very best of intentions."

"What will happen if you do *not* catch this villain?" she asked.

Spiggott gave a shrug. "He'll be back, Lady Hatton," he said, bluntly. "I have absolutely no doubt about that."

The Turk's Head was a large tavern in Clerkenwell, frequented by working men from the area. It was known for the warmth of its hospitality and the quality of its beer. Mother Gudgeon was largely responsible for both. Her husband might be the licensee but it was she who helped to create the welcoming atmosphere. A big, bosomy, effervescent woman in her fifties, Mother Gudgeon knew the names of all their regular customers. When a new face drifted into her bar, she was just as friendly and considerate.

"Welcome to the Turk's Head, sir," she said.

"Beer," grunted the man, eyeing the barrels on the counter.

"The first drink is always on the house for a new customer." She reached for a tankard and started to fill it. "Are you from round these parts, sir?"

"No," he said.

"Then you'll have not heard how wonderful our beer is. You'll find none better."

"I'll judge for myself."

As the beer rose slowly in the tankard, Mother Gudgeon glanced at her visitor. He was a broad-shouldered man in his forties with a broken nose and unkempt hair. But it was his ear that caught her attention. It was swollen to three times its normal size and looked quite raw. Turning off the tap, she put the drink on the counter.

"There you are, sir," she said. "I hope that you enjoy it."

"I will." He took a first sip and nodded his approval. "It's good."

"You'll have to pay for the next pint, mark you."

"It'll be worth it." He looked around the bar. "Nice, big room you have here."

"We've an even bigger one upstairs," she boasted, "and we let it out for meetings and dinners. We're to have haristocracy under our roof soon, you know."

"Are you?"

"Yes, Sir Timothy Hatton will be dining here. Just think of that. A man of his standing is coming to eat a meal that's been cooked in my kitchen. That will be a real feather in our cap." She cackled loudly. "We'll be having royalty next!"

"So the room upstairs is bigger, is it?" he said, clearly interested.

"Almost twice the size of the bar."

He took another swig of beer. "Can I see it?"

Ben Spiggott had been to Newmarket racecourse many times but not to watch the races. He had either been employed as a bodyguard or been retained to arrest some of the pickpockets who descended on the various meetings. On this occasion, he was keeping a friendly eye on Sir Timothy Hatton and his wife. The radical dandy might spurn his aid but Lady Hatton did not. Concerned for her husband's safety, she had written to tell the Bow Street Runner that they were venturing out that afternoon to Newmarket. It was enough to encourage Spiggott to visit the racecourse himself.

He soon found them. They were standing near the paddock as the horses for the next races were being paraded. Hatton was at his most elegant and his wife at her most decorous. They seemed relaxed and happy but Spiggott knew how anxious Lady Hatton must be feeling. From time to time, she glanced nervously over her shoulder. There was, however, no apparent danger. Hatton and his wife chatted quietly until they were joined by a tall, angular, well-dressed individual in his early thirties. Spiggott was too far away to hear what was being said but he sensed an immediate tension among the trio. Though the newcomer was smiling politely, he had obviously said something to upset the couple.

Wanting to know who the man was, Spiggott realized that he had a means of doing so. He had already noticed Ascot Mary, a woman he had arrested on more than one occasion at race meetings. Working with a male accomplice, she mingled easily with the titled and wealthy by wearing the right apparel and adopting the correct voice. Nobody seeing the attractive young woman for the first time would suspect that she was an expert pickpocket. When she came into view again, Spiggott strolled across to her. Ascot Mary nudged her companion and he slipped quickly away.

"Good afternoon, Mr Spiggott," she said, warily.

"I've not come to arrest you this time, Mary," he reassured her with a friendly grin. "I need your help."

"How can I help you?"

"By identifying someone. You spend all your life at racecourses – when you are not cooling your heels in a prison cell, that is." She glared at him. "You always know where the richest pickings are. It's part of your stock-in-trade."

"So?"

"Tell me who that man is over there," he said, pointing towards the paddock. "The one talking with Sir Timothy and Lady Hatton."

She curled a lip. "Oh, *him*," she replied. "That's Lord Egerton Wykes."

"How well do you know him?"

"Well enough to keep clear of him, Mr Spiggott. He's a dreadful man. Lord Egerton knows every gaming house and haunt of vice in London. When he has money, he loses it straight away at the card table. When he borrows it, he never repays it."

Spiggott smiled. "I can see that he's of little use to you, Mary."

"Why dip my hand into an empty pocket?"

He looked across at them again. The two men seemed to be having an argument.

"Sir Timothy does not like the fellow, I think," observed Spiggott.

"He did at one time," she said. "They were birds of a feather. He and Lord Egerton were the best of friends then. They were never apart."

"Why did they fall out?"

"Sir Timothy got married."

"Ah, so Lord Egerton lost his boon companion."

"I feel sorry for Lady Hatton. Poor woman! She deserves better." Mary looked around. "But where's Joe Glindon today? You and he always work together."

"Joe is otherwise engaged, Mary."

"Doing what?"

"Searching for a pistol."

Joe Glindon had called on eight gunsmiths before he found one who was in any way helpful. Most of the others had shown no interest in him when they realized that he was not there to buy anything. Two of them had been openly hostile. Augustus Northcott was the exception to the rule. He was actively cooperative. A small, wizened, hunched man in his fifties, he was bent over his workbench when the Runner came into the shop, cleaning a Ferguson rifle with loving care. Glindon explained the reason for his visit.

"In the last couple of weeks," said Northcott, "I've sold two percussion pistols and a Forsyth sporting gun, but they all went to reputable customers. There's no question of any of those weapons being used to murder someone."

"In other words," said Glindon, wearily, "you're unable to help me."

"Wait a moment, my young friend. I did not say that."

"Oh?"

"You've not heard about the strange cove who was in here some days ago."

"A strange cove?"

"Yes," said Northcott, rubbing his chin. "An ugly devil, he was. I'd not care to meet *him* in a dark alley, I can tell you that."

"Did he buy a pistol?"

"No, he brought one in so that I could sell him gunpowder for it. A fine weapon, it was. Far too good for the likes of that fellow. It was a percussion pistol with a plated turn-off barrel and a walnut stock inlaid with silver." He heaved a sigh. "I offered to buy it off him but he refused."

"I suppose that he wanted bullets as well."

"No, Mr Glindon. That was the other odd thing."

"What was?"

"He already had a supply of ammunition. He showed it to me. It was made in private bullet moulds. Do you see what I mean?" he asked. "Where would a man like that get hold of such a magnificent pistol and such a ready supply of ammunition?"

"Did he seem to know much about guns?"

Northcott laughed. "I think he knew which end was the more dangerous, but that's about all. I had to show him how to put in the gunpowder. No, Mr Glindon," he went on. "He was a rum individual and no mistake. A little frightening as well. To be honest, I was grateful when he went out of my shop."

By prior arrangement, they met that evening at the Black Swan, a small but popular tavern in Coleman Street. Spiggott told him what had transpired at Newmarket.

"Ascot Mary asked after me?" said Glindon, touched that she had remembered him. "I had a feeling that she liked me."

"Only because you let her off with a warning at Epsom last year."

"Some of those swells can afford to have their pockets picked."

"It's still a crime," noted Spiggott. "For once, thank goodness, I did not have to arrest Mary. What she told me was very useful. Mary moves in exalted circles and she certainly knows how to pick up gossip."

"What else did she tell you?"

"That Sir Timothy was not the only suitor of Lady Hatton. Unknown to him, he had a serious rival – Lord Egerton Wykes."

"Is he a politician as well?"

"Hardly, Joe! His only concern is for himself."

Glindon was cynical. "Then he's well suited to a life in politics."

"He's far too lazy to get involved," said Spiggott. "But how did you get on?"

"It was an ordeal, Ben. While you were enjoying yourself at the races, I was tramping around the gunsmiths of London. They were a grim bunch. Only one of them actually tried to help me."

"Oh? Who was he?"

Glindon told him about the visit to Augustus Northcott and described the man who had come into the shop to buy gunpowder. Spiggott snapped his fingers.

"It could be our man, Joe!" he announced. "The witnesses in Hyde Park only had a fleeting glimpse of the man but they all mentioned the broken nose and the swollen ear. That narrows the field at once."

"Does it?" asked Glindon.

"Of course. A man with those mementoes has seen action somewhere. He's either served in the army at some time – though, if he did," he continued, thinking it through, "he'd know something about firearms. That leaves one other possibility."

"He was a pugilist."

"Exactly. The wonderful Pierce Egan can help us there. Go through copies of his *Boxiana* and see if you can pick out our man. There'll be no shortage of broken noses and thick ears but there are other features to look for as well," he warned. "The witnesses at that meeting said the same as your gunsmith. The man was in his forties. That means he'll have deserted the ring years ago. You may have to dig back a long way."

"I'll find him, Ben."

"I'm sure that you will," said Spiggott, confidently. "The fellow may not be able to fire a gun properly but I'll wager that he'll know how to use his fists."

Stripped to the waist, the two men circled each other in the ring before beginning to spar. Their bare knuckles had been pickled to harden them and their faces were still bruised from earlier contests. The aristocrat who was watching them leaned against a wall with his hat tipped forward over his forehead. He did not notice the thickset man with the broken nose and the swollen ear who came into the boxing academy. Sidling up to his employer, the newcomer's manner became obsequious.

"I did as you told me, my lord," he said. "I've been to the Turk's Head."

"And?"

"He dines there tomorrow."

"Did you see the room itself?"

"Yes, my lord. It's upstairs. It will hold sixty people at least."

"Upstairs?" said the other. "I like not the sound of that. How will you escape?"

"Through a window. I'll drop to the yard and be away in seconds."

"*After* you've killed him."

"Yes, my lord."

"I want no mistakes this time, Nat."

"I've been practicing every day."

"Make sure you hit the right man." He slipped a hand inside his coat and extracted a letter. "First, deliver this to Grosvenor Square," he ordered, handing it over, "and do it discreetly. I need a guarantee of his presence. When he reads this," he added with a thin smile, "Sir Timothy will insist on being at the Turk's Head tomorrow."

Spiggott was just about to leave the office in Bow Street when he had an unexpected visitor. A carriage drew up outside and Lady Hatton opened the door. The Runner moved forward to offer his hand to help her alight. She thanked him with a smile.

"Sir Henry Longfoot is not here, I fear," he said.

"It was you I came to see, Mr Spiggott, and not the Chief Magistrate."

"Then you caught me just in time, Lady Hatton. Shall we go inside?"

He escorted her into the building and along a corridor. After leading her into an empty room, Spiggott closed the door behind them. He could see how agitated she was. Her face was pale and drawn, and her hands played nervously. When he offered her a seat, she shook her head.

"This is not a social visit, Mr Spiggott," she said. "I need your help."

"It is yours for the asking, Lady Hatton."

"Please stop my husband from leaving the house this evening."

"Why should I do that?" wondered Spiggott.

"Because he is due to speak at a dinner in his honor," she explained. "It's at a tavern in Clerkenwell called the Turk's Head."

"I know the place."

"He must, at all costs, be kept away from there."

"For what reason, Lady Hatton?"

"My husband received a threatening letter," she said. "It warned him to stay away from the Turk's Head. I've no idea who sent it but it only made my husband more determined to attend the dinner."

"Did the letter say *why* he should stay away?"

"No, Mr Spiggott. It was just a blunt warning. Unsigned, of course."

"And neither of you recognized the handwriting?"

"Alas, no," she replied. "I have to confess that it's not the first time that letters of this kind have been delivered to our house. The name of Sir Timothy Hatton is not universally popular. Ordinarily, my husband simply ignores them. This time, in view of what happened in Hyde Park, I think he should take the threat seriously."

"So do I, Lady Hatton."

"Could you and Mr Glindon go to the Turk's Head to protect him?"

"Oh," said Spiggott, pensively, "we'll do more than that. A lot more." He ran a hand across his chin. "May I speak frankly, Lady Hatton?"

"Of course."

"I understand that you know a certain Lord Egerton Wykes."

"Why, yes. He was a close friend of my husband's."

"I believe that he was also well acquainted with you," he said, tactfully.

She blushed visibly. "What on earth do you mean?"

"You are a very attractive women, Lady Hatton. You must have had many suitors in your time. I had the impression that Lord Egerton might conceivably have been one of them."

"That's vicious tittle-tattle," she said with vehemence. "I'm disappointed in you, Mr Spiggott. I took you for a decent man, not someone who pays attention to such baseless scandal."

"Scandal?"

"Come, sir. You know what I am talking about. You have read that scurrilous periodical, *Ferrers' Magazine*. That is where my name was linked with Lord Egerton. It was a vile attack on me and on my character. My husband was livid when he saw it. Unlike you, he did not believe the foul insinuations about me."

"Neither do I, Lady Hatton," said Spiggott with an apologetic gesture. "I've never even heard of this magazine. It's shameful that anyone should libel you in this way. Do you know who wrote the article?"

"No," she replied, "but it was deeply hurtful."

"Can you not take legal action against the publishers?"

"That would only draw more attention to the lies that were spread about me. I prefer to forget the whole thing, Mr Spiggott. To that end," she emphasized, moving to the door, "I'd be grateful if you never mentioned the name of Lord Egerton Wykes to me ever again. Good day to you."

And before he could stop her, she flounced out of the room and shut the door behind her. Spiggott was baffled. He was annoyed with himself for catching her on such a sensitive spot but he was not entirely persuaded by her denials. He suspected that the man he had seen in their company at Newmarket had a closer relationship with her than Lady Hatton was prepared to admit. Spiggott was still reflecting on the interview when Joe Glindon let himself into the room. His eyes were glazed and he was beaming.

"She touched me!" he said with delight. "I was just walking along the corridor when Lady Hatton bumped into me. She seemed to be in a hurry." He inhaled deeply. "I can still smell that wonderful perfume of hers."

"I fear that I may have upset her."

"What? You upset a gorgeous creature like that?"

"Quite by accident."

Spiggott told him about the conversation with Lady Hatton and how she had flared up at the mention of another man. Glindon chided him for wounding her feelings then returned to the threatening letter.

"What are we going to do about it, Ben?"

"Take it very seriously."

"But you were at Newmarket with Sir Timothy the other day and there was no sign of danger to him. If someone wanted to kill him, they had the perfect opportunity."

"No," said Spiggott. "He is not in peril at a social event like a race meeting. Sir Timothy is only at risk in a political setting. Somebody wishes to make a point by assassinating him in front of his supporters. That first attempt was in Hyde Park, when he was on a platform before an adoring crowd. The next attempt will be made at the Turk's Head when he is making another political speech."

"What are we going to do?"

"I'll come to that in a moment, Joe. First, tell me what you've discovered."

"More than I dared to expect."

"You have a name?"

"Two of them, Ben."

"Who was the man who shot Aaron Peak?"

"My guess is that it was Nat Pusey," said Glindon. "A fearsome looking cove with a good record in the ring. There was a full account of his career in *Boxiana*. The illustration showed him fifteen or twenty years ago, but Augustus Northcott was still able to identify him. The gunsmith will swear that it was Nat Pusey who bought that gunpowder from him."

"Excellent!" said Spiggott. "But you mentioned two names."

"Yes, Ben. I managed to find out the name of Nat Pusey's former patron."

"Well?"

"It was Lord Egerton Wykes."

Nat Pusey resolved to earn his money this time. There was no possibility of error. He had spent the whole morning, firing the pistol in a shooting gallery, and his accuracy had steadily improved. He told himself that he was not to blame for what happened in Hyde Park. Someone must have jostled him as he pulled the trigger. That was the reason that Sir Timothy Hatton has escaped the bullet. The radical dandy would not be so fortunate a second time. The threatening letter had been sent in the certain knowledge that he would defy its warning. Nat Pusey would be able to have another shot at him.

He was circumspect. To make sure that nobody recognized him, he wore a large hat that helped to conceal his telltale ear. As he sat in the bar at the Turk's Head, guests for the dinner began to arrive and troop upstairs. Pusey was not going to join them until the crucial moment. Thanks to Mother Gudgeon, he knew that the upstairs room could be reached by the backstairs from the kitchen as well as by the main staircase. Once inside the room, he had only to fire one shot before escaping through the window. Nobody would impede him. They would all be sitting at their tables with too much beer and food inside them. Pusey could not possibly be caught.

Ordering another pint, he stayed in his corner and bided his time. Over sixty guests were dining in the upstairs room and they were making enough noise for him to hear what was going on. It was towards the end of the evening that he heard thunderous applause. That was his cue. Sir Timothy Hatton was about to speak. Pusey was off at once, slipping through a door at the rear of the bar so that he could climb up the backstairs. When he reached the top, he took out the pistol, cocked it then took a deep breath. His chance to redeem himself had finally come.

Opening the door slowly, the assassin peered through the pipe smoke at the radical dandy. Dressed in his finery, Sir Timothy Hatton was still acknowledging the cheers of his friends. Pusey moved swiftly. Taking a few steps into the room, he leveled the pistol at his target. Before he could fire, however, a warning cry was heard.

"Look out, Joe!" yelled Spiggott.

Distracted for a moment, Pusey discharged the bullet with a loud report but the radical dandy had already taken evasive action. He dived to his left. Instead of killing the man, the assassin had merely grazed his arm. There was worse to come. When he tried to make his escape, Pusey found that the window was locked. As he struggled to open it, he was suddenly hit from behind by a relay of punches. Spiggott was a strong man and, with the advantage of surprise, he soon overpowered the would-be assassin. Willing hands came to his assistance. Nat Pusey was captured.

When the radical dandy strolled across to him, he saw that it was not Sir Timothy Hatton at all. It was a man he had never even met before. Joe Glindon pointed to the tear in his sleeve that had been made by the bullet.

"Sir Timothy will make you pay for this," said Glindon with a chuckle. "You've ruined his best coat."

Lord Egerton Wykes was enjoying a glass of port in his drawing room when he heard the visitor arrive. Expecting to be told that Nat Pusey had done his bidding, he was disconcerted when a stranger was shown in.

"Who are you?" he demanded.

"My name is Ben Spiggott, my lord," said the newcomer, "and I'm employed as a Bow Street Runner. I've come to arrest you on a charge of conspiracy to murder Sir Timothy Hatton."

Wykes was on his feet. "That's a preposterous allegation!"

"It's one that your confederate, Nat Pusey, is happy enough to make. He's in custody. I had the pleasure of arresting him myself. Oh, and by the way," added Spiggott, "I should perhaps tell you that Sir Timothy is unharmed. Nat Pusey failed to kill him for the second time."

"I've no idea what you are talking about Mr Spiggott."

"There was an article in *Ferrers' Magazine*, my lord."

"So?"

"You wrote it," accused Spiggott. "When I saw how much it had distressed

Lady Hatton, I called on the proprietor of the magazine. He was obstinate at first but he was more than ready to volunteer your name when I suggested that you might be involved in a plot to murder Sir Timothy."

"I deny it wholeheartedly."

"Nat Pusey has incriminated you, my lord."

"You accept the word of a brainless pugilist?"

"There's ample proof that you employed him. When he was in the ring, you were his patron and made a lot of money out of his brute strength. Pusey was your creature. He would do anything for you, even kill someone at your behest. That's why you loaned him the pistol, was it not?"

"I loaned him nothing."

"Then you will not mind letting me see your bullet moulds," said Spiggott, taking a bullet from his pocket. "This was part of the ammunition taken from Pusey when he was overpowered. If it fits your bullet mould, my lord, then you are guilty."

Wykes shifted his feet uneasily. "There must be some mistake," he blustered. "I gave that pistol to Pusey so that he could shoot rabbits. The last thing I'd instruct him to do is to kill a dear friend of mine."

"A dear friend and hated rival."

"Sir Timothy and I love each other."

"You did so until he married the woman you coveted yourself," said Spiggott, watching his reaction. "That was why you traduced her in that shameless article. You wanted revenge. You not only claimed that Lady Hatton was liberal with her favors, you also wrote that she was once secretly engaged to you."

"And so she should have been!" asserted Wykes. "Lucy was mine."

"I think that she chose a much better man, my lord. And so does Lady Hatton. When he saw the lies that you were peddling about her, he did what any husband would do in the circumstances. He defended his wife's honor."

"Timothy is too impulsive."

"Not as impulsive as you, I fancy. That article was your death warrant, my lord. Sir Timothy challenged you to a duel." He raised a hand to silence the protest that rose to the other man's lips. "Do not lie about that as well. Sir Timothy has admitted it. I forced him to do so by warning him that I'd arrest him if the duel took place. It's against the law." He took a step closer to Wykes. "So is murder."

"I had no *reason* to want him dead," pleaded the other.

"You had the best reason of all – the wish to stay alive. Sir Timothy is an expert marksman. If a duel took place, he would surely kill you." Wykes's shoulders sagged. "What you devised was a clever plan to throw suspicion off you. If he was assassinated at a political gathering, everyone would think that one of his opponents was behind it, and not the man who was once his best friend. For a while, I was fooled myself."

Lord Egerton Wykes glared at him. Spiggott knew far too much. There was no way that he could shake off the Runner by a string of denials. Pretending to accept the charges against him, he gave a hopeless shrug and lowered his head in shame. Without warning, he then pushed Spiggott violently backwards and ran to the door, hoping to get to the room where he kept his firearms. But the Runner had not come alone. Still wearing his ostentatious attire, Joe Glindon was waiting in the hall to grab him. As the fugitive grappled with him, Glindon struck him on the jaw and sent him reeling to the floor. Wykes looked up at him in dismay.

"Is that you, Timothy?" he asked.

"No, my lord," said Spiggott, coming out of the drawing room. "Allow me to introduce my colleague, Joe Glindon of the Bow Street Runners. We have our own radical dandy, you see."

SLAUGHTER IN THE STRAND

Throughout my life, public libraries have been of immense help to me so I tend to hold librarians in high regard. When I wanted a hero for this tale, therefore, I turned to an obscure and impecunious librarian. It is 1912 and Herbert Syme, a harmless and self-effacing man, is about to fulfil a lifetime's ambition. After years of handling other people's books at the library, he has written one of his own, a mystery set in his native Derbyshire. He heads for London with dreams of fame and fortune but he reckons without the interference of the publisher. Edmund T. Roehampton insists that certain changes are made to Syme's novel and the latter agrees at first. Then he gets a cruel introduction to the awesome power of the publisher.

England, 1912

Herbert Syme had never traveled in a First Class carriage before but nothing else would suffice. It was, in a sense, the most important day of his life and it deserved to be marked by the unaccustomed display of extravagance. Impecunious librarians like Herbert were never allowed to pose as First Class passengers on a train to London. Indeed, they could hardly afford to travel by rail at all on a regular basis. Herbert always rode the six miles to work on his ancient bicycle, weaving past the countless pot holes, cursing his way up steep hills, hoping that the rain would hold off and that no fierce dogs would give chase. Today, it was different. Instead of arriving at the library, breathless, soaked to the skin and, not infrequently, with the legs of his trousers expertly shredded by canine teeth, he was sitting in a luxurious compartment among the elite of society.

The fact that he was an outsider made it even more exhilarating. Habitual denizens of the privileged area were less than welcoming. They saw Herbert Syme for what he really was, a tall, slim, stooping man in his forties with a shabby suit and a self-effacing manner. The whiff of failure was unmistakable. What was this interloper doing in their midst? Murmurs of resentment buzzed in Herbert's ears. The rustling of newspapers was another audible display of class warfare. They were professional men and he was trespassing on their territory. They wanted him out. The elderly lady in the compartment was more vocal in her criticism. After repeatedly clicking her tongue in disapproval, she had the temerity to ask Herbert if he possessed the appropriate ticket.

The librarian withstood it all without a tremor. While his companions took refuge behind their copies of *The Times*, Herbert took out the letter that had transformed his dull existence. It was short and businesslike but that did not lessen its impact. He read the words again, fired anew by their implication.

> *Dear Mr Syme,*
>
> *Thank you for submitting your novel to us. It has found favor with all who have read the book. Subject to certain changes, we will consider publishing it. To that end, we request that you come to this office on Wednesday, May 16th at 3 p.m. precisely to discuss the matter with Mr Roehampton. Please confirm that you are able to attend at this time.*
>
> Yours sincerely,
> Miss Lavinia Finch (Secretary)

There it was – his passport to fame and fortune. Other passengers might be going on routine visits to the capital but Herbert Syme was most certainly not. Thanks to the letter from Roehampton and Buckley Ltd., he was in transit between misery and joy. Long years of toil and derision lay behind him. Success had at last beckoned. Putting the magical missive into his pocket, he reflected on its contents. His novel had found favor at a prestigious publishing house. Instead of spending his days stacking the work of other writers on the shelves of his branch library, he would take his place alongside them as an equal. Herbert Syme would be read, admired and envied. Everyone's perception of him would alter dramatically. Publication was truly a form of rebirth.

"May I see your ticket, please, sir?"

"What?" Herbert came out of his reverie to find the uniformed ticket inspector standing over him. "Oh, yes. Of course."

Newspapers were lowered and each pair of eyes was trained on Herbert as he extracted his ticket and offered it to the inspector. Everyone in the compartment wanted him to be forcibly ejected. They longed for his humiliation. To their utter disgust, the inspector clipped the ticket and handed it back politely to its owner.

"Thank you, sir," he said.

Herbert was elated by the man's deference. It was something to which he would swiftly adjust. From now on, it would be a case of First Class all the way.

The sheer size, noise and bustle of London were overwhelming at first. Herbert had never seen so many people or so much traffic. Garish advertisements competed for his attention on walls, passing vehicles and in shop windows. It was bewildering. Crossing the Strand was an ordeal in itself, the long thoroughfare positively swarming with automobiles, omnibuses, lorries, horses and carts, mounted policemen, rattling handcarts, stray dogs, hurtling cyclists and darting pedestrians. When he eventually got to the correct side of the road, Herbert took a deep breath to compose himself. He needed to be at his most assured for the critical interview with Edmund T. Roehampton. The fact that he would be dealing with one of the partners in the firm, and not with a mere underling, augured well. His novel would finally see the light of day – *subject to a certain changes*. Whatever those changes might be, Herbert vowed that he would willingly agree to them. A publisher was entitled to make minor adjustments and add refinements.

When he located the premises of Roehampton and Buckley, Ltd., he met with his first disappointment. Such a leading publishing house, he assumed, would have palatial offices that signaled its lofty position. Instead, it appeared to operate out of three rooms above a shoe shop. Mindful of the request for punctuality, Herbert checked his pocket watch, cleared his throat, rehearsed his greeting to Mr Roehampton and climbed the stairs. When he entered the outer office, he heard Big Ben booming in the distance. A second disappointment awaited.

The middle-aged woman seated at the desk looked over her pince-nez at him. "May I help you, sir?" she said.

"Er, yes," he replied, finding that his collar was suddenly too tight for him. "I have an appointment with Mr Roehampton at three o-clock."

"What name might that be, sir?"

"Syme. Herbert Syme." His confidence returned. "I'm an author."

"Ah, yes," she said, her tone softening. "Mr Syme. I remember now. I'm Miss Finch. It was I who wrote to you to arrange the appointment. Welcome to London, Mr Syme. Mr Roehampton will deal with you as soon as he returns from his luncheon."

"Luncheon?"

"He and Mr Buckley always eat at their club on a Wednesday."

"I see."

"Do take a seat. Mr Roehampton will be back within the hour."

Within the hour! So much for punctuality. It had taken Herbert all morning simply to reach London. To arrive in the Strand at the stipulated time had required a huge effort on the part of the provincial author. During the wayward journey from the station to the offices of Roehampton and Buckley, Ltd., his provincialism had been cruelly exposed. His instincts were blunted, his accent jarred, his lack of sophistication was excruciating. He was made to feel like a country mouse in a metropolitan jungle. All that would soon vanish, he reminded himself. He was going to be a published author. As he sank down on the chair beside the door, he consoled himself with the fact that that he had made it to the top of Mount Olympus, albeit situated above a shoe shop in the Strand. It was only right that a mortal should await the arrival of Zeus from his luncheon.

Miss Lavinia Finch offered little decorative interest to the observer. A spare, severe woman of almost exotic ugliness, she busied herself at her typewriter, striking the keys with a random brutality that made the machine groan in pain. She ignored the visitor completely. Herbert did not mind. His gaze was fixed on the oak bookcase that ran from floor to ceiling behind the secretary. The firm's output was stacked with a neatness that gladdened the heart of a librarian. He feasted his eyes on the impressive array of volumes, thrilled that he would be joining them in time and deciding that he, too, when funds permitted, would acquire just such a bookcase in which to exhibit his work. Herbert was so caught up in his contemplation of literature that he did not notice how swiftly an hour passed. The chimes of Big Ben were still reverberating when Edmund T. Roehampton breezed in through the door.

A third disappointment jerked Herbert to his feet. Expecting the Zeus of the publishing world to be a huge man with a commanding presence, he was surprised to see a dapper figure strutting into the room. Roehampton was a self-appointed dandy but the fashionable attire, the dazzling waistcoat and the gleaming shoes could not disguise the fact that he was a small man with a large paunch and a face like a whiskered donkey. Seeing his visitor, he doffed his top hat, pulled the cigar from between his teeth and manufactured a cold smile.

"Ah!" he declared. "You must be Syme."

"That's right, sir. Herbert Syme. The author of —"

"Well, don't just stand there, man," continued Roehampton, interrupting him. "Come into my office. We must talk. Crucial decisions have to be made." He opened the door to his inner sanctum and paused. "Any calls, Miss Finch?"

"None, Mr Roehampton," she said.

"Good."

"But you do have an appointment at four-thirty with Mr Agnew."

"Syme and I will be through by then."

He went into his office and Herbert followed him, uncertain whether to be reassured or alarmed by the news that a bare half-an-hour had been allotted to him. Had he come so far to be given such short shrift? Roehampton waved him to a seat, put his top hat on a peg then took the leather-backed chair behind the desk. Raised up on a dais, it made him seem much bigger than he was. Herbert relaxed. The office was much more like the place he had envisaged. Large and well appointed, it had serried ranks of books on display as well as framed sepia photographs of the firm's major authors. Herbert wondered how long it would be before his own portrait graced the William Morris wallpaper.

Roehampton drew on his cigar and studied Herbert carefully.

"How is Yorkshire?" he asked abruptly.

Herbert was thrown. "Yorkshire, sir?"

"That's where you come from, isn't it?"

"No, Mr Roehampton. Derbyshire. I come from Derbyshire."

"I knew it up was up there somewhere," said the other dismissively, opening a drawer to take out a manuscript. He slapped it down on the desk. "Well, Syme, here it is. Your novel."

"I'm so grateful that you are prepared to publish it, Mr Roehampton."

"Subject to a certain changes."

"Yes, yes. Of course," agreed Herbert. "Anything you say."

"Then let's get down to brass tacks," said the publisher, exhaling a cloud of acrid smoke. "Interesting plot. Well drawn characters. Good dialogue. A novel with pace." He gave a complimentary nod. "You're a born writer, Syme."

Herbert swelled with pride. "Thank you, sir."

"But you still need to be weaned."

"I await your suggestions, Mr Roehampton."

"Oh, they're not suggestions," warned the other. "They're essential improvements. Mr Buckley and I could never put our names on a book with which we were not entirely and unreservedly satisfied."

"And what does Mr Buckley think of *Murder in Matlock*?" wondered Herbert. "Your letter said that it had found favor with all who had read it."

"Yes. With Miss Finch and with myself. We are your audience." He heaved a sigh. "Mr Buckley, alas, is not a reader. The perusal of the luncheon menu at our club is all that he can manage in the way of sustained reading. What he brings to the firm is money and business acumen. What I bring," he added, thrusting a thumb into his waistcoat pocket, "is true literary expertise and a knack of unearthing new talent."

"I'm delighted to included in that new talent, Mr Roehampton."

"We shall see, Syme. We shall see. Now, to business." He consulted the notes written on the title page of the manuscript. "Omissions," he announced. "Let us first deal with your omissions."

Herbert was baffled. "I was not aware that I'd omitted anything."

"Yours, sir, is a novel of sensation."

"I see it more as a searching exploration of the nature of evil."

"It amounts to the same thing, man. *Murder in Matlock* inhabits the world of crime and that imposes certain demands upon an author."

"Such as?"

"To begin with, you must have a Sinister Oriental. A murder story is untrue to its nature if it does not have at least one – and preferably more than one – Sinister Oriental."

"But there are no orientals, sinister or otherwise, in Matlock."

"Invent some, man," said Roehampton with exasperation. "Import some. Bring in a Chinese army of occupation, if need be."

"That would upset the balance of the narrative."

"It will help to sell the book and that is all that concerns me."

Herbert was deflated. "If you say so, Mr Roehampton."

"As to your villain, his name must be changed."

"Why? What's wrong with Lionel Jagg?"

"Far too English," explained the publisher. "We need a wicked foreigner. Do you know why Wilkie Collins chose to christen the villain of *The Woman in White* with an Italian name? It was because he felt no Englishman capable of the skullduggery to which Count Fosco sank. I applaud the thinking behind that decision, Syme. Follow suit. Lionel Jagg commits crimes far too horrible for any true-born Englishman even to contemplate. Henceforth, he will be Count Orsini."

"An Italian count in Matlock?" wailed Herbert. "It's unheard of."

"Anything can happen in Yorkshire."

"Derbyshire, Mr Roehampton. Derbyshire."

"Yorkshire or Derbyshire. Both are equally barbarous places."

"That's unjust."

"Let us move on. Criminals must be exposed early on to the reader. Lionel Jagg concealed his villainy too well. Count Orsini must be more blatant. Equip him with a limp and one eye. They are clear indications of villainy. A hare lip is also useful in this context. And he needs an accomplice, just as evil as himself."

"Not another Sinister Oriental, surely?"

"No, no. Don't overplay that hand. A Wily Pathan will fit the bill here."

Herbert was aghast. "Wily Pathans in *Derbyshire*?"

"Metaphorically speaking, they are everywhere. They are the bane of the British Empire and we must remind our readers of that fact. Now, sir, to the most frightful omission of all. A hero. Your novel must have a Great Detective."

"But it has one, Mr Roehampton. Inspector Ned Lubbock."

"Wrong name, wrong character, wrong nationality," insisted the publisher, stubbing out his cigar in the ashtray with decisive force. "Lubbock is nothing but a country bumpkin from Derbyshire."

"Yorkshire," corrected the other.

"There – I *knew* the novel was set in Yorkshire!"

"In Derbyshire. Inspector Lubbock is a Yorkshireman, working in Matlock. I thought I made that abundantly clear."

"What's abundantly clear to me, Syme, is that you need to be more aware of the market you are hoping to reach. The common reader does not want a bumbling detective from a remote northern fastness. He expects style, charm and intellectual brilliance, In short, sir, the Great Detective must be French."

"Why?" groaned Herbert.

"Because there is a tradition to maintain," asserted the other. "Vidocq, Eugene Sue, Gaboriau. They all had French detectives and not simply because they themselves hailed from France. Consider the case of Edgar Allan Poe, the American author. What is the name of his sleuth? Chevalier August Dupin. It's inconceivable that someone called Ned Lubbock should solve *The Murders in the Rue Morgue*."

"It's just as ludicrous to have a French detective hailing from Yorkshire."

"Change his birthplace to Paris."

Herbert descended to sarcasm. "The Rue Morgue, perhaps?"

"And give the fellow more substance," said Roehampton, sweeping his protest aside. "This is the age of the Scientific Detective, the man with a supreme intelligence. Think of Sherlock Holmes. Think of Monsieur Lecoq. Think of The Thinking Machine."

All that Herbert Syme had thought about for years was publication. Elevation to the ranks of those he idolized most would solve everything. It would rescue him from a humdrum life in a small provincial library where he was mocked, undervalued and taken for granted. Five years had gone into the creation of the novel that would be his salvation. In that time, he had grown to love Inspector Ned Lubbock, to marvel at his invention of the dastardly Lionel Jagg and to take a special delight in the meticulous evocation of his native Derbyshire. His hopes were dashed. Edmund T. Roehampton was mangling his novel out of all recognition. He felt the grief of a mother whose only child is being slowly strangled in front of her. Anger began to take root.

"Inspector Jacques Legrand," decreed Roehampton. "That name has more of a ring to it. He uses scientific methods of detection and outwits the villains with his superior brainpower. Needless to say – and I must repair another omission of yours – he must be a Master of Disguise. Just like Hamilton Cleek – the Man of the Forty Faces."

Herbert struck back. "And what does this preposterous French detective disguise himself *as*?" he asked, his Derbyshire vowels thickening in the process. "An Italian Count or a Wily Pathan? Or maybe he can pretend to be the commander of an invading Chinese army. And where do his changes of apparel come from? I should warn you that there are no costume hire shops in the Peak District."

"I'm glad that you mentioned that, Syme."

"Does that mean I've got *something* right at last?"

"Far from it. Your location is a disaster."

"You're going to take Derbyshire away from me as well?" cried Herbert.

"I have to, man. Shift the story to London and we enlarge its possibilities."

Heavier sarcasm. "In which part of the capital is Matlock to be found?"

"Nowhere, fortunately," said Roehampton with a complacent chuckle. "Unlike your home town, we do have more than our share of Sinister Orientals here so that's one problem solved. My shirts are washed at a Chinese laundry and they are obsequiously polite to me but there's still something ineradicably *sinister* about them."

"They're foreigners, that's all, In Peking, you would appear sinister to them."

"That's beside the point. Your novel is not set in China."

"No," said Herbert, desperation taking hold. "It's firmly rooted in Derbyshire. How can a book called *Murder in Matlock* be set in the city of London?"

"By a simple slash of the pen. Here," said the publisher grandly, indicating the title page of the manuscript. "I crossed out your effort and inserted my own. I venture to suggest that it will have more purchase on the reader's curiosity."

Herbert was shaking with fury. "You've stolen my title as well?"

"Improved upon it, Syme. That is all."

"In what way?"

"See for yourself," advised the other, pushing the manuscript across to him. "Ignore the blots. My pen always leaks. Just imagine those words emblazoned across the title-page of your novel. *Slaughter in the Strand.*"

"But there's no mention of the Strand in the book."

"There is now, Syme. I've also included some other elements you failed to include. As well as being a killer, Count Orsini must be a Prince of Thieves just like Arsene Lupin. You see?" he said, eyes glinting. "The Franco-Italian touch once more. Inspector Legrand must solve the crime by playing with a piece of string while sitting in the corner of a restaurant. Notice the hint of Baroness Orczy there? The Old Man in the Corner. It adds to the international flavor of the novel. On which subject, I must point out another fatal omission."

Herbert gritted his teeth. "Go on," he growled.

"There are no German spies in the book. We must have spies for the Kaiser.

Remember le Queux, a true English patriot as well as a brilliant writer. He's warned us time and again about the menace of the Prussian eagle. Yes, Syme," he concluded, sitting back with a grin, "those are the few changes I require. Make them and your book may stand a chance in a busy marketplace."

"Except that it won't be *my* book," snarled Herbert.

"What do you mean?"

"I mean, Mr Roehampton, that you have been hurling names at me that I neither like nor strive to emulate. Vidocq, Sue, Gaboriau, Baroness Orczy, William le Queux. They merely skate on the surface of crime. I tried to deal with the subject in depth," argued Herbert, rising to his feet. "If you want an international flavor, listen to the names of those who inspired me to write *Murder in Matlock*. Dostoevsky gave me my villain. Balzac supplied me with my insight into the lower depths of society. Maupassant taught me subtlety. Goethe schooled my style. You wave Wilkie Collins at me but a far greater English writer suggested the infanticide with which my novel begins – George Eliot, the author of *Adam Bede*. My debt to them is there for all to see. I'll not have it obliterated."

Roehampton blinked. "Am I to understand that you reject my emendations?"

"I refuse to put my name to the rubbish you've concocted."

"Ah, yes," said the publisher, rubbing his hands. "That brings me to my final point. Whatever form the novel finally takes, we cannot possibly put your name on it."

"Why not?"

"Be realistic, man. Syme rhymes with Slime. The critics would seize of that like vultures. Herbert Syme sounds like, well, what, in all honesty, you are, a struggling librarian from a Yorkshire backwater."

"Derbyshire!" roared Herbert. "Matlock is in Derbyshire!"

"That point is immaterial in a novel called *Slaughter in the Strand*."

"I loathe the title."

"It will grow on you in time," said Roehampton persuasively. "So will your new pseudonym. Out goes Herbert Syme and in comes – wait for it – Marcus van Dorn. It has a bewitching sense of mystery about it. Marcus van Dorn. Come now. Isn't that a name to sew excitement in the breast of every reader?"

Herbert exloded. "But it's not *my* name!"

"It is now, Syme."

"You can't do this to me, Mr Roehampton."

"I'm a publisher. I can do anything."

It was horribly true. Herbert's great expectations withered before his eyes. He was not, after all, going to be an author. If this was how publishers behaved, he was doomed. Life would become intolerable. All the people to whom he had boasted of his success would ridicule him unmercifully. He would have to return to the library with his tail between his legs. Every time he put one of Roehampton and Buckley's books on a shelf, the wound would be reopened. It was galling. Publication was not rebirth at all. It was akin to the infanticide with which his novel had so sensitively dealt.

The villain of the piece was none other than a man whom he had revered from afar. Edmund T. Roehampton had not only hacked his book to pieces, he had altered its title and deprived the author of his identity. It was the ultimate blow to Herbert's pride. His gaze fell on his precious manuscript, disfigured by ink blots and scribbled notes, then it shifted slowly to the gleaming paper knife. A wild thought came into his mind.

"Well," said Roehampton, "do you want the book published or not?"

"Only if it's my novel."

"Make the changes I want or it will never get into print."

Herbert stood firm. "I'll not alter a single word."

"Then take this useless manuscript and go back to Yorkshire."

"Derbyshire!"

It was the final insult. As Roehampton reached for the manuscript, Herbert grabbed the paper knife and stabbed his hand. The publisher yelled in pain but there was worse to come. Pushed to the limit, Herbert dived across the desk and stabbed him repeatedly in the chest, avenging the murder of his novel with a vigor he did not know he possessed. Alerted by her employer's yell, Miss Finch came bustling into the office. When she saw the blood gushing down Roehampton's flashy waistcoat, she had a fit of hysteria and screamed madly. Herbert was on her within seconds. Lavinia Finch was an accomplice. She had not only typed out the guileful letter to him, she had read the finest novel ever to come out of Matlock and pretended to admire it. She had deceived Herbert just as much as her employer and deserved to die beside him. He stabbed away until her screams turned to a hideous gurgling. Both victims were soon dead.

Herbert Syme had traveled in a First Class carriage on the most significant journey of his life but his return ticket would not be used. A horse-drawn police van was his mode of transport now. As he sat in handcuffs behind bars, he reflected that he had, after all, achieved one ambition. His name would certainly be seen in print now. Every newspaper in Britain would carry the banner headline – *Slaughter in the Strand*. A treacherous publisher may have provided that title but its author would not be Marcus van Dorn. It would be Herbert Syme, the most notorious criminal ever to come out of Matlock in Derbyshire. He liked that. It was a form of poetic justice.

THE SEA HORSE

This story first appeared in anthology called Death by Horoscope *so its theme was already decided for me. Most of us have mixed feelings about horoscopes and even the cynics tend to sneak a look at them. They can turn out to be embarrassingly accurate. The prediction in "The Sea Horse" is a rather chilling one but it is uncomfortably true. Foresight or coincidence? I leave the reader to judge.*

W elcome aboard the *Sirius!*" said Luke Sanderson, giving her a mock salute. "Your captain is at your service."

"That remains to be seen," she replied with a teasing smile.

"Is that an invitation or a challenge?"

"Who knows?"

"You're being very provocative today, Tania."

"I hope that you don't object."

"Quite the opposite."

"Good." Her smile broadened. "I have a soft spot for sailors."

They shared a laugh then Luke helped her to get the luggage aboard. When it had been stowed away in the cabin, he took a proper look at Tania Kew and signaled his approbation with a roll of his eyes. Short but shapely, she wore a red T-shirt, white trousers and a pair of navy blue deck shoes with white lacing. Luke had only ever seen her before across the table in a restaurant when Tania was immaculately dressed in one of the sober outfits she favored at work. Clients who saw her now would hardly recognize her as the efficient young lawyer with whom they did business. Dark brown hair that was brushed neatly back into a chignon now hung loosely to her shoulders. Luke, too, had undergone a complete transformation. The financial consultant from a top firm in the City was sporting a uniform that would have done justice to the skipper of cruise ship in the Caribbean. It made a pleasantly ugly man in his thirties look decidedly raffish.

"When are the others due?" asked Tania.

"Any moment," he said. "Neil will probably drive down with Kit Greeves."

"What about Faith?"

"Oh, she's coming as well."

"Isn't Neil bringing her?" wondered Tania. "I thought they were an item."

Luke sighed. "Yes, they were until last weekend. I need to warn you about that. Apparently, they had another of their explosive rows and split up."

"Yet they're still *sailing* together?"

"Neil being Neil, there was no way he'd miss out on the treat."

"It won't be much of a treat if Faith is scowling at him all the time," said Tania with a frown. "And I can't see that she'll enjoy being cooped up on a boat with her latest reject. It could make for a very nasty atmosphere."

"Not while I'm around," promised Luke with a grin. "This is a voyage of pleasure. Neil and Faith both accept that. They'll be no problem. Besides," he went on, "they'll be too busy to have a slanging match. Neil will be helping me to sail the boat and Faith will be preoccupied with her new friend."

Tania was surprised. "A new *boy*friend?"

"No," said Luke, shaking his head, "even Faith doesn't work that fast. It's an old flatmate of hers who surfaced again after ten or twelve years. They were at Cambridge together. Faith was delighted when she got in touch again and begged me to let her come along. She said it was like having a wonderful new friend."

"And who is this wonderful new friend?"

"Miranda Hart."

"Is she an academic like Faith?"

"No, Tania. She's a consultant astrologer."

"A what?"

"Miranda casts horoscopes."

"Only for the idiots who believe in such things," said Tania sceptically.

"You don't, obviously."

"Horoscopes are a load of crap."

"I know. Nevertheless, we all take a peep at them in the morning papers. Miranda sounds like an interesting lady," observed Luke. "She could turn out to be a lot of fun."

"Could she?"

"Yes, Tania."

"As long as she doesn't try that Madame Miranda routine on me."

"You underestimate her. Miranda doesn't sit in a tent with a crystal ball. She's much further up the food chain than that. There's serious money in astrology. She writes books, gives lectures, attends conventions."

"There must be a lot of gullible people in the world."

"Than heaven!" said Luke cheerfully. "Most of them are my clients. Three cheers for gullibility! It's what helped to buy this amazing boat for me."

Tania softened. "It's marvelous, Luke," she said, glancing around. "So spacious."

"She can sleep six with comfort, eight at a pinch."

"Who decides the sleeping arrangements?"

He grinned. "Mother Nature."

Luke was very proud of the craft, purchased on impulse at the Boat Show but a source of continuous pleasure for him. He loved to be able to take his friends for weekend trips in the *Sirius*. Assuming the mantle of captain gave him a sense of power and excitement. He showed Tania around the vessel and pointed out its special features. His guest was more interested in the people with whom she would be sailing.

"How old is this stargazer?" she asked.

"The same age as Faith, I suppose. Early thirties."

"Single?"

"Widowed, from what I gather."

"Does that mean she's on the prowl?"

"I hope so," said Luke with a smirk. "I like prowling females."

"Faith will be on the loose again, if she's junked Neil. The boat will be overrun with spare women. That will suit you, Luke." He laughed merrily. "Who was that other chap you mentioned?"

"Kit Greeves? He's a bookseller."

Tania was disappointed. "He works behind a counter at Waterstone's?"

"No, Tania. He specializes in rare books and cartography. Kit is an expert."

"At what?"

"Doing what we all do," said Luke complacently.

"And what's that?"

"Making a healthy profit out of our chosen professions."

"I wouldn't call astrology a profession," she observed sourly.

"Miranda makes a mint out of it."

"I'm a lawyer, remember. I'd call that fraud."

Luke beamed. "I sail pretty close to the wind at times myself," he admitted. "Much of my work is akin a glorious confidence trick."

"That's different."

"Is it?"

"Yes, Luke," she said sharply. "I'm sorry but I have a thing about so-called astrologers. They're complete crooks. Only an imbecile would be taken in by them."

"Miranda may change your mind."

"Don't bank on it."

The men were the first to arrive. Big, bearded and relentlessly affable, Neil Ambrose was a former chef who now had his own column in a national newspaper. As well as helping to sail the boat, he was in charge of any meals eaten aboard and had brought boxes of food with him. Tania liked Neil though she wondered if she could endure his hearty laughter for a whole weekend. Kit Greeves was the oldest of the passengers. Almost forty, he had somehow managed to keep his hair, his slim body and his handsome features. Tania warmed to him immediately. Kit was an intelligent man with a dry sense of humor. He also donated four bottles of Champagne to the galley. Like Neil and Luke, he was clearly determined to enjoy the trip. Tania basked in the glow of their attention.

The women arrived in a flurry of apologies. The train had been late leaving Charing Cross and they had difficulty finding a taxi at Folkestone station. They clambered aboard the *Sirius*. Faith Brightwell was an intense woman of medium height and spreading girth, her striking beauty now encroached upon by bulging cheeks and a supplementary chin. She taught Mathematics at a London Polytechnic that had now been elevated to University status and it gave her a faint air of superiority. Evidently, she and Neil had reached a prior agreement to be excessively nice to each other because they kissed affectionately, exchanged happy banter and went out of their way to indicate that their estrangement would not be allowed to spoil the weekend for the others. Luke was relieved. Tension aboard was bad for everyone.

It was Miranda Hart who was the revelation. After the praise heaped on her by Faith, Luke had expected a female paragon. Instead, he was introduced to a tall, thin, angular woman who stooped badly and who was painfully shy. Her hair was straggly, her face plain and unacquainted with cosmetics. In her woolly cardigan and mustard-coloured skirt, she looked a ridiculous sailor. Luke gave her a cordial welcome.

"I might have named the boat in your honor," he said to her.

"Might you?" she murmured.

"*Sirius*. The brightest of stars."

"Ah, yes."

"Be honest, Luke," joked Neil, giving him a nudge. "You named her after yourself. Sirius is the dog-star. Neil Sanderson is not only a star of the financial world, he's the most lecherous old dog, I know."

Miranda did not join in the general laughter. She seemed to be having doubts about the wisdom of accepting the invitation to join the party. Even when the first bottle of Champagne was opened, she did not relax. Tania began to feel sorry for the woman but she was also relieved. Miranda Hart would pose no threat to her primacy nor would the overweight Faith Brightwell. She had a clear field. Luke, Neil and Kit Greeves were all hers. Tania could play the three of them off against each other. It was the kind of game that she relished.

The crossing was remarkably calm. With Luke at the helm, the *Sirius* glided effortlessly across the water, her powerful engine purring steadily away. Neil prepared a snack for the passengers then relieved Luke so that he could enjoy the refreshment with the others. It was exhilarating to sit on deck with the sun beating down on them and the wind ruffling their hair. They were soon into the third bottle of Champagne. Miranda Hart was monopolized by Faith who reminisced endlessly about their time together at Cambridge.

"I never dreamed that you'd end up in astrology," she said.

"Nor did I, Faith."

"You were a linguist."

"That was a bonus," said Miranda quietly. "I've been able to read French and German astrologers in the original. Nothing is wasted."

"That was your motto at Cambridge."

"I once sold a copy of *Zadkiel's Almanac*," said Kit Greeves, inserting himself politely into the conversation. "A rare early edition. I got an excellent price for it."

"I'm not surprised," said Miranda.

"Who was Zadkiel?" asked Faith.

"Who cares?" muttered Tania under her breath.

"His real name was Richard James Morrison," explained Miranda. "He was an naval officer who became an astrologer and founded the Almanac in 1830. As a sea-faring man, he knew the value of being able to read the stars."

"I could steer by them if I had to," boasted Luke.

Miranda smiled. "I hope that it won't come to that."

"What did your husband do?" asked Tania, irritated that Miranda had now taken centre-stage without even trying. "Was he in the same line of business as you or did he earn an honest penny?"

"Oh, Howard was no astrologer," said Miranda fondly.

"No?"

"He sold swimming pools." She heaved a sigh. "It was ironic, really."

"Why is that?"

"I can't swim."

Luke laughed. "You were hardly well-matched, then."

"We were," said Miranda loyally. "It was a marriage of true minds in every sense. But, unhappily, it didn't last. Howard was killed last year. It was the one time when I felt guilty about being an astrologer."

"Guilty?" repeated Faith. "Why?"

"Because I foresaw his death."

"Nobody can do that," argued Tania.

"I did," said Miranda.

"You're lying."

"No, I'm not," said Miranda solemnly. "I cast his horoscope. It was a chilling moment. I foretold both the time and manner of my husband's death."

Even Tania was silenced by the announcement. There were tears in Miranda's eyes. Faith put a comforting arm around her, Kit looked deeply sympathetic and Luke wondered if he should press for details. Neil's voice rang out across the deck.

"Any of that Champagne left?"

When they reached Boulogne that afternoon, they went ashore immediately to explore the town. Tania linked arms familiarly with Neil and Luke. Determined to be the center of attention, she was peeved when Miranda once again stole her limelight. The dowdy astrologer not only spoke fluent French, she seemed to have a fascination for Kit Greeves. He plied her endlessly with titles of obscure books about astrology, trying to win her favor by a display of arcane knowledge. Faith was prompted into airing her own expertise, talking contemptuously about her students and comparing them unfavorably to the undergraduates with whom she had studied at Cambridge.

Dinner was eaten on the terrace of a restaurant that overlooked the harbor. Tanya was careful to sit between Luke and Kit, flirting with both while exchanging intermittent glances with Neil Ambrose. As the acknowledged chef, he was allowed to choose from the menu though Miranda's command of the language was once again called into play during the discussion with the waiter. Wine flowed freely. It made Faith more intense, Kit more desperate to impress Miranda, and Neil more prone to bursts of incongruous laughter. Luke was in his element, hosting the party and regaling them with tales of how he had cleverly overcharged some clients to the tune of fifty thousand pounds. Tania felt his hand on her thigh. Neil was shooting even more lustful glances at her. She was beginning to enjoy the situation when the whole mood suddenly changed.

"Tania thinks that astrology is a load of crap," declared Luke.

"Most people do," said Miranda tolerantly. "I did myself at first."

"Was that before you saw the commercial potentialities?" said Tania spikily.

"No, it was before I cast my own horoscope and found it uncannily accurate."

"Sheer coincidence!"

"Is it, Tania?"

"Of course."

"Then how do you explain the fact that I foresaw that my husband would be killed in a car accident during the month of April? Was that sheer coincidence as well?"

"He should have given up driving," said Neil with a misplaced laugh.

"He did," said Miranda calmly. "He even refused to let me drive him."

"So what happened?"

"Howard went everywhere by bus or train. Unfortunately, on his way back from a client in Hereford, the train broke down. The passengers had to be ferried to the next station by a fleet of coaches and taxis. Howard was in a taxi," she recalled. "It never reached the station. He was the only person to die in the crash."

"What rotten luck!" said Kit.

Faith nodded soulfully. "It must have been a shattering blow."

"It might still have been a coincidence," said Tania.

"Don't be so cynical," reproved Luke.

"Somebody around here has to keep in touch with reality."

"Howard was killed exactly as I predicted," said Miranda. "That was my reality."

"Have you made any predictions about yourself?" asked Kit.

"Yes," she replied. "I cast my horoscope at the start of each year."

"So what does 2002 hold for you?" sneered Tania. "A meeting with a tall, dark handsome man? Or a string of incredulous clients who pay to listen to your claptrap?"

"It's not claptrap," said Faith defensively.

"Do *you* believe it?"

"Well ... not entirely, perhaps."

"Nor me," added Neil, emitting his thunderous laugh.

"Astrology has a much more scholarly base than you imagine," insisted Kit. "Those who've plumbed its mysteries can make remarkable predictions."

Tania was unconvinced. "Is that what Miranda's done?" she teased. "Plumbed its mysteries? Or is she just lucky with her guesswork?"

The debate was shifted to another level. Luke and Kit spoke up for Miranda but Tania and Neil were openly derisive about the claims of astrologers. Faith was caught in the middle, anxious to support her friend yet having reservations about her ability to make accurate predictions. Miranda said nothing. As the arguments became more heated, she withdrew into her shell. It was Neil Ambrose who drew her out again.

"Prove it!" he taunted. "Come on, Miranda. Prove it."

"Prove what?" she said.

"That there's some truth in all that nonsense."

"Yes," goaded Tania. "Prove it."

Miranda shrugged. "It's not as easy as that." Neil and Tania jeered at her. "Is anyone around this table a practicing Christian?" she asked.

"I am," said Luke, "but no matter how hard I practice, I never get it right." Miranda spoke over Neil's braying laughter. "It was a serious question. Kit?"

"I'm a sort of Pick and Mix Christian," he confessed.

"That would sum up my position as well," said Faith. "In spite of my name, my faith comes and goes. However, I'd insist on getting married in a church," she went on, shooting a look of hostility at Neil, "but the only person who ever proposed was a confirmed atheist."

"Guilty as charged," said Neil with a chuckle. "What about you, Tania?"

"I loathe all religions," said Tania with sudden ferocity. "And with good cause. I was born in China where my father was a Catholic missionary. It was excruciating. I think I was ten when I saw him through the whole charade. I hated my parents for trying to bring me up as a good Catholic. In my view, that's a contradiction in terms."

"Right," said Miranda calmly. "We obviously don't have any potential saints around the table but all of you have had some kind of Christian upbringing. And what was the sign that marked the birth of Jesus Christ? A star in the east. When you believed in that, as you all once did," she pointed out, "you believed in astrology."

The remark set off another barrage of complaint and accusation. Luke ordered two more bottles of wine before joining in the discussion. Stroking Tania's leg under the table with one hand, he turned to Miranda.

"I'm a Taurus," he declared. "What does that make me?"

"The bull of the herd," said Neil.

"I asked Miranda."

"The miserable cow!" said Tania to herself.

"Taurus is a fixed sign," explained Miranda. "If stressed, it will make the mind just, uncompromising, constant, firm of purpose, prudent, patient, industrious, strict, chaste, mindful of injuries, steady in pursuing its object –"

"What is this?" interrupted Tania. "Some mantra that you chant at your clients?"

"I was quoting the most famous astrologer of ancient times – Ptolemy."

"He was writing in the third century B.C," said Kit knowledgeably.

Tania was scathing. "They didn't even know that the world was round then."

"You still haven't *proved* anything, Miranda," challenged Neil.

"What's the point of offering proof to those who wouldn't recognize it?" she said. "*I'd* recognize it," promised Faith.

"So would I," said Luke, emptying his glass as fresh wine arrived. "A moment ago, you described the salient characteristics of a Taurean. Could you do it the other way around, Miranda? When you get to know someone well enough, can you guess the sign under which they're born?"

"Usually," said Miranda. "For instance, even if I didn't already know that Faith's birthday was in December, I'd pick her out as a typical Sagittarian. She belongs to the Fire Element. She's a great optimist who thrives on challenges. Faith never does anything by halves. She pursues her interests with real vigor. Oh, and she's very honest as well. She's not given to deception."

Faith was pleased. "That sums me up perfectly."

"She missed out the fact that you have a foul temper," said Neil bitterly.

"Okay," resumed Luke, filling their glasses with a new bottle, "you've got Faith and me pegged. What about Tania, Kit and Neil? How long would it take you to work out their birth signs."

"Not too long," said Miranda. "I've plenty to go on already."

Kit was amused. "Do we give ourselves away so easily?"

"Certain characteristics always show through."

"Then find them," decided Luke. "Tell me the month in which the three of them were born and I'll never have doubts about astrologers again. Is it a deal?"

Miranda looked around the faces. The expressions on them ranged from curiosity to cold antagonism. She sipped her wine before making her announcement.

"I'll make one prediction," she said confidently. "By the end of this year, one of us will have met a premature death." She gave a knowing smile. "Who it will be?"

By the time they got back to the boat, most of them were too drunk to do anything more than tumble into their bunks. Miranda remained on deck, wrapped in the warm blanket of night as she gazed up at the stars. It was Kit Greeves who eventually joined her.

"You certainly shut them up," he said with admiration.

"Who?"

"Neil and Tania. They were baiting you, Miranda."

"I'm used to that kind of thing," she said wearily.

"That prediction about one us dying really shook them. It takes a lot to put Neil Ambrose in his place," he continued, sitting beside her. "Faith could never manage it. That's why she broke up with him. Neil laughs at everything."

"Yes, I know. Faith told me all about him on the journey down here."

"Deep down, I think that she still loves him. That's her weakness."

"What's yours, Kit?"

"Oh, there's no doubt about that. Books. I can't resist them."

"So I gather."

"They never let you down, Miranda. Books are always there to yield up their treasure whenever you want it. No angry moods, no squabbles, no recriminations. The printed page is the most reliable of friends."

"That depends on what's printed on it, surely."

"Of course," he said loftily. "One has to be selective."

"You sound as if you're highly selective, Kit."

"I am, believe me."

"You only choose the best."

"That's why I'm here," he said, slipping an arm rather clumsily around her. "I got fed up with listening to Neil's snores so I came up on deck. It seems a shame to waste such a beautiful night as this."

Miranda neither resisted nor encouraged him. When he kissed her gently on the cheek, she offered no reproach. Kit pulled her closer and turned her to face him. The look in her eyes made him release her at once.

"What's wrong?" he whispered.

"You chose the wrong book."

"Is it your husband? Are you still grieving over him?"

"Yes, but that's not the reason."

"Then what is? We don't want to be the odd ones out, do we?"

"What do you mean?"

"Oh, come on, Miranda," he said, taking her hand. "You're not that naïve. Luke didn't invite us on this trip to enjoy our intellectual companionship. He's got his eye on Tania. Sooner or later, they'll be sharing the same bunk. The same goes for Neil and Faith, if you ask me," he predicted. "Did you notice the way he squired her back to the boat? When he wakes up in the morning, the first thing he'll do is to reach out for her and Faith will be there for him." He leaned in closer. "That leaves you and me."

"Does it?"

"You don't need to be a mathematician of Faith's standard to work it out."

"Six minus four equals two."

"Three men, three women, three partnerships."

"I thought that you preferred books."

"Not while you're around," he said, about to kiss her on the lips.

Miranda shielded herself with a palm. "No, Kit."

"Why not?"

"Because I just wanted to enjoy a quiet night under the stars."

"That's what we *are* doing, isn't it?"

"I'm afraid not. You have a different agenda, Kit. I don't flatter myself," she said levelly. "I'm not as attractive as Faith or as sexy as Tania. If you really wanted a woman, you could have gone after one of them but you deliberately went for me – the last resort."

"That's not true," he protested.

"Yes, it is. They threaten you. I don't." She eased him away. "But I'm sorry, Kit. I simply can't do it."

"Do what?"

"Help you to prove that you're not gay. Why bother? We both know the truth."

Eyes blazing, he leapt to his feet. "Tania was right about you," he said with vehemence. "You're a bitch, Miranda. A cruel, calculating, nasty little bitch!"

And he rushed back to the cabin.

Sunday morning found them in varying stages of recovery. Neil Ambrose was in high spirits, showing no signs of a hangover and serving breakfast to each new person who emerged from the cabin to join in the *al fresco* meal. As he handed a plate to the somnolent Kit Greeves, he described some of the tricks of the trade he had used as a chef to persuade his customers that they were eating something far more exotic than they actually were. It was clear to Miranda that one prediction had been borne out. At some time during the night, Faith Brightwell had obviously succumbed to her former partner. There was an air of triumph about Neil as he flitted to and fro between the galley and the deck. Faith, by contrast, was grumpy and withdrawn, regretting her capitulation and angry at the way that Neil was, in effect, trumpeting it aloud. Tania Kew was at her most tetchy. A dawn fumble with Luke Sanderson had been deeply disappointing and she had let him know it in the most vivid language. When the skipper of the *Sirius* finally came out into the light of day, he was still suffering the effects of too much wine and brandy. His eyes never dared to stray in Tania's direction.

By mid-morning, Luke had revived enough to take the boat along the coast to a quiet little bay. Anchored well out from the shore, it became a diving board for the swimmers. Neil was the first to go in, eager to show off his physique. Luke went into the water with a spectacular dive, anxious to impress Tania and to show that he had recovered completely from the excesses of the previous night. Faith was eventually lured into the water but she kept well clear of Neil who was thrashing about wildly. Tania, too, could not resist the temptation of a swim on such a hot and sunny morning, though she posed on the edge of the boat for a long time before jumping in, allowing the men to appraise her trim body in its scanty bikini.

Kit was the last to take the plunge. Wearing a pair of neat blue swimming trunks, he was lean, muscled and tanned to a light brown. He looked across at Miranda.

"Aren't you going in?" he asked.

"I told you. I can't swim."

"Then do us all a favor and leap overboard."

Miranda ignored the gibe and the water that splashed over her when Kit dived in. She remained on deck in a blouse and a pair of slacks, glad to be alone at last. When an impromptu game of water polo started, the men became very competitive. Miranda watched them from the safety of the boat, noting how quickly they regressed into childhood. Faith was treading water lazily but Tania was striking out for the shore as if to prove her credentials as a swimmer. An hour soon passed. Having worked up an appetite, they all came back to the *Sirius*. Luke toweled himself off in the sunshine.

"We're still waiting for that proof, Miranda," he said.

"Yes," added Neil, grinning at her. "You haven't told me what I am."

"A prize idiot!" muttered Faith.

"Start with Kit," suggested Luke. "What's his birth sign?"

Miranda pondered. "I think he's a Piscean," she decided. "True or false?"

"True," conceded Kit with a scowl.

"There you are!" shouted Luke. "It *does* work."

Tania was still skeptical. "A fluke guess."

"It was more than that. Tell us how you did it, Miranda."

"By simple observation," she said. "Pisces is the last of the Water signs and the twelfth in the Zodiac. It's in a privileged position. Pisceans are extraordinary people as a rule. Compassionate and understanding. They're very high-minded. In practical terms," she went on, indicating the sea, "they're drawn to water which is why Kit is such a good swimmer."

"I'm a good swimmer," asserted Luke, "but I'm no Piscean."

"No, Luke. You're ruled by Venus."

He chuckled lecherously. "I won't argue with that."

"Kit, on the other hand, is ruled by Neptune, the planet of mystery, escapism and deception. That's the down side of being a Piscean, I'm afraid. They make excellent martyrs but they're also inclined to self-deception." She raised a quizzical eyebrow. "Is that a fair description of you, Kit?"

"Not in the slightest," he retorted.

"I'd say that it was spot on," said Luke. "What about Neil and Tania?"

"I'm still working on them," admitted Miranda.

"Count me out," snapped Tania, drying her hair. "I'm not playing this silly game."

Luke waved an admonitory finger. "It's not a game, Tania. It's a scientific experiment under controlled conditions. So far, Miranda has scored a hundred per cent."

"Nice to know that someone has scored around here," she murmured to him.

"Tania!"

"I'm going to get changed."

She flounced off into the cabin and Luke went after her, gesticulating wildly. Neil read the situation. "Perhaps I should give him a few tips," he said.

"Be quiet, Neil!" reproached Faith.

"Sex is only a form of astrology. Celestial bodies moving in the same orbit."

She was livid. "Do you have to tell everybody?"

"The only person who doesn't seem to know that it happened is you, Faith."

It was her turn to stalk off to the cabin. Neil went after her, showering Faith with a mixture of apology and blandishment. Raised voices continued for some time. Kit finished drying himself off and moved across to Miranda. He seemed contrite.

"I'm sorry for what I said earlier," he began. "You caught me on the raw."

"Your secret is safe with me."

"It's hardly a secret, Miranda. I think that Luke rumbled me years ago."

"Faith hasn't. She told me you were an eligible bachelor."

"Technically, that's what I am."

"One eligible bachelor searching for another."

"No, Miranda. Someone who prefers his own company most of the time."

"Yet you were willing to stretch a point for me last night."

"That was a mistake," he said tartly.

"Was it?"

"An example of that self-deception you talked about."

"Self-deception?"

He was genuinely hurt. "I thought you were my friend."

Neil Ambrose cooked such a superb lunch for them all that even Faith was won over. Rich food and good wine helped to restore a happy atmosphere and they were soon chatting and joking as if there had been no trace of friction aboard. Kit was on his best behavior, Tania seemed to have forgiven Luke, and Miranda was not pestered for any more demonstrations of her astrological skills. Time rolled gently on. Neil ended up with a proprietary arm around Faith, Luke danced slowly with Tania to the music that oozed out of his CD-player and Kit conversed with

Miranda on the neutral subject of books. A mood of contentment reigned. It did not last. Seated apart from the rest of them, Neil and Faith were engaged in a quiet but intense discussion. When she whispered something in his ear, he turned round to fling an accusation at Miranda.

"Is that what you said?" he demanded angrily. "Did you tell Faith that she'd be better off without me?"

"Yes," answered Miranda.

"Why?"

"Because she asked me my opinion."

"It's none of your bloody business."

"Probably not."

"You don't even know me."

"I know enough to see that my advice was sound."

He lurched towards her. "What do you mean?"

"Sagittarians rarely get on with Cancerians," she said evenly, "and I'd bet anything you were born in mid-July. All the indications are there, Neil. You're loving, sympathetic and tender when you want to be. Behind all that laughter, you're a very sensitive soul. You're a true home-lover who likes his creature comforts. You even do the cooking. Well?" she asked. "Am I right? Were you born under Cancer?"

"Get stuffed!"

"You *were*, Neil," said Faith, betraying him. "Your birthday is July 15th."

Neil glared at her as if about to strike her then his ire shifted back to Miranda. "It's a pity you weren't in that taxi with your husband," he snarled.

Still in his shorts and T-shirt, he dived overboard in a rage.

Dinner was a muted affair. Though they returned to the same restaurant in Boulogne, they could not recapture the spirit of the previous night. Miranda could see that she was chiefly to blame. Tania had resented her from the start but, in Kit and Neil, she had made two additional enemies. As the host, Luke felt obliged to jolly everyone along but there was his amiability was half hearted. When Miranda excused herself from the table, the others were able to vent their fury.

"Why the hell did you invite that witch?" said Neil, rounding on Faith.

"Miranda isn't a witch," she countered.

"Well, she's certainly cast a spell on this trip. She's spoiled everything."

"Not necessarily," said Luke. "Try to ignore her."

"If only we could!" sighed Tania.

"She's just not used to this kind of thing," said Kit with asperity. "While the rest of us have all mucked in, Miranda is like the specter at the feast."

Neil nodded in agreement. "Inviting her was a disaster."

"I felt sorry for her, Neil," said Faith.

"You should have felt sorry for the rest of us and kept her well away."

"Miranda's not *that* bad," opined Luke, trying to calm them down.

"She's diabolical!"

"And so fucking pleased with herself!" added Tania, turning to Faith. "Miranda is the pits. What on earth do you see in her, Faith?"

"I don't know," confessed the other. "She's changed so much. Miranda was a lot of fun at Cambridge. We had some great laughs together. But now ..."

Neil was vicious. "The only laugh I'd get from her is if I heard that she swallowed one of her own predictions and choked to death on it."

"That's unkind!" said Faith.

"Oh, I can be much more unkind than that," offered Tania.

"So can I," said Kit softly. "I'd like to kill the bitch."

"That's enough!" ordered Luke, embarrassed by the intensity of their hatred. "We're stuck with Miranda so we've all got to make the most of it. She's not my favorite person by a long chalk but I can put up with her for one more night. So can the rest of you. Agreed?"

The nods of consent were slow and reluctant.

When they got back to the boat, Luke uncorked a couple of bottles of wine then started the engine. While the others bantered on deck, he steered them back to the little bay when they had spent the morning. It was an ideal spot for a quiet night. Dropping anchor well out from the shore, he cut the engine and joined the others. Drink had mellowed them all. Faith was pouring contempt on the Higher Education System, Neil was shaking with mirth, Tania was nurturing fresh hopes about Luke's virility and Kit was at his most expansive. When Luke told them about some of the sharp practice in which he engaged from time to time, Kit saw an opportunity to air his knowledge.

"I feel as if I'm in *Das Narrenschiff*," he said with mock disdain.

"What's that?" asked Neil.

"The Ship of Fools. It's a famous narrative poem by Sebastian Brant. Written over five hundred years ago."

"So why bring it up now?"

"Because you appear in it, Neil," said Kit. "One of the characters on the boat is a dishonest cook. Yes, Luke, there's a usurer aboard as well. He's another arrant fool. There's even an unscrupulous lawyer like Tania and a pretentious scholar like Faith."

"I'm not pretentious!" denied Faith.

"Yes, you are," said Neil, unleashing yet another laugh.

"What about Miranda?" asked Luke. "Is she is this Ship of Fools?"

"Oh, yes," said Kit. "There's a trendy theologian who sounds just like Miranda."

"You're forgetting the Buchenarr," said Miranda with asperity. "The Bookish Fool. He takes pride of place on the ship, sitting on the prow, surrounded by useless books. He might almost have been modeled on you, Kit."

Kit glared back but said nothing. The others sniggered at his expense. When his glass was empty, he was the first to peel off to bed but not because of fatigue. As he lay on his bunk, Kit Greeves was throbbing with anger. Back on deck, Tania allowed Luke to slip and arm around her and fondle a breast. Neil's hopes of any reconciliation with Faith were doomed. Whenever he tried to get close to her, she inched away. He blamed Miranda for coming between them. After a long wait, he took his hurt feelings off to bed. Luke and Tania were the only couple destined to share a bunk. As they headed for the cabin, he remembered something.

"You never told us what Tania's birth sign is, Miranda."

"And she's not going to," said Tania, dragging him off. "We've had enough of that nonsense for one day."

The two women were left alone. Their friendship had been quietly fractured.

"All things considered," said Faith ruefully, "it might have been better if you hadn't come."

"You were the one who pressed me, Faith."

"I wanted you as a buffer against Neil."

"I rather hoped that you'd invited me for my own sake."

"Well, yes," added Faith quickly, "that, too, of course. I'm sorry that it didn't work out. I thought that you'd *like* everyone."

"I did," said Miranda. "The trouble was that they didn't like me."

"Especially Tania. She didn't have a good word to say for you."

"Tania has a lot of problems. Who wouldn't have if they'd been brought up in the Far East by a family of Catholic missionaries?" She gave a hollow laugh. "That's enough to put the curse on anybody."

"Are you coming to bed?"

"No," said Miranda. "I'll stay up here and enjoy the stars. While I can."

It was hours before she finally dozed off to sleep on the deck of the *Sirius*. It was a humid night and the boat bobbed gently on the swell. Miranda Hart did not hear the footsteps that came up out of the cabin and approached her with stealth. Her dreams were suddenly invaded by something hard and metallic that struck the side of her skull. Caught between sleep and waking, she could not resist the hands that eased her over the bulwark and into the unforgiving water. When the anchor was hauled up, the *Sirius* drifted slowly out to sea on the tide. It was soon quite distant from the scene of the crime.

Just before dawn, Luke Sanderson came out of a deep sleep and realised that his boat was no longer at anchor. Climbing over the naked body of Tania beside him, he went up on deck and saw that they were now out in the Channel, being buffeted by waves. He started the engine to establish control over the craft. The noise soon woke the others. They tumbled out on deck one by one. The last to arrive was Faith Brightwell.

"Where's Miranda?" she said.

"Isn't she in her bunk?" asked Luke.

"No, she stayed up here last night. I left her gazing up at the stars."

"She must be on the boat somewhere," said Kit, wiping the sleep from his eyes.

Luke was alarmed. "Where else could she be?"

The search was brief but thorough. There was no doubt about it. Miranda had disappeared. The only explanation was that she had somehow gone overboard. Since they were several miles from their anchorage in the bay, they had no idea where and when her departure occurred. Everyone was thrown into turmoil. Luke felt a personal responsibility for the loss of a passenger. Kit wondered if they should report the missing person to the French coastguard. Tania suggested that Miranda might somehow have made her way ashore, alienated by the general antipathy towards her. Faith pointed out that her friend would not have left without her belongings and she went into the cabin to search for them. It was left to Neil Ambrose to put into words the thought that worried them most.

"Somebody pushed her overboard," he concluded. "Miranda couldn't swim."

"Who would do such a thing?" said Kit with disbelief.

Neil was honest. "There was a moment yesterday when I would cheerfully have done it," he confessed. "The woman just got up my nose."

"And mine," said Tania. "But wanting her dead and actually killing her are two different things. I mean, where's the proof?"

"Someone hauled the anchor up," said Luke. "That's our proof."

"It's only supposition," she argued. "Miranda might have done that herself."

"I agree," said Kit. "Maybe she was trying to play a trick on us all and tumbled overboard in the process."

Neil was not persuaded. "Then why didn't she cry for help?"

"Perhaps she did. We were too drunk to hear her."

"I went out like a light," said Luke. "A typhoon wouldn't have woken me. One thing is certain," he added, looking out across the water. "It's pointless to search for her. Miranda could be anywhere within a radius of miles. We'll never know what happened."

"I'm not so sure," announced Faith, coming back on deck with a large diary in her hand. "I found this in Miranda's bag. It contains that personal horoscope she mentioned."

Kit shuddered. "It was too uncannily accurate. Miranda warned that one of us would meet with a premature death. She didn't know that it would be her."

Faith held up the diary. "Oh, yes, she did. She even named the killer."

"That's impossible!" exclaimed Tania.

"We can't even be sure if she *was* murdered," said Neil.

"Yes, we can," said Faith, looking around them. "You had cause to push her over the side, Neil. So did Kit. She really upset him somehow. And I don't suppose that you were overjoyed with her either, Luke."

"Me?"

"You set up this trip and along comes Miranda to ruin it."

"Not deliberately."

Tania was watchful. "What's this about her naming the killer?"

"I'm coming to that," said Faith. "I can see now why you didn't want to go along with that guessing game about birth signs, Tania. The Sun Signs don't apply to you, do they? You were born in China. They have their own astrology there."

"So?"

"My guess is that your date of birth was early in 1978. February, say."

"What if it was?"

"Then you were born in the year of the Horse. Look what it says in Miranda's diary, Tania," said Faith, thrusting it at her. "Read it. "This year, I will be killed by a horse." In this case, it was a sea horse but it amounts to the same thing. You pushed her over the side of the boat, didn't you, Tania? You're behind all this."

Tania tried to brazen it out but her guilt was plain for all to see. Eyes darting wildly, she backed against the bulwark. Neil and Kit looked on with disgust. Luke was horrified to realize that he had slept with a woman who left his bunk in the middle of the night in order to commit murder. Faith snapped the diary shut.

"Tell them what 2002 is, Tania," she said. "The Chinese year of the Horse."

BLIND EYES

The Mammoth Book of Locked-Room Mysteries and Impossible Crimes *was an anthology to which I felt impelled to contribute. As a fan of John Dickson Carr, I love locked-room mysteries but it was the impossible crime that attracted me in this case. Nelson's Column is the most distinctive feature of Trafalgar Square in London. Supposing that someone stole the statue of Nelson and – even worse – replaced it with a statue of Napoleon. How on earth would they do it? Here's my suggestion.*

The first explosion came at midnight. No warning was given. Oxford Street was surprisingly busy at that time on a Saturday. People waited for buses, hovered for taxis, searched for somewhere to eat, headed for nightclubs or simply walked aimlessly along. Drunks relieved themselves in dark corners. A man with an accordion played evergreen favourites with fitful enthusiasm. A group of young women, fresh from a hen party, laughed and joked their way boisterously along the pavement. Curled up in sleeping bags, self-appointed tenants of the various shop doorways had already counted the day's takings and turned in for the night. Two burly uniformed policeman studied the suits on display in Next and shared their misgivings about the prices. A lone cyclist headed towards Marble Arch.

The explosion sounded far louder than it really was. It came from a card shop near Oxford Circus and terrified everyone within earshot. The plate glass window became a thousand deadly missiles that shot across the road. Cards were scattered everywhere. Those in the Get Well Soon rack were the first to ignite. Women screamed, men yelled, residents lifted bedroom windows or came dashing out of front doors. The two constables abandoned their shopping and ran towards the scene of the blast, one of them raising the alarm on his mobile while the other warned bystanders to keep well clear of the danger area. It seemed only minutes before police cars converged on Oxford Circus to investigate the crime and to control the gathering crowd. A fire engine arrived soon afterwards with an ambulance on its tail. The noise was deafening.

It was a scene that was repeated elsewhere in the city. A second bomb went off in the Euston Road, a third near Victoria Station and a fourth in Baker Street. No sooner had the emergency services reached one devastated area than another explosion was heard. Nor were the bombs confined to central London. Blackfriars, Belvedere, Chingford, Whitechapel, Pentonville, Clapham Common, Greenwich and other sites were targeted. The Metropolitan Police were at full stretch, the Fire Service pushed to the limit. Chaos reigned for hour after hour. The one consolation was that there seemed to be very few casualties.

At the height of the crisis, the biggest explosion of all went off in an electricity sub-station and the whole of the West End was suddenly blacked out. Panic spread uncontrollably. Older inhabitants were reminded all too vividly of the Blitz, younger people were convulsed with fear. Everyone rushed around wildly, wondering what was happening. A foreign invasion? A bombing campaign by Irish dissidents? A visit by aliens? The end of the world? It was only when dawn finally lifted the blanket of night that another crime was uncovered, a theft so shocking that it was totally impossible to believe even though the evidence was there for all to see.

Lord Nelson had been stolen from atop his column in Trafalgar Square. In his place, usurping his position of honour, gazing down Whitehall with a smile of triumph and outraging every true English patriot, was a huge statue of Napoleon Bonaparte.

Fluttering at his boots was a self-explanatory banner.

VIVE LA FRANCE!

Commander Richard Milton was not pleased to be hauled back from his holiday. His week in Cornwall had been curtailed before it had even begun and he was determined to make someone pay for his loss. With his wife's complaints still ringing in his ears, he was flown back swiftly to London to take charge of an inquiry that was dominating the media like the outbreak of the Third World War. A tall, thin, angular man with a face like a Victorian poisoner, Dick Milton had the experience, the guile and the stamina to lead a large team of detectives in the investigation of what appeared to be a series of interrelated crimes. He got results. That was why he was chosen. When he worked in harness with his old friend, Detective-Inspector Kenneth Hurrell, results tended to come quickly.

An incident room was set up in Scotland Yard. By the time that Milton came charging in, Hurrell had already been busy for hours.

"What the hell is going on, Ken?" demanded Milton.

"I wish I knew," sighed Hurrell. "A series of bombs went off all over London last night. Soft targets. Extensive damage to property. Minor injuries but no fatalities. And then – this other bombshell!"

"Nelson can't have *disappeared!*"

"He has, Commander."

"How?"

"That's the bit we haven't worked out."

"And is it true that someone else is up there?"

"Napoleon Bonaparte."

"Bloody hell!"

"The media are calling it a national scandal."

"And that's exactly what it is, Ken!" said Milton vengefully. "My holiday's been ruined. Nothing could be more scandalous than that. I had strips torn off me when I left St Ives. You try telling your wife that she'll have to manage without you while you go off in search of Nelson."

"I'm not married, sir."

"Be grateful. At times like this, celibacy is a blessing."

"I didn't say I was celibate."

Kenneth Hurrell grinned. He was a wiry man of medium height with wavy black hair that was the envy of his colleagues. His immaculate suit made Milton's tweed jacket look positively shabby. The Commander became businesslike. He snapped his fingers.

"How far have you got?"

"This far," said Hurrell, moving to the large wall map. "The pins indicate the locations of the bombs. Twenty-one in all."

"Twenty-one! What did they think it was – Bonfire Night?"

"Oh, no. They were very precise about the date."

"What do you mean?"

"It's October 21st."

"So?"

"The date of the Battle of Trafalgar."

"But that was years ago, Ken."

"A hundred and ninety-five years. October 21st, 1805."

"Is that relevant?"

"Extremely, sir. Some people obviously have long memories. The pattern of bombing proves that." He jabbed a finger at the map. "At first, I thought they were just random explosions to create a diversion and move every available officer well away from the vicinity of Nelson's Column."

"And they're not?"

"No," said Hurrell. "Take this one here, for instance," he continued, touching one of the pins. "Old Bethnal Green Road. The bomb was very close to Nelson Gardens. Then there's this one, sir." He indicated another pin. "On the site of Greenwich Market. Close to Nelson Road."

"Could just be a coincidence."

"Not when it happens in every case," argued Hurrell. "There was a bomb near Nelson Walk in Limehouse, another on Morden Road, close to the Nelson Industrial Estate and a third in Nelson Yard, off Mornington Crescent. So it goes on."

"What about Oxford Street and Victoria Station?" asked Milton. "I don't recall any Nelson Roads in those areas."

"There aren't any."

"So the pattern is incomplete."

"Far from it, Commander. The explosion in Oxford Street was less than forty yards from the Admiral Nelson pub. The one in Victoria Station was directly opposite The Trafalgar. No question about it, I'm afraid. We're dealing with a case of aggravated revenge."

"Some militant Frogs?"

"All the signs point that way."

"So it seems."

"You can't fault their timing."

"Timing?"

"Yes, sir. Until last week, workmen were at the top of the column to give Nelson his habitual clean-up. The thieves didn't just get away with the most famous statue in London. They waited until all the bird shit had been scraped off it. We're up against pros."

"No phone calls from them?"

"Just one, sir. In French."

"What was the message?"

"Short and sweet. We were ordered to leave him where he is."

"Who?"

"The Emperor Napoleon."

"Ruling the roost in Trafalgar Square!" exclaimed Milton with an upsurge of patriotism. "We'll see about that! Nobody gives me orders, especially in Frogtalk. Come on, Ken. Clap on full sail. We're going straight over to Trafalgar Square. You can fill me in on the way. Leave him there indeed!" He gave a snort of defiance. "We'll have the bugger down off that column before he can say 'Not tonight, Josephine.'"

Napoleon Bonaparte had drawn a vast audience. Though the police had cordoned off Trafalgar Square itself, all the approach roads were heaving with sightseers. Every window which overlooked the column had its own private audience. Television cameras had prime positions and sent their pictures to the watching millions. Driven to the scene of the crime, Dick Milton was furious when he caught sight of a French television crew.

"What are *they* doing here?" he growled.

"Somebody must have tipped them off," said Hurrell.

"They're in on the conspiracy."

"If that's what it is, sir."

When they got out of the car, Milton took his first proper look at the statue which had displaced Nelson. He craned his neck to get a good view, realising how rarely he even noticed the usual occupant of the fluted Corinthian column. Nelson was such an essential part of the fabric of London that he could be taken for granted. Like St Paul's Cathedral or Westminster Abbey. In a sense, it was a compliment not to look at him, an acknowledgement of his status and permanence. Only foreign tourists actually stared at the column. Everyone was staring now. The new arrival compelled attention. Napoleon looked bigger, bolder, more authoritative. There was a mutinous rumble among the spectators.

Dick Milton shared their disgust. His faced reddened angrily.

"What, in God's name, is he doing up there?"

"Making a statement, sir."

"I'll make a bloody statement myself in a minute."

"Not when there are so many microphones about," warned Hurrell. "We have to be diplomatic. Keep our own opinions private."

"Well, *he's* not keeping his opinion private, is he?" said Milton, looking up at the banner. "VIVE LA FRANCE! That doesn't leave much to the imagination, does it?"

"No, sir." Hurrell gave a signal and a detective walked briskly across to them. "Let's see if we have any more leads. D. S. Williams was in charge of taking statements from witnesses."

"Good." He appraised the newcomer. "Well?"

"They all say the same, sir," explained Williams, referring to his notebook. "There were over a dozen of them, sleeping here last night or sharing bottles of cheap booze. They saw very little."

"They must have, man!"

"There was a total blackout, Commander."

"Winos are nocturnal. They can see in the dark."

"Not when they're pissed out of their minds," said Hurrell before turning back to the Detective-Sergeant. "Sorry, Jim. Do go on."

Williams nodded and ran a tongue nervously across his lips. He knew all about Dick Milton's hot temper and had no wish to set it off. He consulted his notebook.

"They saw little but they heard a lot," he resumed. "The one thing they all agree on is the helicopter. It seemed to be directly above them and created a terrific downdraft. Well," he said, glancing around the rubbish-strewn square, "you can see the results. The helicopter stayed for ages, they said, and there was another sound. A loud grinding noise. They could even hear it above the whirr of the blades."

"Did they identify the noise?" asked Milton.

"No, sir. They were too scared to stay."

"I don't blame them."

"But I think it was a stonecutter," said Williams, stooping to pick up a handful of chippings from the ground. "You see, sir? These are pieces of Craiglieth stone from the statue of Nelson. They had to cut it clear before they could carry it away."

"By helicopter?"

"How else?"

"But it must have been a hell of a weight."

"Several tons, sir."

"How tall was the statue?"

"Seventeen feet," said Williams. "And the column is a hundred and forty-five. Devonshire granite from Foggin Tor. It supports a bronze capital cast from old guns from Woolwich Arsenal."

"You've done your homework. Good man."

"Thank you, sir."

"An ordinary helicopter couldn't have winched it up," said Hurrell, "but an Army helicopter might have managed it. Several sightings of a flying object were reported. People couldn't pick it out properly in the dark but they saw something when they heard the helicopter go past overhead. They didn't realise it was a chunk of English history."

"No," grumbled Milton. "Anything else, Williams?"

The detective rattled off all the other information he had gleaned before being sent back to interrogate the witnesses for the second time. They were a motley crew, tramps, winos and homeless students. There was one old woman among them, singing hymns at the top of her voice. Milton ran his eye over the group then looked at his companion.

"This was a well-planned operation, Ken."

"Involving several people."

"Do we know of any French extremists capable of this?"

"Not really, sir," said the other, "though I was surprised to find out just how many different political groups there are. Apart from the usual anarchists, nihilists and assorted nutcases, that is. There's a Pro-Euro Ginger Group, a Friends of General de Gaulle Society, a Jacobin Club, a League of French Imperialists and heaven-knows-what else. I'm told there are some pretty dodgy characters in the Gerard Depardieu Fan Club as well. France is a country steeped in revolution. It's in their blood. When something rouses them, they act. Still, one thing is certain."

"What's that?"

"These people mean business."

"Yes, they stole one of our great national heroes," said Milton bitterly. "And what do they give us in return? Those tasteless Golden Delicious apples and seventeen feet of Napoleon Bonaparte."

"Amazing, really. You've got to admire them."

The Commander was appalled. "Admire those thieving Frogs!"

"They whisked Nelson off into the sky."

"They did a lot more than that, Ken. Apart from insulting a naval man by transporting him in an Army helicopter, they achieved an even greater feat." He glanced upwards. "They stuck that monstrosity up there at the same time. *How?* One helicopter, two national heroes. How on earth did they remove one and lift the other into place in such a relatively short period of time?"

"The blackout lasted for a few hours."

"That means they were working in the dark."

"Perhaps they had a second helicopter, sir."

"None of the witnesses heard it."

"I don't think we can rely too heavily on them," said Hurrell with a sad smile. "They were either too drunk to notice much or too frightened to remember what they did see and hear. And don't forget those other reports we had. A number of people saw a hot air balloon crossing the River Thames last night."

"A balloon could never carry a heavy stone statue."

"How do we know that it *is* made of stone?"

"Good point." Milton took out his mobile phone. "Who were those people who cleaned the statue recently? Have you got their number?"

"Yes, sir. They're called Gostelow and Crabtree."

"Sounds like a firm of corrupt solicitors."

"Are they're any other kind, sir?"

They traded a professional laugh. Hurrell gave the Commander the number and the latter rang it at once. After barking a few orders, the latter switched off his mobile and put it in his pocket.

"Gostelow and Crabtree are on their way."

"How will they get up there?"

"Scaffolding."

"Then what?"

"Well," said Milton firmly, "the first thing they can do is to get that VIVE LA FRANCE banner down. It's making my stomach heave." He looked across at the massed ranks of cameramen and journalists. "I suppose that I ought to throw them a bone. Give them the idea that we have everything under control. Ho, ho! You wait here, Ken. I'll go and make a non-committal statement to the media or they'll be hounding us all day." He gazed up at Napoleon again. "By the way, what's French for 'We're coming to get you, you mad bastard?'"

Emblazoned with the name of Gostelow and Crabtree, the lorry arrived within half an hour. In the rear was a large tarpaulin and an endless number of scaffolding poles. The lorry was closely followed by a huge mobile crane. Fresh interest was stirred up in the crowd and the cameras recorded every moment for the television audience. While waiting for the men to arrive, Commander Milton had pacified the media, given his statement and spoken to some of the denizens of Trafalgar Square to hear first-hand their reminiscences of a night to remember. Two of them came out of their drunken stupor to claim that they had seen a balloon in the sky with something dangling from it.

Milton went across to introduce himself and Kenneth Hurrell to the newcomers. They treated him with muted respect.

"Who's in charge?" he asked.

"I am," said a hefty man in his thirties.

"Who are you? Gostelow or Crabtree?"

"Neither, sir. Mr Gostelow died years ago."

"What about Crabtree?"

"On holiday."

"Lucky devil! So was I until this little caper."

"My name's Pete Sylvester," said the foreman, extending a gnarled hand. "I was in charge of cleaning Nelson so I have a real stake in getting him back. You grow to like a man when you've been chiselling away at him for as long as we did."

"I thought you just gave him a wash and brush-up."

"I wish it was that easy, sir. But we're not just cleaners. We're trained sculptors. We actually have to re-carve bits from time to time. Freshen up the contours. It's skilled work. We've sculpted bits of half the churches in London before now."

"What about taking a statue down?"

"That's more difficult."

"But you have done it before?"

"A few times. We'll manage somehow. Leave it to us."

Peter Sylvester's craggy face split into a grin. He had a reassuring jauntiness about him. While he was chatting to the detectives, his men were already starting to build the scaffolded around the column. In the background, another crew was assembling the crane.

"Listen, Pete," said Hurrell familiarly, "when you were working on the Admiral, did you see anything?"

"We saw everything, mate. Best view in London."

"I meant, did you see anything unusual?"

"Unusual?"

"People taking a close interest in what you were doing."

"There were dozens of those. Real nuisance at times."

"Were any of them French?" asked Milton.

"Yeah, couple of girls. They took our picture."

"Nobody else?"

"Not that I recall. When you climb all the way up there, you can't chat to anyone down here. Some people watched us for hours. We felt a bit like performing monkeys."

"Did anyone else come up after you?"

"Oh, no! We wouldn't stand for that."

"What happened over night?" wondered Hurrell. "Presumably, the scaffolding was left in place. Did you ever arrive in the morning and get the feeling that someone had been up there at night?" Sylvester shook his head. "How can you be so sure?"

"Because we had a nightwatchman on duty. If you don't guard them, scaffolding poles have a nasty habit of walking off in the dark. Besides," said the other, "we didn't want idiots climbing all over the column. It's bad enough when they get on the lions" backs. Admiral Nelson deserves to be protected."

Pete Sylvester was a man who clearly liked his work but he was unable to help them with their enquiries. When they released him, he went off to supervise the erection of the scaffolding. It was a long but methodical process. The column was slowly encased in an aluminium square which rose steadily upwards. Hurrell was impressed.

"It must have taken much longer with timber," he observed.

"Timber?" echoed Milton.

"Yes, sir. When they first put up the column, a hundred and fifty years ago, they used wooden scaffolding. The statue itself was raised in 1843 by means of a winch. It must have been a wonderful sight."

"Someone else has been doing his homework, I see."

"I like to be thorough."

"It's the only way, Ken."

Pete Sylvester eventually drifted back across to them.

"I'd suggest that you clear the square completely," he said. "I'm fairly sure we won't drop him but it's better to be safe than sorry. It's a long way to fall."

Milton gave a command and everyone was moved away.

"When you get him down," he said, "our forensic boys will want to give him the once-over. Only not here in the glare of publicity."

"We'll take him back to the warehouse, sir. More private there."

"Good."

"One favour."

"What's that?"

"Could you keep the press off our backs? We don't want them clambering all over our lorry to get exclusive pictures."

"They won't get a chance, Mr Sylvester."

"Thanks."

When the scaffolding finally reached the capital, Sylvester swarmed up it so that he had the privilege of tearing down the banner. To the cheers of the crowd, he hurled it to the ground. A policeman retrieved it then scurried back out of the way. Dick Milton and Kenneth Hurrell watched with admiration from the safety of the steps of the National Gallery. Pete Sylvester was fearless. Using a small pick-axe, he chipped away at what appeared to be fresh concrete at the base of the statue then exchanged the implement for a stonecutter. Its whine soon rang across the square and the noise intensified as it cut into solid stone.

One eye on developments, Milton gave his orders.

"Check out all of these fringe groups," he said.

"Even the loony ones, sir?"

"Especially those. Leave no stone unturned, Ken. If someone so much as asked for Eric Cantona's autograph, I want him checked out for Gallic sympathies. We're supposed to be fellow-Europeans now but that message obviously hasn't got through to the Froggy mentality. Out there somewhere is a sawn-off Napoleon with delusions of grandeur."

"We'll find him, sir."

"And soon."

Hurrell was about to depart when his colleague's mobile phone rang. The Commander snatched it from his pocket and turned it on.

"Yes?"

"Commander Milton?" said a heavily-accented voice.

"Who's this?"

"I told you not to take the Emperor down!"

"It's him!" said Milton, cupping a hand over the mouthpiece. "The anonymous Frog. He's watching us."

"Can you hear me?" said the voice.

"I hear you, *mon ami*," replied the other with polite contempt. "And I don't care two hoots for your orders. Napoleon comes down."

"In that case, we double the price."

"What price?"

"For Nelson."

Milton rid himself of a few expletives but the line went dead.

"They're holding him to ransom," he told Hurrell.

"Where?"

"He forgot to tell me."

"How much do they want?"

"A lot, by the sound of it." He put the mobile away. "Well, let's get rid of one statue before we try to reclaim the other. Meanwhile, you do what I said, Ken. Get your men on the case, chasing down every weird group of French sympathisers they can find. Join me when it's time to take the Emperor for a ride."

Hurrell moved swiftly away to pass on the orders to a small squad of detectives. Milton turned his gaze back to the statue. Pete Sylvester seemed to have cut through the base of the statue and was ready to have it removed. Using thick ropes with great dexterity, he lassoed the statue at various points. He was quite fearless, even climbing part of the way up the solid stone to secure the ropes more tightly. When he finished, he waved to the crane driver and the massive hook swung slowly towards him. Sylvester waited until it had stopped swinging before he began to loop the ropes around it. After tying them off with great care, he and his men descended the scaffolding at speed then stood back to watch.

The crane applied pressure but the statue refused to move at first. A yell of encouragement went up from the crowd. When the driver put extra power into the tug, the statue was suddenly lifted clear of its base, sending rubble hurtling to the ground. Shorn of his majesty, the deposed Emperor made a slow descent until he rested horizontally in the back of the lorry. Sylvester and his men swiftly covered him with their tarpaulin. As the lorry drove away with its foreign cargo, it was greeted with the kind of ovation that only a winning English goal in the final of a World Cup could have evoked. Even Commander Milton applauded.

Before he could get away, he was obliged to make another statement to the media and hinted that he was already in contact with the kidnappers. Hope was firmly planted. Nelson had not been abducted in order to be destroyed. A ransom demand presupposed that no harm had come to him. If the money was paid, he might return unscathed.

"Is this a French conspiracy?" asked an interviewer.

"I'll tell you when I find out."

"What else can you tell us?"

"Nothing at this stage."

Milton excused himself and elbowed his way to a waiting car. He and Hurrell were soon being driven after the lorry. Having discharged his orders, the Detective-Inspector had grown pensive.

"Do you know much about the Battle of Trafalgar?" he asked.

"I know the only thing that matters, Ken. We won."

"But do you know how, sir?"

"Our sailors were better than theirs."

"And our commander. Villeneuve was no match for Nelson."

"Who?"

"Villeneuve. The French Admiral."

"I was forgetting," said Milton, running a hand across his lantern jaw. "Napoleon was a landlubber, wasn't he? The Emperor didn't fight any sea battles." He glanced over his shoulder. "Why did they put him up there instead of the French Admiral?"

Pete Sylvester and his men had been remarkably efficient. By the time the detectives arrived at the warehouse, the rear of the lorry had been tipped hydraulically and the statue had been eased gently out on to a bed of sand. Sylvester waved the lorry off then turned to welcome Milton and Hurrell. Other detectives emerged from a second car.

"He's all yours, Commander," said Sylvester, gesturing.

"Thanks to you."

"It was much easier than I thought."

"Why?"

"Because he's not made of solid stone." The foreman kicked the base of the statue. "This part is, as you can see. But I think your men will find that Napoleon Bonaparte is largely made up of plaster."

"So he could have been carried by a balloon!" said Hurrell.

"Balloon?"

"Nothing, Mr Sylvester," said Milton, taking him by the shoulder to usher him away. "Thank you for all you've done. We won't detain you any further. As long as you're on stand-by for the important part of the operation." Sylvester looked puzzled. "Putting Nelson back up again."

The foreman chuckled. "I can't wait, sir. That's why we left the scaffolding in position. We're so confident that we'll get him back."

"You have my word on that."

Peter Sylvester went out and Milton motioned his men into action. They put down their cases and began an examination of the statue. The base was indeed made of solid stone but there was a hollow ring when they tapped the head and the shoulders. Dick Milton was merciless. He had no qualms about giving the order for execution. With a well-judged kick, one of the men struck the Emperor's head from his shoulders. The Commander peered inside the torso. He could see all the way down to the knees. He gave a grim smile.

"I bet he's got feet of clay as well!"

A uniformed constable entered with a large brown envelope.

"This is for you, Commander," he said, handing it over.

"Where did you get it?"

"Someone in the crowd thrust it at me."

"Didn't you get his name, man?"

"I had no time, sir. He said something in French and ran off."

"In French?" Milton looked at the envelope. "A ransom note."

He tore it open and quailed. Hurrell looked over his shoulder.

"Five million pounds!" he said with a whistle.

"Payable in unmarked notes of specific denominations."

"Is that the going rate for a stolen statue?"

"Look at the signature, Ken."

"I can see it, sir."

"Villeneuve."

It was over three hours before the call came. In the interim, Dick Milton and Kenneth Hurrell left their colleagues to continue their work at the warehouse and returned to Scotland Yard. The first thing which the Commander had to endure was a searching interrogation by the Commissioner. He limped back to the security of his own office.

"He made it sound as if I'd stolen the bloody statue!"

Hurrell looked up from the book he'd been reading.

"What about the ransom?"

"He thinks we should pay it, Ken. If all else fails."

"Never!"

"That was my feeling. The Commissioner's argument was that we're talking about a national treasure. In emotional terms, it's worth far more than five million. He even had some crazy idea about opening a public fund. A quid a head from five million people. I ask you!" sighed Milton. "All I'm interested in is nailing this gang."

"Me, too."

"No word from the lads while I was out?"

"Not a peep, sir. I don't think Napoleon is going to yield up many clues somehow. Seems to have been made out of the sorts of materials you could buy anywhere."

"In that case, we must concentrate on the Army helicopter and the hot-air balloon. See if any have been reported stolen. And chase up the bomb squad. They should have analysed those devices by now. My guess is that they were made by someone with Army training."

"And a friend who can fly a helicopter."

"Yes," said Milton, pacing the room. "The helicopter took Nelson out and the balloon brought Napoleon in. Or did it? Something's been bothering me, Ken. Remember when the statue was lowered from the column? That crane had to make a real effort to shift it."

"It did. The weight made the ropes tighten."

"Yet Napoleon was as hollow as a chocolate Easter egg."

"It doesn't make sense."

The telephone rang to interrupt their cogitations. Milton lifted the receiver and placed it to his ear. He had no need to speak at first. A continuous stream of information came down the line and put a look of utter amazement on his face. Milton asked a few questions then recoiled from the answers he got. When he put the phone down again, he was in a daze. He lowered himself into a chair. Hurrell stood over him.

"Who was that?"

"Mr Crabtree of Gostelow and Crabtree."

"I thought he was on holiday."

"He was. Tied up for two days in his own warehouse. And he wasn't the only one. His wife was there with him so that she couldn't raise the alarm. The pair of them have just been released."

"But we were in the warehouse ourselves."

"No, Ken. That wasn't Crabtree's place."

"Then why did Pete Sylvester take us there?"

"It was all part of the ruse," said Milton, thinking it through. "He pulled the wool well and truly over our eyes. I know that my namesake was blind but I don't think he could have blind as the pair of us."

"What do you mean, sir."

"Crabtree had never heard of Pete Sylvester."

Hurrell gulped. "I'm beginning to guess what happened."

"So am I, Ken. And I certainly don't relish the idea of telling the Commissioner. Peter Sylvester – or whoever he really is – has duped us good and proper. He pulled off the most astonishing trick in front of millions of viewers. And nobody saw it happening." He punched a fist into the palm of his other hand. "Where is the sod?" he said through gritted teeth. "More to the point, who is he?"

"I can tell you where he got his name from, sir."

"Can you?"

"Yes, sir," said Hurrell, opening the book he'd been studying. "While you were out, I read up on the Battle of Trafalgar."

"What's that got to do with it?"

"Everything. He's playing games with us. Do you recall the name of the French Admiral in the battle?"

"Yes. Villeneuve."

"But do you know what his Christian names were?"

"Who cares?"

"We ought to, sir," said Hurrell, putting the book in front of him. "Look at the name under that portrait of Villeneuve. Pierre-Charles-Jean-Baptiste-Silvestre Villeneuve. Do you see now? Pierre Sylvestre."

Milton grimaced. "Peter Sylvester!"

When the cargo had been unloaded on to a bed of sand, the lorry was taken away to be disposed of with its false number plates. The gang congratulated themselves on the success of their plan and celebrated with bottles of beer. There were ten of them in all, each of them due to pocket a half a million pounds when the ransom was paid. In the meantime, everything had been laid on at the warehouse. Food, drink, comfortable chairs, beds and two television sets had been installed. There was even a stolen microwave.

The preparation had been faultless. It was time to relax.

"We should have asked for more than five mill," said one man.

"We will," promised their leader. "Let them sweat it out first."

"What did old Crabtree say when you released him?"

"Swore like a trooper." He glanced at his watch. "He had no idea why we commandeered his lorry and his tackle but I daresay he's found out by now. That means the boys in blue will be searching every warehouse in London while we live it up here in Milton Keynes. It'll keep them off our backs." He gave a harsh laugh. "Know the bit I enjoyed most? Having that Commander bloke call me "Mr Sylvester". I really fooled him and his mate."

They savoured the details of their crime and the hours oozed past with ease. Hamburgers were heated in the microwave. More beer flowed. They lost all purchase on time and all sense of danger. When the police burst in, the whole gang was taken completely by surprise. They fought hatd but were hopelessly outnumbered. All but their leader were dragged off to the waiting police vans. Dick Milton and Kenneth Hurrell waited until the man had been handcuffed before they questioned him.

"Did you really think you'd get away with it?" he asked.

"We did get away with it!" insisted the other. "Nobody rumbled us."

"Until now, Mr Sylvester. Oh, I'm sorry, that's not your real name, is it? You're Charles Villeneuve, aren't you? Or, in plain English, good old Charlie Newton. Late of Her Majesty's armed forces. It takes a lot to get a dishonourable discharge, Charlie. Your record makes colourful reading."

"How did you get on to me?" snarled the other.

"Ken must take the credit for that," explained Milton. "Always been the reading type. When you threw all those clues at him, he read up on the Battle of Trafalgar. Learned about your French namesake, Admiral Villeneuve. You obviously had an obsession with him. So we followed that through. A series of bombs, a helicopter, a balloon, the removal of a statue in broad daylight. All the hallmarks of a military mind. That's where we started looking for you, Charlie. In the Army."

"It deserved to work!" protested the other. "It did work!"

"Only up to a point," said Milton, strolling across to the statue of Napoleon Bonaparte that lay in the sand. "Your stage management was admirable. Only instead of giving them live theatre, you blacked out London and gave them a radio play instead. What they heard was a statue of Nelson being hoisted away by helicopter and one of Napoleon being put in its place. But the simple truth is that dear Horatio didn't move one inch during the night, did he?"

"No," added Hurrell, bending down to pull away the Emperor's fibreglass hat. "Now, then, what do we have here? I do believe it's Lord Nelson's hat hidden underneath." He tapped it with his knuckles. "Solid stone. That won't come off."

"You didn't steal him from his column," said Milton. "You merely disguised him as Napoleon so that you could take him legitimately – or so it appeared – today. No wonder you wanted us to keep the media off your back. You didn't want them around when made the switch. The fake Napoleon was already under the tarpaulin when you laid the real Nelson beside him. All you had to do was to unload the plaster version and drive off with this one instead. Ingenious."

Newton was sullen. "We could never have got away with the statue in the pitch dark. There had to be another way. If you've seen my record, you know my hobby. I'm a bit of a sculptor. Much easier to disguise Nelson with moulded fibreglass. It fitted him like a glove. Who could tell the difference from down below?"

"You covered every option," said Milton. "But made one mistake."

"Yes," agreed Hurrell. "You tried to be too clever. You played the Nelson game to the hilt and it was your undoing. You just couldn't resist the final trick. Villeneuve. New Town. You were taunting us, Charlie. Telling us exactly where you were."

"There aren't all that many new towns to choose from," said the Commander. "Milton Keynes was the most obvious. We made enquiries with the local police and they checked the footage on their motorway cameras. Sure enough, there you were. Gostelow and Crabtree."

"Or," said Hurrell with a grin, "Nelson and Napoleon."

"Two for the price of one, Charlie."

They took him by the arms and marched him out. As they headed towards the police van, the Commander gave a quiet chuckle.

"It wasn't a brilliant deduction," he admitted frankly. "Luck came into it. But, then, I've been due a bit of good fortune for some time and this was it. You were so busy playing clever games with your own names, that you never thought to consider mine. Dick Milton. Poet by name and policeman by nature. And where did you decide to hold up and toast your success? Milton Keynes. There's a poetic justice in that."

He pushed the prisoner into the rear of the police van.

"Any room in there for Nelson?" he asked.

SECOND FIDDLE

During the long reign of Sir Simon Rattle, I enjoyed endless concerts given by the City of Birmingham Symphony Orchestra, and I was always struck by the sight of those nameless musicians, who toiled away in the second violins. Did they never aspire to greater heights? How did they feel when a virtuoso like Nigel Kennedy or Maxim Vengerov played one of the great violin concertos with the orchestra? Did they fantasize about being in the limelight themselves? Or were they content to stay in the shadows? Second Fiddle is about a man who yearns to escape the anonymity of the second violins but finds that he has to commit a murder in order to do so.

Jeremy Bakewell was a quiet, unassuming, law-abiding man. It had never occurred to him that he would one day contemplate murder. Then, out of the blue, Constance Holliday came into his life. Without even realising it, she managed to turn a friendly, reliable, decent human being into a potential killer. It happened during the second movement of Beethoven's Ninth Symphony.

From the very start, Jeremy had been doomed to play second fiddle. He had been born on the second day of the second month of the year at the second attempt – so to speak – his twin brother having entered the world several minutes before him and therefore in a position to welcome Jeremy's own appearance with lusty howls of protest. Jeremy's polite whimper marked him down from the start as the also-ran.

It was James Bakewell who had the privileged childhood and the glittering career as a concert pianist. Jeremy remained in his shadow – a competent musician who had been conditioned to aspire to no higher a place than one among the second violins. While James Bakewell became an international star, Jeremy became an anonymous member of the Royal Philharmonic.

Twenty years brought no change in his status. Jeremy's position in the second violins was as intact as ever. His unassuming personality prevented his relationships with woman from going any further either. For a while he maintained a fleeting obsession with Lynette Cooper, the bosomy cellist who grappled with her instrument as if making passionate love to it, but by the time Jeremy gained enough courage to invite her out for a meal, he discovered that she had already succumbed to the blandishments of a bearded Lothario in the brass section. It was disheartening but not entirely unexpected. Programmed to settle for second best, Jeremy gritted his teeth and played on in resigned silence, a difficult pose to maintain in an orchestra, especially when it is giving a performance of Mahler's First Symphony.

It was Martin Kemble who finally took pity on Jeremy. A talented flautist, Kemble was something of a joker, who – along with most of the other musicians – had often teased Jeremy. However, there had always been an affection behind his mockery. During a break in rehearsals, he took his friend aside. "I've just heard," he confided, "that Alistair is going to retire."

"Never!" said Jeremy with surprise. "Alistair Lumley is one of the best violinists in Britain. He lives for his music. He'll never retire."

"Mother Nature has other ideas. She's started to remind him how old he is. The arthritis has got a real hold on his hip now. There are other problems as well. Suffice it to say that Alistair has decided to quit while he can still hold his instrument. That will create a big gap in the first violins, Jeremy. I think you should fill it."

"Me?"

"Yes. You've been playing second fiddle for too long."

Jeremy was hesitant. "Am I ready to move up?"

"Of course you are," encouraged Kemble. "Your brother feels the same."

"James?"

"Yes. After he played the Grieg Piano Concerto with us, the great James Bakewell said that you didn't really belong in the second violins."

"Is that what he told you?" asked Jeremy, hurt that his brother had never spoken to him directly on the subject.

"Those were his very words, according to Lynette."

"Lynette Cooper?"

"Yes," explained Kemble with a grin. "Over a brandy, I daresay. Didn't you know that your brother whisked her off to the Ritz Hotel after his performance? That's where she got her latest nickname from."

"Nickname?"

"The Bakewell Tart."

Jeremy cringed. His brother's renown as a virtuoso was matched only by his reputation as a compulsive womaniser. Even though James Bakewell was married to one of those beautiful, ethereal blondes that concert pianists always seem to attract, he felt the need to spread his love generously among the female members of the world's best orchestras. Jeremy wished that, of all people, it had not been

Lynette Cooper's turn to play a nocturnal duet with him and he smarted at the fact that the brotherly remark about his deserving promotion to the first violins had reached him second-hand.

"Go for it!" urged Kemble. "You deserve it, Jeremy."

For once in his life, Jeremy felt the flames of ambition flicker. The tip-off from Kemble gave him an early advantage over any of his colleagues who might apply for the vacant position. It allowed him vital extra time to practice what he knew would be the conductor's audition piece. Tarquin Roebuck was a Sibelius man through and through. The dark, brooding violin concerto in D minor, opus 47 was his preferred choice. It was also – Jeremy later came to realize – an overture to murder. His first meeting with the intended victim took place weeks later.

"Hello," she said with an imperious smile. "I'm Constance Holliday."

"Jeremy Bakewell," he muttered, sheepishly.

"Brother of the more famous James, I gather."

"Yes."

"Poor man! That must be a crippling disability." It was more of a gibe than an expression of sympathy.

Constance Holliday bared a row of hideous teeth before sweeping off to her date with destiny and Jeremy was left gasping in her slipstream. The vacant post would be filled by one of them. Others had applied for it but only two now remained in contention. The haughty Constance was marginally older than Jeremy – a tall, stringy woman with the face of a Gorgon but a talent that had gotten her into the London Symphony Orchestra and a distinguished string quarter. Eager to play symphonic music again, she had applied for the post with the Royal Philharmonic, seeing it as a stepping stone in her bid to become leader in due course.

Jeremy smouldered with anger. To be pushed into second place yet again would be galling enough but the thought that a supercilious woman with serious dental problems might oust him was humiliating. It put steel into his resolve. When the time came, he did not play Sibelius like a no-hoper trying to lift his head above the parapet of the second violins. He attacked the piece as if his life depended on it. Tarquin Roebuck, a neurotic stick insect with arms like supplementary batons, was patently impressed by the way he tackled the first-movement cadenza, the long, serene melody of the second movement, and the pulsing rhythm of the finale. Jeremy Bakewell did not merely play the concerto – he explored its darkest frontiers.

"Brilliant," said Tarquin, clapping his hands.

"Does that mean I have the position?" asked a breathless Jeremy.

"I'm afraid not. Frankly, there's nothing to choose between the two of you. You both gave faultless performances. However, Constance Holliday's range of experience gives her a slight edge. Also ... I shouldn't really tell you this, I suppose, but I feel that you have a right to know. Alistair recommended her."

Jeremy blinked. "Over me?"

"Yes."

"Did I have no chance at all, Tarquin?"

"Of course. But you were pipped at the post by Constance."

He saw the distress in the other man's face and sought to comfort him. "Next time, however, there'll be no need to audition. When a second vacancy occurs in the first violins, Jeremy, it's yours."

It was small consolation. Jeremy had been defeated by someone with equal, but by no means, superior talent. A kind word in her favour from Alistair Lumley had consigned him to a supporting role once more. Whatever happened to friendship? Why didn't Alistair show loyalty to his colleague? It was agonising. What made the pain more intense was the victor's overweening arrogance.

"I was inspired in there today," she boasted. "I've never played Sibelius better."

"Nor have I," countered Jeremy.

"Yes, but you lack my flair. Besides, the Bakewell family already has one musical genius in it – your brother James. To have two would be asking for the impossible. Stay in the safety of the second violins," she said with a patronising smirk. "They also serve who sit and support."

The woman was insufferable. Moving into the Royal Philharmonic as if she were its acknowledged star, Constance Holliday managed to upset, offend, or alienate almost everyone around her. The one person who liked her was Tarquin Roebuck, the anorexic conductor. And she was, undeniably, a fine violinist. Jeremy was the first to admit that. But he had also come to appreciate his own talent as a musician and to feel that it was time to fight for some kind of recognition.

During the second movement of Beethoven's Ninth, a wild idea took hold of him. The orchestra was playing at the Birmingham Symphony Hall, a splendid arena for music but not until then, perhaps, a breeding ground for homicidal inclinations.

From his lowly position in the second violins, Jeremy could see her clearly, sawing away at her instrument with the vigour of a lumberjack yet producing divine music in the process. Constance Holliday had to go. Not only was she the most hated member of the Royal Philharmonic, she was a constant reminder of Jeremy's own failure. At every opportunity, she crowed over him with a pleasure that was almost sadistic.

The best way to create a vacancy in the first violins was to remove her, thereby advancing himself and gaining revenge all in one swipe. As his mind toyed with the possibilities, he played on by means of automatic pilot. A musical death would be the most appropriate. A small canister of deadly cyanide gas, concealed in her instrument so that it would explode at the first touch of the bow? A poisonous spider lurking between the pages of her music, ready to strike when her fingers reached out? A venomous snake hidden in her violin case? Pleasing notions but far too impractical. Jeremy had to bide his time. It would mean that he would have to soak up scores of fresh insults from her, but this would only serve to stiffen his commitment to kill her.

His chance finally came in Turkey. After a triumphant performance in Istanbul, the orchestra had a few days to relax before flying on to Athens. Most of them decided to take a boat trip on the Bosporus. Jeremy was keen to join them but arrived just as the boat was pulling away from the quay, collecting jeers of derision from his colleagues. He was forced to wait for a second boat. And there was an added handicap. Another violinist had been too slow off the mark.

"Why didn't they wait for me?" demanded Constance, surging up to him.

"The boat was full," said Jeremy.

"That's no excuse. They could have made room for me somehow."

"There's another boat due in five minutes."

"I suppose that will have to do," she moaned. Her teeth glinted in a sly grin. "Well, we might as well make the most of it, Jeremy. The two of us – alone at last. It will give us the opportunity to get to know each other a little better."

It was a grim thought – one which was quickly supplanted by a slightly more palatable one in Jeremy's fevered mind. None of their colleagues would be aboard. No witnesses.

"Can you swim, Constance?" he asked, artlessly.

"Heavens, no! A violinist has to protect her hands."

"Quite so."

"Water always makes my palms look like stewed prunes."

When the boat drew up alongside the wharf, the pair of them got into it with the other passengers. The vessel soon set off. Constance was as waspish as ever.

"Your brother thinks that your career is on the slide," she observed.

"James?" he said vaguely. His mind was busy weighing the possibilities of his next move.

"He played with the London Symphony orchestra recently. Mozart, I believe."

"And he mentioned me?"

"According to Hannah Margrave. An oboist. She's a friend of mine."

Jeremy could imagine the circumstances under which the comment was made. It was embarrassing to be reminded that the only time James was sufficiently interested in passing judgement on his twin brother's work was when he was between the sheets of an adulterous bed with his latest conquest.

"You're not really twins at all, are you?" prodded Constance.

"What do you mean?"

"Well, you're so different in every way. James Bakewell is really successful."

That was it. The final insult that sealed her fate. Jeremy was determined. When the boat reached the deepest part of the water, circumstances suddenly worked in his favour. The two musicians were alone in the stern. All of the other passengers had their backs to them. Constance thrust a highly expensive camera into Jeremy's hands and insisted that he take her photograph. Hands on her hips, she stood near the bulwark with a condescending smile on her face. Jeremy sensed that his moment had come.

"Back a little," he advised. "A little further."

"Make sure you press the right button," she said, moving back.

"Of course. Sit on the bulwark, Constance."

"It's too dangerous."

"Nonsense," he said, crossing to her to arrange her pose. "Just rest lightly against it. One leg up. That's better. It'll make the perfect picture."

The perfect picture of Constance Holliday could only be taken at her funeral – that was his considered opinion. Pretending to adjust her position by touching her shoulder, he instead gave her a sudden push that sent her over the stern of the boat into the foaming water. She disappeared from sight and his heart lifted. But he had to appear innocent of her murder and that could only be done in one way. Running up the boat, he waved his arms in despair.

"Someone overboard!" he cried. "Help! Help!"

Crew and passengers looked at him in surprise, not understanding him at first.

"Help!" he shouted. "My friend fell overboard."

Grabbing the first lifebelt, he hurled it over the stern, then sent three others trailing in its wake none of them anywhere near the stricken violinist. By the time the boat had slowed and turned, he reasoned, a woman who could not swim would have drowned – dragged down to the bottom of the Bosporus by the weight of her own malice. Jeremy had committed a murder that would send waves of delight through the rest of the orchestra. Moreover, he had gotten away with it. Or so he thought. But Constance Holliday was not ready to meet her Maker just yet. Coming to the surface with sudden urgency, she threshed around madly and yelled at the top of her voice, "Save me, Jeremy! Please, please! Save me!"

The murder victim had turned into a damsel in distress. Having plotted her demise, Jeremy Bakewell was now overtaken by a fatal impulse of gallantry.

Instead of gloating over her predicament, he dived headlong into the water, swimming powerfully in her direction. Crew and passengers cheered him on in his bold rescue bid. Constance vanished, reappeared, vanished once more, then bobbed up for the last time. Her strength had gone and she had no more breath to call out. At the very moment when she was about to sink beneath the waves forever, Jeremy got to her, turned her on her back and, in a manoeuvre that he had been taught as a boy, secured her with one arm while he kicked his legs and swam backwards.

Minutes later, the pair of them were hauled aboard the boat. Jeremy was cursing himself for his bravado. Given the chance to dispose of a hated rival once and for all, he had instead saved her life. When she recovered from the ordeal, she would surely point the finger at him as the man who had deliberately tried to kill her. He was caught. But his fears proved to be illusory. When the panting Constance had expelled a few pints of water from her mouth, she opened her eyes and looked up at him with a gratitude that bordered on worship.

"My hero!" she exclaimed.

Success had come at last. When the rest of the orchestra heard about his bravery, Jeremy Bakewell became the centre of attention. It was he – and not his brother, James – who was the virtuoso now, praised highly on all sides. Lynette Cooper threw herself at him, arguing that there was only one way to celebrate his triumph and allowing him the supreme pleasure of turning her down. Tarquin Roebuck kept kissing him on both cheeks and Constance Holliday actually winked roguishly at him. Men who had mocked him now shook his hand. Women who had sniggered now competed to get near him.

It was Martin Kemble who pointed out the main consequence of his heroism. "You'll be on all the front pages tomorrow, Jeremy," he said.

"Will I?"

"In one mighty leap, you've achieved international stardom."

"Have I?"

"You'll never have to play second fiddle after this."

But the prediction proved cruelly inaccurate. Jeremy Bakewell's dreams of fame were soon shattered. On the very day that he rescued the woman he had tried to murder, an earthquake occurred in Eastern Turkey, a military coup was attempted in Ankara, and the country's most popular vocalist won the Eurovision song contest. The following morning, Jeremy scanned the pages of every newspaper he could get his hands on, but they were dominated by domestic concerns. There was not even the tiniest mention of his heroism in the cold water. It was as if it never happened. Constance Holliday made a vain attempt to cheer him up.

"Never mind, Jeremy," she said, helpfully. "It may turn up in the second editions."

SEA VOICES

This is my favorite story in the whole anthology, perhaps because it has autobio-graphical elements in it. Some years ago, The Times, *the most famous British newspaper, ran a competition for ghost stories. Since the judges included Kingsley Amis and Patricia Highsmith, I felt that I had to submit an entry. Simply to have a story read by writers of such caliber would be a pleasure. Fortunately, my entry was one of the thirteen chosen for publication in* The Times Anthology of Ghost Stories. *"Sea Voices" is also a mystery story with an unsolved crime at its core. Its setting is one that I knew well – an out of season holiday resort on the Welsh coast. I spent my youth cycling to such places to play games with friends on deserted, windswept beaches or to risk life and limb as we climbed the rocks. Byron Morris retraces my steps and uses his Byronic voice to lure ladies into his bed. But how would he manage if he were deprived of that voice?*

The past is a ghost.

And Byron Morris, with his car roaring over coastal roads, sped into a future that was clamorous with promise. Experience, samples, jokes, toothpaste, attack. Byron knew how to pack for these trips. Surging between one life and the last, he exploited time to the full. His left hand fumbled, located, switched on, lifted the microphone. At seventy miles an hour, he poured words smoothly into the machine, like a barman pouring egg flip into a silver tankard. Replies, requests acknowledgements, orders. At the end, separated from his business voice by a pause, then a lower octave, a personal and very personal message to Pat, his secretary. Pat would type up the letters. Plugged in behind a desk, Pat would listen to the ghost of Byron's voice and advance his business interests on an Adler Standard. Pat, like so many other Pats, would giggle and remember as she heard the recorded intimacy, which was meant for her and all the others alone.

The sea is a ghost. Those whispers are ghost stories.

Yet the wind did not disturb them. As it howled across the beach in search of new territory to terrorize, it had no effect on the two figures wearing anoraks on the rocks. The gulls cried above them and they offered up something to the gulls and all parties seemed happy with the transaction. From his parked car and now strident radio, Byron Morris looked out to ignore the anoraks and to wonder about the girl. Was she working in this cold? Was she creating an out-of-season masterpiece? Crouched over her board, she laboured quietly. Occasionally, she looked up in the direction of the sea and listened. She was a young girl, eighteen maybe. She was a solitary girl. She was an accessible girl. Three reasons for making Byron Morris defy the whistle of the wind and leave his vehicle behind him.

Art is a ghost. It consorts with phantoms of the imagination.

"Painting, are you?"

The girl smiled at Byron. He corrected his mistake with grinning pedantry. "Sketching, anyway. Used to be a dab hand with charcoal and pad myself."

She smiled again. Nineteen, he decided. At most.

"Hardly need those sun-glasses this weather, my love. Hopeful, eh?"

A third smile in succession. Yes, Byron. A potential Pat. "On your own, then?"

Her nod triggered off his golden voice, his special Byronic voice, his dark and manly voice, his patter for this and every Pat. A few minutes of gold and her smile broadened into agreement. A probable Pat, Byron. Details. Now.

"The Ship. Eight. Always stay at the Ship."

Why not, Byron? Attempt a metaphor, if you like.

"I've weighed anchor at the Ship many a time. Put port into every girl."

Laughter from behind the sun-glasses.

"Interesting picture ... can I see?"

Leave her, Byron. No need to stay. She's landed.

"But what's this figure on the beach ... a body ... man, woman? ... I can't see any body. Are you drawing from Life or Mind?"

Expressive dimples in her cheeks. She's quite Byronized.

"We'll talk about Mind tonight, my love ... and bodies."

Mutual laughter in the wind. A definitive Pat.

And all day long the voice of Byron rolled. He sold himself, his soul, his wares, his hope of salvation. Thrusting cases of samples before widening eyes, he demonstrated and assured, amused and impressed. Byron Morris on the make. Toy-selling was a toy in his hands. He filled windows with bendy rubber and whirring windmill.

He loaded shelves with plastic cars and fragile dolls. He trinketed display stands and clogged up storerooms with buckets and spades and trumpets and This Is Something Entirely New. Participation, that was his secret.

"What about these masks? Dracula – Frankenstein's monster – the lot?"

He tried them on and achieved frightening verisimilitude.

"Novelty joke packs. A winner at any price."

And he scattered itching powder on himself, or smoked a non-smoking cigarette, or drove a nail through his blood-soaked finger, or acquired a growth on his nose. Proprietors shook with merriment. When the season started in a few weeks, they knew they would be able to sell as easily as Byron sold. Byron conveyed such a feeling of confidence in a toy.

"And if you decide on anything else, Mr, Mrs, Miss, you can always get me, before closing time, at the Ship."

The Ship is a ghost. Through the bottoms of its beer-glasses, you can see apparitions floating on froth.

"Have you heard the one about …?"

Strange. This ability of Byron's to clear a bar.

"Or there's the one about …"

Men, for the most part. Byron does not connect. They ease away.

"And one I must tell you …"

He makes the latest of late-nighters an early-bedder.

Byron cannot go on buying their drink and their attention indefinitely. Profit margins. Expense accounts. Commonsense. There are limits.

"Looking for someone, Mr Morris?"

" 'Byron" to you, my love."

" 'Mrs Elias' to you, Mr Morris."

The licensee is emphatic. Byron has been Byron to her once, long ago. She heard the golden voice and went to his room that same night, no doubt to inquire about his comfort. Later, she returned to sleep in her own bed with the awakened ghost of the late Mr Elias. Byron has widowed her familiarity. She will endure him as a customer once a year, but that, Mr Morris, is all.

"Let you down, has she?"

"Not at all, not at all."

Byron has looked at that watch every hour and still the girl from the beach has disappointed him. Seven, eight, nine, ten o'clock. Art students can tell the time, surely?

"Local girl, is she?"

Mrs Elias presses home her advantage. Years too late.

"What's this, then? Someone lost?"

Sergeant Owen has called in for his habitual half and his annual spot of friction with Byron Morris, Sales Manager, Welsh Area.

"Can I be of any help, Mr ... um ..."

"Morris!"

In the mouth of Mrs Elias, the word sounds like a disease.

"What can I get you, Sergeant ... Usual? Half, isn't it?"

And with that phenomenal memory and his reflex affability, Byron talks into a uniformed ear with zeal. He's not waiting for anybody, but he did notice somebody. On the beach. That morning. Girl. But the Sergeant must have. Couldn't miss her. Fair hair. Nineteen. Pretty? I'll say, boy! Name? Pat, or so I thought. Drawing all morning. A body washed up on the shore. Pat wore sun-glasses.

"We'll get *you* some sun-glasses, Mr Morris!"

Law-enforcement humour. Heavy and functional as a cell door.

"And a white stick to go with it."

Mrs Elias sniggered her revenge after all these years.

"Seeing what isn't there, not seeing what is ... well, Mr Morris. Tell us this, then: Are you a blind man or a visionary? Is it Byron the Blind or Morris the Messiah?"

Two farmers, who had been conversing agriculturally in Welsh in order to exclude Byron, looked up as Sergeant Owen guffawed royally. He obligingly translated his joke into their native tongue and Byron was mocked anew. He made a ghost of the whisky in his glass and commissioned that a new life be born there.

"Well, must get back on duty ..."

Byron gave thanks inwardly.

"Hope we'll have no ... trouble from you this time, Mr Morris. Eh?"

And with this warning reference to Byron's peccadilloes in the normally moral and law-abiding town, the Sergeant strode out.

"Yes, no trouble, Mr Morris."

Mrs Elias underlined the warning, then withdrew to the other bar. Byron swallowed more alcohol and cursed silently. Trouble? From him? Never. What real trouble had he ever caused this small Welsh holiday resort? His behaviour that night had not been in the least scandalous. In any case, that policeman should not have shone the torch in there and then. Particularly there. The girl, named Pat, was over age. Byron had, once he found his clothes, been able to produce a licence. The car did have its lights on. Trouble? Anything but. Ask Pat.

Trouble is a ghost and it will always haunt you with its former acquaintance even when it is out of season.

"Would you care to join us?"

Byron looked up at the anorak. A woman, fortyish, English, lived inside.

"For a drink. My colleague and I have been most interested in what you've been saying throughout the evening."

The word "colleague" gave status to the other anorak. It, too, was woman. Older. Plainer. More intelligent.

"I'd love to. Look, what can I get you both?"

And waving aside the anoraked protests, Byron Morris responded to the glow of an audience once more. They both wanted him to talk. And talk. Friendship can defeat time. Temporarily. Years fell from the two ladies with each drink that Byron consumed. The colleagues had become his lifelong companions for the rest of the evening.

"And once, when I first went into selling – encyclopaedias, I think, no, wait, *medical* encyclopaedias – a woman invited me in to explain to her why I thought these expensive volumes, which I had never even opened, were the publishing event of the decade, as I had so persuasively described them."

"What happened, Mr Morris?"

"That would be telling!"

"Then tell us."

So he did, and they smiled approvingly, shedding more years. They were both down to their twenties now. Neither of them were exactly up to the Pat standard, individually. But together, well, why not, Byron? Colleague Pats. Joint possibilities.

"Did you see her on the beach, the artist, the young girl?"

They had not, but then they had been too busy with their research and with the gulls above the rocks.

"What kind of research?"

"We're scientists, Mr Morris. Of a kind."

"We'll go into all that later, Mr Morris."

" 'Byron,' please."

And they Byroned away to his heart's content. The older of the two scientific anoraks, who was now less than twenty-five, moved closer to him and pressed for clarification.

"Are you married or are you not?"

"Yes and no."

They laughed dutifully and Byron explained.

"I do have a licence somewhere, and a wife somewhere else – God bless her – yes, and we even had a child. A girl, I think. Must be four, nine, twelve, by now. My wife and I parted, you see. That's to say, I can run faster than she can; and she's never caught me yet nor ever will."

Mrs Elias called for last orders and Byron stood his friends and himself a nightcap.

"Yes. Her name was Patricia. My wife."

A wife is a ghost if you can see right through her, and if she walks out through the walls of a marriage.

"It's not far, Byron."

How had he got into their van and what was all this equipment?

"Go on talking. We love your voice."

Where was he driving between two teenagers in anoraks?

"Talk. We love your voice."

"We know about voices."

"Sound. That is what we research. Sound."

"Scientists in sound."

Had he talked for an hour before the van stopped?

"Here we are, Byron. Come on in."

In which direction had they come and how would he return?

"Let's have a drink, shall we, Byron?"

No matter. The joint possibilities had matured as they had grown younger. Both were positives in the Pat sphere. Double Pats. A before and after Pat. A first then second Pat. A left and right Pat. A beneath and on top Pat. Yes, he would have another whisky, Pat.

The anoraks hanged themselves on hooks and the girls reclined on warm sofas. The cottage was large and well-appointed. Sound scientists did well, obviously. Perhaps there was something among all this gadgetry that could be adapted to Byron's purpose and palmed off on holiday children. Might he see this? How does that work? I bet those cost a bit, Byron. Ask more about these. Then, as he was about to divide and rule the Pats, as he was about come to terms with them, the offer.

"A thousand pounds!"

"In cash, Byron."

"Here it is, Byron. See for yourself."

He felt the notes. Crisp, real, immediate.

"You want to give me one thousand pounds for my voice?"

"It's worth far more but that is all our Foundation allows us."

"It's ridiculous … all I have to do is to speak into the mike …"

"And you're richer by one thousand pounds, Byron. Feel them again."

"No need. You're on."

And though the scientists in sound did look a trifle older and did put on dark spectacles for the recording, Byron was not dismayed. Technical fun beforehand would only heighten his desire. There were still two consecutive Pats waiting. Not to mention a thousand pounds by way of an honorarium. But first you must drink to science, Byron.

"What is it, girls?"

"It will help to clear your throat. For the recording."

How much had the gulls been paid for their voices?

Into his mouth Byron poured the liquid. It was sharp, cleansing. His mouth felt bigger. Examine that mouth, Byron. Take a mirror and study the ghosts around those lips. The shades of spent words, of betrayals, of boasts, of marital vows, of midnight promises. Spectres of kisses for this Pat or that. Drink, food, nicotine. A lot has come in and out of that mouth, Byron. A lot more will come in and out of it before this night is over. Yes, take the card. You can read.

"I, Byron Morris, do hereby give my voice for scientific purposes, in return for the payment of one thousand pounds."

"Louder, please."

Adjustments, earphones, amplifiers.

"I, Byron Morris …"

"With more urgency, please."

"I, Byron …"

"Faster".

"I, B—"

"Faster still."

"I—"

"All over."

"All over, Byron."

"There's your thousand pounds."

A woman in her forties handed him the money. It was all there.

"Thank you, Byron."

"You've been an immense help."

"One can only do so much with gulls."

"You have assisted our researches no end."

They age with each second. Where have the two Pats gone?

"Goodbye, then, Byron."

"Find your own way out."

"And thank you again."

"Did you want to say something, Byron?"

WAIT! Byron is mouthing madly. The loudmouth who is skilled in mouth-watering promises agitates his mouthpiece. It is as well that the two scientists can lip-read.

"Where is your voice?"

"On the tape, of course. We own it now, Byron."

"You sold it to us. Remember?"

It is not a joke, Byron. It is not one of your plastic gimmicks which you can thrust upon the juvenile population in order that it can irritate its elders. This toy works. This toy is real. This toy is not for sale, least of all at a thousand pounds. They will give you a demonstration if you will only stop thrusting the money into their faces. One of them, an anti-Pat, is depressing the switch.

"What the hell have you done with my voice?"

"Bought it, Byron."

"Stop playing games, will you?"

"It was a fair agreement, Byron."

"Fair. You give me my voice back or I'll –" Click.

Poor old dumb Byron. Cut dead by a female finger. Silenced by science. Work it out if you can, Byron. Five yards away is a machine and your voice. You here, it there. Thoughts within you, means of expressing them without. It is no use looking menacing. They have legal arguments. A finger presses another switch.

"I, Byron Morris, do hereby give my voice ..."

Out of your own mouth you have been condemned. And you repeat your bargain louder, with more urgency, faster, faster still.

"I shouldn't do that, Mr Morris."

Mistake, Byron. To try and grab the machine.

"Goodnight, Mr Morris."

Down-graded to "Mr Morris" now. Morris the Mute.

"This is loaded."

Two scientists with a real gun. Are they really kicking him out?

Night is a ghost. It haunts nightly.

Steal their van, Byron. Drive madly in all directions. Obey the pointing of all these fingerposts that flash by. You must get to town soon. But what then? How will you explain your predicament? Write it down. Of course. And what about your voice? Consult the gulls. Have they, too, been cheated by science of their means of speech? You must have a voice to voice your complaints, Byron. And you do! On your own tape-recorder back at the Ship. Find the town. Find the Ship. One of these fingers must point aright. There – lights, shapes, sea. Defy speed-limits, man. This is a matter of life and the death of a voice.

"Don't knock the door down!"
    Nothing amiss with the voice of Mrs Elias.
    "I'm coming, I'm coming!"
    And a dozen oaths confirm that her vocal abilities are intact.
    "What are you trying to say, man!"
    But Byron has lost patience with the former Pat and pushed past her to rush up to his room. There, he stops, transfixed. A picture on the wall is lit by the beam from a street-lamp. A picture that was not there before. A picture of the beach and the sea and a body which is clearly a man's. The girl's picture. Completed. She did exist. She did call at the Ship, after all.
    "Come as soon as you can, Sergeant. Gone berserk, he has."
    Down below, Mrs Elias plays the traitor. No time to reason with night-duty Sergeants. Grab your tape-recorder and go. Run, Byron. Make for the van. Drive, off you go, drive. You've got more power under your bonnet than the police car. You'll soon shake it off.

Forks and twists and bends in the road help Byron to shake off his pursuers long enough for him to switch on the tape-recorder. He will draw comfort from his own voice. He will be reassured by his own requests and replies and vocal nudges to Pat. Switch on.
    "I, Byron Morris, do hereby give my voice ..."
    You should not have thrown it out of the van like that, Byron. It will not be covered by your expenses. The firm is particular about the safety of its equipment.
    A light ahead. A farmhouse. No, *the* farmhouse. The one that houses two anoraks and a stolen voice! Stop the van, creep up, look through the window. Over strong coffee, the scientists chat about sound and consider the day's takings. Don't

rush, Byron. The tape recorder is there for the taking, but do not forget the gun. That stick will be ideal. Quietly. In you go. The door is on the latch.

"Mr Morris. What do you want?"

"I thought we told you to … aw!"

The gun smashed from her hand by the weight of the stick.

"Leave that alone. It cost thousands."

So did your voice, Byron. One thousand, anyway. Take the machine.

"Take your hands off it, or … ugh."

Women have to be struck sometimes. Knock the other one out, too. They look better in repose. Now take the machine and go.

"Go round the back, Jones. And be careful. He may be dangerous."

The law approaches.

"Hurry, Jones. He must be inside."

Sergeant Owen is no court of appeal, Byron. You need time and apartness. Face a policeman with the theft of a car, breaking and entering, grievous bodily harm, a stolen machine, a lost voice and a previous warning for causing trouble and where will it get you? Find the back door and get away, even if the machine is heavy.

"This way, Sarge! He's making a run for it!"

"Come here, Jones."

"But, Sarge."

"These women need attention. Quick, man!"

Policemen turn nurses, then speak into transmitters.

Alone in a ditch, Byron Morris stops long enough to appreciate that the machine, true to the money expended upon it, operates on battery or mains. He flicks the switch marked "battery", then presses another. Gulls call endlessly. He stops their sound, tries another switch.

"I, Byron Morris …"

Again, he kills the sound. A third switch.

"What on earth are you going to do, Byron?"

Himself. His own voice, strangered but loyal.

"Think. How are you going to get out of this one?"

He could go to the police.

"With all they've got on you? That Sergeant would think this was another of your jokes."

Back home. Back to the office. Back to Pat.

"What use are you to any of them without me?"

The dialogue between two old friends is interrupted by whistle and dog. Where have all these men and animals come from? The police station in the town only runs to a few constables. Why the reinforcements? It is almost like a murder hunt.

"You did belt that woman hard."

There was no blood, replies Byron.

"None visible, you mean. Hey, come on, let's get out of here."

Barking encircles and Byron lugs the machine down the ditch. His voice gets heavier at every step, but it is a burden he must carry. The dark is lightening into morning so he must make cover soon. A noise, a restlessness. He must be near the sea. He must have worked his way back to the shore. Rocks have pools. Water bears no scent.

Byron runs and strains and zig-zags and breathes violently though without noise. He wades through water and climbs over rocks. He ignores cuts and bruises and takes risks over crevices. At last, a hiding place. Safety. Dogs will never sniff him here in the salt air. High tide will never wash him out of this lair. The gulls who circle above cannot alert his pursuers because they have wings but no voice. You have made it, Byron. You are free. They will look in vain.

"Here. I'm over here!"

"That way, Sergeant!"

"Here I am! Come and get me."

Why is the machine yelling at the top of its voice? Why is Byron unable to check the treachery of his own voice?

"Over here! Come on!"

"Follow me, men."

"I'm waiting, Byron Morris is waiting."

Try that switch, no, that, well pull out the batteries.

"I, Byron Morris, do hereby give notice ..."

And with a long scream the voice and its undertaking are thrown far and deep into the sea. Byron has abandoned his voice. He has murdered his sound. But a voice is a ghost, too.

A voice is a ghost with a voice. From beneath the waves it calls to Byron with the golden harmony of a Byronic voice. It whispers in his ears the intimate messages which only he can whisper. It weakens, it convinces, it compels. With shivering policemen approaching over the rocks, a man stands up and yells at them with the voice of a hundred gulls then hurls himself into the sea. The manner of his fall from the high promontory suggests that he is searching for something down there, but we shall never know if he found it or not.

When the body was washed up two days later, it proved awkward under questioning. The Sergeant adjourned to the Ship.

"I've never seen that picture before, Mrs Elias."

Beach, sea, drowned man. As before.

"Had it for ages, Sergeant. Always meant to hang it in the bar."

Look closer, Sergeant. The artist has signed the name of "Pat," quietly, in the corner.

PSALM FOR A DEAD DISCIPLE

If you have read these stories in the suggested sequence, you'll see that we have come full circle. Iddo the Samaritan is back again, in a longer and more complex story. Having heard so much about the Healer, he goes to hear the man preach to a large crowd. A would-be disciple first enthralls everyone by singing a psalm but it is cut short when he is stabbed to death. Since the murder weapon is Iddo's dagger, the merchant is lucky to escape with his life. Imprisoned and interrogated by the Romans, he has to find a means of escape and solve the crime for which he is unjustly blamed. "Psalm for a Dead Disciple" shows how closely politics and religion are intertwined, and it underlines the danger of being an outsider. Iddo, the eternal outcast, has to be at his most alert to survive.

*W*e reached our destination by nightfall on the third day. Amok, my bodyguard, as was his wont slept on straw with the animals in the stable of an inn but I sought more wholesome accommodation. She and I were having breakfast the next morning when I heard my first mention of The Healer.

"It is wonderful to see you once more," she purred.

"You are the perfect woman," I said with feeling. "I would travel ten times the distance to sleep in your enchanting arms." An involuntary yawn. "Not that we had much sleep last night." That bewitching smile of hers. "You are insatiable."

"Is that a complaint?"

"It's a cause for celebration, Naomi."

"How long will you be in Galilee?"

"Long enough to come here again," I said.

"Is that a promise?"

"To both of us."

"I will hold you to that."

Naomi is always my first port of call in Galilee. She is a most delightful harbour. Dedicated to pleasure, she does things for me that most women would not dare to contemplate, still less to execute with such delicate precision. Naomi is a place of

240

refuge from a hostile world. A fount of love in a Jewish town where a Samaritan like me is despised, Naomi's love has to be bought but it is all the more reliable for that reason. A merchant by trade, I know how to get value for money.

Tall, slim and sensuous, Naomi is no mere companion for a weary traveller from Sebaste. She is also my intelligencer. She sees and hears everything that happens in Galilee. That is why I pay her so handsomely. To keep watch. A merchant needs to have a ready supply of news.

"Who have you come to see?" she asked.

"You, my angel."

A lazy grin. "Who else?"

"Zebedee the Fisherman."

"He is not in town today."

"Is he out on the lake?"

"No," she explained. "He is going to see The Healer."

"The Healer?"

"A man from Nazareth. He cures the sick."

"Oh?" I said, interest quickening. "Is that why Zebedee wants to visit this man? Is the testy old fisherman ill?"

"No, Iddo. He wants to see The Healer out of curiosity. James and John, his sons, have abandoned their nets to follow this Nazarene. Andrew and Peter, the brothers of Bethsaida, have also declared themselves to be his disciples."

"Disciples? Of some roadside conjuror?"

"He is much more than that, Iddo. They say that he performs miracles. No other man alive could have enticed Zebedee's sons away." Her mouth hardened into a rueful line. "Or stolen one of my best clients."

"Who is that?"

"Levi, son of Alphaeus."

"The tax collector?"

"Yes," she sighed. "But he will never collect taxes again. Levi – or Matthew as we must now call him – has renounced everything to follow this Healer."

"He preferred this itinerant Nazarene to *you*, Naomi?" I said in utter astonishment. "Why?"

"That's a long story."

"I can't wait to hear it."

But I did just that. At that moment, Naomi's divine left breast (my favourite) slipped artlessly into view from beneath her raiment and deprived me of the wish to listen to a story of any length. The olive-skinned mound of flesh had a silken sheen and its gleaming nipple blossomed under my eager gaze. Breakfast was summarily abandoned and we devoured each other instead. It was an hour or more before I had breath enough to ask her a question.

"What is this Healer like?"

"He is dangerous."

"I want to see him," I decided.

It was a disastrous mistake.

The road was busy. Amok and I were part of a sizeable crowd which was moving – largely on foot – in the same direction. Could they all be going in search of The Healer? How could he tempt so many men away from their places of work and so many women from their domestic chores? What was the secret of the Nazarene's appeal?

We were an incongruous sight. Short and squat, I was as usual mounted on Jubal, the huge stallion I won in a wager in Cilicia. Amok, by contrast, my big, shaggy, bear-like scribe and protector, sat astride his flea-bitten donkey and let his heels drag idly through the dust.

We rode in silence. There was no point in attempting meaningful contact with Amok. He is a man of few words. Even his grunts are severely rationed. But then I do not employ him for the joy of his conversation. He is there primarily to safeguard me. In a country where Samaritans are hated I need Amok beside me to discourage my enemies from adding blows to the familiar insults. His stench keeps most people at bay. I was grateful that Naomi's perfume still haunted my nostrils.

As the crowd thickened I recognised a sturdy figure on foot ahead of us and nudged Jubal forward until I drew level with him.

"Good morrow, Levi!" I said.

"Iddo!" he replied with uncharacteristic warmth. "What on earth are you doing here?"

"Looking for The Healer."

"You are only looking," he said proudly. "I was called. He chose me as one of his disciples. Oh, and by the way, he gave me a new name. I am Levi no longer. I am Matthew."

"Naomi told me."

"I have put that harlot aside."

"Madness!"

"I have resolved to live a cleaner life."

"Whatever for, Matthew?"

"It is a condition of following him."

"I prefer to be a disciple of Naomi."

Levi – or Matthew as I will henceforth call him – is an old acquaintance. We knew each other for years before we realised that we had someone in common. Naomi. That indicated to me that he was a man of taste. And moderate wealth. Naomi sets a high price on her favours and rightly so. She does not consort with paupers.

A stocky man of medium height, Matthew dresses well and has an air of seedy prosperity about him. He was a tax collector at the frontier town of Capernaum, a quick-witted fellow with an unctuous charm. Tax collectors are a loathsome species at the best of times but he was also reviled for co-operating with the Roman administration, taking money from his own people to put into the coffers of their overlords.

Jews look upon tax gatherers with the same contempt they reserve for murderers, robbers, rapists and other undesirables. Like Samaritans. It was another bond between Matthew and me. Both of us were despised and shunned. Since his job entailed the collection of customs dues on all articles going in and out of Capernaum, I made sure that we came to an amicable arrangement early on. A merchant must know who to bribe.

Jubal ambled alongside the unlikely disciple.

"Have you really given up all to follow him?" I asked.

"Yes," he said with glowing certitude. "I have seen the error of my former ways and renounced them completely."

"Naomi is an *error*?" I gasped in disbelief.

"She is a sinful woman."

"That is her attraction."

"Not to me. I have turned my back on her."

"That is a terrible sacrifice to make."

"I do it willingly, Iddo. I serve a new master now. The light of purity shines out of him. He has the gift of healing. He restores sight to the blind and hearing to the deaf. When he laid hands upon a cripple the poor wretch was made whole again and danced with joy. My master has magic fingers."

"So does Naomi."

"You have grown coarse, Iddo."

"I am the same as you once were, Matthew."

"Yes," he admitted freely, "that is true. When I sat behind my table and collected taxes I enjoyed a crude jest to break the monotony of the work. But that man has died. I have been reborn in a more godly image."

"I liked the old Levi."

"Wait until you meet our master."

We came round a bend in the road and saw them ahead of us. There were hundreds of people, gathered in a rough circle around a rocky outcrop, looking upwards at the small group of men on the rock itself. Matthew was so keen to join them that he broke into a trot. Amok and I dismounted near the fringe of the gathering and tethered our animals to an olive tree.

I checked that my knife was in my belt. You can never be too careful in a public place. Even with Amok beside me, I like to have a means of defence. The knife has a long, curved blade and a decorated handle of the finest ivory. Its copper scabbard is a work of art. The weapon imparts reassurance.

Anxious to see The Healer I soon found my height a severe disadvantage in such a large throng. Amok noted my distress and pushed a way through the press. One hand on the knife, I followed in his wake. A crowd as large as that is normally loud and boisterous but this one was strangely subdued. It was eerie. Nobody even cursed Amok as he bullocked past them. Attention fixed on the rock, they hardly noticed us.

When a man's voice was raised in the singing of a psalm a hush fell on the whole congregation. The mellifluous words floated on the wind like so many doves of peace. Accompanying himself on the lyre, the musician had a deep, resonant voice which lent beauty and authority to his words. Even to ears as sceptical as mine the sound was persuasive and moving. It also helped us to get our bearings. Follow the psalm and it would lead us to The Healer.

> "The Lord lifteth up the meek;
> he casteth the wicked down to the ground."

That has not been my experience but the melodious voice almost had me believing in it. The singer was positively beguiling us with his art, investing every phrase of the psalm with the sheer power and harmony of his conviction.

> "Sing unto the Lord with thanksgiving;
> sing praise upon the harp to God:
> Who covereth the heaven with clouds,
> who prepareth rain for the earth,
> who maketh the grass to grow upon the mountains."

When we finally reached the singer we found ourselves gazing at a big barrel-chested man of mature years with a red beard and long red hair which hung in ringlets. His fingers plucked deftly as his voice soared.

"He giveth to the beast his food,
and to the young ravens which cry.
He delighteth not in the strength of the horse;
he taketh not pleasure in the legs of a man."

There were thirteen other men on the rock with him. Matthew was directly behind the singer and I also recognised James and John, the sons of Zebedee, but I could not pick out The Healer. Which of those smiling onlookers had brought us all to that hot and dusty place outside the town? My eye ran slowly over the thirteen men. Before I could even guess which one might be the Nazarene, tragedy struck in mid-psalm.

"Praise the Lord, O Jerusalem; praise thy God, O Zion!"

As the words rose up into the air there was a sudden movement behind us and we were pushed towards the singer in a surging wave. Hit by the human deluge he let out a cry of agony, dropped his lyre and fell like a stone to the ground. Having spent its force, the wave ebbed quickly back to reveal the victim. Lying on his back, his mouth frozen in praise of his Lord, he gazed up at heaven with a mixture of yearning and reproach. Only angels would accompany his psalms from now on.

When I studied the corpse more closely my shock was tempered with alarm. Sticking out of his chest was the ivory handle of the weapon which had evidently killed him. I identified it all too readily.

The taut silence was broken, improbably, by Amok.

"Look, master," he said, pointing. "Your knife."

It was all the proof that the crowd needed. They attacked with ferocity and fought each other for the privilege of reaching me. My protests of innocence went unheard in the swirling hysteria. The last thought which went through my mind before I was beaten unconscious was that if I survived the onslaught to hold that knife in my hand once more, I would use it to cut out Amok's tongue.

A man of few words had used them to incriminate me.

Thrown into my face with vicious force, a bucket of black, brackish water finally brought me to my senses again. My face was a mass of aching bruises and a continuous avalanche of sharp stones was taking place inside my skull. My apparel was torn, my body throbbing with pain and my legs made of wax. What disturbed me most of all was that my arms were paralysed.

A second bucket of water concentrated my mind and allowed me to open a first wary eye. It liked nothing of what it saw. Arms pinioned, I was perched on a stool in a featureless room, held upright by two Roman soldiers with drawn swords in their other hands. A third soldier stood before me with two empty wooden pails and a grin as broad as the Tiber. He had enjoyed the task of reviving me for interrogation.

The bucketeer stepped back smartly as an officer came marching into the room. My guards kicked the stool from beneath me and jerked me into an upright position. The newcomer was short and muscular with the strutting arrogance of a man in a position of command. My two supporters were Syrians, pressed into service in the Roman army, but their superior was the genuine article. A Roman soldier from Rome itself. A member of the conquering élite.

It put an imperious note into his clipped Latin.

"What is your name?" he demanded.

"Iddo," I mumbled.

"Speak up in my presence."

A thorough shake by the guards loosened my vocal cords.

"Iddo," I repeated aloud.

"Where do you live?"

"Sebaste."

"What is your occupation?"

"I am a merchant."

"Why did you come to Galilee?"

"To do business."

"With whom?"

"Zebedee the Fisherman."

"Where did you spend last night?"

"At an inn."

"Alone?"

"With my travelling companion. Amok."

Arms folded, legs wide apart, he gave a curt nod.

"You have a good command of Latin," he said with grudging approval. "Do not use it to lie to me."

"I am not lying."

"Then why tell me you slept at an inn with that smelly servant of yours when you spent the night between the thighs of a harlot?" He gave a cold smile. "True or false?"

"A bit of both," I confessed, wondering how he could possibly have come by the information. "The beating I took left me confused."

"Perhaps you would like another bucket of water to refresh your memory. This time your head will be held in it for a few minutes until you learn the difference between truth and dishonesty." He let the threat hang in the air for a moment. "You were lucky," he added.

I raised an ironic eyebrow. "This is *luck*?"

"In the hands of the Jewish authorities you would have been killed an hour ago. A Samaritan stabbing a Jew to death in broad daylight? They would have slaughtered you without even the formality of a trial. You were fortunate to escape. But for the courage of your bodyguard you would have been torn to shreds by that mob. Amok saved your life. My men rescued you both in the nick of time but Amok is your real saviour."

"Where is he?"

"Helping us with our enquiries."

"He's *talking* to you?" I said in amazement.

"Constantly. Through an interpreter."

"What has he told you?"

"That is our business," he snapped. "All I am concerned to establish now is whether or not your story agrees with his. We have already stumbled on one discrepancy – where and with whom you spent the night. I hope we do not find any more." He took a step towards me. "Now, Iddo. Answer me this and be careful with your reply. Why did you kill that man?"

"I did not kill him!" I denied hotly.

"Your knife was in his chest."

"I swear that I did not put it there!"

"Then who did?"

"Whoever took it from my belt."

"Amok, perhaps?"

"Of course not. Amok is my bodyguard."

"He was the one person in the crowd who knew that you carried a knife and he was close enough to take it."

"It would have been an act of suicide," I argued. "You said it yourself a moment ago. A Samaritan murdering a Jew at an exclusively Jewish gathering. Even Amok's strength would not have kept that mob at bay indefinitely."

"True. He took a buffeting on your behalf."

"Because he was more concerned with protecting my life than seeking the death of an anonymous musician."

"Josephus."

"Who?"

"That is the name of the murder victim," he explained. "Josephus of Cana. A fine singer by all accounts."

"He had a most beautiful voice."

"Who decided to silence it?"

"Not me. Nor Amok. We were innocent bystanders."

"That remains to be seen."

"I had no *reason* to kill the man."

"None that has so far emerged."

"I've never seen him before in my entire life."

"We will need to verify that fact."

"Speak to Zebedee. He will vouch for me."

"Do not try to tell me my job," he warned, "or I will have you soundly whipped then thrown into a cell to repent your folly. You are my prisoner. That means you have no rights beyond those I choose to grant you. Frankly, Iddo, I've half a mind to throw you back to the Jews so that they can deal with you. It would save me time and trouble. And you would probably get no more than you deserve." He wagged an admonitory finger. "Do as I tell you or I'll make you wish you were never born."

It was time to fight back and my brain had now cleared sufficiently for it to remember the one fact that might save me. I had no chance of justice at the hands of this self-important brute. My only hope lay in appealing to a higher court. Shrugging off the guards, I drew myself up to my full height and managed a semblance of dignity.

"I wish to speak with Caius Marcius," I said calmly.

He was visibly shaken. "Repeat that," he ordered.

"Caius Marcius. The commander of this fort. Your superior. I want him to witness how shabbily I've been treated by one of his underlings. Send my name to him. He will recognise it."

"You know Caius Marcius?" A note of caution intruded. "What exactly is the nature of your relationship with our commander?"

"I have often done business with him."

"Of what nature?"

"That is highly confidential," I said. "I could not possibly divulge any details because Caius Marcius trusts me implicitly. I have earned that trust and turn to him now to speak up on my behalf."

"He will not defend a murderer."

"Nor will he send an innocent man to his death."

I spoke with more conviction than I felt but it seemed to do the trick. My interrogator moved away and ran a pensive hand over his smooth-shaven chin. I had planted a doubt in his mind. It was a relief to see that all those favours I had done for Caius Marcius over the years might now bear fruit. A merchant should always ingratiate himself with his political masters. A friend high up in the Roman administration is a friend indeed.

My captor swung round to face me again.

"Caius Marcius is not at the fortress," he said.

"Then I will come back when he is."

"He returns from Caesarea tomorrow."

"Good," I said. "Release me at once from this unwarranted imprisonment and you have my word that I will be back here tomorrow to discuss this whole matter with your commander."

My suggestion was met with a sneer of contempt.

"Lock him up!" he decreed.

"Alone?" asked one of the guards.

"No. Put him in with the others. A night in a cell with real criminals will tell us if he is one himself."

Lifting me bodily, the two guards carried me out.

"Caius Marcius will hear about this!" I yelled.

"It will be included in my report."

"He would expect me to be treated with respect."

"You have been."

The prison quarters consisted of a series of low, dark, airless stone cells with sunken floors. Dragged through the dust, I arrived in an even more dishevelled state than before. The one concession to my bodily comfort was the removal of my bonds. My hands and arms belonged to me again. Before I could rub them back into life however, the door of a cell was unlocked and I was hurled unceremoniously in through it.

Somebody punched me as I landed on top of him and I rolled into a corner for safety. The door slammed shut with awesome finality. I felt as if I would never again savour the sweet taste of freedom. More immediate problems pressed in on me. The first was the stink. The cell was flavoured with the accumulated excrement of its past and present inhabitants, enriched by the reek of rancid food and the stench of despair. I retched for several minutes which afforded some amusement to my companions. Their sniggers buzzed in my ears like angry bees in search of stolen honey.

My fellow-prisoners were the second problem. It took me some time to work out how many of them there were. One tiny slit in the stone, high in one wall, admitted only a finger of light to penetrate the darkness. When my nostrils finally adjusted to the smell I was able to let my eyes get used to the gloom. Shapes were slowly conjured into view but they had no real definition. I was incarcerated with ghosts.

There were two of them. Huddled against the opposite wall, they sat close enough to each other to exchange nudges and whispers. I caught the odd curse in Hebrew. They were talking about me and keeping me under scrutiny. Who were they? What hideous crimes had they committed to get themselves thrown into such a foul prison? Murder? Kidnap? Robbery? Assault? Rape? I shuddered. They were creatures of the pit, denizens of the darkness who were as much at home in that black mire as the rats I could hear snuffling in the clotted straw.

They belonged. I did not. I was trespassing on their territory and they resented it. How would they express their resentment? That was the question which tormented me.

"Amok!" I cried to myself. "Where *are* you?"

I sat up with a start when I remembered that it was Amok, my own loyal, reliable, incorruptible Amok, who was directly responsible for my arrest. It was he who told the world that the murder weapon which had interrupted a psalm was mine. It was Amok, my closest associate, ridding himself of a week's verbiage in one calamitous speech, who tossed my Samaritan carcass to the ravening Jewish wolves. Had he maintained his habitual silence I would not now be fearing for my life in a military prison. Amok had rebelled against his master.

Evil has its own distinctive odour. It emanated slowly from my companions until it filled the cell and made my head pound. Menace was tangible. They were biding their time. Having sized me up, the two men would know when to strike with maximum effect. Vigilance was essential. Whatever happened, I told myself, I must not fall asleep.

When your body has been pummelled into fatigue such advice is easier to issue than to accept. Sitting upright against the dank wall was an effort in itself. I could feel my strength being sapped by the minute. There was no hope of my being able to stay awake throughout the night to defend myself against an assault. My whole being seemed to be closing its doors on the world one by one. It was impossible to believe that my numb anatomy had so recently thrilled to Naomi's soft caresses.

I clung on until the finger of light drooped, turned grey and waggled a farewell before vanishing through the slit. A blackness deeper than anything I had ever known before enfolded me in its arms and squeezed all resistance from me. I was asleep in an instant. How long my slumber lasted I have no notion but I was brought out of it in the most inconsiderate manner.

The kick in the stomach awakened me then I was hauled upright by a powerful arm and pinned against the wall. Light was just starting to feel its way in through the slit so it must have been dawn but I was given no chance to make an accurate assessment of the time of day. The villain who had me flattened against the wall was bigger, broader, heavier and stronger than me. He also had a weapon.

Grabbing me by the beard, he put the blade of his knife across my throat. From the smell of his breath I knew that we could never be close friends.

"What's your name?" he growled.

"Iddo."

His eyes narrowed suspiciously.

"Are you a Samaritan?" he accused.

I gave him my most obliging smile.

"Not necessarily."

It was not the occasion for complete honesty.

"If you were I'd slit your throat right now. We have our standards. We may be criminals but we do not deserve to be locked up with a rotten, lousy, cheating Samaritan. It'd be an insult to us. Understand?"

"Only too well."

"So what are you in for, Iddo?"

"Murder."

It earned a momentary respect from them. They nudged and whispered again then the knife was twisted to draw a warning trickle of blood from my neck.

"With us or against us?" hissed my assailant.

"With you," I affirmed. "All the way."

"We mean to escape."

"But that's impossible."

"Not with your assistance," he said. "We have a plan."

"How do I come into it?"

"Call for help."

"Who from?"

"The guards. There are only two of them. Stupid Syrians who come on duty at first light, still half-asleep. Yell out that we're attacking you and they'll stagger over here. When they open that door we'll be ready for them."

"You'll kill them?" I gulped.

"We'll kill anyone who stands in our way."

"What about me?"

"You escape with us, of course."

I know a grotesque lie when I hear it. Merchants are students of character. We develop intuition. I did not need a long acquaintance with the pair to know that they had no intention of letting me leave the cell alive. When I had served my purpose they would dispose of me as callously as they would of the two Syrians. My brain whirred madly.

"Will you do it?" he demanded.

"What must I say?"

"Just howl for help. Say that we're hitting you."

"Or we will," added his friend. "Hard."

They held the advantage over me but I did have one secret means of fighting back. A merchant needs to speak in many languages. Unknown to them I was fluent in Aramaic. When I battered on the door of the cell and cried out for help in the Hebrew which they understood I also slipped in a warning in words that the Syrian guards alone would recognise.

"This is a ruse!" I cried. "I'm pretending to be in danger to lure you to the cell. They are behind the door and one of them has a knife. Beware!"

My voice became one long screech of pain and footsteps were heard thundering down the passageway outside. Crouched behind the door, the two villains waited to pounce on the unsuspecting guards but these were Syrians with the benefit of Roman military training. When the door opened they came through it with their shields held before them, giving them complete protection and allowing them to force the two prisoners back against the wall. Other guards came running to their aid. Instead of escaping the men were overpowered and fettered within minutes.

I was taken out of the cell for my own safety.

"You betrayed us!" shouted my would-be assassin.

"Shameful, isn't it?" I teased. "Learn your lesson."

"What lesson?"

"Never trust a Samaritan."

His howl of rage was heard as far away as Sebaste.

I prefer to think that it was my brave action in foiling a prison escape which earned me my release but two other factors were paramount. Amok, my silent associate, suddenly discovered the power of words and used them to persuade the Romans, if not of my innocence then at least of the unlikelihood of my guilt. But it was the return of Caius Marcius which was decisive. We are old trading partners. Over the years I have provided him with rich foods, heady wines and all the other delicacies a soldier needs when he is isolated from the civilised world of Rome. More to the point, I introduced him to Naomi and he has been unfailingly grateful to me.

"You are free to go, Iddo," he said magnanimously.

"What about Amok?"

"Take him with you. He is charged with no offence."

"Thank you, Caius Marcius."

"Ride hard in the direction of Samaria," he counselled. "Leave Galilee while you have the opportunity."

"But I was falsely accused of a murder."

"The Jews still believe you stabbed Josephus with your knife. Show yourself in the streets and they will take the law into their own hands. Trade elsewhere until this whole affair has blown over."

"How can it until the crime has been solved?"

"We will look into the matter."

"I was there," I reasoned. "You were not. The only person likely to get to the truth is me. I owe it to myself to track down the killer. And I owe it to Josephus. I have never heard a psalm sung so well."

"Stay in Galilee and you court danger."

"I thrive on it."

"Go now," he urged. "While you still may."

"Only when I have unmasked the real assassin."

Caius Marcius turned away to ponder. A noble Roman, he has the kind of handsome profile which would grace the imperial coinage and withstand the wear and tear without losing any definition. When he looked back at me he clicked his tongue and shook his head sadly.

"You are a brave fool, Iddo."

"I want my name cleared."

"Let others try to do that for you," he said. "How can you possibly solve this crime? You would not even know where to start looking."

"Yes, I would."

"Where?"

"In the psalms."

Torn between anger and gratitude, I was not sure whether to berate Amok for bringing the wrath of the mob down on me or to thank him for saving me from their worst excesses. In the end I settled for a brief reprimand followed by a pat on the back. Amok retreated into a hurt silence.

Remaining in Galilee meant assuming a disguise and he was very unhappy about that. As anyone who has stood next to him will testify, Amok has not changed his garments for at least a decade and I had to force him to put on a clean robe. My own flamboyant apparel – a merchant needs to be visible – was traded for the most sober raiment I could find. Our animals had been brought to the fort by the soldiers who arrested us and it seemed sensible to leave Jubal there for the time being. A white horse is a rare sight among the asses and camels of Galilee. For once in my life I did not want people to look at me and take due note of my status.

Two men and a donkey left the fort to solve a murder.

"Your task is simple, Amok," I told him. "Watch my back. That is all you have to do. Guard your master. Is that clear? And the next time my knife ends up in someone's chest you are to hold your tongue. Do you hear? Say nothing!"

Amok said nothing.

He waited outside the house while I made my first call. Amok would never dream of crossing such a sinful threshold. Naomi was puzzled until she realised who was concealed beneath the black burnoose. Relief gave way to sheer delight and she showered me with kisses.

"Thank heaven you are safe!" she said.

"You heard what happened?"

"Everyone in Galilee has heard."

"I did not kill him, Naomi."

"I never thought for a moment that you did."

"Somebody used me as his scapegoat," I said, taking her by the shoulders. "I need you to help me find him."

"How?"

"Tell me all you know about Josephus of Cana."

"It is little enough," she apologised. "Report has it that Josephus was a lawyer, a learned man of good reputation. When he heard The Healer preach however, Josephus lost all interest in his clients and talked only of the law of the Lord. His ambition was to become one of the disciples but twelve had already been chosen. Josephus found it difficult to cope with rejection. Why should an upright man like himself be turned away while a rogue like Levi, son of Alphaeus, was accepted as a fit companion to The Healer?"

"A good question."

"It preyed on his mind."

"What action did he take?"

"You witnessed it for yourself, Iddo," she said. "He elected himself as one of the chosen. Whenever and wherever The Healer went to preach Josephus of Cana went also and inspired the crowd by singing them a psalm. It was his way of being part of The Healer's ministry."

"I think I hear what you are telling me, Naomi."

"Josephus was an interloper."

"An unlucky thirteenth disciple."

After a visit to the temple I set off in search of Matthew. It took an age to track him down. In the old days he would have been easy to find, sitting behind his table in the open air, collecting taxes, dispensing ribald jokes and swindling the gullible citizens with a skill born of long practice. Our search began at his home then took us on a circuitous route through the whole of Galilee. We eventually caught him outside a house on the fringe of the town. When I revealed to him who we were Matthew was duly startled.

"I thought you were languishing in prison," he said.

"Until this morning I was. Quite unjustly."

"I know, my friend. Whoever killed poor Josephus, it was certainly not you. I tried to say so at the time but the crowd was in no mood to listen." He embraced me warmly. "Your travail is over. God has seen fit to deliver you."

"With a little help from the Roman army," I corrected. "As for my travail it continues unabated. Were it not for this disguise I would probably have been stoned to death by now. In the eyes of your people I am still the prime suspect. Murder is bad for a merchant's business. I must exonerate myself."

"Count on my full support, Iddo."

"That is why I came to you." I glanced up at the fine mansion behind him. "But what are you doing out here at this splendid residence? I thought you had renounced your rich friends and your life of indulgence?"

"I have, I have," he insisted. "My master was summoned here because the daughter of the house is grievously sick and likely to die. Only his healing powers can save her."

"Are the other disciples here?"

"Some of them. I stayed outside to keep watch."

"For what?"

"Enemies. My master is not popular in some quarters I fear. His preaching unsettles the Pharisees, his miracles arouse much envy and scorn. After what happened yesterday we feel that it is wise to take certain precautions."

"Who killed Josephus of Cana?"

"I wish I knew."

"Do you have no idea, Matthew? You were standing as close to Josephus as anyone. Did you not see the knife being thrust into his chest?"

"It happened so quickly and amid such commotion."

"What of the faces in the front row of the crowd?"

"I recognised none apart from your own."

"Did Josephus have any particular enemies?"

"Several. He was a lawyer."

"Has anyone sworn to kill him?"

"I do not know, Iddo. He was not one of the chosen. He merely lurked in our master's shadow and tried to befriend him by singing psalms." He put an anxious face close to mine. "This is a desperate business, my friend. I tell you this in confidence. We are appalled at the murder of Josephus of Cana and mourn his demise but some of us, privately, have a deeper fear. Was the hapless Josephus, in fact, the killer's intended target? Might not your knife – stolen deliberately from your belt – have been destined for another heart?"

"Your own, perhaps?"

"Or my master's. They wanted to silence him."

"They?"

"His enemies."

"Do you have their names?"

"They are legion."

"Where was your master standing?"

"Just behind Josephus."

"Then why was he not stabbed?"

"Who knows?" he said with a shrug. "All I can suggest is that when the crowd surged forward it was difficult to control the thrust of the knife. My guess is that the murderer had a confederate further back in the press and that it was he who caused that sudden lurch forward in order to conceal the stabbing. You unwittingly provided the murder weapon."

"Come back to Josephus," I said.

"Why?"

"Is there any significance in the timing of his death?"

"What do you mean?"

"The thirteenth disciple was killed at the very moment he was about to sing the thirteenth verse of his psalm. Do you know what that verse is, Matthew?"

"Not offhand."

> "For he hath strengthened the bars of thy gates;
> he hath blessed thy children within thee."

"Your knowledge of the psalms astounds me, Iddo."

"Even a sinner needs something to sing."

"But you are a Samaritan. You only accept the Pentateuch."

"The Five Books of Moses could do with a psalm or two to lighten their tone," I said with an irreverent grin. "But I will not deceive you. The psalm sung by Josephus has a special meaning for me. I called at a temple on my way here to seek it out in full lest it should contain some vital clue."

"And does it?"

"I am not sure. I need to sing it to myself a few more times. And in honour of Josephus of Cana."

"Josephus?"

"A psalm for a dead disciple."

"We all grieve at his passing."

"What does The Healer say?"

"My master?"

"He was there at the crucial moment and in a perfect position to witness the outrage. Does he not have some idea who delivered the fatal thrust with the knife and which breast the blade was really destined for?"

"He spoke only of you, Iddo."

"Me?"

"With great sympathy."

"But he does not even know me."

"He knows your situation," said Matthew gently. "Knows and understands. You are a Samaritan, a natural outcast in a Jewish enclave like Galilee, a man so despised for an accident of birth that he will be suspected of the most heinous crimes. You are the ritual sacrifice, Iddo. A man is killed. Your knife is in his chest. Proof positive of Samaritan villainy."

"I am beginning to like your master," I conceded.

"Then hearken to his advice."

"What is it?"

"Two crimes were committed yesterday, Iddo. The second was the murder of Josephus and it was so hideous an act that it obscured the crime which preceded it."

"The theft of my dagger."

"Who knew that you carried it?"

"Amok and myself."

"Are you sure?"

"What do you mean?"

"Only this, my friend," he said with a consoling hand on my shoulder. "Someone deliberately put the blame for this killing on you. Someone who hates you enough to want you dead. Someone who trailed you through that crowd. Someone who knew that you had that weapon in your belt."

"What are you saying, Matthew?"

"Leave us to worry about who the real target was. All that you need to concentrate on is your own predicament."

"Give it to me in a sentence."

"Look to your enemies."

It was sound advice and we acted on it promptly. The problem lay in the sheer numbers. Success breeds envy and I have been highly successful as a merchant. I have created so many enemies in Galilee that it would take a month or more to get around them all. Speaking aloud, I counted the leading suspects on my stubby fingers. All would be happy to see me dead.

It was Amok who provided the breakthrough. He refused to speak but he did rise to an elaborate mime, taking back one hand before bringing it smartly forward and opening his palm. I saw invisible dice rolling in the dust and let out a cry of triumph.

"Amok!" I congratulated. "You are a genius."

A faint smile lit his inscrutable features.

"Nathan!" I continued. "He must be involved here. Why ever didn't I think of Nathan of Galilee?"

The answer was simple. It would be hard to imagine anyone less likely than Nathan to make the effort to see The Healer. Nathan is one of the most godless and unscrupulous human beings in existence, the sort of grasping merchant who gives the rest of us a bad name. What Amok had reminded me was that Nathan knew that I carried the knife in my belt. It was something he would not forget because I had won it off him in a game of dice and he had cursed me when parting with it.

Could Nathan be involved in the murder of Josephus?

We set off to find out, trailing him through the dingier parts of the town where he preyed upon the poor and ignorant. As expected we found him at an inn, sharing a jug of wine with a thin, angular man. Nathan was sleek, fat, middle-aged and far too cowardly to wield the murder weapon so he would need an accomplice of sorts. The sly smile of his companion alerted me at once. The two of them were celebrating and had already drunk too much wine to be aware of eavesdroppers.

I stationed Amok outside the inn and went in alone. Taking care to keep my face turned away from them I sat at the adjoining table and ordered food and drink. As time passed their celebration became steadily louder and their comments more indiscreet. I leaned in to hear the tell-tale phrases.

"Iddo," said Nathan with a chuckle. "Iddo the idiot."

"A Samaritan dog!" sneered the other.

"I could not believe our luck when I saw him there."

"His knife went in like a dream."

"My knife, Phanuel," insisted Nathan. "My knife. That wretch won it off me in a game of dice. I still believe that he cheated. But it was my knife that did the deed. And I caused that ripple. I played my part."

"Almost too well, my friend. When the crowd surged forward, I was almost knocked off my feet." His lips parted in a grin. "But my weapon found its mark."

"We worked well together."

"Next time it will be *his* turn."

"You have not paid me for Josephus yet."

"Here," said Phanuel, taking a bag of coins from his belt and slipping it to Nathan with faint disgust. "There is your wage, hireling. What I did was done out of true conviction but you needed to be bought."

"I am a merchant."

"You drive a hard bargain."

"That is what Iddo the Samaritan found out."

I had heard enough. Finishing my drink, I went back outside and told Amok what I had discovered. He was all for charging into the building and dragging the pair of them out by the scruff of their necks but I warned against intemperate action. We had to choose a less public place for our confrontation.

As it turned out, Nathan chose it for us. When he and Phanuel rolled out of the inn we simply had to follow them from a discreet distance until they came to a grove of olives. Too much wine prompted both men to step among the trunks in order to relieve themselves. They were standing targets.

I sauntered up behind them on my own.

"Hello, Nathan," I said jocularly. "Remember me?"

"Iddo!" he exclaimed, drenching his legs in alarm.

"I wondered if you had time for a game of dice."

"We thought you'd be dead by now."

"I know. That's what I wanted to discuss with you."

Phanuel was quick to recover. Swinging around, he slipped a hand into his sleeve and produced a long dagger. There was a glint of madness in his eye.

"I should have killed you when I had the chance!" he said.

"Tell that to the authorities."

"It was Phanuel who did it," bleated Nathan, losing his nerve. "I'm no murderer. He stole your knife, Iddo."

"Shut your mouth!" snarled his accomplice.

"Yes," I said. "I heard all I needed to back at the inn. You are as guilty as this villain. You'll both hang."

Phanuel brandished his dagger menacingly.

"Who says so?" he challenged.

"Amok does," I explained.

"Who?"

"Amok. Let me introduce you."

But my bodyguard was in no mood for the niceties. His mode of introduction was brutally direct. One blow across the back of the neck felled Nathan then a kick in the groin doubled Phanuel up. Before he could regain his breath his dagger had been expertly snatched away by Amok who lifted him high above his head, rotated him several times, then hurled him against the trunk of a tree with great force.

The killer of Josephus of Cana sat on the ground amid an impromptu hailstorm of olives. Amok reached down to pick one up and pop it into his mouth. It was a deserved reward.

The capture of the two conspirators absolved me from the charge of murder and allowed me to resume my career as Iddo the Merchant. Nobody was more overjoyed at the turn of events than my old friend Matthew, the quondam tax collector.

"Well done, Iddo!" he said. "You and Amok have done us all a great service. I am surprised that Nathan was implicated but not that Phanuel was involved."

"You know him?" I asked.

"Only by reputation. A religious zealot. Part of a small but dedicated group who have tried to infiltrate the Sanhedrin in recent years. They see our master as a serious threat. He inspires people with his miracles, leading them away from the influence of Phanuel and his sect."

"The Healer was their next target, Matthew."

"So we feared."

"This first murder was simply a test of their cunning."

"They will pay the full price for their crime."

"Caius Marcius had a cell waiting especially for them."

"Thanks to you a horrible crime has been solved."

"Amok did his share," I reminded him. "He was the one who plucked the name of Nathan from the long list of my enemies."

"You have won many friends, Iddo. But I daresay you will not wish to linger here among them. Galilee treated you very badly. You will wish to get away as soon as possible."

"I will stay for the funeral, Matthew."

"Funeral?"

"I must," I said. "I want to pay my respects to Josephus of Cana. After all, he and I have an unfortunate bond."

Matthew heaved a deep sigh of regret.

"You were both in the wrong place at the wrong time."

I remembered that beautiful voice raised in song.

"Yes," I said. "Wrong place, wrong time, wrong psalm."

SOURCES

Murder and Miracles first appeared in *Past Crimes: Perfectly Criminal III*, the Crime Writers Association Annual Anthology, edited by Martin Edwards. Severn House, 1998.

The Hunchback and the Stammerer first appeared in *Ellery Queen Mystery Magazine*, edited by Janet Hutchings, February 2003.

War Hath Made All Friends first appeared in *Shakespearean Detectives / More Shakespearean Whodunnits*, edited by Mike Ashley. Robinson, 1998.

Domesday Deferred first appeared in *Crime Through Time II*, edited by Miriam Grace Monfredo and Sharan Newman. Berkley, 1998.

The Shoulder Blade of a Ram first appeared in *Murder Through the Ages*, edited by Maxim Jakubowski. Headline, 2000.

Perfect Shadows first appeared in *Royal Whodunnits*, edited by Mike Ashley, Robinson, 2000.

Black Death first appeared in *Royal Crimes*, edited by Maxim Jakubowski and Martin H. Greenberg. Signet, 1994.

A Gift from God first appeared in *Murder Most Medieval*, edited by Martin H. Greenberg and John Helfers. Cumberland House, 2000.

Squinting at Death first appeared in *Much Ado about Murder*, edited by Anne Perry, Berkley, 2002.

Murder at Anchor first appeared in *Crime Through Time*, edited by Miriam Grace Monfredo and Sharan Newman. Berkley, 1998.

Murder, Ancient and Modern

Murder, Ancient and Modern by Edward Marston is set in 11-point Garamond on 13.5-point leading (for the text) and 14 point Zapf Chancery Light on 16-point leading (for the running titles). It is printed on sixty-pound Natures acid-free paper. The cover design is by Gail Cross. The first edition was printed in two forms: trade softcover, notchbound; and two hundred twenty-five copies sewn in cloth, signed and numbered by the author. Each of the clothbound copies includes a separate pamphlet, *The End of the Line* by Edward Marston. *Murder, Ancient and Modern* was printed and bound by Thomson-Shore, Inc., Dexter, Michigan and published in October 2005 by Crippen & Landru Publishers, Inc., Norfolk, Virginia.

CRIPPEN & LANDRU, PUBLISHERS

P. O. Box 9315, Norfolk, VA 23505

E-mail: info@crippenlandru.com; toll-free 877 622-6656

Web: www.crippenlandru.com

Crippen & Landru publishes first edition short-story collections by important detective and mystery writers. The following books are currently (October 2005) in print in our regular series; see our website for full details:

The McCone Files by Marcia Muller. 1995. Trade softcover, $19.00.

Diagnosis: Impossible, The Problems of Dr. Sam Hawthorne by Edward D. Hoch. 1996. Trade softcover, $19.00.

Who Killed Father Christmas? by Patricia Moyes. 1996. Signed, unnumbered cloth overrun copies, $30.00. Trade softcover, $16.00.

My Mother, The Detective: by James Yaffe. 1997. Trade softcover, $15.00.

In Kensington Gardens Once by H.R.F. Keating. 1997. Trade softcover, $12.00.

Shoveling Smoke: by Margaret Maron. 1997. Trade softcover, $19.00.

The Ripper of Storyville by Edward D. Hoch. 1997. Trade softcover. $19.00.

Renowned Be Thy Grave by P.M. Carlson. 1998. Trade softcover, $16.00.

Carpenter and Quincannon by Bill Pronzini. 1998. Trade softcover, $16.00.

Not Safe After Dark by Peter Robinson. 1998. Trade softcover, $17.00.

Famous Blue Raincoat by Ed Gorman. 1999. Signed, unnumbered cloth overrun copies, $30.00. Trade softcover, $17.00.

The Tragedy of Errors by Ellery Queen. 1999. Trade softcover, $19.00.

McCone and Friends by Marcia Muller. 2000. Trade softcover, $16.00.

Challenge the Widow Maker by Clark Howard. 2000. Trade softcover, $16.00.

Fortune's World by Michael Collins. 2000. Trade softcover, $16.00.

Long Live the Dead by Hugh B. Cave. 2000. Trade softcover, $16.00.

Tales Out of School by Carolyn Wheat. 2000. Trade softcover, $16.00.

Stakeout on Page Street and Other DKA Files by Joe Gores. 2000. Trade softcover, $16.00.

The Celestial Buffet by Susan Dunlap. 2001. Trade softcover, $16.00.

Kisses of Death: by Max Allan Collins. 2001. Trade softcover, $17.00.

The Old Spies Club by Edward D. Hoch. 2001. Signed, unnumbered cloth overrun copies, $32.00. Trade softcover, $17.00.

Adam and Eve on a Raft by Ron Goulart. 2001. Signed, unnumbered cloth overrun copies, $32.00. Trade softcover, $17.00.

The Sedgemoor Strangler by Peter Lovesey. 2001. Trade softcover, $17.00.

The Reluctant Detective by Michael Z. Lewin. 2001. Signed, numbered clothbound, $42.00. Trade softcover, $17.00.

Nine Sons by Wendy Hornsby. 2002. Trade softcover, $16.00.

The Curious Conspiracy and Other Crimes by Michael Gilbert. 2002. Signed, numbered clothbound, $42.00. Trade softcover, $17.00.

The 13 Culprits by Georges Simenon. 2002. Trade softcover, $16.00.

The Dark Snow by Brendan DuBois. 2002. Signed, unnumbered cloth overrun copies, $32.00. Trade softcover, $17.00.

Jo Gar's Casebook by Raoul Whitfield, edited by Keith Alan Deutsch [Published with Black Mask Press]. 2002. Trade softcover, $20.00.

Come Into My Parlor: by Hugh B. Cave. 2002. Trade softcover, $17.00.

The Iron Angel and Other Tales of the Gypsy Sleuth by Edward D. Hoch. 2003. Signed, numbered clothbound, $42.00. Trade softcover, $17.00.

Cuddy – Plus One by Jeremiah Healy. 2003. Trade softcover, $18.00.

Problems Solved by Bill Pronzini and Barry N. Malzberg. 2003. Signed, numbered clothbound, $42.00. Trade softcover, $16.00.

A Killing Climate by Eric Wright. 2003. Signed, numbered clothbound, $42.00. Trade softcover, $17.00.

Lucky Dip by Liza Cody. 2003. Signed, numbered clothbound, $42.00. Trade softcover, $17.00.

Kill the Umpire: The Calls of Ed Gorgon by Jon L. Breen. 2003. Signed, numbered clothbound, $42.00. Trade softcover, $17.00.

Suitable for Hanging by Margaret Maron. 2004. Trade softcover, $17.00.

Murders and Other Confusions by Kathy Lynn Emerson. 2004. Signed, numbered clothbound, $42.00. Trade softcover, $19.00.

Byline: Mickey Spillane by Mickey Spillane. 2004. Trade softcover, $20.00.

The Confessions of Owen Keane by Terence Faherty. 2005. Signed, numbered clothbound, $42.00. Trade softcover, $17.00.

The Adventure of the Murdered Moths and Other Radio Mysteries by Ellery Queen. 2005. Numbered clothbound, $45.00. Trade softcover, $20.00.

Murder, Ancient and Modern by Edward Marston. Signed, numbered clothbound, $43.00. Trade softcover, $18.00.

FORTHCOMING TITLES IN THE REGULAR SERIES

Murder! 'Orrible Murder! by Amy Myers
More Things Impossible by Edward D. Hoch
The Mankiller of Poojeegai and Other Mysteries by Walter Satterthwait
A Pocketful of Noses: Stories of One Ganelon or Another by James Powell
Quintet: The Cases of Chase and Delacroix, by Richard A. Lupoff
Thirteen to the Gallows by John Dickson Carr and Val Gielgud
A Little Intelligence by Robert Silverberg and Randall Garrett (writing as "Robert Randall")
The Archer Files: The Complete Short Stories of Lew Archer, Private Investigator, Including Newly-Discovered Case-Notes by Ross Macdonald, edited by Tom Nolan
14 Slayers by Paul Cain, edited by Max Allan Collins and Lynn F. Myers, Jr. Published with Black Mask Press
Tough As Nails by Frederick Nebel, edited by Rob Preston. Published with Black Mask Press
You'll Die Laughing by Norbert Davis, edited by Bill Pronzini. Published with Black Mask Press
Hoch's Ladies by Edward D. Hoch
Suspense—His and Hers by Barbara and Max Allan Collins

CRIPPEN & LANDRU LOST CLASSICS

Crippen & Landru is proud to publish a series of *new* short-story collections by great authors who specialized in traditional mysteries:

The Newtonian Egg and Other Cases of Rolf le Roux by Peter Godfrey, introduction by Ronald Godfrey. 2002. Trade softcover, $15.00
Murder, Mystery and Malone by Craig Rice, edited by Jeffrey A. Marks. 2002. Trade softcover, $19.00.
The Sleuth of Baghdad: The Inspector Chafik Stories, by Charles B. Child. 2002. Cloth, $27.00. Trade softcover, $19.00.
Hildegarde Withers: Uncollected Riddles by Stuart Palmer, introduction by Mrs. Stuart Palmer. 2002. Cloth, $29.00. Trade softcover, $19.00.
The Spotted Cat and Other Mysteries by Christianna Brand, edited by Tony Medawar. 2002. Cloth, $29.00. Trade softcover, $19.00.
Marksman and Other Stories by William Campbell Gault, edited by Bill Pronzini; afterword by Shelley Gault. 2003. Trade softcover, $19.00.

Karmesin: The World's Greatest Criminal — Or Most Outrageous Liar by Gerald Kersh, edited by Paul Duncan. 2003. Cloth, $27.00. Trade softcover, $17.00.

The Complete Curious Mr. Tarrant by C. Daly King, introduction by Edward D. Hoch. 2003. Cloth, $29.00. Trade softcover, $19.00.

The Pleasant Assassin and Other Cases of Dr. Basil Willing by Helen McCloy, introduction by B.A. Pike. 2003. Cloth, $27.00. Trade softcover, $18.00.

Murder – All Kinds by William L. DeAndrea, introduction by Jane Haddam. 2003. Cloth, $29.00. Trade softcover, $19.00.

The Avenging Chance and Other Mysteries from Roger Sheringham's Casebook by Anthony Berkeley, edited by Tony Medawar and Arthur Robinson. 2004. Cloth, $29.00. Trade softcover, $19.00.

Banner Deadlines: The Impossible Files of Senator Brooks U. Banner by Joseph Commings, edited by Robert Adey; memoir by Edward D. Hoch. 2004. Cloth, $29.00. Trade softcover, $19.00.

The Danger Zone and Other Stories by Erle Stanley Gardner, edited by Bill Pronzini. 2004. Cloth, $29.00. Trade softcover, $19.00.

Dr. Poggioli: Criminologist by T.S. Stribling, edited by Arthur Vidro. 2004. Cloth, $29.00. Trade softcover, $19.00.

The Couple Next Door: Collected Short Mysteries by Margaret Millar, edited by Tom Nolan. 2004. Cloth, $29.00. Trade softcover, $19.00.

Sleuth's Alchemy: Cases of Mrs. Bradley and Others by Gladys Mitchell, edited by Nicholas Fuller. 2005. Cloth, $29.00. Trade softcover, $19.00.

Philip S. Warne/Howard W. Macy, *Who Was Guilty? Two Dime Novels*, edited by Marlena E. Bremseth. 2005. Cloth, $29.00. Trade softcover, $19.00.

Dennis Lynds writing as Michael Collins, *Slot-Machine Kelly*, introduction by Robert J. Randisi. 2005. Cloth, $29.00. Trade softcover, $19.00.

FORTHCOMING LOST CLASSICS

Rafael Sabatini, *The Evidence of the Sword*, edited by Jesse Knight

Julian Symons, *The Detections of Francis Quarles*, edited by John Cooper; afterword by Kathleen Symons

Lloyd Biggle, Jr., *The Grandfather Rastin Mysteries*, introduction by Kenneth Biggle

Erle Stanley Gardner, *The Casebook of Sidney Zoom*, edited by Bill Pronzini

Max Brand, *Masquerade: Nine Crime Stories*, edited by William F. Nolan, Jr.

Hugh Pentecost, *The Battles of Jericho*, introduction by S.T. Karnick

Mignon G. Eberhart, *Dead Yesterday and Other Mysteries*, edited by Rick Cypert and Kirby McCauley

Victor Canning, *The Minerva Club, The Department of Patterns and Other Stories*, edited by John Higgins

Ellis Peters (Edith Pargeter), *The Trinity Cat and Other Mysteries*, edited by Martin Edwards and Sue Feder

Elizabeth Ferrars, *The Casebook of Jonas P. Jonas and Others*, edited by John Cooper

Anthony Boucher and Denis Green, *The Casebook of Gregory Hood*, edited by Joe R. Christopher

SUBSCRIPTIONS

Crippen & Landru offers discounts to individuals and institutions who place Standing Order Subscriptions for its forthcoming publications, either all the Regular Series or all the Lost Classics or (preferably) both. Collectors can thereby guarantee receiving limited editions, and readers won't miss any favorite stories. Standing Order Subscribers receive a specially commissioned story in a deluxe edition as a gift at the end of the year. Please write or e-mail for more details.